A SNOWBALL'S CHANCE

A SNOWBALL'S CHANCE

A Novel by TED DUNCAN

Pleasant Word
A Division of WINEPRESS PUBLISHING

Printed in the United States of America

Packaged by Pleasant Word, a division of WinePress Publishing, PO Box 428, Enumclaw, WA 98022. The views expressed or implied in this work do not necessarily reflect those of Pleasant Word, a division of WinePress Publishing. Ultimate design, content, and editorial accuracy of this work are the responsibilities of the author.

ISBN 1-57921-622-6
Library of Congress Catalog Card Number: 2003102180

TABLE OF CONTENTS

Appendices

FOREWORD

Nearly twenty years ago, my studies of the Scriptures caused me to question the generally accepted views of the rapture of the church and the nature of the accompanying tribulation period. The more I studied, the more convinced I became that there was a whole new approach to those questions that, as far as I could tell, no one had examined.

I waited for someone else to expose what I considered to be the obvious holes in the standard theories and to suggest the totally different, but thoroughly biblical, alternative I had come across; but no one did. Instead, with the phenomenal success of the *Left Behind* series, the old standard approach became almost canonized as gospel truth.

So, I decided that I would attempt to tackle it myself. When I discussed my plans with my wife Marge, she suggested that if I seriously wanted anyone to read what I wrote, I should put it in the form of a novel, rather than a critical thesis. She said she personally would much rather read a fast-paced novel, full of romance, drama, and suspense, than some stuffy document, filled with boring facts and figures.

Frankly, I had never considered that possibility, but it sounded intriguing. I had written stories and poems and articles that people found interesting and informative. Why not try my hand at a novel?

Thus, *A Snowball's Chance* was conceived. But as I put it together in my mind, I didn't want to introduce yet another post-rapture tribulation drama, many of which were already available in various formats by several different authors. I wanted a new and refreshing setting to go along with the new and refreshing ideas I planned to introduce.

Therefore, you will discover that *A Snowball's Chance* unfolds entirely prior to the rapture, with no apocalyptic special effects at all. Nonetheless, you will find that it has all the elements that make for a rousing novel, including a surprise ending that will blow you away, and enough unanswered questions to leave you wanting to know more.

The characters and story line are purely fictional, resembling only on occasion, people I've known, things I've done, and places I've been. But the doctrinal implications are purely intentional and absolutely serious.

In order to keep the story line from bogging down, much of the doctrinal and historical support for my views has been relegated to a series of appendices. I challenge you to read them after you've finished the novel to confirm the scriptural accuracy of what I suggest through the events and dialogue of the story itself.

As you will discover, I have implied that the rapture will occur in the early years of this twenty-first century. That is not necessarily because I'm convinced that it will indeed occur at that time. It could well be delayed for years, decades, or even longer. But, being neither a prophet, nor the son of a prophet, I have no idea what life might be like twenty or thirty years from now. Hence, I've set it to take place in the very near future so I could at least have a chance of describing places and events with some semblance of accuracy.

You will also notice that I have challenged many of the doctrinal implications of the popular *Left Behind* series. However, that does not imply that I challenge the integrity or orthodoxy of Dr. Tim LaHaye, the series' creator, who espouses those doctrines. He and I agree absolutely on all the essential doctrines of the Bible, and I have the utmost respect for him as a scholar and as a man of God. We just happen to disagree on many of the non-essential doctrines of predictive prophecy. Good and honest men have been doing that ever since such prophecies were first penned by the apostles and prophets, and they will continue to do so until Jesus comes and sets the record straight once and for all.

Finally, I want to thank my wife, who inspired me to undertake the writing of this novel in the first place, and who offered invaluable suggestions along the way to help improve it and make it more readable. Also, I owe a debt of gratitude to the many other good people who have read it, and whose observations and corrections have added greatly to its content and style.

Enjoy your read. Immerse yourself in the lives and events of *A Snowball's Chance*. But pay particular attention to the doctrinal and spiritual implications it introduces, and may our good Lord bless you richly as you do.

Ted Duncan

CHAPTER ONE

THE FIX

Jamal Davis sat on a training table, deep in the bowels of UCLA's massive Pauley Pavilion, as Fred Baker, the trainer, applied layers of tape to the athlete's left ankle. It was little more than an hour before the game was to start and there was an air of excitement in the adjoining locker room. The players were getting dressed in their home uniforms and bantering back and forth, trying to ease the persistent pre-game jitters. The noise from the jubilant crowd, already filling the huge stadium upstairs, could be heard through the ceiling above them, and it did little to calm their nerves.

"Hey kid, you're gonna kill dem bums from Houston tonight," said Fred, as he applied the last piece of tape from one roll to Jamal's ankle and reached for another. He had been wrapping ankles and massaging sore muscles at UCLA for nearly thirty years now, but he still talked like he had when he was growing up in the Bronx. "Dey got dat Jackson fella from Geo'gia, but udder dan dat, dey got nuttin'. And besides dat, you're gonna toin dat Jackson kid inside out. Nobody's better'n you around da basket. You're everybody's choice ta repeat as a foist team all-American. You do know dat, don'cha?"

"Yeah, Freddie, that's what they say," replied Jamal absently, his mind obviously on other things.

"Well, dat outta do it, kid," said the trainer as he applied the last piece of tape to the masterpiece he had created. "Dat bum ankle ain't goin' noplace tonight. No sir, not wid Freddie Fleetfingers on the job, it ain't."

"Thanks, Freddie, I don't know what I'd do without you, man." Jamal slipped off the table and picked up his sock and shoe and headed back toward the locker room.

"And justa show ya how sure I yam," Fred called after him, "I'm bettin' a bundle on ya ta win it big tonight."

Those words stabbed at Jamal's heart like a dagger as he heard them. "Now don't be doing that, Freddie," he said as he turned back and looked at the trainer. "It's illegal to bet on the game you know, and besides that, it isn't smart. Anything can happen when two teams are on that court out there for forty minutes."

"Not when you're on dat court, big fella. It's in da bag." Fred gave him the thumbs up signal and a big grin as he turned back to the next player who had meanwhile climbed up on the table.

Jamal sighed and walked back into the dressing room and sat down heavily in front of his locker. Normally he would have been brimming with enthusiasm at this point before a home game in front of thousands of adoring fans. UCLA was undefeated halfway through the season and ranked number one in all the polls. This year they were predicted to win their thirteenth national championship in the school's history and their second in a row. He himself had appeared on the cover of *Sports Illustrated* the previous month and the article had said that he was certain to be that year's top draft choice in the NBA. But instead of exhilaration he felt the cold chill of guilt and self-condemnation.

"How can I throw this game?" he screamed at himself, silently. "I've always played to win! I can't just lie down and let a team that isn't even in the top twenty beat up on us on our home court! We haven't lost in Pauley Pavilion in all the four years I've played here . . . and we've played the best in the country!"

But as he sat there lecturing himself on these matters, inside he knew that throwing the game was exactly what he was going to do. After all, he really had no other choice. Hadn't those thugs in Vegas made it real clear that unless UCLA lost to Houston, both his kneecaps would be smashed and he would never play another game of basketball in his life?

Why had he ever gone to gamble in Las Vegas with his brother in the first place? And why had he allowed himself to get talked into playing that game of five-card-draw with those high rollers? And why hadn't he suspected anything when he, a raw amateur, had been winning consistently against a table full of obvious experts? And why had he stayed in the game and bet money he didn't have on that phony hand? Why indeed?

As he thought about it now, it was clear that the game had been rigged. They had let him win early on to get him hooked, and then they dealt him that ten-high, straight flush he was sure was unbeatable. So sure was he of winning that he raised every bet until every dime he had won earlier was now heaped in the middle of the table. But when he ran out of money, there were two other players who were still in the game, who not only called his last bet, but raised him and each other even higher. He was faced with the grim prospect of either calling their bets or folding his hand. Since he was broke, he was about to throw down his cards in anguish when Mr. Apparicio, or whatever his name had been, offered to cover him . . . that is if he was certain he was going to win.

He knew from his study of mathematical probabilities that the possibility of anyone having a better hand than his in a game of five-card-draw were astronomical. So he assured the man that his money was secure and continued to call as the other two raised each other back and forth. Finally, much to his relief, no one raised after the last bet, and they had reached a showdown.

He remembered saying something stupid like, "Read 'em and weep," as he laid down his cards and reached for the huge pile in the middle of the table.

One of the other players threw down his cards in apparent disgust, but the other one, a fat, Latin-looking man, chewing on an equally fat cigar, stopped Jamal. He apologized profusely as he revealed his queen-high, straight flush and proceeded to rake in his winnings. But there was a gleam in his eyes that betrayed the true satisfaction of one who had baited his trap and sprung it at just the precise moment to capture his prey.

Jamal experienced three distinct emotions in rapid succession: first, shock, that his winning hand had been beaten; then, outrage, when he realized he'd been suckered; and then, raw panic, when it dawned on him what a mess he was in. So confident had he been of winning and so absorbed in the thought of the great amount of money he was soon going to possess, that he had never considered the possibility of losing, nor what it might cost him if he did. He was flabbergasted when his supposed benefactor told him that he owed him over twenty thousand dollars and that he expected his money within forty-eight hours.

When Jamal confessed that he had no way of raising the money, the room that had been full of sports fans who had admired the all-American and welcomed him into their friendly game was suddenly transformed into a gathering of hardened gangsters, ready to eliminate the punk who had crossed them.

In desperation, Jamal assured them that he would be signing a pro contract in a few months and that he had been promised a huge bonus. He would gladly pay his debt at that time, along with whatever amount of interest they required. But his former benefactor laughed in scorn and reminded Jamal that he wasn't running a savings and loan institution. He expected his cover to be repaid in the customary forty-eight hours.

Jamal's brother Marcus, who had been watching over his shoulder and sweating heavily for the past twenty minutes, spoke up in his brother's defense. He started talking excitedly, trying to explain that Jamal hadn't realized what he was getting into and they should let him go and that he, Marcus, would somehow repay his debt.

But one of their goons shoved him into a chair and told him to "Shaddup!" They obviously were not interested in Marcus. They had the one they were interested in, and they had him right where they wanted him. Jamal was in debt big time to these hoods. He couldn't pay, and they seemed to take delight in deciding how they were going to "take care of him."

It was then that Mr. "A" came up with the suggestion that Jamal throw the game with Houston and he would forget about the twenty grand he owed him. Everyone acted surprised at first and some even opposed the idea for a respectable period of time, but soon they all came around to agree that it was an acceptable compromise.

It was then that everything had became clear to Jamal. He had been suckered into a well-orchestrated sting operation. No wonder he had met so many friendly fans in the casino downstairs, so anxious to buy him drinks, and to brag about his exploits on the basketball court. No wonder he had been befriended by the owner of the casino himself and invited to join him and a few friends for a private game in the penthouse. No wonder he had been so popular and so successful early on. What a sap he had been! They had just been setting him up for the kill. They couldn't have cared less about the money in question. What they had been after all along was *The Game*.

At first Jamal refused even to consider the thought of throwing the upcoming game, but these men were not to be denied. A big one they all called Sal, obviously somebody real close to Mr. "A", grabbed Jamal by the shirt and backed him up against a wall. He was nearly as tall as the athlete, and Jamal almost gagged on the smell of the tobacco, and the liquor, and the garlic, and who knows what else he breathed in his face.

"Look, wise guy," Sal growled, "you got two choices here. You either see that UCLA loses next Friday or we smash botha you knees. Capeesh? Now, whatzit gonna be?"

Jamal had hated himself back then for backing down so easily and agreeing to throw the game, but he hated himself even more now. He was filled with an overwhelming sense of self-loathing as he sat on the bench less than an hour before he was to go out on the court and betray thousands of loyal fans in this building, and perhaps millions more watching on national TV. But what was he going to do? These guys meant business. UCLA was favored by at least three-to-one odds and the mob stood to win millions of dollars if he was able to ensure Houston's victory. If he failed to pull it off, he was sure they would not be content with just breaking his legs. They stood to lose a bundle if UCLA won, and he was confident they would make him pay for it with his life.

He couldn't let that happen, not with a life as important as his. After all, wasn't he the hottest thing going in college basketball today? Hadn't sports writers already compared him to such legendary greats as Magic Johnson and Michael Jordan? Wasn't he going to bring a brand new charisma to the NBA the next year that would revitalize the whole industry? If any life was worth saving, it surely had to be his . . . . If that was so, then why did he still feel so rotten?

Perhaps Jamal's doubt was due to the fact that, deep inside, he wasn't as convinced as everyone else seemed to be of the innate greatness of Jamal Davis. He had been born a black child in a dysfunctional family in South-Central Los Angeles. Neither his father nor his mother had much influence in his life during his formative years. They spent most of their time on the streets, and both had been in and out of jail until he was fifteen. Drugs were their problem, as it was for so many others in their neighborhood. Robert and Tasha Davis were in trouble repeatedly for either possessing drugs, or selling drugs, or stealing something to get money to buy drugs.

Bobby, as everybody called him, spent eight years in prison at one time for robbing a gas station and pistol whipping an attendant to get less than $100 to buy some smack.

The fact that both Bobby and Tasha had spent so much time behind bars probably accounted for the fact that they had only two children. Actually, it was that eight years in prison that separated their sons so much in age. Marcus, now 30, was born six months after Bobby was locked up, and Jamal, at 21, came along a year after he had finally been released.

But even eight years in prison had not reformed Bobby Davis. It hadn't been long before he was back in trouble again. For twelve years he alternated between the streets and the slammer. Fortunately for him, it was before the Three Strikes Law had been passed, or he would have spent the rest of his life in prison, rather than just short stretches at a time. When Marcus was 21 and Jamal 12, Bobby was convicted again for dealing drugs and sent to the state prison in Corcoran for three years. The cycle might have continued on indefinitely had not something happened there that changed his life forever. Jamal hadn't understood it back then, and he still didn't understand it now, but somehow, in prison, the streetwise Bobby Davis got religion.

He started writing letters about what had happened to him and how he had changed and how he couldn't wait to share all these things with his family when he got home. The boys knew that their grandmother Georgia, and their mother, had gotten religion a year or so prior to that, but that wasn't so hard to understand. After all, religion was basically for women and small children anyway. But not long after their mother became ill and later died of AIDS, Bobby crossed that line as well. The news that their father had been converted too nearly blew them away. Both of them agreed that it wouldn't last. They gave him two months after his release before he was right back on the streets again. But they were wrong.

Bobby had been out of prison for six years and he hadn't missed a beat. Not only did he not go back to the streets, he actually started working at the church in Compton where their mother and grandmother attended. He started out as an assistant to Reverend Wilcox, but when the old pastor died the previous year, the church voted almost unanimously to call Bobby to take his place.

Their father became a man Marcus and Jamal hadn't known before. Something had really made a change in him, but they weren't sure what it was. He gave himself wholeheartedly to the people of the church, but especially, he gave himself to the task of rescuing his sons from the destructive path he himself had been leading them down only a few years before.

Jamal was only fifteen when his father was released from prison the last time. He was still in school and living with his grandmother and somewhat open to his father's influence, but Marcus was long gone and appeared to be beyond Bobby's reach.

By now, Jamal was out on the court with his teammates, going through the pre-game warm-up ritual. Pauley Pavilion was already rocking to the sound of the huge band and the exuberant crowd, which was already approaching the maximum capacity of 12,819. The seating in the large student section, as always, had been unassigned, so the students had started arriving hours before the game to get the best seats. Everyone came early if they could. These days, with UCLA being the hottest team in America, the pre-game hoopla was about as exciting as the game itself.

But instead of being exciting, it was excruciating for the superstar Jamal Davis. He went through the motions and took his shots, but his mind wasn't focused on the game as it should have been. Instead, it was torn with guilt over what he was about to do, and it was preoccupied with thoughts about himself and his family, especially his older brother.

Marcus had grown up while Bobby was in prison, and he started following in his father's footsteps. He dropped out of school at sixteen and started living pretty much on the streets, working a few odd jobs now and then. He started running with a gang whose members had given him the nickname of "Snowball." They called him that, neither because he had actually come in contact with a snowball at any time, nor because he resembled one in any way; but because his drug of choice was heroin, often referred to as "snow" on the streets. The name also may have stuck because its definition was so completely opposite of anything that might have been used to describe Marcus physically. His complexion was actually darker than that of the average African-American living in the U.S., and his 190 pounds did little to fill out his lanky 6'6" frame. He was the very antithesis of a snowball.

His actions hadn't been very snow-like either. Besides the drugs and the gang fighting and the petty thievery, he had slipped deeply into immorality and criminal activity. He had slept with dozens of different women, but really cared for none of them. He fathered a daughter by a beautiful young woman named Sarah nearly nine years prior, but never seriously considered becoming either a husband or a father to them. He knew his family had stayed in contact with Sarah and her daughter Tamika, but he never bothered to do so himself. He knew that Sarah had married a policeman named Carl something, and that they lived over near MacArthur Park someplace, but he had kept his distance, especially since her husband was a cop.

Marcus had a natural athletic ability, like his younger brother, but life on the streets, and in and out of jail, had given him little opportunity to develop it. He was a likable person with a great personality and a ready laugh, but he had never let anyone get very close to him. He saw his family only on rare occasions, and he preferred it that way. He didn't feel comfortable around all their talk of Jesus' love and saving faith and stuff like that, so he kept his distance. He had been living life in the fast lane for too long to get slowed down by things like family relationships and religion.

The one exception was Jamal. His younger brother had been cool through all of this. He had become successful and famous and all that, but he never let it go to his head. Jamal stayed close to the rest of the family, but he never really became like them. When he and Marcus were together, it was just like old times. There wasn't much of anything they hadn't done together. Marcus always felt that Jamal was the only one who really understood him and the only one to whom he could really relate.

Perhaps that close relationship with Marcus was what was bothering Jamal most right now. The pre-game warm ups were completed and the team was back in the locker room beneath the massive seating section at the west-end of the Pavilion. The coach was going through his pre-game speech, telling them not to be overconfident, that Houston had a powerful team, that they needed to pay special attention to Billy Jackson, and all the other predictable stuff coaches always say before a big game, but Jamal wasn't listening. His mind was on his own life, and that of Marcus, and the value he placed on each of them respectively

He tried to convince himself that if it were Marcus' life on the line here, it wouldn't be such a serious matter. After all, his brother was a drug user and part- time dealer, a womanizer, a petty thief, a compulsive gambler, and who knows what all. No one but his family and a few friends cared anything about him, and few others even knew of his existence. On the other hand, Jamal was supposed to be the clean-cut all-American hero, known and admired by millions all over the country. That perceived difference in worth was what bothered Jamal most as the team prepared to return to the court for the start of the game. Down deep, he knew that there wasn't as much difference between himself and Marcus as one might think.

It was true; Jamal had all the obvious advantages. He was taller. He measured just over 6'8", but was listed in the program at 6'9". Every team fudged a little on the height of its players, and Jamal didn't mind the exaggeration. With his shoes on, he was at least that tall, anyway. He was also in much better physical condition than Marcus. His well-fed, well-trained, and well-muscled body weighed in at 237 pounds, while Marcus' lifestyle kept him always thin and a little sickly most of the time. It was also obvious that Jamal was the better looking of the two. Marcus was good looking enough himself, but Jamal was downright handsome. He looked more like an artist's rendition of the ideal African-American male than he did a seasoned college athlete. His complexion was free of any blemish and his facial features were all in proper alignment and proportion: from his strong jaw and his straight white teeth, to his broad forehead and his intense brown eyes, he was pretty-much flawless.

But what was supposed to be the biggest difference between the two of them didn't seem to be any difference at all right now to Jamal. Marcus was known as the evil older brother, and Jamal was the virtuous and innocent one; but in his heart, Jamal knew that wasn't so. It was also true that he had stayed in school and out of any serious trouble with the law. He had excelled in basketball since he was in grammar school and had become a national celebrity. He had stayed at home and even attended church with his family infrequently. But he knew he wasn't the clean-cut Christian the media made him out to be.

Actually, Jamal loved the same things Marcus did. He smoked pot with him whenever they got together, and he had gotten drunk with him on several occasions as well. He had the same eye for the ladies too. As handsome and popular as he was, he had young co-eds making themselves available to him constantly, and he rarely turned any of them down. And, oh yes, he also loved to gamble. It was that vice that had gotten him into all his present troubles in the first place.

The buzzer sounded and it was time to go out onto the court for the team introductions. As he passed Coach Barnes, the older man asked, "You okay, Jamal?"

"Sure, Coach, I'm fine. Why do you ask?"

"Oh, you just seem distant . . . preoccupied maybe."

"No, I'm fine, really," Jamal lied as he followed his teammates out the door to be greeted by a thunderous roar from the capacity crowd. The band played at peak volume and the cheerleaders bounded about the floor as the team took its place at the side of the court. Jamal should have been feeling at his best right now, but as he stood there, he couldn't remember ever feeling quite so miserable.

He looked around, and there was Marcus in his bleacher seat right behind the home team bench. Immediate family members of the players had such seats reserved for them, and Marcus never missed a game. He flashed him a nervous grin and shot him the thumbs up sign. Jamal tried to return the grin, but it died on his face.

The visiting team was introduced and each player was politely cheered, with the exception of their center, Billy Jackson. He was tall and massive at 7'1" and 290 pounds, and he had boasted openly how he was going to shut Jamal down and lead Houston to a victory over the national champions. He was booed loudly by the raucous partisan crowd.

When the home team was introduced, the cheers were enthusiastic; but when Jamal Davis' name was called, it became deafening. Jamal managed a smile and a wave, but his heart was in none of it.

"At least Marcus is what he appears to be," Jamal scolded himself. "With him, what you see is exactly what you get, but I'm the biggest hypocrite on the planet. I'm every bit as messed up inside as he is; but here I am, pretending to be everybody's hero. What a scum bag!"

With the introductions over, the team returned to the bench for that last-second word of inspiration from the coach. Jamal felt a wave of nausea wash over him as he stood there. When Coach Barnes reminded him just how much the team was counting on him, he was sure he was going to puke. He was leading the nation in scoring, but right now, the only bucket he felt he could hit was the bottom of a wastebasket with the remains of his lunch.

As the buzzer announced the beginning of the game, Jamal unsteadily joined four of his teammates at the center circle to await the tip off. The only possible consolation he could imagine right now was that, as totally miserable as he felt, he would not consciously have to throw the game at all. He was confident that he could easily lead his team to defeat without even trying.

CHAPTER TWO

THE SCHEME

As thousands of college students and assorted fans leaned forward in their seats, awaiting the tip-off, two such students had an advantage thought to be held exclusively by Jamal and Marcus Davis and various members of the underworld. These two were neither members of the mob, nor did they know either of the Davis brothers; yet they knew exactly what was going down here. They cared little for the UCLA Bruins, or for the Houston Cougars, for that matter; yet they were on the edge of their seats with excitement. They were not thrilled with the prospect of either team winning a big game, but they were extremely optimistic about their own prospects of winning it big.

Scott Graham and Tony D'Angelo looked at each other and grinned like schoolboys up to a playful prank. "This is so cool!" gushed Scott. He was the larger of the two, at 6'2" and 196 pounds. He was not especially handsome, but his powerful athletic build, his strong chin, and his piercing blue eyes gave him a striking appearance. His hair would have been brown, had his head not been shaved, but many hours in the California sun had given him a deep tan that added to his attractiveness.

"I wouldn't miss this for the world," agreed Tony. He was slightly shorter than Scott, but he more than made up for his smaller size by his striking good looks. His muscles were well defined and his facial features were chiseled like those of a movie star. His teeth were white and perfect and his deep brown eyes were captivating. So conscious of his looks was he that he had refused to shave his head like all the other members of their swim team. He was willing to sacrifice the few hundredths of a second it might cost him in a race in order to save the wavy dark locks that helped make him so irresistible to the ladies.

They had been so excited about the upcoming game that they had been among the very first to arrive. They sat about half way up on the south side of Pauley Pavilion, right under the blue and gold basketball banner, which heralded the Bruins' first national NCAA championship back in 1964. Around the perimeter, clockwise, hung eleven more just like it. Most of them were earned in the 60's and 70's under Coach John Wooden when they had won ten titles in twelve seasons. After those wonder years, UCLA had not been nearly so prolific, gaining only one additional banner before the end of the century, that one representing their championship back in 1995. Completing the circle was the banner they had garnered just the previous year, defeating Oklahoma for the title in Portland.

But Scott and Tony had been only mildly impressed when they had surveyed these badges of honor earlier. Neither of them had ever been in Pauley Pavilion prior to that Friday evening, and they were more impressed with the building itself than they were with its furnishings. Indeed, as college gymnasiums go, it was pretty amazing. It reminded them more of the Staples Center, where they had seen the Lakers play, than of any other building they could think of.

Both Scott and Tony were students at California State University at Long Beach, and they had been impressed with the large pyramid-shaped field house where their own Forty-Niner teams competed, but they both agreed that it paled by comparison with their present surroundings.

But what really impressed them, more than anything about the building itself, was the special knowledge that they now shared inside it. They knew UCLA was going to lose the game, and more importantly, they also knew that each of them was going to become more than $10,000 richer in the process.

Their knowledge, and correspondingly good fortune, had come rather fortuitously. Actually, Tony had literally stumbled onto it. He was a powerfully built, twenty-one year old captain of his CSULB swim team, who swam with the grace of a seal in the water, but who, unfortunately, could at times be almost as clumsy as one on the land.

He was in his room studying on the previous Monday evening when he got up from his desk to go to the bathroom, and he inadvertently stepped on a tennis ball left in the middle of the floor. The ball rolled under his foot and he lost his balance, falling headlong onto the floor next to the wall. He was ready to curse loudly when he heard muffled voices coming through the heater vent next to his ear. He recognized one of the voices to be that of his father, but the other one was unknown to him.

He glanced at the clock on the wall and saw that it was well after eleven. "Who could Dad have over here this late?" Tony asked himself, "and why are they meeting in his study, instead of in the family room?" Michael D'Angelo's private study was directly under Tony's bedroom, and the vent openings to the two rooms were fairly close to each other off the main heating duct. The close proximity of the vents allowed Tony to hear the conversation taking place below him.

He wasn't actually able to understand the words themselves, but he could tell that the conversation was indeed a serious one. His curiosity was immediately aroused. Because many of his father's activities had been cloaked in mystery and secrecy, Tony had often hoped for an opportunity to find out more of what his dad was actually involved in.

On the surface, Michael D'Angelo was an accountant for Global Imports, an import-export firm operating out of Long Beach Harbor, but Tony had always suspected that he was involved in something more than just shipping bananas in from Panama and sport shoes from China. He didn't have to be a genius to figure out that a simple accountant couldn't afford the palatial home on ten acres in Rancho Palos Verdes where their family lived. Nor could he afford the lavish lifestyle they all enjoyed.

Michael drove a new BMW and his wife Margo cruised around town and to her bridge club in a new Lincoln Navigator. She claimed she needed the massive size of the SUV for crash protection, and the four-wheel-drive for stormy trips up and down the steep roads that wound their way throughout their exclusive neighborhood. Tony drove back and forth to school in a new Mustang convertible, and his sister Camille, had not only received a new car, but her parents had spent at least $60,000 paying for her wedding the previous year. They all had what they wanted, and did what they wanted, and never was there any concern about money.

Tony had been pretty sure that the underworld had connections with Global Imports, and that they were using it as a cover to transport drugs into the country and to launder dirty money. It had never been discussed at home, but all the pieces seemed to fit into place.

Tony strained to hear what the two were discussing downstairs, but being unable to do so, and suspecting that something big was going down, he decided to creep down and find out for himself.

His mother had already retired for the night and the house was otherwise empty. Tony found it easy to slip undetected down the stairs and through the hall to the door outside his father's study. The door itself was of heavy oak and nearly soundproof, but by lying on his stomach, he found that he could hear quite well through the crack between the bottom of the door and the plush carpet stretched beneath it.

"I'm telling you, Mike, it's a sure thing," Tony heard an unfamiliar voice assuring his father.

"But, Leon, how can you be so sure that this Davis kid will pull it off?" Tony's father countered. "He's been one big winning machine for UCLA. Once he gets in the game, his competitive spirit could take over and he's likely to play to win in spite of any agreement to throw the game."

"Oh no he won't," this Leon reassured him. "The boys got him good in a sting in Vegas. I was there. He dropped over twenty grand to Mr. Apparicio, and the price for lettin' him walk was throwing the game against Houston this Friday. If he doesn't come through, he's gonna find his kneecaps all busted up and he ain't gonna be playin' no basketball, for nobody, ever again. I'm so sure it's in the bag, that I'm bettin' twenty grand on Houston myself."

"So why are you telling me?" Tony heard his father ask.

"Well, whattya think I'm tellin' you for? Because you're my friend, that's why. Without your expertise, Global Imports wouldn't be goin' nowhere. You keep the books, man. You keep everything lookin' legit, and the feds haven't given us no trouble at all. You made me a rich man, and I wanna let you in on this deal so you can make a few easy bucks yourself."

"Thanks, Leon. I appreciate all you and your associates have done for me and my family. It's been a pleasure working for all of you. And thanks for driving all the way out here to tell me about this situation. So, you're sure Houston's going to win on Friday?"

"Trust me, Mikey, it's gonna happen. You haven't been with the family as long as I have. When they set somethin' up like this to happen, then it's *gotta* happen. You can take it to the bank."

"Speaking of the bank," Michael said, "just what are the odds, and how much do I stand to win?"

"Well, as it stands right now, UCLA's favored by more than three to one, and a bet of ten grand will pay off more than thirty. But don't be tellin' nobody about this. I'm not even supposta be telling you. If a lotta people go bettin' a lotta money on Houston, the odds are gonna go down for sure, but if we keep a lid on it, they may be gettin' even better by Friday."

"Alright, count me in," Michael consented. "Can you take care of placing my bet for me?"

"Sure thing, buddy, just tell me how much."

Tony then heard the sound of a chair being scooted back and soft footsteps on the carpet. At first he began to panic, thinking his father was approaching the door, till he realized he was going to the opposite wall where his wall safe was located.

"The ten thousand you mentioned sounds like a good round number to me. I think I got that much right here," Tony heard him say. "Is that okay?"

"Sure, but are you sure you wanna trust me with the cash?"

"Hey, since I've gone to work with you people, I've learned to trust you with my life. I guess I can trust you with a few dollars as well."

"Yeah, you got a point there. You know what they say about honor among thieves and all. I'll take real good care of it for you, and come next Monday morning at the docks, I'll have a nice envelope for you with more'n thirty grand in it."

Tony heard movement in the room and could visualize the exchange of money and the sealing of the deal with a handshake.

"Now I really gotta be goin'," he heard Leon say. "I didn't wanna be talking about this at work or on the phone or nothin', cause you never know who's listenin'. I was workin' late and this was sorta on my way home, so I thought I would just stop by and handle it personal and all."

"Well, I'm glad you did," Michael replied. "I appreciate you thinking of me. This will be a really nice bonus, especially considering the fact that Christmas is almost a year off now."

Both men laughed, and Tony knew he'd better clear out since the other two had almost certainly started moving toward the door by this time. He scrambled to his feet and hurried down the hall and around the corner just before he heard the heavy door open behind him. He bounded up the stairs, undetected by his father and Leon, thankful for the fact that stocking feet on padded carpet make virtually no sound at all.

He stood just around the corner at the top of the stairs as the two older men exchanged farewells in the entryway, not wanting to miss out on any last-minute details. Hearing none, he slipped back into his room and turned out the light so his father would not suspect anything when he passed by on his way to his own bedroom.

Tony undressed and got in bed just in case his dad might poke his head in to check on him as he sometimes did. But he heard his father walk by his door without pausing, and as he heard the door open and close at the end of the hall, he was sure that his presence downstairs, and the knowledge he had thus acquired, had remained completely undetected. As he lay there in the dark, hearing nothing but the pounding of his own heart, he had already begun scheming about what he was going to do with this new windfall of information.

At first, Tony considered keeping quiet and just making a killing for himself, but human nature being what it is; he found that it was just too good not to share. As gifted and good looking as he was, he had always suffered from a poor self-image, always striving to impress others with his abilities and accomplishments. Now he had the formula for instant wealth, and it would be a shame not to let someone else know about it. If he kept it all to himself this whole thing might go down without anyone else ever realizing just how cool he really was.

His obvious choice was Scott Graham, a good friend who lived just up the hill and around the corner from him. They had been friends since Tony's father had bought their house and moved his family there when Tony was in junior high school. Scott was a fellow member of the swim team at CSULB, and they had spent a lot of time together. But most importantly, Scott was someone who could keep his mouth shut. On one occasion, he had walked up as Tony had been going through the contents of a teammate's locker in what was an otherwise deserted locker room. Tony had offered a flimsy excuse for his actions, and Scott had apparently accepted it, never divulging the other's actions to either the teammate or the coach.

Besides that, Tony was sure that Scott could use the money. His father provided well enough for his every legitimate need, but he provided him with little else. Scott was left to scrounge around for any extra cash that he might need to pay for things that were of some particular interest to him. He would have been willing to get a part-time job to provide him extra cash, but with his classes and homework and the time spent working out with the swim team, there simply was no time left in the day. Sometimes he borrowed money from others, sometimes he hocked or sold possessions, and sometimes he simply did without.

Tony made his decision to cut Scott in on the scheme, and after practice Wednesday evening; he felt that the time was right to confront him with it. He called out to him as they were walking to their respective cars in the parking lot, "Hey Scott, wait up!"

"Yeah, man, What's up?"

"Hey, dude, I need to talk to you about something really important. You got a few minutes?"

"Yeah, I guess so. You wanna talk right here, or go somewhere else?" Scott asked.

"Nah, let's stop at Starbucks for a cuppa coffee," Tony responded. "It's on our way home. Why don't you just follow me?"

"Okay, lead the way," Scott agreed as he unlocked his green Chevy Blazer and got in. He waited until Tony had gotten in his Mustang and started it up before he pulled in behind him and followed him out of the parking lot.

Once they were settled in at Starbucks on the Pacific Coast Highway, Tony began his story. While nursing a steaming cup of espresso, he related the events of Monday night, watching Scott become and more animated as we went along.

"You have got to be joking!" Scott blurted out, gulping down the last swallow from his cup of vanilla roast.

"No, man, swear to God, it's the gospel truth," Tony gloated. "That's just how it happened, and I'm not gonna let those two old buzzards be the only ones who cash in on it either."

"What can you do about it?" Scott protested. "Do you have thousands of dollars to bet on a wild hunch?"

"It's not a wild hunch," Tony countered. "If my dad and his boss both bet such big bucks on it, it's gotta be a sure thing. And, yes, I do have thousands to bet on it, my good man. Five thousand, to be exact."

"Where'd you get that kind of money so fast? You knock over a 7–11 or something?"

"No, it was easy. I just showed my dad that brochure the coach gave us last week about traveling to Europe next summer. You know, that one where we would travel with a special team of Olympic hopefuls and swim against some of the best teams in Europe."

"Oh yeah," Scott recalled. "That's the same one my dad tossed in the wastebasket, saying it was too expensive. He said if I want to make the Olympic team, I need to do it by staying home and working harder at it, not by gallivanting all over Europe spending his money."

"Well, that's where our old men are different," Tony shot back. "My dad thought it was a great idea. He even wrote me out a check for five big ones to cover the cost without batting an eye."

"So how are you gonna cash a check made out to somebody else, wise guy?"

"You think I didn't think about that? I had him leave that part blank. He couldn't figure out who to address it to, and I sure as heck wasn't about to tell him. I already wrote my name on it and cashed it yesterday."

"But, remember your dad's an accountant. He's gonna see you dummied up that check soon enough when he gets it back from the bank."

"Look, Scott," Tony started to become annoyed, "by then Davis will have thrown the game to Houston and I'll have fifteen thousand extra dollars in my hot little hand. From my winnings I'll pay for the trip to Europe myself in cash, and I'll have the receipt to show my old man. I'll just tell him I cashed the check myself so I could impress the people in the office by turning in that much in cash. He'll be a little ticked at me, and I'll get one of his lectures about being more fiscally responsible, but he knows how I like to show off, and it won't be any big deal. I'll get my trip to Europe paid for, and an extra ten grand to spend on the night life while I'm there."

"It sounds like you've got it all figured out, alright," Scott conceded, "but it's not gonna be that easy for me."

"Well, you're just gonna have to figure out a way to get the money. Your old man is a big hotshot attorney for that corporate law office on top of a high-rise building in downtown Los Angeles. He ought to be rolling in dough."

"He is, but he sure doesn't roll much of it my way. Besides, what am I going to say, 'Hey, Dad, loan me five thousand, so I can bet against UCLA, cause I know Jamal Davis is gonna throw the game?' Besides that, he and my mother are out of the country till the middle of next week."

"Oh yeah, I forgot. They've gone on that religious trip to Israel or something, haven't they?"

"Yeah, but it doesn't make much difference. I don't think I could get the money even if they were here."

"Well, it's up to you, my friend," Tony said with some resignation. "I think it would be so cool for us to go to the game this Friday and watch the Bruins get their butts kicked for a change. I never liked them that much anyway. Besides that, we'd get to make a pile of money in the process. Hey, you're a smart kid, you'll figure something out, but you gotta do it quick. You need to give me the money by tomorrow night so I can place our bets first thing Friday morning. That's when they say the odds will be the highest in favor of UCLA."

"Okay, Tony," Scott tried to sound enthusiastic, "I'll see what I can do."

CHAPTER THREE

THE GIRL

Scott and Tony left shortly thereafter, and on the way home Scott drove subconsciously, his mind totally absorbed with the conversation he had just concluded with Tony. Down deep, he knew that he should have nothing to do with the get-rich-quick scheme, but instead, he was captivated by it. This was his chance, he thought, not only to get a pile of much-needed cash, but to finally do something on his own, to establish his own identity and gain a measure of independence from his parents.

Scott was the youngest of three brothers. Matthew and David were eight and six years older, respectively, and he had always grown up in their shadow. They had both been taller and tougher and better at football and basketball than he was. Scott was a natural athlete and had been good at both sports, but his brothers had been great. Between them, they had set new records in most of the major categories in both football and basketball at Roosevelt High School, and most of those records were still standing. Perhaps that had been the reason Scott had made one of the few independent decisions in his life and dropped out of basketball and taken up swimming in his sophomore year. He had excelled in the sport, even getting a full-ride scholarship to nearby CSULB, but he had been a disappointment to his parents, especially his father, who had himself been an all-American basketball sensation back in his college days.

Both Matt and Dave had accepted basketball scholarships to major universities out-of-state and had distinguished themselves throughout their college careers, but neither had done as well as their famous father Bruce

Graham. He had held out hopes that his youngest son would have eclipsed them both, but when Scott had chosen swimming over basketball, he had been devastated inwardly. Thereafter, Bruce had never quite trusted Scott's judgment, nor had he been too impressed with his accomplishments. No doubt, that had something to do with his insistence that his youngest son live at home and go to college nearby, and why he had kept him on such a tight leash financially.

With his mother, it had been simply due to the fact that Scott was her baby that she continued to smother him so much. She hadn't really cared that much which sport he chose, or no sport at all, for that matter, but she was even more insistent than her husband that Scott live at home while going to college. This was especially true since both of her older sons had now married and were raising their families out-of-state. She simply refused to let Scott grow up and become a man, and insisted on doting over him as she had always done. She continued to make his bed, clean his room, do all his laundry, and took delight in packing him a lunch each day, which he always hid, and usually tossed when no one was looking.

Scott was neither a sissy nor a mama's boy, and he struggled under her constant attention. He often chided himself for not taking one of the many scholarship offers he had received from schools out of the area, but he had basically been bribed into accepting the one to CSULB. Had he gone elsewhere, he had been told that he would have been on his own, but he had been promised the new Chevy Blazer at his high school graduation for agreeing to stay at home.

He loved the vehicle and the freedom it afforded him, but he had convinced himself that it had not been the reason he had accepted the offer at Cal State. After all, they did have a great swimming program, and besides that, Tony had agreed to swim for them, and he was his best friend. It had been a logical decision, he convinced himself, but down deep, he continued to resent the control his parents maintained in his life. He had even majored in pre-law at his father's insistence, despite the fact that he wasn't at all sure that he even wanted to be an attorney.

So controlling had they been, it surprised him when they had informed him that they were going to take this two-week trip to the Holy Land with a group from their church and leave him all by himself. Of course, his father had lectured him about being responsible, not getting into any trouble, not having any girls or booze in the house, and a whole list of other do's and don'ts. His mother had wept over him and promised to call him every day, which she had faithfully done for the past week. She had also prepared separate meals for him for every day, and had left them in the freezer, complete with the date each one was to be used and microwave instructions.

Even so, it surprised Scott that both parents had left together for so long a time. He was delighted, of course, but they had never done anything like that before. But then, come to think of it, since they had started going to the big Community Christian Church in Long Beach the previous summer, they had started doing a lot of strange things. They had started going to services every week, when before it had been mass only a couple of times a year at the old church. They had started reading the Bible together and praying out loud at meals and at other times as well. He had heard them talk about giving sizable sums of money to various causes at the church, which had offended him because they continued to be so tightfisted with him. But what offended him most was their insistence on converting him too.

He had been willing enough to go with them to church when they had first started inviting him back in July. He had enjoyed the music, and the preacher, Dr. Schumway, was a great speaker, able to combine humor and amazing stories and statistics together in such a way as to present really interesting messages. But Scott soon started resenting both his parents and their preacher. His parents kept telling him he needed to get saved, accept Jesus into his heart, be born again, and a lot of other phrases he didn't understand. And he was sure they had been prompting their pastor too, because his sermon each Sunday seemed to reinforce everything his parents had been harping on during the previous week.

Scott would have refused to continue attending long before had it not been for Candace Mercer. He had seen Candi at Cal State before, where she was a starting outside hitter on their powerful women's volleyball team, but he had never actually met her personally. He spotted her immediately one Sunday at church back in August, just before the beginning of the fall term. She stood out, not only because she was nearly six feet tall, but also because of her striking appearance.

She had the slender, well-proportioned body and the fluid grace of a gifted athlete, and the face of a beauty contestant. Her long, honey blond hair, which he had only seen tied back in a ponytail for volleyball matches, now hung in long curls, framing that lovely face. Her light blue eyes were quick and radiant, wide set and intelligent. Her nose, he thought, was just right, not too big, and yet not upturned and pixie-like either. Her lips were full and very kissable, he noticed. Her chin was strong and her cheekbones high. Her complexion was clear of any blemish, but he noticed a small congregation of freckles scattered across the bridge of her nose. However, he found them to be more of an asset than a liability, adding an element of wholesomeness and simplicity to her otherwise movie star-like appearance.

The fact that he noticed her had been no surprise to him at all, as he assumed she was noticed by nearly everyone, everywhere she went. The thing that surprised him is that she noticed him as well. She smiled and walked up to him and his parents and introduced herself, "Hi, I'm Candi Mercer. Aren't you Scott Graham?"

Scott stuttered and blushed, and hated himself for it. He wished that he were cool and confident around girls like Tony was, but most of all, he wished that his parents would disappear. But it was clear that neither was going to be the case, so he stammered instead, "Yeah . . . uh . . . I mean . . . yes, I am. How did you know?"

"Oh, I love swimming. I go to all the meets I can, and I've seen you swim lots of times. You're pretty good." Then, noticing how uncomfortable Scott's dad and mom seemed to be, she added, "These must be your parents."

Now Scott was really embarrassed; first, because he had just met the most gorgeous girl in the world, and his parents were standing right there watching him squirm; and second, because he had been so nervous that he hadn't even thought about introducing them.

"Oh yeah, I'm sorry. Candi, these are my parents, Bruce and Florence Graham," he managed to get out. "Mom, Dad, this is Candace Mercer. She plays volleyball on the women's team at Cal State."

"Now, how did you know that?" she asked with a grin.

"Oh, I think everybody at school knows who you are," he said self-consciously. "I love volleyball, and I go to all the matches I can. I've seen *you* play lots of times, and I think *you're* pretty good yourself."

Candi laughed at his obvious reuse of her own words, and as they looked at each other, there was a definite moment of connection that made Scott's heart leap in his chest.

Right then, Florence Graham extended her hand and interjected, "How do you do, Miss Mercer? It's always good to meet other students who go to school with our Scotty."

Scott, just for an instant, really wanted to strangle his mother right there in the church foyer, because he knew she had chosen her words purposefully. She had wanted Candi to know, right up front, that *Scotty* was *her* little boy, and that he didn't need any other woman in his life.

He managed to smile and not show his anger as he suffered through the exchange of greetings and necessary pleasantries all around, but his fists were clenched all the while. He would like to have stuffed one of them in his mother's mouth to keep her from making a complete fool of him.

Just when he thought all was lost, hope was rekindled when Candi turned from his parents, smiling knowingly, and invited him to meet with their college group at church that evening at six o'clock. She explained that she had just returned to school from her home in Washington over the summer break and was looking forward to getting back with her college group here at church.

Scott couldn't have cared less about any college group, but he would have done about anything to actually be with Candi again, especially without his parents around. He accepted her invitation and went willingly, and Candi was there to meet him at the door and to introduce him around.

The director of the large college group, Pastor Don, was a lot of fun, and he led the evening's time of singing songs Scott didn't know, eating sweets he didn't like, and meeting strangers he didn't care anything about. But in spite of all that, Scott thoroughly enjoyed himself, for the simple reason that Candi was by his side the entire evening.

Afterward, as he walked her to her car, he mustered up enough courage to ask her to go with him to a movie later that week. Her response blew him away. She asked him if he was a born-again Christian. He stammered again and confessed that he didn't really understand what that term meant, but that, yes, he considered himself to be a Christian. He assured her that he had been baptized as a baby and that he had lived a pretty good life.

His answer had obviously not impressed her, because she got real serious and told him just how things were going to be between them. She informed him that she was most certainly a born-again Christian and wasn't interested in dating anyone who wasn't. She didn't fool around and wasn't interested in being with anyone who wanted to. She fully intended to serve the Lord the rest of her life and was looking to find the right guy who shared that same commitment.

All that was way too much for Scott, and he was sure she was about to tell him that he had been eliminated from the equation, when she took his hand in hers, with just a hint of tears in her eyes. She confessed that she had been attracted to him for some time, not because of his looks so much, but because of the way he handled himself: his intensity in sports, yet his ability to lose graciously; his confidence around guys, yet his politeness and shyness around girls; his seriousness about his studies, and yet his carefree-like spirit.

She went on further to tell him that she had been looking for an opportunity to meet him and that she had been so pleased when she had seen him at church that morning. She had really enjoyed getting to know him a little that evening, and she would probably regret it, but she would like to see him again, and get to know him better.

Scott was about to go into orbit emotionally, when she brought him right back down to earth with her conditions for any further communication between them. They were not to date, nor were they to be alone together. There would be no hugging or kissing or physical involvement between them. They could see each other only at school and at church. And only when Scott seriously gave his life to Christ, would she consider becoming more involved with him.

Scott was, by then, experiencing serious conflicts of emotions. First, he was offended that she had obviously rejected his claim at being a Christian. Then, he was delighted that she had actually been attracted to him and wanted to see him again. Then again, he was frustrated that she had insisted on keeping such a distance between them. But when it came right down to it, he was so attracted to her that he was willing to accept almost any conditions just so he might be with her again.

He assured her that her conditions were fine with him. He lied and gave her further assurance that he wasn't interested in any sort of physical relationship at this point in his life either. The truth was that he would have liked nothing better than to have taken her in his arms and kissed her right then.

They parted with a handshake that night, and for the next five months, she held him to his agreement. They saw each other often on campus and at church, but she never indicated a desire to become more involved in any way. Scott became an avid volleyball fan, never missing a match if he could help it, even traveling to many of the away matches that were within driving distance.

Candi had an outstanding season, helping her team win the Conference Division-One title, losing only later in the national tournament in a close match to Stanford, who went on to win the national title.

Scott had his own swim practices in preparation for his upcoming season, but he invested every spare minute in supporting Candi through her matches. About the only times he saw her at school were before and after their practice sessions, her volleyball matches, and his swim meets. It became even more difficult to see her after his swim season started in late October, but both of them made the effort and they grew closer over the months.

Of course, he attended a lot of church services with her during those months as well, and enjoyed all the college group activities they were able to attend. During that time, he heard a lot of sermons too. He came to realize that he had not been a truly born-again Christian after all, at least not as Dr. Schumway had defined one from the Bible. He had not been willing to admit that he was a condemned sinner before God's righteous judgment and that he could not do anything to contribute to his salvation. He had not yet humbled himself and accepted Jesus Christ as his own personal Savior, receiving the free gift of eternal life, trusting in nothing but Christ's death, burial, and resurrection in his behalf.

Everyone was encouraging him to make that commitment, but somehow, he was not willing to bring himself to do it. Part of his reluctance, he realized, came from the fact that his parents, especially his mother, was so insistent that he *get saved!* His foolish pride welled up and he balked, not wanting to grant his mom and dad the satisfaction of working their will in his life, yet one more time.

Another thing that caused Scott to avoid the decision was the dilemma he had been wrestling with from the beginning. Candi had made it clear that she would not date him until such a time as he became a Christian, and though he most assuredly wanted to date her, he wasn't willing to feign a decision just to garner her affections.

But perhaps the most compelling reason for his unwillingness to accept Christ was his own selfish pride. He was unwilling to admit that he had been so bad a sinner that he really needed to be saved. He had spent the last five months desperately trying to convince everyone, himself especially, that he already was good enough to be accepted by God, and by Candi too, for that matter. But he had grown fearful that in all that time he had convinced none of the above, not even himself.

Scott began to be depressed over the whole situation, for by this time, he had fallen hopelessly in love with Candi, even though he had hardly done so much as hold her hand. His mind was consumed with thoughts of her constantly, and he would have done anything to win her love. That's where he encountered so great a conflict.

If he made an attempt to accept Christ now, the decision would not be sincere. It would simply be a way to win Candi's approval and her affection. He knew that any real decision for Christ would have to be genuine and from the heart, or it would be of no value whatsoever. So absorbed was he in his love for Candi and his determination not to lose her, that he pretended to be very close to making that commitment, but in truth, his own hardened heart was still rebelling against it.

He was sure that Candi had grown to care for him deeply by now as well. She had as much as told him so, but she had also reaffirmed her commitment not to get involved with an unsaved guy. Scott sensed that she was beginning to pull away. Perhaps she had already come to the conclusion that Scott was not going to accept Christ after all, and that she had best break it off before she too fell in love and become romantically involved against her convictions.

Scott felt a sense of panic. He tried more than once to pray and accept the Lord privately, and not tell anyone but Candi; but every time, the words stuck in his throat. He came to understand that until he was willing to declare publicly his faith in Christ before his teammates at school, before his college group at church, and especially before his parents at home, he wasn't really willing to declare Christ at all.

CHAPTER FOUR

THE DECISION

It was in this sad mental and emotional state that Scott arrived at his parents' home high in the Palos Verdes hills that cold January night. Palos Verdes was one of the most exclusive districts in all of the LA area, located where the Pacific coastline stops its southernly descent below Los Angeles and makes a sharp turn to the east toward Long Beach. Wide, tree-lined roads wound their way through the high, rolling hills of this exclusive peninsula, and the land was sectioned off into large, palatial estates, owned by some of the wealthiest and most influential families in the county. Scott had always been proud of where he lived, but on this night, he felt no sense of satisfaction as he rounded the last curve and pulled into the driveway of the Graham estate.

He parked his Blazer in their large three-car garage and walked into the deserted house. It was a sprawling, ranch-style home, built back in the seventies on five manicured acres, with a circular drive in the front and a swimming pool in the back. It even had stables beyond the pool where horses had been kept at one time. But as the boys had grown up, they had lost their interest in riding, and the horses had been sold years before. Florence Graham now used the converted stable building as a storage shed for all the scores of boxes of Christmas decorations she put up and took down each year.

Scott turned on the light and sat down heavily at the oak table in the breakfast nook. He had not eaten since grabbing a snack at noon, but he had no thoughts of food. He now had a decision to make, and he found that he could think of little else until he made it.

On the one hand, he could slip to his knees and give his life to Christ right then, which was what nearly everyone wanted him to do. He could call Candi and tell her of his decision, which, he was sure, would delight her. He then could pass the news on to his mother later that night when she would most assuredly call. He could call Tony and tell him to count him out of his scheme to cash in on Jamal Davis' misfortune. Then he could set forth to live the Christian life and to pursue his future wife. Not only did it rhyme, it made perfect sense. There was only one problem. He simply found no faith inside himself to do it.

Oh, he tried to believe all the stuff he had heard from the Bible, but it all seemed so far-fetched. Could a loving God really send good and sincere people to hell just because they hadn't received Jesus? And what about those who had never heard of Him at all? The God he had always believed in just couldn't be that narrow and heartless.

He was reluctant to really study the Bible or any other serious books written about its doctrines, but at Candi's suggestion, he read several apocalyptic novels first published in a series back in the late 90's. They were about what happens to a bunch of people during the tribulation who had not accepted Christ, and were left behind here on earth after the rapture. He pretended to be impressed with them so he might, in turn, impress Candi. But in all honesty, he found them way too fanciful. He even got Tony to read a couple of them, and they shared some good laughs over some of the books' more bizarre episodes. No, he had not been able to buy into all that stuff, and still wasn't, at least not at this time.

On the other hand, he could stop playing games and be honest with himself and everyone else. He could tell Candi that he was in love with her and that he wanted to go out with her, but that he was not ready to accept Christ at this time. She would have to decide whether or not she could accept him as he was. He could then go along with Tony and win the cash that would allow him to get out from under his parents' control a little bit, and to pursue Candi in somewhat the style she deserved. This option, frankly, appealed to him much more than the former.

Suddenly, his decision was made. He would do the deed! A sense of relief came over him, and it felt as though a load had been lifted from his shoulders. He got up from the table and headed for his father's study. He had already come up with a pretty good idea where he might find the money he would need to place his bet on Houston.

In Bruce Graham's study, buried in the concrete, concealed under the carpet in the closet, was a large floor safe. Scott had known of its existence for years, but he had never seen it open. Only about a month before, he had come across the combination to it, quite by accident.

His father had been out of town and Scott was working at his father's desk, using his computer, when he inadvertently knocked the phone line loose from its jack under the desk with his foot. He immediately lost contact with the Internet. Sensing what had happened, he crawled under the desk to reattach the line, and that's when he made his discovery.

Scott had left one of the desk drawers partially pulled out when he had opened it to retrieve a pen, and while under the desk, he glanced up and saw a couple of numbers penciled on the bottom of the drawer. They caught his attention right away, because one number had been preceded by an R and the other by an L. He suspected immediately that they were part of a safe combination, and he pulled the drawer out the rest of the way. Sure enough, there were five numbers altogether written on the bottom of it, all preceded alternately by R's and L's.

He knew then that the combination was almost surely that of the floor safe in the closet. His father must have written it there as a precaution, just in case he should ever have forgotten it or had a need to tell someone else how to access the safe. Scott wondered at the time what might be in the safe, but having no compelling reason to look in it, and respecting his father's privacy, he had not tried to open it. But, that had been then, and this was now.

Now he went directly to his father's study, turned on the light, and crawled under the desk again. Only this time, he copied the numbers from the bottom of the desk drawer onto a piece of paper. He then opened the closet door and pulled back the carpet to reveal the top of the safe. He tried the combination, and on the first attempt, it opened freely as he turned the handle.

As he began removing the contents of the safe, he was careful to place everything in order so he could replace things properly and prevent his father from suspecting the intrusion. At the top of the safe, Scott found the obvious items he had expected: insurance policies, a will, some stocks and bonds, the deed to the house, etc. But under the top layer of documents, "What was this . . . two *Playboy* magazines?" Scott smiled to himself, "So, the good ole' born-again Christian isn't quite as sanctified as he would like me to think he is." But Scott couldn't be too condemning. On a different occasion, he might well have checked out the contents of those magazines himself, but he had no time for such diversions now. He was a man on a mission.

At last, there under the magazines, he saw what he was looking for: a bundle of currency. But when he retrieved it, he was sorely disappointed. Instead of the thick pile of hundred-dollar notes he had been hoping for, it was a bundle of assorted old bills instead. On examination, Scott found it to contain a large assortment of old Silver Certificates and two-dollar bills. There wasn't more than a few hundred dollars in total, but it wouldn't have mattered anyway. They obviously were collector's items and would have been irreplaceable.

Scott was about to give up hope of finding anything both negotiable and replaceable, because the only thing left in the bottom of the safe was a metal container, about the size of a cigar box. He assumed it contained a similar assortment of old coins to go along with the bundle of currency, but he decided to have a look inside it anyway.

As he retrieved it, he found it to be much heavier than he had expected. "The old man must have been collecting these things for decades," he thought to himself. But as he opened the box he was both surprised and relieved. For along with a large assortment of old coins, Scott identified a whole section of large gold ones. He took them out and counted thirty-five American Double Eagles. They were about the size of an old silver dollar and Scott understood them to contain exactly one ounce of pure gold apiece. More importantly, he also remembered hearing that gold was worth about $400 per ounce on the exchange.

Now he remembered. Back at the turn of the century, everyone had been worried about the horrors of Y2K. Because of a numbers glitch, many experts had predicted worldwide chaos when millions of computers were to have shut down, having been unable to convert to the year 2000 from 1999.

People everywhere had stockpiled food and survival equipment to help them make it through the crisis. Bruce Graham had done some of that as well, but mostly he had decided to convert some of his assets to gold. He had said you could always use gold no matter how tough things might get.

Scott remembered his dad showing him all those shiny gold coins back then, but he had assumed that when the crisis never materialized, the coins had been sold, or at least secured in a safe deposit box in the bank somewhere. He had never imagined that they could still be right here in the house.

But, believe it or not, they were still there, and nothing could have pleased him more. Gold coins could easily be converted to the cash he would need to place his bet, and then converted back again from his winnings. When he replaced them in the safe, his dad would never suspect a thing. After all, one double eagle looks pretty much the same as the next one.

Not knowing exactly what the current price of gold was, Scott selected fifteen coins, just to be sure, and returned the others to the box. He then replaced the box and all the other contents to the safe and put everything back as it had been before. If the Grahams were to return home that evening, Bruce would never detect that anyone had been in his study, much less his safe.

As Scott tossed and turned in bed later that night, sleep eluded him. He was filled with anticipation over the upcoming *Tony and Scott's Great Adventure,* but he also struggled with the knowledge that in the process, he might well sacrifice that which was of far greater value than whatever pleasure and profit he might hope to gain.

The next day, Thursday, was a busy one for Scott Graham. After his last class had let out at 1:30, he drove down to the office of a precious metals dealership on Pine Street in Long Beach. He had looked up the address in the phone book earlier that morning and found it with little difficulty. He was nervous, but the clerk who waited on him, a fat little man with a goatee, named Silas, handled the whole transaction rather matter-of-factly. He asked to see Scott's identification, and remarked that if Scott had come in a month earlier he wouldn't have been able to help him had he not been accompanied by one of his parents. Scott was in his junior year at the university, and had just turned twenty-one the day after Christmas.

With the commission charges, it took thirteen of the coins to net Scott the necessary five thousand dollars. He noticed that it would take somewhat more than that sum to buy them back on Monday, but since he planned to have over fifteen thousand dollars by then, he didn't balk at the thought of the additional charge.

Next, he took the cashier's check he received from Silas to the Bank of America branch near the university. He had just opened an account there under his own name with some money he had received from his grandparents for his birthday and Christmas combined. As a child, he had always resented having been born near Christmas because it always seemed that he had thereby been cheated out of his fair share of presents. His brothers had always received separate presents on their birthdays and then again at Christmas, but he had usually been doubled up on, receiving only one present for both.

But that wasn't on his mind at this time. He was just thankful that he now had his own account and independent access to it. As requested, he slid his new bank card through the machine on the counter and punched in his PIN number, trying to act as though he had done so thousands of times, when in fact, it was his maiden voyage. He was pleasantly surprised when everything went through smoothly, and the pleasant, middle-aged teller, identified as Liz by her nametag, asked him how he would like the cash. He said in hundred-dollar bills, and she counted them out matter-of-factly, as though she had done so thousands of times, which she probably had.

He locked the cash in his glove box and drove back on campus to meet Candi. He had called her early that morning and had asked her to meet him at their usual spot in the student union at 3:30. He managed to arrive a little early, but she was already there, waiting for him. On seeing him approach, she smiled and pushed back a chair for him.

"Hi Scott," she said, as he sat down across from her, "what's so important that you had to see me before your big meet tonight?"

She looked so beautiful to him and he sensed such love for her, that he nearly abandoned the idea of telling her what he had intended to say, but he screwed up his courage and forged ahead.

"Hi Candi, thanks for meeting me on such short notice. I've got something really important to tell you and I wanted to do it in person."

Her eyes lit up immediately and she leaned forward expectantly. "What is it, Scott?"

He then realized that she had misunderstood his intentions and was expecting him to tell her some great news, like he had just been converted or something. He hated himself for what he was about to say, but he knew he had to do it. "Candi, I've thought a lot about this and I need to level with you," he said. "Please, I want you to listen and let me get it all out at one time, without interruption, okay?"

Her expectant look turned to a quizzical one, but she agreed to hear him out in silence.

"I've never had a steady girlfriend before," he began. "I guess I still don't have one now, but the past five months have been great being with you.

"I know I wasn't supposed to do this, but I've gone and fallen in love with you. I want you to love me too, I want you to marry me when we graduate, I want you to have my kids, I want to grow old with you, I want it all."

At this point he began to choke up, and Candi was about to say something, but he put up his hand, regained his composure, and continued.

"I would do almost anything to please you, Candi, and I know how much religion means to you, but I can't pretend any longer. I can't believe like you do, not yet anyway, and I need to let you know before you should ever start caring for me too."

Now it was Candi who choked up and through her tears she blurted out, "How can you be so blind, Scott? I love you too! I've loved you from the beginning. I told myself I wasn't going to fall for you, but it didn't do any good. I want all the same things you do, but dammit, I'm *not* going to marry a non-Christian!"

By this time, she was sobbing. Scott tried to reach out to her, but she pushed his hand away. He was surprised that she had confessed to loving him too, but perhaps even more surprised that she had just sworn at him. He had never heard her say anything that had even remotely resembled profanity before. She totally lost her composure at this point and got up to leave.

"Wait, Candi, we've got to talk about this," he pleaded.

"Oh, no we don't!" she choked out, "I don't want my heart to be broken any more than it already is. I don't want to talk to you again at all. Not until you come to Christ. But don't you dare do it for my sake! You have to make that decision for yourself. I'll manage to live if I have to go on without you, but you'll never have life at all if you continue to go on without Jesus. Goodbye, Scott!"

With that she pulled her jacket around her shoulders and ran out of the building. Scott, almost overcome with emotion himself, wanted to run after her, but he knew that it would have been to no avail. They had come to an impasse, and there wasn't much of anything that could be done to remedy it at the moment. He just stood there and watched her go, his heart filled with sorrow and anger.

He was angry with himself for his own stubborn unbelief, he was angry with Candi for her fanatical insistence on his conversion, but perhaps most of all, he was angry with God. Why had He granted Candi such complete and simple faith, and at the same time, withheld it from him? Why had He allowed them to come together and fall in love, and then for Him to be the one and only obstacle now driving them apart?

Later that evening, Scott swam in the dual meet against UC Santa Barbara. In spite of his depressed emotional condition, he won both the 50— and the 100-meter freestyle events in the best times he had had all season.

Perhaps the competition gave him an opportunity to vent some of his pent-up frustrations. Tony, of course, won all of the breaststroke and butterfly events, as he had done in every meet so far that season. He was one of the best swimmers in the nation and a cinch to make the upcoming Olympic team. Aaron Muller, an outstanding Jewish boy on the team, won the backstroke events, and the three of them teamed up with Jake Turner to sweep most of the relay and medley events as well. In all, their team won all but four of the events in the meet and soundly defeated one of their archrivals.

However, the victory was a hollow one for Scott. He looked for Candi in the stands where she had always been before, but she had not come. After the meet, when she still failed to appear, he went out with Tony to get something to eat. There, he told his friend that he had the cash and was ready to go ahead with the scheme. Tony was delighted with the news and suggested they skip their first period class and place their bets the first thing in the morning.

Upon arriving home later that evening, Scott hurried to check if he had received any messages from Candi, but there was none. There was only one from his mother, calling him from Jerusalem to tell him, for the sixth time, that they were having a great time, and they were praying for him to do well in his swim meet.

He spent another restless night struggling with his frustration over his breakup with Candi, if you could call it that. He had never officially been going with her in the first place, but he felt awful, nonetheless. He sensed that he had lost a big chunk right out of his heart. He wanted to call her and make it all better, but he knew that unless he was able to tell her of his newfound faith in Jesus Christ, no other words would be of any avail. He knew he wasn't ready for that sort of a commitment yet, so he didn't bother trying to call.

Besides, there was the thrill of the big payoff coming after tomorrow night's game. He lay awake thinking of all the ways he would be able to spend his newly acquired, ill-gotten gain. He tried to convince himself that with this added advantage, surely he would be able to win Candi over, with or without a conversion. But inside, there was that nagging voice telling him not to count on it.

Friday, the big payday, finally arrived. Scott, having been able to sleep very little anyway, was up before the sun and off to school by 7:30. He met Tony at eight and joined his friend in his Mustang to go place their bets on the game. Tony drove without hesitation through a busy section of the downtown Long Beach area, and parked outside a nondescript office building. As he jumped out and started for the door, Scott put a hand on his shoulder and stopped him.

"Hey, dude, how do you know this is the right place, and how did you know how to get here?"

"Well, you see, my good man," Tony said with a smug grin, "there are a few things about myself that I've neglected to tell you. I've actually been here and placed a bet or two before, but never with this kind of money and never with this kind of an advantage."

With that, he feigned a punch to Scott's stomach and, with a laugh, opened the door and led his friend into the reception area of the Worldwide Travel Agency. There he greeted the pretty receptionist, Heather, who immediately perked up when she saw who it was.

"Oh, hi, Tony," she cooed, her hazel eyes flashing under her thick auburn hair. Obviously attracted to the handsome young athlete, she winked and said, "Come this way, Mr. Dini is expecting you."

With that, she got up and straightened her mini skirt and led them through a large area, where several secretaries appeared to be hard at work, to an office at the rear of the building. Scott could not help but notice Heather's long slender legs and attractive figure as she wiggled her way in front of them. He suspected that she hadn't really needed to escort them to the office, because Tony undoubtedly knew the way. But Scott noticed his friend also checking her out as she walked, and he figured Heather had planned it that way so Tony could get a clear view of what might be available to him if he were so inclined.

"After tonight," Scott could almost hear Tony thinking, "I'll have plenty of money to spend on you, pretty woman, and on a lot of other ones just like you."

Scott realized that Heather hadn't so much as given him a second glance, and it really didn't surprise him. He knew he wasn't unattractive, but next to Tony, he might as well have been the Hunchback of Notre Dame. No one would have had much of a chance of being noticed standing alongside Tony. Scott had gotten used to feeling invisible around girls when he was with him, so enamored were they always with his friend's striking good looks.

That had been one of the many things that had attracted him to Candi so much. Tony obviously noticed her right away, and tried to move in, but she dismissed his advances completely. Tony's pride was wounded, of course, but he recovered quickly, commenting on of all the other fish out there in the sea.

Now, after Heather knocked and gained entrance to Mr. Dini's office, she introduced Tony D'Angelo and his friend, somewhat embarrassed that she hadn't even thought to inquire about Scott's name. She smiled at Tony once again as she turned to return to her station, and Scott was sure she purposefully brushed up against him as she passed.

The meeting with Mr. Dini was uneventful. Tony had called before they came and the transaction took less than five minutes. The two had combined their money earlier, and Mr. Dini, a handsome man, in a business suit, in his mid-forties, with brown hair and eyes to match, took the bundle, matter of factly. He thumbed through the stack of 100 hundred-dollar bills in his hand and mentally weighed them, not even bothering to count. Satisfied that it felt right, he placed it in a drawer and handwrote Tony a receipt for a $10,000 wager on Houston that night.

After a few pleasantries, they shook hands all around and Tony and Scott left the office. As they passed Heather's desk on their way out, she again spoke sweetly to Tony and completely ignored Scott. Tony promised to call her later, to her obvious delight, and the two young men left the building.

On their way back to the university, Scott voiced his disappointment at his only experience at doing business with the underworld. He had expected a smoke-filled bookie joint, populated with beady-eyed little men with sleeve holders and visors demanding secret handshakes and passwords.

Tony explained to him that things in real life were not always like they were portrayed in the movies. He assured him that once he had been proven trustworthy, a phone call and an explanation was all that was necessary to set up the deal. After all, they were businessmen, not gangsters, for Pete's sake.

Scott asked about the tickets to the game that night, and Tony pulled them out of his pocket.

"Way ahead of you, man," he quipped. "I got these last Tuesday."

"But how did you even know I would be going with you?" Scott protested.

"I didn't, but I had a pretty good hunch you would. Besides, even if you didn't go, I didn't think I'd have had any trouble getting someone to accompany me to the game, and she would have been a lot better looking than you, let me tell you."

After a nervous day of sitting through boring classes, and a light workout at practice, they left early for the game. They drove in Tony's car up the San Diego Freeway from Long Beach, past the Santa Monica Freeway interchange, and exited east on Wilshire Blvd. in the west Los Angeles area. They turned north on Westwood Blvd. and followed it right into the UCLA campus. They stopped at the kiosk and paid for their parking permit and followed the road until it dead-ended next to parking structure number six. After parking on the second level, they took the short walk northward to the massive Pauley Pavilion, already beginning to fill, more than two hours before the game.

Now, here they were on the edge of their seats, after only a few days of anticipation, which had seemed like a month. They were eagerly awaiting the opening tip off of the game, and of the beginning of a brand new chapter in their lives.

CHAPTER FIVE

THE GAME

Jamal Davis stood with his toes crowding the stripe at the center circle awaiting the opening tip off of the game he had dreaded for the past week. He looked around the circle at the faces of the four teammates he was about to betray. He saw looks of excitement and anticipation; looks of innocent hopefulness, anticipating the victory to which, they were confident, their super star would most surely lead them. He tried to smile and look upbeat, but could not bring himself to actually look any of them in the eye.

In the middle of the circle, about to jump center against Billy Jackson for the initial tip off, was Alexander King. He was smaller than Jackson, at 7'0" and 245 pounds, but he had amazing leaping ability. (*"Especially for a white boy,"* everyone thought, but didn't actually say.) Coach Barnes had given him the nickname of "Sky King," after one of the favorite TV personalities he had watched growing up as a child.

Alex actually looked nothing like the stocky, middle-aged actor who had played Sky King, the airplane pilot, so long ago. It was his last name, of course, that had made the original connection in the coach's mind, but it was the athlete's ability to *sky* without the use of an airplane, that had confirmed the title. Although few of them had ever heard of the original Sky King, much less seen an episode of his program, Alex's teammates, and even sportscasters, had picked up on the name, and it had stuck. Around the country, Sky King was known to be the big center for UCLA.

Sky, as a junior, was a talented athlete, with quick hands and a soft touch on the ball. When unmolested, he was deadly under the basket, whether shooting or rebounding. The problem was that under the basket, one was rarely unmolested. He lacked the bulk and the aggressiveness of some of his counterparts around the country and, though he always made his presence known, he was not considered one of the truly great post players, as Houston's Billy Jackson was proving to be.

To Jamal's right, and separated from him by a Houston player, was Samuel Clayton, UCLA's big power forward. At 6'10" and 265 pounds, he did indeed contribute a lot of power to his team. He was known as college basketball's "Slammin' Sammy," because of the powerful way he loved to dunk the ball. Under the basket, he helped make up for any appearance of weakness Sky King's presence may have given.

Like Jamal, Sammy had grown up a poor black kid in the inner city, but he had blossomed at UCLA. He was a good student and was well liked on campus, and though only a sophomore, he had already become a dominant force on the basketball team.

Across the center circle, Jamal could see Jared Andersen, eager to get things underway. He was the remaining African-American in the starting lineup. Though a senior, he had just recently earned that position, proving himself to be worthy of starting as their shooting guard. Prior to that, Jamal had played in that position, and Denton Foster, a tough senior at 6'8", had filled Jamal's present forward slot. Jared, at 6'5', wasn't as tall as Jamal, but he handled the ball almost as well, and was a good outside shooter. With Jared in the game, Jamal's presence in the forecourt gave the Bruins considerably more firepower around the basket.

Rounding out the starting five was Russell Thomas, an amazing addition to their squad that year. On the surface, he didn't seem to have much going for him. He was a freshman, a skinny white kid, and only 6'2". He didn't have the look of an athlete. As he walked, he was clearly knock-kneed and pigeon-toed. With his flattop haircut, his teeth slightly bucked, and his shoulders slightly stooped, he looked more like he had come out of the hills of West Virginia, than from a top high school in Beverly Hills, which he had.

But put a basketball in his hands, and he was transformed. He was one of those players who only comes along once in a lifetime. The ball seemed to be an extension of his body. Whether he was dribbling, passing, or shooting, he was always in total control. He seemed to have a sixth sense about him, having command of everything that was going on around him. He would sometimes pass the ball behind his back, without even looking, to an empty spot on the court just as one of his teammates broke into it. He just seemed to *know* that he was going to be there.

Russ was one of the most highly recruited players in the history of college basketball, but he had made it clear from the beginning that he was going to go to UCLA and play at least one year with his hero, Jamal Davis. Coach Barnes couldn't have been more pleased, nor could the rest of the team. Russ was just eighteen, and a big cutup most of the time, but get him in a game, and he played with the heart and skill of a pro. He was their point guard and playmaker par excellence.

More than anyone else, Jamal hated the thought of letting Russ down. The Kid, as they called him, played with such passion and abandon, and he practically worshipped Jamal. How was Jamal going to face him and the rest of the team after throwing the game and screwing up their chances of going undefeated for the whole season?

But as he looked at the Houston team, he consoled himself a little with the thought that perhaps he wouldn't have to work too hard to lose the game. The Cougar team was taller than theirs at every position, and they appeared to be heavier too. Billy Jackson looked like a mountain in the center of the circle, and Bo Sutherland, standing next to Jamal right now, was nearly 7'0" himself. Jamal had a feeling the two of them were going to be all over him that night.

Then, they also had Winston Daniels, a black kid at 6'5" from Harlem, who was reported to be a wizard in the backcourt. He and his teammates would give Jared and The Kid all they could handle.

Still, Jamal was confident that they could and should win this game. The only thing that was really going to stop them was not the Houston team, but his own treasonous intentions. He had never felt such disgust with himself as he did right at the moment the referee tossed the ball high into the air to start the dreaded contest.

Billy Jackson gathered himself in preparation for the toss of the ball. As it arched above him, he leaped high into the air, fully expecting to control the tip, just as he had always done. But just as he was about to reach the ball, a slender white hand extended several inches above his, and Sky King easily tipped it in the opposite direction.

Jackson gasped in disbelief and turned to see Jamal Davis jumping up to retrieve the ball. In midair, he caught it, turned, and tossed it down the court, all in one fluid motion. Sammy Clayton was already sprinting toward the basket and caught the ball in mid-stride. He was well in front of the surprised Houston defenders, and was able to plan his attack.

He sailed high into the air and brought the ball with both hands back over his head, arching his back. Then with a snap, he brought his shoulders forward, catapulting the ball toward the basket at the end of his long, powerful arms. The ball smashed into the net with a tremendous snap, and Sammy's hands hit the rim with such force that it caused the entire backboard apparatus to rattle and sway.

He held onto the rim momentarily, making sure his feet were under him, before dropping gracefully to the court. The partisan crowd exploded its approval as Sammy trotted back down the floor. He pointed at Jamal with and big grin and shouted, "Nice pass, Jamal."

Three seconds had not expired from the huge, four-sided scoreboard clock hanging from the ceiling overhead, and already UCLA had jumped out in front. The happy fans were eagerly looking forward to the rest of the game unfolding equally to their liking.

Jamal felt that familiar rush as he took his place on defense under the Houston basket. The game was in progress and he was in control. Then it dawned on him what he had just done. "Hey, stupid," he scolded himself, "you can't be playing like that. Not tonight."

As Winston Daniels brought the ball down for the Cougars, he spotted Bo Sutherland underneath, pretty much by himself, because Jamal had purposefully backed off from him. With amazing quickness, Daniels fired the ball into Sutherland, who spun to face the basket. Jamal had closed on him by now and could have swatted the ball from Sutherland's hands, but he didn't even make an attempt at it. As Sutherland crouched to jump, Jamal sensed when he should have timed his own jump so he could block the shot, but he hesitated a fraction of a second. When he reached the top of his jump, Bo had already released the shot, and the ball sailed over the top of Jamal's fingertips. It wasn't a pretty shot. The ball caromed off the backboard and rattled around the rim before it finally fell through, but it counted as a field goal, nonetheless.

As both teams returned to set up at the other end of the court, Jamal could see the confidence returning to the faces of the Houston players as well. Oh, how he hated what he was feeling! No one was blaming him for what had just taken place at the other end. They were too busy admiring the way Sutherland had executed the play. But Jamal knew he could have prevented him from making that basket in at least three different ways. He knew the caliber of play of which he was capable. How could he continue to play at a level so far beneath that, and see the game slip right through his fingers? But, like it or not, he reminded himself, that is exactly what he was going to have to do.

As difficult as it was for Jamal, he did manage to control himself throughout the first half. No one in the building, who hadn't already known of his agreement to throw the game, suspected he was deliberately slacking off. He led his team with 14 points, 6 rebounds, and 5 assists, and he indeed made some brilliant plays. But he purposefully passed up some clear opportunities, both to score points for his own team, and to prevent Houston from doing likewise.

He deliberately passed up shots he could have taken, as well as passes he could have made to an open man. Of the shots he did take, he consciously missed some of the more difficult ones, and he even missed three free throws, which would never have happened ordinarily. He failed to get some rebounds he would normally have pulled down, and he let himself get tied up for a jump ball on two occasions, which would not have normally happened either. But the hardest part for him was the way he forced himself to let up on defense.

Billy Jackson was pretty much having his way with Sky King under the basket, and already had 21 points and 10 rebounds. Jamal could have helped Sky with him on several occasions, but chose not to do so. Jamal's primary responsibility was to guard Bo Sutherland, and ordinarily it would have been an easy task. Bo was a big kid, and aggressive, but he wasn't particularly skillful. On many occasions Jamal could have taken the ball from him or blocked his shot, but he forced himself to pass up most of those opportunities. As a result, Bo was having the game of his life. He had 12 points and 7 rebounds at half time, and he was feeling cocky.

Both he and Jackson were beginning to taunt Jamal. They were leading their team to a 51–42 halftime lead over the number one team in the nation, and they were feeling pretty darned good about it. On one occasion, after making a basket over Jamal, Sutherland chided him as they headed for the opposite end of the court, "Hey Jamal, what's the matter? You finding it hard to play against the big boys?"

"Nice shot," Jamal replied with a forced smile, but inside he was boiling. He didn't know if he would be able to continue to hold back for the rest of the game or not.

As the horn sounded at the end of the first half, the stunned audience wasn't nearly so loud as it had been at the beginning of the game. As the teams returned to their dressing rooms, there was a sense of apprehension hanging over the formerly jubilant crowd.

Their fears were justified, because Houston had clearly outplayed UCLA for the first twenty minutes. The rest of the team seemed to have taken their lead from Jamal, and had all been playing below their potential. Sky King had 10 points and 5 rebounds, but it was clear that he had pretty well been beaten up on by Jackson under the basket. Sammy Clayton had 8 points and 4 boards, and had been playing hard, but it was obvious that he had not had the same exuberance that normally would have characterized his game. Even The Kid had been having his problems. Houston's Winston Daniels had been giving him fits, not allowing him to drive to the basket. The Kid had managed to hit only two for four from behind the three-point circle, and he had gone into the locker room with only 6 points, well below his normal output.

There were a good number of fans in the crowd cheering for Houston. Some had flown out from Texas just to see the game, but the majority of them were from the LA area. Some had a previous loyalty to Houston for one reason or another, but most of them were USC fans who would have rooted for any team playing against the Bruins. These fans were having the time of their lives, cheering wildly at every successful play executed by Houston and every miscue by UCLA.

None of them were more enthusiastic than Scott Graham and Tony D'Angelo. They had spent much of the first half on their feet, loudly expressing their approval of the way things were going, much to the displeasure of the Bruin fans around them.

"This is my kind of game," Tony beamed as they sat back in their seats during the half time break.

"Yeah," agreed Scott as he looked up again at the big scoreboard to confirm the sizable Houston lead, "I don't remember when I've had quite so much fun watching the home team get beat."

"Just twenty more minutes and we can go out and celebrate," Tony added, "and we won't have to worry about how much it'll cost either."

"That's for sure, I can hardly wait. I just hope Davis doesn't change his mind and turn things around toward the end of the game."

"I don't think we have anything to worry about, Scott. He would never risk his life over one ball game. He'll continue doing just what he's been doing, and he'll be off the hook with the mob, and we'll be rolling in dough. I love it!"

In the UCLA locker room, Coach Barnes wasn't loving it at all. As a matter of fact, he was loudly expressing his displeasure. He was in his late fifties, overweight, and had a heart problem, but he couldn't have cared less about his own health right then. His only concern was how sickly his team had performed in the first half.

"What's the matter with you guys?" he demanded. "You're playing like a bunch of old barmaids out there! Houston's got a good team, but they're not a *great* team. Most of the teams you've played this whole year are better than they are, yet you're making them look like all-stars." The veins stood out on his thick neck, and his round face was approaching crimson in color.

"All of you are dragging, but Jamal, you're the worst," he said, looking directly at the tall athlete. "You should be eating Sutherland's lunch, but you're letting him get away with murder out there. You need to be helping Sky with Jackson more too. Those two are killing us under the bucket, and you don't seem to be willing to do too much about it.

"Sure, you're having a good game," he conceded, "but you should be having a *great* game against these guys. You're going to have to pick it up this next half, or we're gonna lose our shirts out there. And that goes for the rest of you girls too!"

"Okay, Coach," Jamal lied, "I won't let you down. We can take these guys. Come on, Let's do it!"

Jamal was on his feet and acting excited and determined, but there was something about his performance that just didn't ring true. He didn't know whether the others noticed it or not, but he was sure Coach Barnes picked up on it. As the coach sent the rest of the team back out on the court to warm up, he asked Jamal to wait behind.

"What is it, Jamal? Are you sure you're feeling alright?"

"Yeah, Coach, I'm fine," he replied, not wanting to sound too convincing. "Oh, I do feel like I might be coming down with some kind of little bug or something, but it's no big deal." He thought it best to give the coach some explanation for his sub-par performance. He might be able to fool most of the people out there, but Chuck Barnes wasn't one of them. He wasn't playing up to his potential and his coach knew it almost as well as he did.

"Well, you let me know how you're feeling, son," Barnes said, as he put an arm around Jamal's shoulder. "You're the key to this team's success, and I'll pull you out before I'll let you injure yourself or make yourself sick. We don't have to win tonight, but we do have to have you healthy as we head into the national playoffs."

"Thanks, Coach, but I'll be fine," Jamal responded as he left the room with the older man to rejoin his teammates on the court.

This had to be the most miserable day of his life, Jamal thought. Here he was, betraying this good man, along with his team and his fans, and yet his coach was genuinely supportive of him and concerned about his well-being.

He just wanted it to be over, and yet he had to be careful. If he played too well, they might rally and win the game; and as much as he would have liked that emotionally, he just simply could not allow it to happen. But on the other hand, if he played too poorly, the coach would surely bench him; and his team was perfectly capable of turning the game around and pulling off a win even without him. He couldn't allow that to happen either. So he would have to play just well enough to stay in the game, and just badly enough to keep his team from winning. It wouldn't be easy, and it surely wouldn't be any fun.

The second half began pretty much as the first half had ended, with Houston putting on the pressure and controlling the tempo of the game. At one point they had increased their lead to as many as thirteen points, and it looked as though they might not only win the game, but actually blow

UCLA away in the process. Yet, with about twelve minutes left in the contest, the Bruins began slowly turning things around.

This was due in part to the fact that the Houston players simply were getting tired. Their starting five had played their hearts out for nearly three-quarters of the game, with very few opportunities to rest, and it was catching up with them. Also adding to the turnaround was the fact that the rest of the Bruin team began to adjust to Jamal's inconsistency, and to compensate for it. Alex "Sky" King became more aggressive under the basket and was able to keep Jackson at bay. "Slammin' Sammy" Clayton began taking the ball to the hoop with more authority, and Russell "The Kid" Thomas started penetrating inside and making some sensational plays.

Jamal found himself walking a tightrope. He too picked up the pace towards the end of the game, especially when he had a chance to burn Jackson or Sutherland. But he had to be careful not to play too well. He was determined to make a respectable showing and not humiliate himself or his teammates, but he had to make sure, at the same time, that they did in fact lose the game.

With five minutes left in the contest, the Bruins had narrowed Houston's lead to only six points, and it seesawed back and forth around that margin until nearly the end of the game. Jared Anderson, who had suddenly developed a hot hand, sank a twenty-foot jump shot from the corner, with a minute left on the clock, to bring UCLA within three. But Houston came right back, as Winston Daniels drove the lane and buried a left-handed lay-up over Jamal's outstretched hand.

Jamal felt he could have blocked the shot, but with the score that close, he knew he could not risk it. Now trailing by five points, with less than a minute to play, he was confident that they would go ahead and lose, but that they would be able to do so with some dignity.

As they set up at their end of the court, the Bruins were looking to get a quick score so they would have time to get the ball back in time to score again before they ran out of time. Knowing that at least one of the baskets had to be from the three-point range, The Kid found himself open on the left side and fired up a jumper from just outside the circle. The shot looked good, and the crowd jumped to their feet in anticipation, but the ball struck the back of the rim and bounced high into the air, just to the right of the basket.

Jamal found himself right under the ball as it started its descent. He jumped up to meet it just as Billy Jackson also bounded up after the rebound. Jamal had the advantage and got to the ball first. He could have attempted to tip the ball in, which would have been fairly routine for him, but that would have put them within striking distance of winning the game, and he dared not risk it. He could have pulled down the rebound and passed it to Sky, who was open on the other side of the key, but then he would surely have scored an easy basket, and that would have amounted to the same thing. So Jamal did the only thing he felt he could do under the circumstances.

He grabbed the ball with both hands, but instead of pulling it down to protect it, he held it over his head, just for a fraction of a second. But that brief instant was all the time it took for Jackson to get his big hands on the ball as well. Jamal held on with all his strength to keep the stronger Jackson from wrenching it out of his hands, and as they were descending to the court, locked together, the referee was already blowing his whistle, signaling a jump ball.

Jamal had saved face, but he might just as well have given the ball over to Jackson. He knew that the possession arrow was in Houston's favor, and any jump ball would simply be given to the Cougars to bring it in from out of bounds. With 43 seconds left to play and with Houston in possession of the ball and a five-point lead, Jamal was confident that the final outcome of the game was secure. Jamal had taken care of everything-except for Jackson's size 22 feet.

Houston's huge center hit the court an instant before Jamal did, and Jamal's left foot landed on the side of Jackson's big Nike-clad right one. Freddie Baker had done a good job in taping Jamal's ankle, but even that was not sufficient enough to sustain it under so much torsion. The tape ripped, the ankle rolled, ligaments stretched, and tendons popped, and the tall athlete collapsed in agony on the court.

An injury time-out was called, and Coach Barnes ran to Jamal's side. The all-American tried to stand up and assure his coach that he could continue, but it was obvious to everyone that he was through for the night. Sammy and Jared assisted him to the bench, and Freddie immediately took off Jamal's shoe and sock, cut off the tape, and put an ice pack on the already swelling ankle. Denton Foster checked in for Jamal, and the team huddled around Coach Barnes for their final instructions.

"I don't know what to tell you, fellows," he said with some resignation in his voice. "There's no sense in fouling them at this point. Daniels will be handling the ball for them, and he hasn't missed a free throw all night. We would just be putting ourselves in a deeper hole. Put pressure on them and try to force a turnover. Don't let them get any easy shots. Let's get the ball back as quickly as possible and get a score, then we'll call time out and figure out what we're gonna do after that. I'm proud of you guys. You've played a hellava game. Get out there now and let's pull this one out for Jamal! Whaddya say?"

They all yelled their approval and moved back onto the court, but down deep, few of them entertained any real hope of actually being able to pull it off. The plan was to let the Cougars inbound the ball and then to put the pressure on and try to force the turnover before they could get down the court and set up a play. But only one Bruin had an idea how they were going to do it, and that player wasn't so much thinking it, as he was simply sensing it instinctively.

A referee had given the ball to Houston's other guard, a talented blond player named Chappell, who was preparing to inbound the ball from the sideline to their great ball handler, Winston Daniels. There was no particular pressure on him in doing so, as no Bruin defender was within ten feet of Daniels. Chappell tossed the ball in Daniels' direction and prepared to move down the court in the unlikely event that Winston got in trouble and needed to pass the ball back to him.

But the ball never got to Daniels at all. The Kid had his back to the play, and hadn't even looked over his shoulder. But suddenly, as though he had picked the ball up on some invisible radar screen, he swiveled and dived back to intercept it. He tipped the ball just before it reached Daniels' outstretched hands and sent it bouncing toward UCLA's basket.

The Kid's body was fully extended and perpendicular to the floor, and there was no way he could land upright, so he simply tucked and did a forward roll when he hit the hardwood. He bounced immediately back to his feet, losing no momentum, and sped off in pursuit of the retreating basketball.

The surprised Daniels was in hot pursuit himself, determined not to let The Kid get an easy lay up.

The Kid caught up with the ball in full stride and bounced it once before he leaped with it up toward the basket. Daniels jumped at the same time and took a desperate swipe at the ball, trying to dislodge it from The Kid's grasp before he could release it in a shot. He hit The Kid's wrist solidly and moved the basketball, but he got the shot off anyway.

It was, without a doubt, the ugliest shot of the night. It banged around wildly between the backboard and the rim, but almost miraculously, it finally slowed down and, at last, it dropped quietly through the net. The referee had already blown his whistle, signaling a foul on the part of Daniels, and suddenly UCLA was back in the ball game.

The Houston coach immediately called time out to put extra pressure on The Kid so hopefully he would choke and miss the free throw. In the Bruin huddle, Coach Barnes never even looked at The Kid, nor did any of the players. They certainly did not want to add to the immense pressure he must already be experiencing. Instead, the coach simply told them that after The Kid made the shot, they were to retreat to the other end and play tight defense. There were still 40 seconds on the clock and Houston would have to take another shot. If they couldn't force a turnover, they must at least get the rebound. At that point they were to call time out and set up their last play to win the game.

Everyone in the Pavilion was keenly interested to see if The Kid would make his foul shot; but four people in particular were breathless as the youngster toed the line and looked at the hoop fifteen feet away. Scott Graham and Tony D'Angelo looked at each other in quiet desperation. This was not the way it was supposed to happen. With Davis out of the game, there was no way he could torpedo the UCLA comeback, and things were way too close for comfort. They grimaced in frustration and fear as the young athlete prepared to take his shot. Scott even offered up a clumsy silent prayer that if God would somehow preserve the Houston victory, he would try to be a better person. But somehow he sensed he wasn't making many points with the Man Upstairs.

Someone else who was sweating it out right then was Marcus Davis. He knew people from the underworld had to be closely watching the game as well, and they couldn't be happy with what they were seeing. Marcus could almost sense their frustration and anger. If the Bruins somehow pulled this game out, he knew Jamal would instantly become a marked man.

He had that sickened feeling of being in a horrible situation and being absolutely helpless to do anything about it.

The other person in the Pavilion agonizing over the outcome of the game was, of course, Jamal Davis. He, like everyone else in the building, had been amazed at what The Kid had just done, and there was a part of him that dearly wanted his team to pull out a victory. But cold chills went down his back when he thought of what might happen to him if they should actually be able to do it. He was on his feet, like everyone else, even though the pain in his ankle protested loudly. All he could do was watch and wait, his insides being torn apart as he anticipated the longest 40 seconds of his life.

If The Kid was feeling any pressure, one could never tell it by looking at him. He calmly took the ball from the referee and politely thanked him with a smile. He seemed oblivious to all the screaming and balloon waving carried on by the Houston fans in the stands behind the basket. He bounced the ball twice, bent his knees, and shot the ball cleanly through the basket with as much ease as though he were shooting at the hoop hanging above the garage door in his driveway at home.

The Pavilion roared its approval, but The Kid was on autopilot. He simply looked around and assumed his defensive position. The game wasn't over yet and somehow you got the feeling that The Kid wasn't through yet either.

Chappell threw the ball in again to Daniels, this time making sure there was no possible chance that anyone would be able to pick it off. As the agile point guard dribbled up the court, he glanced up at the scoreboard. It showed the visitors leading by two, 105 to 103, with 38 seconds remaining. Another glance at the thirty-five second clock revealed only 33 seconds. That meant that he would not be able to run out the clock, and would have to take a shot. But he was determined to control the ball up to the very last moment, hoping to score with only six seconds left, thereby putting the game out of reach for the Bruins.

Jared and The Kid pressured him relentlessly, but he dribbled with such precision, they were unable to tie him up. He passed the ball off on occasion when he started to get boxed in, but as soon as he was free, he got it right back again. He kept looking for an opportunity to get the ball inside, but the Bruins had it boxed up completely.

When the shot clock showed only eleven seconds remaining, Daniels started maneuvering for the last shot. He passed the ball over to Chappell and then cut toward the basket, but then broke back out again just as Chappell shot the ball back to him. He was open for an instant, and he took advantage of the opportunity by jumping high, turning in the air, and getting off a shot just inside the three-point line.

The Kid had anticipated Daniels' move and was on him almost instantly. He also went high into the air and attempted to block the shot. He was unsuccessful in his attempt, barely touching the ball with the tip of his middle finger, but it may have been enough. The ball arched high and came down headed right for the basket, but it was just a little short. It hit the front of the rim and bounced almost straight up.

Billy Jackson was determined to get the rebound and preserve his team's victory. He muscled Sky King out of the way and jumped high to bring down the ball. He was just about to grasp it when he was visited by the same ghost that had frustrated him on the opening tip off. Two white hands seemed to appear out of nowhere and snatched the ball away from him. King had out-jumped him again, and this time it could mean the ball game.

As soon as Sky had control of the ball, he was signaling for time out. The referee blew his whistle and everyone in the house looked at the clock. Five seconds remained in one of the highest scoring games that had been played in the NCAA so far that year. Five seconds and two points stood between UCLA and their dream of continuing an undefeated season.

In front of the Bruin bench, Coach Barnes gave his team their instructions for their final play. The Cougars would be expecting them to get the ball to The Kid for the final shot, so he told Sammy to fake the inbound pass to him above the top of the key, and then to hit Jared on the side, who would take the shot from there. Jared had hit several from that spot throughout the game, and everyone agreed he was the best man for the unenviable task at hand.

The horn sounded, calling the teams back out on the court. The Houston players took their defensive positions with uniform looks of determination on their faces. The Bruins also lined up in a formation that appeared to favor The Kid to receive the inbound pass near the center circle. The official handed the ball to Sammy near the half court line and began his silent count to see that the ball was inbounded within the allotted five seconds.

Sammy moved to avoid the pressing defender and faked a pass to The Kid, who was breaking toward him. Then he turned and fired the ball down the side to Jared, who was temporarily in the clear. But as he turned to take his shot, Chappell was all over him. In an instant, Daniels was there too, looking for an opportunity to tie him up or swat the ball away. Jared had no chance of getting a clear shot off in time, so he turned and made a desperation pass out to The Kid, who was sprinting toward him from the half court line.

The Kid caught the ball about thirty-five feet away from the basket, and without hesitation, jumped into the air to take a frantic shot. There was one second showing on the clock, and it was now or never.

Billy Jackson had seen what was taking place and had run out to intercept The Kid before he could get the shot off. He saw that he couldn't get there in time to prevent him from shooting, but he was determined to block the shot before it ever got started toward the basket.

The Kid saw the hulk of Jackson bearing down on him, and he shot the ball, what appeared to be, almost straight up to avoid the huge hand sent up to swat it down. The ball barely cleared Jackson's extended right hand just as the final buzzer sounded. The clock said the game was over, but the shot was on its way. Victory and defeat hung in the balance, just as the basketball seemed to hang in the air, high above the hardwood court, with ten transfixed players staring up at it from below.

The arc of the ball had to be one of the highest ever made in the history of the game. The ball seemed to go up forever. It would have undoubtedly hit the ceiling in many lesser gymnasiums, and few observers would have given such a shot any chance of ever finding its mark. But even before the ball had reached the top of its arc, The Kid threw both of his hands straight over his head and began bouncing up and down as he watched the ball home in on the basket far below.

That's exactly how it appeared to the nearly 13,000 fans who held their collective breath and watched the ball top out and begin its downward path. It seemed to be guided by some unseen force that directed it straight for the center of the basket. It had gained considerable speed by the time it finally reached its destination, and it shot right through the center of the rim without touching anything until it rifled through the nylon at the very bottom of the net.

The stretched net snapped back and draped itself over the top of the rim, an unusual sight indeed, but not one person in the building even noticed it. The whole place exploded in an uproar. UCLA had just pulled off an impossible comeback and had beaten Houston 106 to 105. Everyone in Pauley Pavilion was staring at the skinny white kid, still bouncing, stiff-legged, up and down near the center of the court with his arms stretched high over his head.

His teammates on the court got to The Kid first, followed quickly by those storming in from the bench, and then by hundreds of fans that came streaming in from all directions. He was swept up in their arms and carried around the court on their shoulders. The UCLA band played thunderously, if not well, and the whole place was in pandemonium.

The whole place, that is to say, with the exception of Billy Jackson and his teammates. They stood in shocked silence, unable to comprehend for a time what had just taken place. Finally, most of them began to make their way through the crowd back to their bench, but Jackson simply sank to the floor in disbelief and despair. Sitting flat with his feet drawn up, he put his head down between his knees and began to mourn quietly. His shoulders shook as hot tears began to roll down his cheeks, joining in with the streams of sweat already dripping off his face. Together they began to form a salty puddle on the varnished hardwood beneath him.

Scott and Tony sat spellbound in their seats, ignoring the jubilant Bruin fans around them who were trying to get their attention so they could gloat. They had just seen one of the greatest basketball games ever played, but they couldn't have cared less about that. They had just lost $5,000 each, and they cared a great deal about that. They were still too much in shock to realize the depth of the trouble they were in, but they were thoroughly heartsick, and they knew it was only going to get worse.

Jamal Davis had been overwhelmed with elation like everyone else on his team when The Kid made his circus shot to seal their victory. He had been jumping around with the rest of them, unaware temporarily of the pain in his ankle, until suddenly he woke up and realized what had actually taken place. The commitment he had made had been broken. The game he had promised to lose had been won. The career that he had so desperately tried to save had just been flushed down the toilet. And the life that had been so precious to him was now up for grabs.

Before, the mob had only threatened to smash his knees, and that was if he refused to throw the game. But now, it was a different story. They had lost a huge amount of money because he had failed to deliver on what he had promised, and he was sure the price of failure had just gone up. As he stood there trembling in the middle of the court, with one shoe on and one shoe off, now oblivious of the multitudes celebrating around him, he wondered how long it would be before some hit man stuck a knife between his ribs or fired a bullet into the back of his head.

CHAPTER SIX

THE AFTERMATH

Marcus Davis was another one in the Pavilion who was devastated by the outcome of the game. After Jamal's injury, he hoped that somehow Houston would have been able to hang onto its narrow lead, but as things began to unfold in the last forty seconds, he sensed that Houston's edge and all other things he held sacred were inevitably going to be destroyed. He wasn't even surprised when The Kid's final shot ripped the net. It was as though the whole game had been previously designed by some mastermind, and that fate would not allow anything or anyone to deviate from the predetermined script.

It seemed as though the whole thing unfolded just to make his already miserable life even more unbearable. All his life he felt that he had been running away; running from the law, running from his family, and especially, running from God. With the money he was to have won from this game, he would finally have been able to run away from them all. But it was clear now that God would never let him get ahead, and never let him get away.

He had talked Jamal into going to Vegas to gamble. He introduced him to those who got him in that fateful game. He talked Jamal into agreeing to throw the game in order to settle his debt with the mob. He liquidated everything of value he owned in order to get money to bet on the game, and now it had blown up in his face. He had not been a good person, and God was going to punish him for it, and punish him good.

"Yeah, well go ahead and punish me all You like," he mumbled to himself as he sat dumbfounded in his seat, "I deserve it, but why do You have to go and destroy Jamal's life while You're at it? He's a good kid, he didn't do nothin' wrong. He couldn't help losing that game, but now the mob's gonna make him pay for all the money they lost, and they're not gonna be satisfied with just breakin' his legs."

Suddenly it dawned on Marcus the stupidity of what he was doing. First of all, the stupidity and self-centeredness to think that everything that had taken place was all about him; and secondly, the stupidity of still sitting there sulking when Jamal's life was in real danger.

He jumped to his feet and ran out onto the floor, weaving his way through the crowd to get to Jamal. He glanced around as he went, looking for any suspicious character who might have been zeroing in on him and his brother. He didn't see anyone, but that didn't necessarily mean he wasn't there.

"Come on, Jamal, we gotta get outta here!" he yelled at his brother when he got to his side.

"What's your hurry? The damage is already done. Besides, nothin's gonna happen to us in here anyway. We're surrounded by thousands of people."

"Man, you really don't know the mob, do you? You just did 'em dirty and blew the deal you made with them. They lost big time on this game and they're gonna make you pay; and me too cause I know all about it. They could have a man with a sniper rifle up there right now," he said, pointing at the metal superstructure in the top of the building. "Or one of these fans celebrating around us could have a knife up his sleeve. In a crowd like this, who would ever notice if he was to do one of us right here?"

"Ok, you made your point, let me get my stuff."

"Stuff your stuff, we gotta get outta here, right now!"

"Look, I don't even have one of my shoes on," Jamal protested.

"Forget your shoes!" Marcus said as he grabbed his brother by his arm and started leading him toward an exit.

Jamal pulled away and turned toward the UCLA bench. "Look, I can't leave here barefooted, in my sweaty uniform. I don't want the coach and the guys on the team to figure out what I was up to, and if I disappear now, they're bound to suspect something. You go ahead if you want to, but I'm not going to leave yet!"

"I can't believe you're saying this," Marcus lamented. "What're you gonna do?"

"I'm gonna go get my stuff, I'm gonna go take a shower, I'm gonna get dressed, and I'm gonna leave with everybody else. That's what I'm gonna do."

"Yeah, and what're you gonna do when one of their goons is waitin' outside to put a bullet in you when you come out?"

"I'll just take my chances, I guess," he said. "Besides, who's to say he's not waiting out there for me right now? No, if they want me, they know they can get me anytime. I don't think they're gonna risk doing anything drastic in front of so many people. You go ahead. I'll be fine."

"Oh, no you don't," Marcus came back, starting to calm down and think more rationally. "You're right, we don't need to panic, but I'm not gonna leave you here tonight. You do whatever it is you gotta do, but I'll be in your car, waitin' for you right outside the gate when you come out with the team."

"Ok, I'll see you in about thirty minutes."

Jamal heaved a sigh of resignation as Marcus left, and he limped back to the bench and gathered up his shoe and sock and his warm-ups. He wound his way through the still celebrating crowd to the home dressing room, shunning several news people wanting to get a statement or an interview from him.

Scott and Tony left the building in virtual silence. It wasn't until they had escaped the crowd and were in Tony's Mustang, driving south on the San Diego freeway, that they began to discuss their situation.

"I wanna thank you for setting me up with this great deal, Tony," Scott said sarcastically as he stared out the window.

"How was I to know Davis was going to sprain his ankle at the last minute," Tony defended himself, "and that Thomas kid was unconscious out there. He couldn't do that again in a million years. It was just one of those freak situations you can't do anything about. Besides I don't remember having to twist your arm to bring you in on this thing."

"I know," Scott conceded. "I have nobody to blame but myself. But the real question is, what are we gonna do now?"

"I know, my dad will kill me if he finds out I blew his five grand betting on a basketball game. We've got to figure out how we can get that money back before he gets his bank statement and discovers I cashed his check myself. I won't be able to go outta the house, much less to Europe this summer."

"I don't have that much time." Scott interjected. "My parents get back from Israel next Wednesday, and I better have my dad's gold coins replaced by then or I'm done for."

"What makes you so sure he'll even notice they're gone right away?"

"Oh, he'll notice alright," Scott assured him. "When they unpack from their trip, he'll put their passports and stuff back in his safe, and he's bound to check to see if everything else in there is in order. You don't just leave fifteen thousand in gold when you go, without checking on it when you get back; at least Bruce Graham doesn't, that's for sure."

"Okay then, you've got to liquidate some stuff to get the cash. What do you have that you can sell quick?"

"Are you kidding? My parents keep me destitute all the time. I couldn't raise five hundred, much less five thousand. The only thing I have that's worth that kind of money is my Blazer, and it's still technically in my dad's name. Besides, even as unobservant as he is, I think he might notice if I didn't have a car anymore and started hitchhiking back and forth to school."

"Come to think of it," said Tony, "I don't know how I'm going to get the money either without my dad finding out, and he's not going to be a happy camper about it when he does. He just dropped ten grand himself tonight, and he's gonna be really sore about it. It's funny how parents come down the hardest on their kids when they find out they've started imitating the sins that they themselves have been committing all along."

"Yeah, I've noticed that too," agreed Scott.

"Well, what are we gonna do?" Tony brought them back around to the original question at hand.

"I don't know," admitted Scott, "and we're probably not going to come up with an answer tonight. We need some time to develop a plan."

"Hey, I got an idea." Tony brightened up. "Why don't we take your dad's boat out tomorrow? You said he told you that you could use it while they were gone. We don't have practice or a meet tomorrow, so we could take the whole day."

"Good idea," Scott agreed, "We could do some fishing, drink a few beers, and figure out what we're gonna do. Besides, we better enjoy ourselves now while we have the chance. If we can't get out of this mess, I'll never be allowed to take it out again."

Scott had left his Blazer at home that day and had ridden to school with Tony, knowing they would be going to the game together that evening. That way they could return home right after the game without having to retrieve Scott's vehicle from the university. As Tony negotiated the familiar route to their neighboring homes high in the Palos Verdes hills, he sought confirmation of their agreement: "So it's settled then; we're taking the yacht out tomorrow?"

"Yeah, let's do it. I'll drive tomorrow since my Blazer has a parking permit sticker on it. I'll pick you up at 8:30 in the morning, if that's okay with you?"

"You're on."

Tony dropped Scott in front of his house at about 11:30, and Scott went right to bed, but sleep eluded him again. He lay there for what seemed hours, condemning himself for getting caught up in Tony's scheme. Instead of solving his problems, he had only complicated them many times over. He felt farther away from both Candi and from God than he ever had before.

But what could he do now? He had gotten himself into a mess and he was going to have to get himself out of it. He decided that when he got everything straightened out financially, he would then try to rectify things romantically and spiritually. But as he finally drifted off to sleep, he was still far from being at peace with himself. The events of the future were dark and unknown, and he had an uneasy feeling that they were going to lead him even farther away from reconciliation of any kind.

Jamal woke slowly on Saturday morning, disoriented and confused. He looked around and found nothing familiar in his surroundings. He was not in his dorm room at UCLA, nor was he in his room at his dad's home. Then he remembered he and Marcus had checked into a motel in Compton late the night before. Marcus had insisted Jamal go to neither of the other places lest some hit man be waiting for him. They couldn't go to Marcus' place either because it would be easy to trace them there too. Hence, they had wound up in this cheap motel.

Marcus was still asleep in the other bed as Jamal checked his watch to find that it was only 7:30. He slipped out of bed and headed for the bathroom, his bladder reminding him that he had business to attend to.

He winced slightly as he felt pain in his left ankle, but it wasn't that bad. Freddie's taping had prevented any serious injury and he was able to walk to the bathroom without limping badly. He had lost count of how many times he had sprained that ankle since that first terrible injury in junior high, which had put him in a cast and on crutches for four weeks. Since then, further injuries had come more readily, but with decreasing severity. As the years had gone by, it seemed that things had loosened up inside his ankle. It was easier to turn it over, and it hurt like crazy when it happened, but it didn't seem to do much lasting damage to it.

He would experience some soreness in it for a few days, but with it taped, he would be able to resume practice and be ready for next week's games against USC and UNLV. Right now, that was the least of his worries anyway.

When he returned from the bathroom, Marcus was stirring, having been awakened by the sound of the flushing toilet. "Hey, Jamal," he muttered, "how's that ankle? You seem to be moving pretty good on it this mornin'."

"It's gonna be fine, thanks," he responded. "Let's check outta this flea bag and go get some breakfast."

"Oh no you don't," Marcus came back at him, now getting out of bed and heading for the bathroom himself. "You're not going anywhere until I have a chance to check things out. It may take a coupla days."

"A couple of days? No way! I'm not gonna stay in this motel room all weekend. Let's at least go over to your place."

"No, it's still too risky. There's lot's of bad guys out there, and we don't know what they're up to yet. Besides you wouldn't like it at my place. At least you can watch TV here."

"Why couldn't we watch TV over there?" Jamal protested.

"Cause there ain't no TV over there. No VCR, and no stereo neither. I hocked 'em all to get money to bet on the game last night."

"Oh man, why did you go and do a thing like that?" Jamal asked, shaking his head.

"Hey, I thought it was in the bag. It was easy money. How was I to know that bum ankle of yours was gonna decide to conk out at the last minute and The Kid was gonna go ballistic?"

"You didn't sell your car too, did you?"

"Yeah, the car too, and everything else I had that was worth anything. But that's not our problem right now. If I'm dead, I'm not gonna need any of that stuff anyway."

"I see what you mean," Jamal said. "So, what's our plan?"

"*We* ain't got no plan," Marcus corrected him. "*I* got a plan. You're gonna stay right here in this motel room, and I'm gonna bring you some food. Then I'm goin' out there and find out what's the word on you."

"You think they might have a contract out on me?"

"Of course they might have a contract out on you, little brother. You did 'em wrong, and they don't take kindly to that. But they might not go too hard on you either. You couldn't help gettin' bunged up, and it wasn't you who pulled the game out. Maybe they'll cut you some slack. I don't know. I'm just gonna have to go out there and find out what's goin' down."

"Well, don't take too long," warned Jamal. "I'm outta here by Monday. I'd rather be a wanted man out there on the streets, than *safe* here in this hole."

Later that same Saturday morning, Scott and Tony arrived at the parking lot south of Shoreline Village, a trendy shopping center on the Long Beach waterfront. They had driven in Scott's Blazer down the Harbor Freeway to San Pedro where they had turned left on Highway 47 and taken the high Vincent Thomas Bridge over the Cerritos Channel and onto Terminal Island. They took another bridge across another channel, and yet another one across the Los Angeles River, finally exiting to the right onto Shoreline Drive at the southern tip of Long Beach. This wide street led them along the exclusive waterfront area, past the aquarium and the convention center on the left, and dropped them off on the right at Shoreline Village at the water's edge.

The village was located on the east and south side of Pacific Terrace Harbor, and was not a village at all. It consisted of 29 different establishments whose common purpose was to relieve tourists of their money. Most of them were either places to eat or to buy gifts and souvenirs, but there were also places where one could rent a bicycle or a small sailboat, or sign up for a cruise of the harbor. To the south of the parking area was the large downtown marina, with its armada of boats, but there was also a smaller marina on the north side of the village within the harbor itself. This was the destination sought after by the two young men.

Scott parked his Blazer in the area designated for boat owners, and he and Tony unloaded their ice chest and sack lunches, and a big zip-lock bag of thawing squid they had brought along for bait. They locked the vehicle and carried their cargo north between the Japanese restaurant and the candy shop to the ramp leading down to the dock area.

There was a ten-foot wide floating dock that was permanently attached to the high sea wall and which followed it around the entire perimeter of the eastern part of the harbor. Attached to this dock at the south side of the harbor, and extending out into it, were three separate docks, to which the boats were moored. The center dock was the longest, being about a hundred yards in length. The ones on either side of it were less that half as long, cut short, of necessity, by the irregular shape of the relatively small enclosure.

Scott and Tony were on their way to the short dock on the right where the Graham's boat was located. As they got to the bottom of the ramp and began to head off in that direction, they were greeted by a familiar voice.

"Hey ya, Scotty, long time no see! And Tony. Where you guys been keepin' yourselves?"

It was the voice of Eddie, the self-appointed mascot of the marina. He must have had a last name, but no one seemed to know or care what it was. He was there virtually every day, and he knew all of the owners, and most of their frequent guests, by name. A retired longshoreman and a widower, he had nothing better to do with his time. He was in his early seventies, but he was healthy and agile, and his mind was as sharp as a whaler's harpoon. He had no official position at the marina, but he was pleasant and well liked and provided excellent security, so the managers grew to welcome his presence.

"Hi, Eddie. How's it going?" Scott responded with a smile.

"Hey, Eddie, I thought you'd be dead by now," added Tony.

"Watch it, pretty boy, you don't wanna mess with me. I might havta mess up that gorgeous face of yours," Eddie bantered playfully, assuming a boxing stance.

Eddie didn't look much like a boxer, though. His gray hair was thinning on top, and his exposed skin was badly weathered. His ears were big, but not cauliflowered, and his nose was sharp, instead of being flattened all over his face. He was not a big man, and his soft eyes and ready smile made him look more like a cuddler than a contender.

"Okay, Champ," said Tony, with mock fear in his voice, "don't hurt me. I'll be good."

"We decided we've been working too hard lately, Eddie," Scott interrupted. "We're gonna take the day off and do a little fishing."

"Good idea," agreed Eddie, "and this is a great day for it. The water's nice and calm out there right now, but it'll probably start actin' up later on this evening, gettin' ready for the big storm that's supposed to blow in tomorrow."

Scott and Tony exchanged some more small talk with Eddie, but they were anxious to get underway, so they excused themselves and made their way nearly to the end of the short dock at the east end of the marina where the Graham boat was tied up. It was technically a yacht, being nearly forty feet long and powered by two big Volvo inboards, which put out 370 horsepower apiece.

The Viking Sport Cruiser had been built in England about five years previously, and had been purchased by some member of the Mafia for about half a million dollars. The owner had been arrested on racketeering charges and Bruce Graham defended him in court. The evidence against him was overwhelming and even Graham wasn't able to get him off, but the gangster had grown fond of his attorney during the long process of the trial. Before being sent to prison, he had to liquidate his assets, so he sold the yacht to Graham for a fraction of what he had paid for it.

That had been over a year ago, and the Graham family had thoroughly enjoyed it since then. They had owned a string of boats over the years, but never anything so luxurious.

It had large accommodations below, complete with a living area and galley, which shared a head with a two-berth guest cabin. It also had a master cabin with a queen bed and private head. Above was the completely enclosed helm station, with its own luxurious sitting area. This was great for piloting the craft during cold weather or rough seas, but when conditions permitted, the obvious choice was the flying bridge. This open cockpit on top of the yacht had an additional helm station and provided a great view and plenty of fresh air.

When Scott and Tony untied the mooring ropes and climbed aboard, they chose the lower helm station. They were hardy and adventurous young men, and the weather was calm, but it was still in January, and the temperature was only in the low fifties. Besides, it was much quieter inside, and they had much to talk about.

Scott had piloted the craft many times and felt confident at the helm. He backed the yacht out and brought her around. He ran her out and around the end of the dock and sharply turned left to stay clear of two other boats moored to the dock on the north side of the small harbor.

The harbor was actually sort of t-shaped. A rather narrow inlet opened to the north from the bay and then branched both to the east and to the west. The east branch contained the marina and was the smaller of the two. It was bordered by Shoreline Drive on the north, and by the Shoreline Village on the east and south. The west branch of the harbor went on for some distance, and was bordered by private facilities with their own docks and boats.

Scott's objective was simply to run west till he had cleared the marina's last dock and then turn south, down the inlet till he joined the estuary where the Los Angeles River ran into Long Beach Bay. With this maneuver accomplished, he brought her around to the east until she had passed the *RMS Queen Mary*, permanently anchored near the point on the opposite side of the estuary. Then he turned south again and headed out toward the open sea.

Marcus had been gone most of the day and Jamal was about to go stir crazy. There was no cable available, and the regular TV programming had little to offer. He was able to pick up a Laker game in the afternoon, which kept him interested, but when it was over, he turned the set off and began pacing the floor.

At about five o'clock, Marcus came in with some Chinese food, a newspaper, and a big grin on his face. He looked tired but relieved, like a big burden had been lifted from his shoulders.

"I've got some good news and some bad news," he said as he walked through the door.

"Let's have it all, Snowball. I've been about to go nuts cooped up in this rat hole all day without knowing what's goin' down out there?"

"First of all, you owe me. I been riskin' my butt out there all day. I musta talked to fifty people before I finally got to somebody who could give me the straight word on you."

"Okay, okay, I owe you!" Jamal almost shouted. "Now, out with it!"

"The good news is that I just found out they're willing to lift the contract they had out on you. They decided you was doin' your part till you got hurt, and that you wasn't personally responsible for that fluke win at the end. But they're only willing to do it on one condition."

"What's that?" Jamal demanded.

"Well, that's the bad news. They're insistin' that you agree to throw another game in the future."

"No! Absolutely not! That game was the worst thing I ever experienced in my life, and I'd rather be dead than go through it again!"

"Well, that's exactly what you will be if you don't agree to do it," Marcus said, "and you'll be takin' me with you. They lost a shipload of money on that game, and if you don't give them the chance of gettin' it back, they're gonna kill us both, real slow and painful-like."

"Oh man! I'm already the goat after last night's game. I can't go through that all over again!"

"No, you got that goat part wrong, Jamal," corrected Marcus. "Here, take a look at the sports page. They're sayin' you and The Kid are the ones who pulled the game out at the end. Hey man, you had 29 points and 15 boards. That's more than anybody in the game except Jackson. Nobody's blaming you for nothin'."

"You gotta be kiddin' me," Jamal protested. "I haven't played that bad since I had the flu one game back in high school."

"Well, that's not the way the sports writers saw it. Course, they gave most of the credit to The Kid. He scored eighteen in the second half alone and that Ally Oop at the end. Well, it was pure magic. The little jerk. Why did he have to choose that particular game to pull one outta the hat?"

"I don't know," Jamal echoed his brother's dismay. "Because of his heroics, all I went through to blow the game was wasted effort. Now I gotta do it all over again. What game do they want me to take a dive in?"

"They didn't say. They're gonna choose the one they figure they stand the best chance of winnin' the most money."

"Oh great," Jamal sighed. "Now I'll never know when to expect it." He swore bitterly, and then continued, "If I know those lowlifes, they will probably wait until we get into the playoffs, and then make me blow a big game, maybe even the national championship."

"I don't know what they'll do, brother," conceded Marcus, "but we'll never live to find out if you don't agree to their terms. Who knows what might happen in the next few weeks, but we need to buy some time so we can figure out what we're gonna do."

As distasteful as the idea of throwing another game was to Jamal, he had to admit that it seemed like his only option at this point. Even if he were somehow able to pull some strings because of his celebrity status and get out of this mess, they would still hunt his brother down and kill him, and he would never be able to live with that on his conscience.

"Okay, I'll agree to do it," he said at last. Marcus was visibly relieved to hear the news. "But I don't think I'll be able to follow through when it actually comes right down to doing it." Those words brought the anxious look right back to his brother's face.

"We'll worry about that when the time comes," Marcus concluded, "but right now we need to let those people know you're on board before one of their goons spots you and gets trigger happy."

"Okay, how do we do that?"

"I've got the number right here. You can talk to the man himself, and then we all can breathe a little easier."

Jamal made the call from the phone in the room and, after talking to a couple of underlings, he was connected to Mr. Apparicio. The mob boss tried to sound friendly, forgiving, and reassuring; but Jamal got the message loud and clear that he was deeply angry, and that he wouldn't tolerate the slightest deviation from his instructions in the future. Jamal assured him that he would do whatever he was told, and hoped he sounded more convincing than he felt.

After he hung up the phone, they ate their dinner pretty much in silence as Jamal read the paper, giving special attention to the sports section and its coverage of UCLA's astounding victory the night before. He was amazed the writers had treated his lackluster performance with such kindness. He concluded his superstar status had bought him some votes he really hadn't deserved.

Jamal wanted to check out and go home, but Marcus convinced him they needed to lay low until the message not to kill them had been passed down to absolutely every possible bounty hunter. So Jamal consented to stay for one more night on one condition: that they go to church in the morning and hear their dad preach, and then spend some time with the family. He found it curious how spiritual and domestic things had become so much more important to him, now that he had been confronted with the distinct possibility of dying in the near future.

Marcus agreed to go along with his younger brother, though he surely wasn't as enthusiastic about it. He was so committed to the goal of escaping the imminent threat of death that he would have agreed to just about anything to better his chances of survival. What neither of them had any way of knowing was that the future held such dark and terrifying realities, they would need all the fraternal and divine help they could get.

CHAPTER SEVEN

THE SOLUTION

The sun had set and it was getting dark when Scott Graham piloted the sleek *Pacific Pearl* back around the point and past the *Queen Mary* on their way back to the marina. As they slipped past the hull of the giant ocean liner, their own otherwise substantial craft, seemed dwarfed and insignificant. Scott couldn't help but think that his own life and dreams, as big and important as they were to him, would probably seem just as small and inconsequential compared to the eternal scheme of things.

As Tony looked at the mammoth ship, he was thinking differently. He voiced his thoughts to his friend, "Look at that baby, would ya, Scott. She's unstoppable and unsinkable. That's how I feel about us and the plans we made today."

"Yeah well, that's what you said about the basketball game last night, and that's what they said about the *Titanic* too," Scott reminded him.

"Okay, okay, last night we were on the *Titanic*, and we hit an iceberg and got sunk. But now we're on the *Queen* and nothing can stop us."

"Well, maybe the *Queen Mary* never faced the kind of obstacles we're up against here. If she came across an iceberg, she might have gone down just like the *Titanic* did," Scott said, not realizing how pessimistic he sounded.

"Now that's where you're wrong, buddy boy. The *Queen* here is a lot bigger and faster and tougher than the *Titanic* ever thought of being. She crossed the Atlantic over a thousand times in over thirty years before they docked her here back in the sixties. She dodged hundreds of icebergs during that time and never hit one of them. During World War II, they painted her gray and she transported troops and bombs and stuff back and forth to Europe to help whip up on Hitler. She was so big and carried so much stuff the German U-boat captains wanted to put her down in the worst way. Hitler even offered a huge reward to anyone who could sink her, but she never took a hit. They called her the *Gray Ghost* because she was so elusive. They lay in wait for her, but she zig-zagged her way through them every time. Even if they ever spotted her, they couldn't catch her. Her top speed was almost forty miles an hour!"

"Alright already," Scott interrupted. "I don't need a history lesson. How do you know so much about the *Queen Mary* anyway?"

"Hey, I'm not just another pretty face," Tony acted offended. "I read books too, ya know. This kind of stuff fascinates me."

"Well, this isn't history. This is now," Scott reminded him. "She's not carrying troops and dodging U-boats anymore. She's a floating hotel and museum, and she hasn't budged an inch in nearly forty years, and our plans might leave us just as dead in the water if we're not careful."

That last comment seemed to subdue Tony a little and he started talking about something else. As Scott brought his own craft into the marina, he rehearsed in his mind the events of their expedition.

They had taken the sleek white yacht out beyond the breakwater and down the coast a few miles to a spot where they had always caught fish before. There, he cut the engines and they just let her drift. The sea was calm and they didn't notice their position changing much at all over the course of the afternoon.

Bruce Graham kept fishing gear permanently stowed onboard, so all they had to do was bait up and start fishing. For the first couple of hours, they only made small talk. They were too busy bringing in fish to concentrate on much of anything else. Soon, they both caught their limit of bottom fish, mostly rock cod and a few red snapper. After they filleted them and put the meat-filled, zip-lock bags in the ice chest, they hosed off the deck and ate their lunch.

After a successful turn at fishing, with a good lunch and a couple of beers under their belts, they were feeling pretty good. As they settled back on the comfortable couch in the helm station, they began to discuss their options for recovering the money they had lost the night before.

"So, what have you come up with for a plan, my friend?" Tony inquired, with a twinkle in his eye.

"I've only been able to think of one thing, and I already know it won't work," Scott confessed.

"Well, let's hear it. Maybe it's not such a bad idea that we can't revise it and make it work."

"No, I've thought about it all day, and there's just no way."

"Just tell me, and let me decide for myself," Tony insisted with a little irritation showing in his voice.

"Okay," Scott consented, "but remember, I told you it was a bad idea. I thought about staging a break-in at my parents' home and ripping off enough stuff to cover our debts."

"That's a great idea," Tony said. "Why didn't I think of that? It would be easy to pull off since your parents are away, and the insurance would cover the damages. So what's the problem with it? And don't say it would be dishonest. We're way beyond that now."

"No, that's not it," Scott assured him. "I would *hate* doing something like that, but we're in desperate straits now, and it will take desperate measures to get us out of them. No, it won't work for these simple reasons. We have no means of hauling off any big stuff like furniture, and we wouldn't have any place to put it even if we did. The money we would get from fencing the TV's, VCR's, stereos, computers, and stuff wouldn't net us more than a couple of thousand, tops. My mom has some really nice jewelry, but she took all the good stuff with her to show off on the tour. What she left here is junk. They do have some expensive paintings, but they're all registered and we would never be able to sell them on such short notice without tipping off the authorities."

"Wow!" Tony broke in. "You really have thought this thing through, haven't you?"

"Yeah, I have," he agreed. "If we had a lot of time and had all the right resources and knew all the right people, we might be able to pull it off, but just you and me, in the next few days? No way!"

"Well, what about their cars? I bet we could get plenty for them at some chop shop somewhere."

"I already thought of that," Scott had said. "It would be a great idea except for one small detail: neither one of their vehicles are at the house. Dad left his car in the parking garage at work and Mom picked him up in her Suburban on the way to the airport. They left it someplace in a long-term parking lot near LAX, but I have no idea where."

"Well, so much for that idea. What else you got?"

"Well, I've got the Blazer, of course, but my dad just signed over the title to me for my twenty-first birthday, and I haven't even got the pink slip back from the DMV yet."

"You could try to sell it cheap at a chop shop and tell everybody it was stolen," Tony suggested. "But then, that's what I was thinking about doing with my Mustang. No way could we both get away with that at the same time. You got any other ideas?"

"No, that's it," Scott said, holding out his empty hands. "I'm fresh out of ideas. We could knock over a convenience store, but they'd never have the kind of money we need. And if we tried a bank, with all their alarms and armed guards, somebody could get hurt . . . probably us. I want to get that money back, but not bad enough to shed any blood over it, especially my own."

"I hear you, man," Tony agreed. "Well, it looks like we're gonna have to resort to my backup plan."

"What plan is that?"

"Okay, now hear me out on this one, Scott. I know it's gonna sound crazy, but I've done a lot of thinking about it, and I'm sure it'll work. Remember when we swam against San Diego State last month and we rode down there in the van with Aaron Muller?"

"Yeah, sure I remember," Scott said. "What about it?"

"I'm getting to that. Remember, he was talking about how concerned he was about his grandfather who owns that grocery store up by MacArthur Park?"

"Oh, no you don't! We're not robbing some poor old Jewish man. I already told you there's no money in convenience stores anyway."

"Just a minute," Tony sounded perturbed. "I told you to hear me out on this, and then you can decide if it's worth considering. Besides, you already said you were fresh outta ideas."

"Okay, go ahead, but this better be good."

"That's better," Tony brightened up immediately. "Now remember how Aaron had said his whole family was worried about his grampa because he didn't trust banks and kept all his money right there in the store in two different safes. He's been there for decades and has to have made a lot of dough. All his kids are married and have moved to the suburbs, and they've been trying to get him to sell out and move in with them ever since his wife died. But he's too stubborn, and insists on keeping the dumb store open even though the area's gotten real bad around there and they're afraid somebody's gonna bump him off to get his money."

"Yeah, I remember him saying that, but what makes you think we could get his money when nobody else has been able to?" Scott asked.

"That's because we know about the safes and they didn't. Aaron said he's been robbed two or three times in the past, but they only got away with what was in the register. That's small change compared to the stacks of money he must have stashed away in those safes."

"And just how are we gonna get him to open those safes? He sounds like a tough old bird. We'd probably have to beat the combination out of him, and I'm not willing to do that. Besides, he might not give it to us even then. It doesn't sound like he's got much to lose, with his wife and family gone and all."

"Yeah, I thought of that," Tony agreed. "That's where we're gonna have to use some leverage. I figure we'd have to take a hostage or two and threaten to shoot them if he doesn't open the safe. He might not care about himself, but by the way Aaron described him, I bet he wouldn't be willing to sit by and let some innocent customer get killed."

"Hold on there, Tony," Scott interrupted angrily. "If I'm not willing to hurt the old man, I'm darned sure not going to be willing to shoot anybody!"

"I'm not either, that's the whole point. We'll just make a lot of noise and threats and point guns at people, and he'll crack those safes in no time to protect them. I'd bet my life on it."

"Yeah, that's exactly what you'd be doing, and mine too," Scott pointed out.

"Look, it wouldn't be that much of a risk at all," Tony said reassuringly. "We'd just have to sit out in the car and watch the store until nearly closing time. Then when some customers went in, preferably old folks or women with kids, we'd go in and do the deed and be outta there in no time at all."

"You know, it just might work," Scott said, more to himself than to Tony. "I remember Aaron saying that his grampa hated guns and wouldn't keep one in the store. That's one of the reasons they're all so worried about him. He insists God has taken care of him all these years and he's trusting Him to continue to do so."

"Yeah, I thought about that too," Tony agreed. "I sure wouldn't want to go into his store and have him pull a shotgun on us or something."

"Now that I think about it, we'd actually be doing him, as well as everybody else, a favor by pulling this job off."

"How do you figure that?" Tony asked, obviously pleased that his friend had begun to take an interest in his plan."

"Well, it would be good for us, obviously, because we would get the money we need to get our butts out of hock. It would be good for the old man too because we wouldn't hurt him, but with his money gone, he'd have to sell the store and move, thus preventing him from really getting hurt or killed by some real bad guys down the road. And it would be good for his family as well, because they would have him living with them where they could take care of him and not have to worry about his welfare."

"Now you're talkin!" Tony couldn't have been more pleased. "I feel a lot better about the whole thing myself. I thought we were planning a robbery, but now I realize we're actually contemplating a wonderful act of human kindness for the betterment of all concerned."

They both laughed at their obvious and clumsy attempt to rationalize and justify their nefarious intentions.

"Before you get too excited, there are some conditions I have before I'll actually agree to don my mask and six-guns and embark on a life of crime," Scott added cheerfully. But even as he spoke, a chill went down his spine as he realized the truth in the words he had just so lightly spoken.

"I agree to all of them," Tony said, elated that Scott had as much as committed himself already.

"No, you better hear me out first."

"Okay, shoot . . . no pun intended," Tony agreed, obviously having a good time.

"That shooting business is my number one concern," Scott said seriously. "You gotta promise me that nobody gets hurt. If we see this thing going south, we walk away. I mean it, no shooting, no violence."

"Agreed! The last thing I want is for somebody to get hurt . . . especially me."

"Okay, that's settled. Now my second condition is that we go up there tonight and check the whole thing out. I want to know exactly what to expect before we walk into that store."

"Gotcha!" Tony agreed, "I was thinking the same thing. Let's case the joint tonight and, if everything looks good, we'll hit it tomorrow about closing time." He was clearly enjoying the use of gangster cliches, which made Scott more than a little nervous. In his mind, this thing was going to be a necessary evil, not the fun adventure Tony seemed to anticipate.

"Now, for number three. We take only enough money to cover our debts. If Aaron is right, there's no tellin' how much money the old man might have in those two safes. We take only ten grand. It's bad enough we're ripping him off, I refuse to get rich at his expense."

"I'm not sure I agree with you on that one," Tony mumbled. "If we're gonna take the risk of staging this robbery, we might as well go for all the gusto we can get. We're taking just as big a risk going for ten grand as if we were going for a hundred."

"I don't care, it's the principle of the thing, I guess. Ten thousand, that's it. Do I have your word on it?"

"Well, yes and no," Tony said. "I agree that if we get enough out of the first safe, we don't need to go for the second one, but I'm not going to sit down and count out exactly ten thousand dollars. It would take too long and it would create a lot of suspicion that might find some way of coming back to haunt us."

"Yeah, you're right," Scott conceded. "We can't afford to be too deliberate or obvious, but when we're stuffing money in the bag, we need to stop when we know we've reached ten grand, okay?"

"Okay, you got it," Tony agreed, but it was clear that he wasn't too happy about it. "Is that it, or do you have any more conditions up your sleeve?"

"Just one, but it's an important one. This has got to be the end of it. When it's over we're outta the gangster business for good: no more gambling, no more robbing, no more nothin'. We don't talk about it, we don't even think about it. I want to put all this behind me once and for all."

"Sure," Tony said, "After we pull this off we'll have no need to do anything else anyway."

"I mean, even if something goes wrong and we have to bite the bullet. I'm not ever going back to the drawing board and cooking up another scheme. One thing could lead to another and we could wind up professional criminals, or in prison, or maybe even dead. So, we better do this one right because, win or lose, it's my last!"

"No problem," Tony agreed, "I want outta this business just as bad as you do."

Scott heard him say it, and he was determined to hold him to it, but inside, he wasn't at all sure that Tony's conviction was nearly as firm as his own.

They talked about a few more details and set the time of their stakeout for ten o'clock that night. Then they fired up the big engines and turned around and headed back to the marina.

It was dark by the time Scott and Tony tied up the yacht and gathered up their gear together on the dock. Scott made one last walk through before locking up. His dad was a real stickler for details, and if Scott wanted to take the boat out again, he had to make sure everything was shipshape. Satisfied that all was as it should be, he locked the sliding glass door at the aft of the main cabin and unzipped one of the cushions on the rear deck and hid the key inside as he had been instructed.

With the cushion re-zipped and returned to its proper place, the two young men left the yacht and retraced their steps of the morning back to Scott's Blazer. The drive home was uneventful. They talked about school, about swimming, about the previous night's basketball game, and various other things, but they avoided any conversation about their upcoming robbery. Neither one of them saw any need nor had any desire to discuss it further at that time.

At the D'Angelo home, Tony's mother was delighted with the fish her son presented her, and promised to prepare a great dinner with them the next evening. She made sure to invite Scott to attend since his parents were still out of town. Margo D'Angelo was a pleasant woman, a little overweight perhaps, but still beautiful. It was clear Tony had gotten his good looks from her because his father wasn't all that handsome. On this particular night, he had a downright ugly cast about him. He only grunted as the boys greeted him as he walked through the room.

Mrs. D'Angelo apologized for him and said she didn't know what had gotten into him. He had been acting that way ever since last night and she didn't know why. Scott and Tony winked at each other knowingly. They could understand how losing ten thousand dollars on a sure thing could easily ruin your whole day.

When Scott got home a few minutes later, he checked the answering machine first of all to see if Candi had left a message, but there was only another one from his mother, wondering where he had been every time she'd called. It had been only two days since he had talked to Candi, but it seemed like a month. So much had happened, and was about to happen, that he wondered if things would ever get back to normal again.

Scott put his bags of fish in the freezer, sure that his mother would be equally pleased with his success as had been Mrs. D'Angelo with Tony's. Then he sat down at the desk and struggled with the telephone. Finally, he mustered the courage to pick it up and dial Candi's number.

As the phone began to ring, he almost lost his nerve and hung up, but he forced himself to stay on the line. He was almost relieved when, after the fourth ring, her answering machine kicked in. With the sound of her voice, he realized again how very much he loved her, and how very much he hated his present circumstances.

When he heard the beep, he stumbled through some jumbled message about being real busy and missing her and promising to call again real soon. What he didn't realize was that she was listening at the other end, wanting to pick up and tell him she loved him and she wanted him to come over right away, but she dared not. She heard nothing in his words and detected nothing in his voice that would have led her to believe anything had changed since Thursday, so she simply told him those things without picking up the phone.

Having left the message, Scott had nothing to do for the hour before he was to go pick Tony up again, so he nuked one of his mom's prepared meals in the microwave and sat down to eat it as he watched the news on CNN.

He was particularly interested in the story about the increased tension in Jerusalem between the Jews and the Palestinians over the construction going on at the site of the new temple. He wasn't so much interested in the building of the temple as he was in the possibility of conflict, since his parents were still over there and in harm's way.

He was relieved to learn that Constantine Augustus, the new President of the United States of Europe, which now included parts of North Africa and the Middle East, was personally committed to maintaining the peace between the two sides. That man had been successful in everything he had attempted in his meteoric rise to power, and there was no reason to believe he would fail in this effort. After all, it had been he who had negotiated the truce between the two sides a year earlier and had put an end to years of killing by Palestinian bombings and Israeli counterattacks.

Satisfied that there was no immediate danger of violence in Israel, Scott turned his attention to the local weather. A storm out in the Pacific was headed for the Southland and was scheduled to hit land sometime Sunday afternoon. That pleased him, as a good rainstorm would keep both vehicle and pedestrian traffic at a minimum. He didn't want an audience around when he and Tony made their move.

When the sports came on, they began to recap the great UCLA come-from-behind victory the night before, but that proved to be too painful for him, and he turned off the TV.

Two hours later, Scott and Tony sat in the Blazer near the corner of Alvarado and Beachum a few blocks north of MacArthur Park, watching people come and go at The Corner Store. It hadn't taken them long to identify the location. It was right in the area where Aaron had said the store was located and it was on the northeast corner, just as he had described it.

They had decided on the Blazer instead of Tony's Mustang convertible for two reasons. It was much less conspicuous, and they definitely did not want to attract attention to themselves on this occasion. Besides that, the wind had started picking up and the temperature was dropping as the front approached from the Pacific, and the Blazer was a lot warmer place to sit and watch.

If they had to pull off a robbery, they decided this was a good location to do it. It was just north of Wilshire Boulevard, the main east-west thoroughfare through the park, and just west of the Harbor Freeway, which ran north and south along the west side of downtown Los Angeles. They could make a speedy getaway if the occasion called for it.

They sat there awhile, watching the traffic in and around the store, and then they decided they needed to actually go inside and check things out. They agreed that it wouldn't be a good idea for both of them to go in together, since the owner might get suspicious and watch them more closely. That would not be good. During the actual robbery the following night, he might be able to remember them, even with their faces covered, and then give the police a detailed description.

Tony was anxious to be the one to go in and "case the joint," as he put it, but Scott insisted on going instead. He pointed out that Tony's movie star appearance attracted attention everywhere he went, and they needed to stay as inconspicuous as possible. Tony argued awhile, but soon realized

Scott was right and agreed to sit in the car and keep an eye on things from outside.

Scott got out and pulled his fisherman's hat down as far as it would go and turned the collar up on his jacket to conceal as much of his face as possible without being too obvious about his intentions. He walked across the street and down about half a block to The Corner Store. As he walked casually through the front door he was planning to notice as much detail as he could without attracting attention to himself. There were about half a dozen other people milling around inside, which helped him to blend in.

He estimated the store to be about thirty feet wide and about fifty feet long. It was obviously old, with a high molded ceiling and a worn wooden floor. There were plate glass windows across the front, with the door opening in the center. There were magazine racks inside the window on the right, totally obstructing any view up to about seven feet or so, and there were no windows along the street side of the building. "Good," Scott thought to himself. "It won't be easy to see what's going on inside from the street."

He glanced up and saw a surveillance camera in the upper right hand corner. Or did he? It looked genuine enough, with a little red light and everything, but somehow, he suspected its authenticity. It would be just like the conservative old man to invest $19.95 on a dummy look-alike camera to discourage would-be robbers than to put out the big bucks to maintain a real surveillance system. It just sat there motionless, pointing at the counter area. Scott concluded that it was probably there for cosmetic purposes only.

The counter was located along most of the right side of the store. The old cash register was sitting on top of it, up front near the magazine racks. No doubt, the owner wanted to be up there to keep an eye on the door and to keep teenage boys from looking at the girly books. Inside the counter and on the wall behind it was all the stuff the old man wanted to keep away from the eager hands of would-be shoplifters; stuff like cigarettes, electronic gadgets, cameras, perfume, etc. It meant more work for him, waiting on customers, but it gave him more control over his more expensive inventory.

The rest of the store was given over mostly to groceries. It was clear that much of the business was characteristic of the average convenience store; with a large assortment of cigarettes, beer, soda, candy, chips, and the like, but there were real groceries as well. There was even a display of fresh produce and another one stocked with bakery goods. Toward the back of the store Scott noticed a respectable assortment of clothing for sale along one side, and some household items and hardware on the other. It appeared to be one of those old general stores from a bygone era. He wouldn't have been too surprised to see a cracker barrel or a potbellied stove standing in one of the corners.

Scott noticed a door at the rear of the store, which must have opened to a storage area in the back. Against that back wall he also saw a stairway, no doubt one that led up to the living quarters where Aaron's mother and her siblings had been raised, and where his grandfather still spent the limited number of hours each day he was not with customers.

Scott didn't linger. He selected some chips and a six-pack of Pepsi. He would have liked a beer better, but he didn't want to have to show any identification, and he was sure the old man would have asked to see it. He picked up a copy of *Sports Illustrated* as well, and took everything to the register.

The owner, Saul Frieberg, was a busy man. He appeared to be about seventy, but he seemed to be full of energy even though it was going on ten-thirty in the evening. He was of average height and looked to be in good health. His otherwise bald head was trimmed with a fringe of gray hair, which matched the thick mustache, which in turn, separated his comparatively small mouth from his comparatively large nose. His bright eyes danced behind his horn-rimmed glasses, and he seemed to take in everything that was going on around him.

Scott liked him immediately, and his store too, which made him feel even guiltier about what he and Tony were going to do to him the next night. Mr. Frieberg was busy talking pleasantly to an elderly woman who was buying some generic brand cigarettes, and he didn't seem to be paying any particular attention to Scott. This was fine with the would-be robber. He just wanted to pay for his purchases and get out of there before he got any more enamored with the old man and changed his mind about what his ultimate intentions were.

Scott had purposefully been bending his knees slightly and slouching a little so as to appear shorter than he really was. He didn't want anything about him to appear familiar during the actual robbery. He was determined not to speak either so the owner would not be able to recognize his voice later. But he didn't know Saul Frieberg. No customer of the old man ever got away without speaking.

"Good evening, young fellow," said Saul pleasantly, "I don't think I've seen you here before."

"Nope, first time," Scott said, making his voice a little higher than normal.

"What brings you our way so late at night?"

"Uh, I'm a student at UCLA and I'm on my way back to school. I just caught a movie downtown."

"Yeah, what did ya see?" Saul asked, just making conversation as he rang up the items Scott had set before him.

Scott was panic-stricken for an instant. He hadn't seen a movie in weeks, and at the moment he had no idea what was even playing.

He suspected if he tried to snow the old man and make something up, the old guy would nail him on it, so he just decided to end the conversation before it really began.

"I'm sorry," he said, trying to remain calm, "I'm kinda in a hurry. I just stopped to get something to help keep me awake. I've got a term paper due Monday morning, and I'll be up most of the night working on it."

"No problem," said the owner with a shrug. "Seems like everybody's in a hurry these days. That'll be $7.87 please."

Scott handed him a ten and pocketed the change without further conversation. He responded with a "You're welcome" when the owner thanked him, and again with a "G'night" when the old man offered the same farewell as he went out the door.

"So much for not saying anything inside the store," he mumbled to himself as he walked back up the street to report to Tony in the waiting Blazer. All in all, though, it hadn't gone badly, he thought. The owner hadn't seemed to suspect anything, and he had gathered all the information he needed to prepare him and Tony for the heist the next night.

They sat in the car eating chips and drinking Pepsi till closing time at eleven. Scott filled Tony in on all the particulars about the store as they watched the traffic in and around it. There were a few too many people and a few too many cars to suit them, but after all, it was Saturday night and that was to be expected. Sunday nights were always quieter, and especially if it rained, the place could be practically deserted when they came to transact their own risky business.

Satisfied that the job was doable and that they were committed to it, they drove home. Along the way, they discussed their plans in detail. It was decided that Tony would steal a car for the holdup. Scott was against it at first, but Tony convinced him that one of their own vehicles might be spotted by someone, and that could lead the police right to their doorstep.

They were to dress like bikers, in leathers and boots. They would wear gloves and ski masks so as to be identified neither by their fingerprints nor in a lineup. And they were to carry real guns, loaded with live ammunition.

Again, Scott objected at first to the loaded guns, insisting on not even the possibility of anyone getting hurt. But again, Tony talked him into it. He reminded him they would probably need to coerce the old man into opening the safes, and a live round fired into a can of spaghetti sauce would be very convincing.

Scott finally agreed reluctantly, realizing that Tony, as usual, was right. Scott was certain that he wasn't cut out for this gangster business, but he was just as certain that Tony was. Tony seemed to be a natural at it. He seemed to know all the right questions to ask and how to come up with all the right answers. But what bothered Scott most of all was that Tony seemed to enjoy it all so much.

They planned the rest of the details for the robbery during an animated drive home down the Harbor Freeway. They agreed to each get everything they would need separately and then get together at Tony's at six for dinner and to prepare for the big night ahead.

Having dropped Tony off in front of his house at about 11:40, Scott drove around the corner and on up the hill to his own home. He parked his Blazer in the garage and went into the empty house. He put the two remaining Pepsis in the refrigerator and checked the answering machine. There was still nothing from Candi.

He thought for a moment that he would go to church in the morning in hopes of seeing her, but he dismissed the idea almost immediately. He felt badly enough about what he was about to do; he didn't need her unabashed reverence making it even worse for him. Besides that, it would be just his luck for Dr. Schumway to be preaching on, "Thou Shalt Not Steal."

He went to bed and, strangely enough, fell sound asleep rather quickly. Before he drifted off, he tried to pray and ask God to forgive him for what he was about to do, but he gave it up. He couldn't sincerely ask for forgiveness for something, and then go right ahead and do it anyway. He decided he would just wait until it was over, then he was sure that he would feel guilty about what he had done, and he could ask for forgiveness then with more sincerity. He wasn't at all sure God would buy any of it, but it made him feel a little better, and his conscience didn't bother him as badly about it.

CHAPTER EIGHT

THE GATHERING

Georgia Davis rose early Sunday morning as she did every day. She had some difficulty getting her large frame out of bed because of her arthritis. In spite of her seventy-plus years, she was in good health, except for that pesky disease. It had not crippled her, but it had surely made her joints hurt, especially on winter days like this when it was about to rain.

She shuffled into the bathroom and, after relieving herself, she stepped on the scales as she did every morning. It pegged out at just under 250 pounds. "My lands," she said out loud, "I've put on two pounds since yesterday. I must be goin' on a diet first thing tomorrow mornin'." Actually, her weight hadn't changed overnight, nor had it in the last ten years. Her old scales were so inaccurate, they could register as many as five pounds differently each time she stepped on them.

She undoubtedly knew that, but she had no intention of replacing the errant machine. Its variant readings added variety to her life. She was able to experience the elation of having lost a few pounds, and the concern over having gained a few, several times each week. Nor was she likely to go on a diet any time soon. She loved to cook and she loved to eat. She had grown quite accustomed to her way of life, and was comfortable with it.

She was not particularly fat, anyway. She stood nearly six feet tall, even after age and arthritis had shortened her a couple of inches. Besides that, she was what she called, big-boned. She did have a large frame and, though somewhat overweight, she carried her bulk quite handsomely on it, especially in the fashionable clothes she always wore.

She really was an attractive lady. She always kept her thick gray hair styled nicely, and her brown skin was amazingly wrinkle-free for one her age. Her son and grandsons, no doubt, had inherited both their size and their good looks in part from her, as well as from her first husband.

Georgia had been married twice, but for a total of less than three years. She first fell in love with Ben Simpson, a 6'6" basketball star, while still in high school in Watts. He had received a full scholarship to USC, and they planned to wait until after he finished college before they got married, but she became pregnant, and that changed everything.

They married right away, when Georgia was only seventeen, because that is what was done in those days. Ben decided to postpone college until after he had taken care of his family. He got a job driving a truck and was making good money, and they were planning on buying a little house, then he received his draft notice. The Korean War had just started heating up, and young men were being called up from all over the country.

Ben might have been able to defer his induction because of the proximity of the birth of his child, but he was anxious to go and get it out of the way so he could get on with his life. However, he was to have no life to get on with. He was killed the first month he was in Korea by a land mine, exactly three weeks before his son was born.

Georgia was devastated by the death of her husband. She had to move back in with her parents, she and Robert Alonzo, her infant son. But she forced herself to recover quickly and was determined not to be dependent on her folks. At that time there was no welfare system to support her on her own, so she got a job at a bank as a teller and began saving her money. She was soon able to rent a little place for herself and little Bobby.

Her mother took care of her son for her while she was at work until he started to school. After that time, she and Bobby were completely self-sufficient. Georgia was promoted to the position of loan officer, and they were doing quite well financially. But they weren't doing so well socially. Georgia had to work long hours and Bobby had already started to run with the wrong crowd, even at twelve years of age. She decided he needed a father figure in his life.

Buford Davis had been coming into the bank for years. He owned a TV sales and service store on Imperial Highway in Watts. He could have sent an employee to the bank, but after he met Georgia, he insisted on going himself. He was thirty-five and had never married, and he was thoroughly smitten with this young widow in the loan department. He asked her out on numerous occasions, but she had always turned him down before. He was surprised and overjoyed when she finally said yes.

Mr. Davis, as Georgia always referred to him, was an inch or two shorter than she, but it never seemed to bother him. He courted her enthusiastically for a year until she finally agreed to marry him. That was in the spring of 1963. They were married on the Fourth of July, and she always liked to say, "That's when the fireworks really started!"

Buford loved Georgia with all his heart, and he loved her troublesome son as well. He bonded with Bobby quickly, and the two of them became fast friends. He officially adopted him on his thirteenth birthday, and it looked like Bobby had really turned the corner. He was doing better in school and even started working at the store afterwards to pick up some extra spending money.

Buford and Georgia put off trying to have any more children so they could give themselves entirely to helping Bobby, and it had paid off. He seemed to have made a complete turnaround, so in the summer of 1965, they decided to try to have a baby. But that was also the summer the riots broke out.

She could not remember how or why those terrible riots had broken out that hot July in Watts, but she could still remember vividly the horrible sound of gunshots, the smell of smoke, and the taste of fear in her mouth.

Buford sent all the employees home and locked up the store when the rioting broke out, but he insisted on staying on to keep any would-be looters away. He knew his TV store would be a prime target in such a situation, but he was convinced that if he were there with his shotgun, he would be able to keep them at bay.

He was wrong. His windows were smashed and when he fired a warning shot into the air, someone put a .45 slug through his heart. He died almost instantly, and with him died Georgia's dreams of a stable, happy home for her and her son.

The store was gutted and then set on fire, and the insurance company declared it a total loss. The settlement did little more than pay for the lost inventory. Georgia was forced to go back to the bank; and Bobby, bitter and disillusioned, chose to go back to the streets.

Though still in her early thirties, Georgia had never married again, nor had she entered into any serious relationships. She spent the next thirty years trying to provide for and protect her troubled son. She was able to accomplish the former, but she was completely unsuccessful with the latter. Bobby soon dropped out of school and spent his time on the streets and in and out of Juvenile Hall.

She was delighted when Bobby married his girlfriend Tasha, and when they presented her with her first grandson Marcus sometime later. She hoped the responsibility of a wife and child would help settle Bobby down, but he and Tasha were no better together than they had been apart. They both had serious drug habits, and they and their son suffered from their abuse. Georgia now found herself trying to rescue her grandson from the hell they were creating for him.

It wasn't until long after their second son Jamal was born, and Bobby was serving yet another stretch in prison, that things had begun to finally turn around. Tasha moved back in with her mother-in-law, because she had become so ill she could no longer live on her own. At Georgia's insistence, she went to the clinic and then to the hospital, only to learn that she had an advanced case of AIDS.

Devastated by the news, neither woman knew what to do. A friend at the bank spoke of being a Christian and had invited Georgia many times in the past to visit her church with her; and now, in her time of great need, she sought her out. The woman, Zelma Parsons, wept with her and prayed for her and Tasha. So sincere and so compassionate was she, that Georgia decided to go to church with her the next Sunday.

Although the Antioch Baptist Church, just off Rosecrans Avenue in Compton, had been packed that morning, everyone seemed genuinely interested in Georgia and made her feel loved and welcomed. She wept during most of the service, which was noted by the elderly Rev. Wilcox. After its conclusion, he greeted her at the door and prayed for her right there on the front steps of the church.

So impressed had she been with her experience, and so insistent was she in her persuasion, that Tasha agreed to accompany her the following week. The whole church must have been praying for them, because they both fell under deep conviction during Rev. Wilcox's message. Each of them had hardly been in church before, but when the invitation was given, they went forward together.

There, Rev. Wilcox embraced them and sent them to a counseling room with Zelma Parsons and another lady. In privacy there, the ladies explained to them that God loved them and that He had sent His Son to the cross to die for all their sins. They explained that salvation was a free gift and that, if they would confess their sin and accept Jesus Christ as their own personal Lord and Savior, He would forgive them and grant them eternal life.

Both Georgia and Tasha readily confessed their need and gladly prayed to receive the Lord. All four ladies hugged and laughed and cried as they celebrated their new life in Christ. They both were baptized the following week, and remained as faithful in church as Tasha's health allowed her to be.

She blossomed as a Christian, and grew a great deal in the following six months, but her sojourn on earth was destined to be a short one. In spite of the consistent prayers of the faithful and the aggressive treatment of the medical profession, her disease grew progressively worse, and she finally slipped away the day before her forty-second birthday.

Georgia too grew strong in her Christian faith, and was able to accept Tasha's death as the will of the Lord. She was grateful for the months of sweet fellowship she and her daughter-in-law had enjoyed since they had both accepted the Lord, where there had been only tension and arguing before. Her greatest regret was that Bobby and his two sons were not able to share in the blessed time they had together.

Bobby had been in prison during the whole process, and had been unresponsive to their attempts to share the gospel with him via letters and personal visits. He grieved at Tasha's illness and death, but he showed no apparent interest in spiritual things. Marcus had already been out of the house for years and had wanted nothing to do with religion. He attended his mother's funeral, and was visibly moved, but he left immediately afterward, and displayed no apparent changes in his lifestyle. Jamal was still in junior high school, and was too interested in basketball and girls to pay much attention to what was going on in the life of his mother and grandmother. He wept at his mother's funeral, but he soon got over his grief. Tasha had never been much of a mother to him before, and he attributed her more recent affection to the fact that she was dying and was trying to atone for her past life of sin.

But all had not been sadness and disappointment in Georgia's family life. In fact, three great things had happened which had brought her tremendous joy and satisfaction. The first was her great-granddaughter Tamika, who had been the result of a brief relationship between Marcus and a beautiful young girl named Sarah. The relationship had lasted less than a year because of Marcus' life on the streets and his unwillingness to leave it, but Sarah had remained close to the family, especially to Georgia. She allowed and even encouraged Tamika, now eight, to spend as much time with her as she wanted to, knowing how much she loved the older lady, and how much she benefited from being around her godly behavior. Tamika, with all her questions and youthful exuberance, was the delight of Georgia's life.

The next blessing she constantly thanked God for was the conversion and subsequent growth of her son. About six months after Tasha's death, Bobby called his mother excitedly; informing her he had accepted Christ in prison. She was pleased with the news, but cautious. Bobby had been known to feign religious and psychic experiences in the past if they could somehow be used to his advantage, but this one was for real. He remained faithful, even after getting out of prison, and was now the pastor of the Antioch Baptist Church. He had insisted on her moving in with him at the church parsonage after he became the pastor and she retired from the bank, so they had been able to share their home and their lives together these last several years. Every Sunday, as she heard him preach the word, she thanked God for her son and how good the Lord had been to him.

The last thing that pleased her so was the way Jamal had turned out. He was such a nice boy, and such a good basketball player too. It gave her great satisfaction when people wanted to know if she was the grandmother of the famous Jamal Davis. Her only concern was over his apparent lack of interest in spiritual things. She even doubted if he were truly a Christian at times. She enjoyed him immensely, and prayed every day for the confirmation of his faith in Christ.

This particular day had the promise of being an especially good day for several reasons. First of all, because it was Sunday and she would get to worship her Lord in the House of God and hear Bobby preach again. Also, Tamika was spending the whole weekend with them, and she looked forward to the fun and excitement the little girl always added to their Lord's Days together. Besides that, Jamal had called the night before and both he and Marcus would be meeting them at church and then joining them for dinner. "It just didn't get much better than this," she thought to herself.

After church that night she would be taking Tamika home on the bus, which was the child's idea of high adventure. She was looking forward to it too because it would give her a chance to witness to old Saul at The Corner Store again. He was Jewish, but he was a nice man and Georgia wanted him to know about her Jesus. She would then spend the night with Tamika and Sarah and Sarah's nice new husband Carl, and then take the bus back home in the morning.

She winced a little as she gingerly walked back into her bedroom. She read her Bible and prayed, and then got dressed and went downstairs to put a roast on for dinner. She didn't like the idea of getting older, but with God so good and life so rewarding, who could complain about a few little aches and pains and a few little bumps in the road?

Later that afternoon, Aaron Muller pushed his chair back from his desk and stood up to stretch. He had been sitting there for several hours, studying from the third volume of his Hebrew Interlinear Old Testament. The Hebrew text was printed out with the English equivalent appearing directly under each Hebrew word. This enabled Aaron, who was just learning Hebrew, to confirm his translation in English. He was going over the prophecies in the Book of Isaiah, which spoke of Israel's coming Messiah. He had become fascinated with anything having to do with messianic prophecy lately, and since Sunday was a day off for him, he had taken advantage of it by studying most of the day.

Aaron had the same strong, athletic build that was characteristic of most of the members of the swim team at Cal State Long Beach. He was a little shorter than Tony D'Angelo and not as good looking, but then, who was? However, he was a handsome young man, and was often told he *didn't look Jewish.* He had a light complexion with hazel eyes, and his facial features were rounded, not sharp and angular. He may not have looked Jewish outwardly, but he was becoming more and more Jewish inwardly with every passing day.

He had been born into a liberal Jewish home, which had not taken religious things very seriously at all. His family had celebrated Hanukkah and Passover with about as much reverence as most nominal Christians celebrate Christmas and Easter. They were simply times for feasting, gift giving, and merriment. But in the past two years, Aaron had found himself ever-increasingly compelled to examine the fundamentals of his racial and spiritual heritage.

At the end of his sophomore year in college, he left his liberal synagogue and joined an orthodox one. He voluntarily accepted the dietary restrictions and started keeping the Sabbath religiously. The Jewish Sabbath being from sundown to sundown, he refused to swim on Friday evenings or during the day on Saturday. His coach had a fit, but Aaron was adamant about his convictions, and since he was such a good swimmer, the coach finally agreed to accommodate him.

He even started wearing a yarmulke, the traditional little skullcap worn by orthodox Jewish men. His parents were beside themselves with Aaron's strange behavior, and tried to talk him out of what they considered his fanaticism, but he was not to be deterred.

Frankly, he did not even understand it himself. He had never been interested in religion before. His interests were in sports, girls, and enjoying life, like every other young man he knew. But lately, he felt compelled to pursue holiness, as strange as that sounded, even to him.

It was especially strange and unacceptable to his girlfriend, Anna Berger. She was a wholesome and pretty girl whom he had known since elementary school. They had become sweethearts in high school, and planned to get married right after college, but things had been going badly between them of late.

Anna was interested in being cuddled and romanced, but all Aaron wanted to do at present was talk about the Scriptures and spiritual things. Whenever she approached him to embrace and kiss him, he withdrew from her. This, of course, hurt and offended her, and it mystified him. He loved her sincerely and wanted to be with her, but ever increasingly, his love was becoming more platonic than romantic.

She had broken up with him in tears, just two weeks before, and it had not devastated him. Instead, he sensed a strange relief. His pursuit of messianic truth in Scripture had become his chief priority, and quite frankly, he had lost all interest in things romantic, and especially in things sexual. Whatever was happening to him was beyond his control, and even beyond his ability to comprehend, much less explain, so he simply apologized and let her go.

Right now he was in the middle of one of the greatest events of his life anyway. He could not be bothered with lesser matters. The famous Old Testament scholar, Rabbi Joshua Ben Gamlin, was in Los Angeles for two nights, lecturing on, "The Rebuilding of the Temple in Jerusalem in Light of Old Testament Messianic Prophecies." The advance interest had been so great that the lectures had been moved to the large Music Center in downtown Los Angeles, near the Civic Center.

Aaron had been there the night before and sat spellbound for over two hours as Dr. Ben Gamlin expounded on the prophetic reasons for expecting the imminent arrival of Israel's long awaited Messiah. Aaron had spent the better part of the day confirming what the rabbi had said, and he couldn't wait to go back that night.

He had been fascinated with the rebuilding of the temple ever since he first learned that it was finally, after all these centuries, actually going to take place. He had even flown all the way to Jerusalem the previous summer to be there for the groundbreaking ceremony. Now he was learning how the temple's presence would fit into God's ultimate plan for the spiritual rebirth of Israel and the coming of its kingdom.

He was especially excited about the meeting that night, because he had been able to talk his own father, Joseph Muller, into attending with him. His father had been deeply concerned about Aaron and the changes he had seen in him, so Aaron had used that as leverage to get him to attend. It would allow Mr. Muller the opportunity to hear firsthand the facts that had so captivated his son for the past two years.

Besides that, the Music Center was right off the Harbor Freeway, and afterwards, they would be able to drop over and see Papa Saul. He never got away from the store anymore and it had been quite some time since they had been over to see him. They both dearly loved the old gentleman and this would give the three of them a good chance to kick back and really visit without a bunch of women and little kids around.

His stomach knotted up and beads of sweat balanced on his forehead as Scott Graham turned the heavy gun over in his hand. "How have I ever gotten myself into this mess?" he asked himself as he tried to balance the Colt .38 Special so that somehow it might feel natural in his grip. But try as he would, it still felt just as foreign to him as it looked.

It was his father's gun, and he had held it on only one other occasion. His dad had been so proud of his new weapon that he insisted Scott "check it out" when he brought it home. After the Los Angeles riots following the Rodney King verdict, the senior Graham decided that he needed a handgun to protect his family. But Scott hated guns and made excuses whenever his dad invited him to go with him to the range and fire it.

It had been kept in the top drawer of the nightstand next to Bruce Graham's bed for nearly ten years, and Scott had been quite content to let it stay there permanently. But that was before Friday night. That night had changed everything. Now he sat on his parents' bed, holding his dad's gun in his sweaty hands, trying to convince himself that he could, and would, use it in committing a violent crime.

As the realization of his conclusion gripped him, so did waves of nausea. He dropped the gun on the bed and stumbled to the adjoining master bathroom where he was barely able to make it to the commode before the remains of his lunch splattered into the basin.

As he crouched, bent over the commode, his body racked with convulsions and now dripping with sweat, a sense of self-loathing came over him. "Pull it together, punk!" he commanded himself. "You got yourself into this mess, and you're gonna to have to get yourself out of it."

After some minutes, he was able to get to his feet and flush down the foul contents of the basin. He willed his weakness and shame to be gone with it, but as he turned to wash his face in the sink, he saw a ghastly image in the mirror. The ashen face staring back at him through watery eyes did nothing to bolster his confidence.

"You *can* do this thing! You *will* do this thing!" he insisted, looking directly at his reflection in the glass. "In a few hours you and Tony are gonna walk into that store, and you *will* pull this off!"

Scott dried his hands and face and turned to walk back into the bedroom, still shaky, but with more resolve. He picked up the handgun and pushed the lever that allowed the cylinder to swing out. He spun it around, like he had seen actors do in movies, to make sure there was a shell in every chamber. That constituted only six bullets, but he didn't care. He was determined not to use even one of them.

He wished his dad had purchased an automatic pistol. He was sure it would have been easier to operate, but Bruce Graham was an avid listener to a talk show host who called himself "The G-Man," and he insisted that a real man would settle for nothing less than a hefty revolver. So a revolver it had to be.

Scott clicked the cylinder back in place and stuffed the pistol into a duffel bag, already filled with the leather jacket, boots, gloves, and a ski mask, which he had taken out of Matt's old room. His brother had been an avid sportsman and had been involved in about every challenging sport there was, from scuba and skydiving, to skiing and motorcycle riding. But after he had gotten married and started his family, his wife insisted he not participate in the more dangerous ones, so most of his equipment and clothing had been left or returned to his parents' home. That suited Scott just fine. He didn't have to even go outside the house to accumulate all the stuff he needed for that night's business.

As a final act of preparation, he tossed a couple pair of cheap sunglasses into the duffel bag. He found them in his mom's junk drawer, and figured they would come in handy to complete their disguises. The ski masks would practically cover their entire heads, with the exception of their eyes. That much protection might seem safe enough, but Scott knew that the eyes were the most distinguishing feature on anyone's face. People in that store would surely get a good look at their eyes that night if they were left uncovered, and they might be able to identify him and Tony later by them if they were to see them up close. The glasses were inexpensive and wouldn't offer much protection if they were to actually wear them in the bright sunlight, but they would be perfect for this job. He remembered the store was rather dimly lit, and he wouldn't want good dark glasses that would obscure their vision anyway.

He glanced at his watch and noticed it was nearly six. He was due at Tony's in just a few minutes to enjoy the famous fish dinner Mrs. D'Angelo had promised him. He would go, but he didn't know how much, if anything, he would be able to eat.

He checked the front door to make sure it was locked and turned off all the lights before heading out to the garage. He tossed the duffel bag onto the back seat before sliding in under the steering wheel of his Blazer. As he backed out of the garage, rain splattered on his windshield. He had been so preoccupied inside that he hadn't even noticed when it had started.

"Good," he thought to himself. "If it keeps this up, it will discourage spectators from being out on the streets when we hit the store later tonight."

An hour later, he and Tony were in the Blazer, headed down the hill in the rain to prepare for the job ahead of them. Scott had been surprised with himself. In spite of the bout with nausea he had earlier, he was able to eat a good helping of everything Mrs. D'Angelo set before him. Italian food had always been his favorite, and Tony's mom was a great cook. Even Mr. D'Angelo was in a better mood at the table. There's nothing like a little time and some good food to take the edge off even the most painful of experiences.

As they drove down the hill to get on the freeway, Scott explained to Tony how the embarrassing experience he had at The Corner Store the night before had given him at idea for an alibi just in case they were ever questioned concerning their whereabouts that night. They had told Tony's parents they were going to go to a movie and then spend the night at Scott's house, and that is precisely what Scott told Tony they needed to do.

"I told the old man I had been to a movie when he asked what I was doing out so late, and then I couldn't even tell him what I'd seen when he asked about it. We still have plenty of time, let's go see a movie right now so we won't get caught like that again."

"Yeah, but how would we ever prove we were there at the time of the robbery?" Tony asked.

"I already thought about that." Scott answered confidently. "We go to a movie right now, and throw away the stubs, and when it's over we buy more tickets for a later showing of the same movie. Then we leave with the stubs in our pockets."

"I gotcha," said Tony. "We'll have stubs in our pockets saying we were at the show during the time of the robbery, and we can tell 'em all about it if we're ever questioned later on. You're a genius, man. Let's do it!"

That is precisely what they did do. At Scott's suggestion, they drove down to the Long Beach Mall off the 605 Freeway, even though it was somewhat out of their way. There was a huge movie complex there that had three different connected theaters and a total of twenty-six screens, an excellent setting to move around in without being conspicuous.

Scott bought the initial tickets to the movie. He pulled a hat down to shield his face and was careful not to do or say anything that would be memorable. He had chosen some futuristic thriller called *Desert Planet*, not because he was interested in it, but because it had just started and would be out by nine-fifteen. He gave one of the tickets to Tony and they entered separately, each making his own way to the darkened theater. They paid close attention to every computer-enhanced scene in the disappointing movie, sitting in separate areas of the theater so as to be as inconspicuous as possible. After it was over, they left separately and met a few minutes later in front of the ticket counter.

This time they went together and Tony bought the tickets. He flirted openly with the pretty brunette behind the counter and even asked her what time she got off. She blushed and said her boyfriend was picking her up, but she was clearly impressed and flattered. She probably wouldn't remember Scott, but she would most definitely remember Tony.

Once inside the lobby, they again went together, this time to the concession counter, and ordered a large popcorn and two Cokes. The cute little blond behind the counter was obviously enamored with Tony and responded eagerly to his playful banter. They stayed and talked long enough to ensure that Tony, at least, would be firmly implanted in her memory as well, and then they took their wares and headed down the corridor toward their designated theater.

They each ate some popcorn and took long draws from their drinks, but as soon as they were clearly out of sight from anyone in the lobby, they dumped everything into a trash receptacle and headed for the door marked exit at the end of the hall. Once outside, they walked around the building and found their vehicle where they had left it in the parking lot. They got in and drove away, confident that no one would remember having seen them leave.

With the radio tuned to a country music station and the windshield wipers keeping time, they drove for about half an hour northward up the San Diego Freeway, which more or less paralleled the Pacific coastline. Their destination was the Los Angeles International Airport. They figured they could steal a car from one of the long-term parking lots there without it being reported missing till long after they had discarded it. Besides, it was a considerable distance from home and would not point any future investigators in their direction.

They exited and drove west on Century Blvd. and then turned north on Sepulveda into the heart of what seemed like hundreds of acres of parking lots. Tony directed Scott to a deserted side street next to one of the lots and had him pull over to the curb.

"How can you just go out and steal a car?" Scott asked skeptically. "They don't have their keys just sticking out of the door locks, you know."

"They might as well have," Tony responded. "You would be surprised how many people have a fear of locking their keys inside the car. To avoid having to call somebody to their rescue, they stash a spare key in a magnetic box under the car someplace. Just sit back and watch the master at work."

With that, he fished a flashlight out of his duffel bag and stepped out into the rain. He walked a short distance to the entrance of the fenced-in lot and then disappeared into the sea of automobiles. Well out of sight of anyone on the street, he turned on his flashlight and started poking around under several cars as he went down a row. At the sixth one he stopped, disappeared for a few seconds, and then emerged triumphant, holding a key in his hand. He came back to the Blazer and got in, having been gone less than a total of five minutes.

"It's an older beige Toyota Corolla, made back in the nineties," Tony said, brushing rainwater off his jacket, "and it's a little banged up, but at least it doesn't have an alarm system, and this one key will fit all the locks. It'll work just fine."

"You're amazing," Scott marveled. "Not only is no father's daughter safe with you around, neither is his car!"

They both laughed loudly, but nervously. They realized they had reached the point of no return. Up to now it had all been planning and speculation, but the moment Tony got in the Toyota and drove off, they would become felons, and there would be no turning back.

"Well, I guess it's about that time," said Tony, looking all around to make sure no one was in their vicinity or looking in their direction.

"Yeah, I guess so, I'll meet you at the Wal-Mart parking lot over in Inglewood."

"Okay, I'll see you there."

With that, Tony got out of the Blazer and walked back to the entrance and disappeared into the lot again. He located the Corolla and unlocked the driver's door and got in. In a moment he had started it up, turned on the lights, and had driven to the tollbooth on the opposite side of the lot. The ticket stub left on the dashboard indicated that the car had been parked there only two days previously. That was good news for two reasons. First of all, it wouldn't cost him much to pay the fee at the booth, but even more importantly, the owner probably wouldn't be returning for several more days, and they would be done with it long before he ever reported it missing.

He had his big hat pulled down over his face in case there were any cameras pointed his direction, and as he paid the determined amount at the tollbooth, he was careful not to look up at the attendant, or to attract attention in any way. There was little need for his caution. The attendant was so absorbed in a basketball game he was watching on a portable TV that he paid only enough attention to determine the amount due and to collect the money. Afterwards, he couldn't have described the car, much less the driver.

By now, Tony was feeling really confident. The Corolla ran fine, with plenty of get up and go for a smaller car. "It must have a V-6 in it," he thought to himself, which was an absurd conclusion. A V-6 had never been available on the Corolla model, but Tony had never been much interested in minor details like that. What was important was that it ran well and that it had almost a full tank of gas. He wouldn't have to worry about attracting any attention at a service station. He had been careful to put on a pair of thin leather gloves before he ever got in, so he wouldn't be leaving any fingerprints. He drove north to Manchester Ave. and then east, across the San Diego Freeway, and into the City of Inglewood, feeling almost cocky. Everything had gone like clockwork so far, and he fully expected it to continue that way.

But Scott wasn't feeling so confident. He sat in his Blazer for some time after Tony had left, deeply troubled. There was something inside that told him to simply go home and forget this whole sordid scheme, but Tony would be waiting for him, and besides, he had already decided to see this through, and he was not going to back down now. So he started the Blazer and turned on the lights and wipers and followed the same route Tony had taken a few minutes before. But as he drove, his stomach tightened, and he shivered, but not from the cold.

As he drove east on Manchester, he passed the Great Western Forum where he had seen the Lakers play, and the Hollywood Park Racetrack, where he had seen the thoroughbreds run. It all reminded him of more pleasant days when he had done those things as a boy with his dad. His dad had driven him there, his dad paid his entrance fee, his dad explained everything that was going on; and all Scott had to do was to sit back and enjoy himself under the protection and provision of his father. Strange, as much as Scott had wanted to be free of his father's control over his life, he sorely missed him at that moment. The little boy who still lived inside him would love to have had his lawyer father there as his advocate right then, to plead his case, to pay his fine, to set him free.

But that wasn't going to happen, and he knew it, so Scott shook his head and tightened his grip on the steering wheel and looked for the street that would take him to the Wal-Mart. They had previously decided to leave Scott's Blazer there because the store was open twenty-four hours a day and its parking lot was well lit and always had cars in it. They could leave the vehicle there and it would be both safe and inconspicuous.

When Scott arrived, he spotted the Corolla parked away from the entrance, but still in an area where other cars were parked. He pulled in beside it and Tony got out and climbed in beside him. They changed into their biker clothes in the Blazer and put their own clothes in the duffel bags to be left there.

Tony complimented Scott on the excellent outfit he had put together as his friend got dressed beside him, especially with the sunglasses. Not only would they give them more anonymity, Tony was sure it would make their appearance even more intimidating. Scott gladly accepted the praise and didn't bother to mention he had been able to requisition every bit of it without even leaving his house. But, as he had expected, Tony had outdone him. His leathers had, without a doubt, protected some biker for many a mile down who knows how many streets and highways, complete with chains and decals. His gloves even had a leather fringe on the cuffs. His boots were well worn and scuffed, and his ski mask was the scariest Scott had ever seen.

"Where'd you get all that stuff, man?" he inquired.

"From garage sales, my friend. Sunday morning is the best day of the week to find the really good stuff. Wait'll you get a load of this."

With that, Tony pulled a sawed-off, double-barreled shotgun out of his duffel bag and broke open the breach.

"Oh, my God!" gasped Scott. "Don't tell me you got that thing at a garage sale!"

"I sure did. Only it didn't look quite like this when I bought it this morning. The guy I bought the leathers from sold me the shotgun as well. He broke his back in a motorcycle wreck a couple of years ago, and he can't ride anymore. He can't hunt either, so he sold me everything for a couple hundred bucks. I spent most of the afternoon sawing the stock and barrels off this thing and grinding off the serial numbers. It outta make Aaron's grampa sit up and take notice, doncha think?"

"Yeah, I'll say. Don't point it in this direction."

"Don't worry. It's not loaded yet. The guy even threw in a box of shells, so I'm all set. What kinda gun did you get?"

"Nothing quite so impressive, I'm afraid. I got this .38 Special," he told Tony as he showed him the handgun.

"That'll work great. You done good, Bugsy. I'll make a gangster outta you yet," Tony laughed, as he checked his watch. "Hey, it's after ten o'clock. We better be on our way."

With that, they got out and locked the Blazer and climbed into the Corolla. Tony drove back to Manchester and then east to the Harbor Freeway, which they took north to their desired destination. Tony was filled with excitement and anticipation as he drove and sang lustily along with Buck Owens on the radio, something about *I got a tiger by the tail.*

Scott tried his best to join in, but he had a deep sense of foreboding he could not shake, and only managed to mouth a few of the lyrics. He couldn't help but wonder how true the words of that song might turn out to be.

Carl Singleton sat on the couch, watching a movie on TV, listening to the rain on the roof above his head. He was warm and dry and comfortable, and had every intention of staying that way; but he also had a pregnant wife, and his situation was just about to change. His wife Sarah had retired earlier, but was now up, wrapped in a housecoat, and coming into the living room of their apartment.

"Honey, could I get you to do me a great big favor?" she asked sweetly.

By the tone of her voice, he knew he was in for an unpleasant experience. "Yeah, sure, Babes. What can I do for you?" he replied, but his voice lacked some of the enthusiasm he tried to project.

"I'm worried about Grandma Georgia and Tamika. They should have been here by now. I don't know why I let them talk me into letting them come home on the bus tonight, especially in this rain. Would you be a dear and walk down to Wilshire and meet their bus? I just want to make sure they get home safely."

Now he was caught. His true inner-self wanted nothing to do with going out in the rain after ten o'clock at night. His mind rapidly flipped through all its files to come up with an excuse that at least might sound legitimate, which would allow him to stay home. But his beautiful wife, six months pregnant, was asking him to assist her eight-year-old daughter and her elderly grandmother home on a dark and rainy night. Besides that, the area around MacArthur Park wasn't the safest, even in the daylight. He had only been married to Sarah for eighteen months and he was still trying to prove himself the faithful and devoted husband that he had promised her he would be. No, he either had to reveal the fact that he was basically selfish and lazy, or he had to go out in the rain and get cold and wet.

"Sure, Hon, no problem, just give me a second to get dressed," is what he said, but what he wanted to say was, "They shouldn't have taken the dumb bus in the first place, and besides, they're probably nearly home already. I'll just go out and get drenched and then meet them half a block down the street. Furthermore, have you taken a good look at your grandmother lately? She's so big no mugger would mess with her anyway. Let's just wait a few more minutes and see if they don't show up."

But he didn't say that, and he was determined never to say anything like that to his lovely bride. He felt he was the luckiest man alive to be married to this classy lady, and he was committed to proving to her that she hadn't made a mistake in marrying him. After all, she had been tall, slender, and gorgeous when he pulled her over two years before for rolling through a four-way stop, and he had been overweight, not particularly handsome, and beset by a lot of bad habits. She had worked her way up into lower management in a computer firm and was certain to advance farther, and he was a motorcycle cop destined to stay right where he was for the rest of his career. About the only things they did seem to have in common was that they were both young and African-Americans.

He had tried to act in a professional manner as he asked for her driver's license and registration, but he was so taken with her appearance and personality, he stumbled through the whole procedure. He wasn't able to bring himself to give her a ticket, so he gave her a warning and let her go. But in his infatuation, he failed to return her documents. He just stood there holding them in his hand as she drove off. He noticed his mistake almost immediately and could easily have pursued her and returned them, but he decided not to. Instead, he waited a few minutes and then he drove to the address printed on her license.

It was about 5:30 and he assumed she was on her way home from work. He wanted to see her again and, perhaps, establish some kind of a rapport with her that would allow him to call on her later. But he was wrong about her being on her way home. No one answered the door when he rang the doorbell outside her apartment, and he stood there wondering what to do.

"What if she's married to, or living with some professional wrestler or something?" he asked himself. "I'm going to look really stupid standing here when she shows up with some gnarly dude." He decided to write her a note and attach it to her door and leave, then he heard footsteps on the stairs.

"Now what am I going to do?" he thought, as he turned around to face the music. But he was pleasantly surprised when he saw her top the stairs holding a pretty little girl by the hand. She recognized him right off, which pleased him, and she laughed with embarrassment when he explained about the license and registration. She had completely forgotten about them as well.

He returned them to her with his apologies, but he wasn't willing to leave without knowing more about her. He introduced himself as Officer Carl Singleton, and she responded by telling him she was Sarah Fitzpatrick and her daughter's name was Tamika. She explained that she had just picked her up from the school's day care facility and that's why they hadn't been there when he had arrived.

"And where might Mr. Fitzpatrick be?" Carl asked, and immediately felt like an idiot for having asked such a crude question, painfully obvious, to find out if she were married or not. But he didn't really care. He just had to know.

Sarah smiled knowingly at him and didn't seem to be offended at his inquiry. "Oh, I'm not married. Never have been. My job and Tamika keep me plenty busy."

So their relationship had begun. Carl had fallen in love with Sarah and Tamika almost immediately, but had proceeded very cautiously. Sarah made it clear that she had her fill of dashing, good-looking men, who were only interested in one thing. She had become a Christian through her relationship with Tamika's great-grandmother, and if she were ever to marry, it would have to be to a good and godly man, and she was in no hurry to find him. If the right man were ever to come along, she said she would know it in due time.

Carl decided that he would become that man. He cleaned up his language almost at once. He tossed out all the pornography he had stashed in his apartment. And he even managed to quit smoking after a three-month battle, which had been much harder on him than had been his decision to give up sweets and junk food in order to drop that twenty extra pounds. He still liked a cold beer now and then, but he never drank anything while around his family.

He started out by going to church with Sarah and Tamika and by taking them to the park, to movies, and to ball games. It was several months before he even asked Sarah to go out, just the two of them, on a date. He was a perfect gentleman during the following period of courtship, and he even professed to be a born-again Christian, although he wasn't at all sure what that really meant. All of his efforts paid off, and after six months, he was overjoyed when she agreed to marry him.

He had been a good husband for the past year and a half, and now they were expecting their first child together. They were even saving up to buy their own home. He wasn't about to jeopardize what they had going by refusing to brave a little cold and rain for the sake of his wife and her family.

"Oh, by the way, Sweetie," Sarah added, "while you're out, would you mind stopping by The Corner Store and picking me up a box of Quaker Oats? It's right on your way and it's open till eleven."

Now it became clear to Carl that Sarah had an ulterior motive behind her request. She, no doubt, was concerned about Georgia and Tamika, but she had even a greater concern for raw oatmeal. Recently, during her pregnancy, she had developed an intense craving for oatmeal. She would sit watching TV with an open box of Quaker Oats in her lap, munching out of it as though it were popcorn or peanuts. Doubtlessly, the baby needed whatever the oats provided, because when the craving hit, nothing would pacify Sarah until she had her fill of them. She had finished the last of a box before she had gone to bed, but the baby had awakened her and signaled that it was time for more, and Carl knew that neither one of them was going to be talked out of it.

"Sure thing, Babe. I think I'll pick up two boxes while I'm at it. I want it to last until this rainy season is over. You sure I can't get you some pickles and ice cream too while I'm out?" He was careful to smile and wink as he said it.

"No, Dear, the oatmeal will be quite enough, thank you very much." She too smiled, knowing he had seen through her little ploy. She had grown to love her husband dearly and was appreciative of the care and consideration he always showed her.

A few minutes later, Carl was locking their apartment door and walking down the stairs, ready to go out and brave the elements. After the initial decision to go out into the rain had been made, he actually looked forward to this little adventure. He was plenty prepared. He had a coat and hat and umbrella to protect him from the weather, plus he had his spare, snub-nosed revolver strapped to his ankle for protection, and his cell phone in his pocket in case he needed to call home for anything. Besides, it wasn't raining that hard, and the total distance, there and back, was less than a mile. The night air and exercise would do him good.

But the real reason he had become so keen about this mission of mercy was due to the fact that he had developed a powerful thirst over the past fifteen minutes. A couple of cold ones down at Papa Saul's would really hit the spot. He would get some breath mints too, and he would wait for Georgia and Tamika to arrive, then he would return home, the hero of the evening, with family and fodder in tow.

Aaron and Joseph Muller had just returned to the parking garage after a long session with Rabbi Ben Gamlin at the Music Center. Aaron was bubbling with excitement over the plethora of information they had just received from the famous scholar.

"Dad, wasn't that the greatest thing you ever heard?" the young man asked his father.

"What thing?"

"You know, all about the completion of the temple and the coming of the Messiah. It should be done in less than two months, and according to Dr. Ben Gamlin, the way will be prepared for the Messiah to return and set up his kingdom right from Jerusalem."

"Oh, I don't know, son. He's a smart man and all, but it all seemed pretty confusing to me. I don't think we should get all excited about what he said. Smarter men than him have been predicting the coming of the Messiah for thousands of years. What makes you think he knows more than any of the others did?"

"I can't believe you said that, Dad. It was all so clear and convincing. C'mon, let's go over and see Papa Saul. I want to talk to him about it. I'll bet he'll agree with me."

"Now, hold on there, Aaron," Mr. Muller cautioned his son. "We're going to go see him, but I don't want you confusing or upsetting your grandfather. He's bound to be tired after a long day in the store, so we'll just pay him a short, friendly visit. No heavy duty discussions, agreed?"

"Okay, okay," Aaron agreed. "Only get in the car already. He'll be locked up and in bed before we ever get there if we keep standing here talking."

CHAPTER NINE

THE HEIST

Georgia Davis looked at her watch and shook her head. She knew Sarah and Carl would be concerned about her and Tamika out here so late and in the rain and all. She had intended to have her great-granddaughter home long before now, knowing that she needed to get her rest before going to school in the morning, but time had just seemed to slip away. She had enjoyed a glorious day and wouldn't have wanted to miss any part of it. So, she would take full responsibility for their tardiness in hopes that Sarah would understand and not be too upset with her.

She loved the little girl so very much, who now sat beside her with her little hand tightly clasped in Grandma Georgia's much more substantial one. She cherished every minute she was allowed to spend with Tamika and she wanted to make the most of every opportunity. She and Bobby had her all weekend, and what a joy she had been. She had been especially good and, as a reward, she had been granted her utmost wish: to ride across town on the big bus with her grandma.

The church services at Antioch Baptist had been such a blessing that morning. Georgia still sang in the choir, and she especially enjoyed the lively spiritual they sang. Bobby's preaching was powerful and convicting, and many had gone forward at the altar call. She was convinced Bobby was one of the finest preachers she had ever heard. Of course, the fact he was her son may have influenced her opinion somewhat.

After church, it was wonderful having all the family together for dinner. Marcus had to leave that afternoon, but Jamal stayed all day, and even went back with them for the evening service. Afterwards, they all went to the local pizza parlor and ate, talked, and laughed well into the night. By the time they finished and were driven to the bus station, it was nearly nine-thirty. So here they were, after changing buses downtown, almost an hour later, approaching their stop at Alvarado and Wilshire.

As the bus slowed to its stop, Georgia rose slowly from her seat, her arthritic joints protesting loudly. With the help of a steadying hand from the driver, she was able to get Tamika and herself off the bus safely and, with her big umbrella canopied above them, they began their short walk north on Alvarado.

As the two walked hand in hand, Georgia smiled down at Tamika, who was making a point of splashing a foot in each puddle they encountered on the uneven sidewalk along the way. What a great day it had been, she reminded herself again. If her life were to end tomorrow, she would have no regrets. She had the love of God in her heart, and the love of her family and friends all around. Besides, her old body was wearing out, and she wouldn't mind getting a brand new one in heaven, one that didn't hurt when it moved.

But she wasn't ready to go just yet. She still had some unfinished business to attend to, namely sharing the love of Jesus with Papa Saul at The Corner Store. She had come to know him well over the years as she visited and stayed with Sarah and Tamika, and more recently with Carl. She did the shopping when she had been there and she always looked forward to seeing Saul Frieberg again.

Saul was a fine human being, but he hadn't been interested in hearing the gospel heretofore. He was Jewish, from a long line of Jews, and that was good enough for him. At least that is what he always said. But Georgia sensed a dissatisfaction somewhere underneath all that purported confidence, and knew the only thing that would give him real peace was a personal knowledge of his Messiah Jesus Christ.

So, as they neared The Corner Store, both she and Tamika were looking forward to it. Tamika was excited about the prospect of selecting the treat her grandma had promised her, and Georgia was anticipating the lively conversation she was about to have with the proprietor.

Unbeknownst to the elderly lady and the little girl, Scott and Tony sat in the Corolla across the street, watching their approach. They had been sitting there for about twenty minutes, waiting for the best time to make their move. There hadn't been much activity in or around The Corner Store since they arrived. A few young men went in and out, but they wouldn't make suitable hostages. If they were going to get the old man to open those safes, they were going to need better leverage.

They both spotted Georgia and Tamika approaching from down the street, and were trying to silently will them into the store, like a bowler tries to scoot his ball over to the head pin after he has already released it and it's rolling down the alley. Everyone else they had seen go in had already come out, so they were convinced no one besides the owner was in the store. When the two of them turned and went inside, Tony let out a whoop and punched Scott in the shoulder.

"That's our cue, partner," he said as he started up the engine and prepared to drive around the block and park alongside the store. Both of them put on their woolen ski masks so they could pull them down over their faces before they went into the store. They got out the sunglasses as well, and had them ready to complete their disguises.

Saul Frieberg looked up from the newspaper he had been reading as he heard the door opening, and smiled as he saw Georgia and Tamika come in. Business had been so slow because of the rain and the lateness of the hour; he had almost decided to close up early. But he never had done so before in over forty years of doing business on this corner, and he had decided that it wouldn't be a good idea to start in now.

He had kept regular hours all those years: open from seven to seven, every day except Saturday, the Sabbath, on which day he had always been closed. In fact, he closed Friday evening an hour early, at six o'clock, so as not to profane the holy day.

Since the death of his wife Rita five years previously, he had started opening the store at 6:00 P.M. on Saturdays and staying open until eleven. He did so much business that he decided to stay open till then on Sunday nights as well. It helped his income even more, but more importantly, it gave him something to do. With Rita gone, evenings had gotten awfully lonely sitting upstairs all by himself. So finally, he just decided to stay open till eleven every night except, of course, on Friday.

Saul was proud of his store and his way of life. The Corner Store had been his home, his business, his very identity, ever since he and Rita had purchased it back in the late fifties. They had raised their three children there. They had served their community there. And Rita had died there. She suffered a massive heart attack stocking shelves early one morning and died before the paramedics arrived. Old Saul fully intended to go out the same way.

Sure, his kids worried about him. They all had beautiful homes in the suburbs and wanted him to close the store and move in with one of them, but what was he gonna do then? He couldn't see himself puttering around the garden or a golf course, or sitting in the house watching soap operas all day. No, this store was his life, and he was going to stay right there.

It was true; the neighborhood had changed over the past half-century. He could well remember closing the store and taking his family to the synagogue every Friday evening, and then Saturday was spent in the park.

At that time, the MacArthur Park area was the center of the Jewish population in Los Angeles. The children would play in the park as their mothers watched over them and their fathers sat on the benches and talked politics, economics, and religion.

Now the park was filled with illegal aliens and homeless people. It was a scary place in the daytime and few would venture there at night. Most of his Jewish friends had moved away years before, and the better businesses had closed down as well, to be replaced by less reputable establishments. For example, the famous Westwood Theater had closed years before, and now a swap meet operated out of what had been its spacious lobby.

But it hadn't been all that bad. Some of his old friends still lived in the neighborhood, and Saul had made lots of new ones too. He always treated everyone with friendliness and respect, and they responded in kind. He supported worthy community causes and hired neighborhood boys to help him stock shelves and clean up after school. He ate most of his meals downstairs, between customers, not because he had to, but because he simply loved people and preferred to be with them as much as possible. He had become a beloved institution in his own lifetime.

"Well, I declare, if it isn't Miss Tamika, and her lovely Grandma Georgia," he said with a chuckle as he greeted his customers. "What are you ladies doing out so late on a night like this?"

"Hi, Papa Saul," Tamika chirped. "I've been riding on the bus with Grandma and she's gonna buy me some candy."

"Well, you've come to the right place, young lady. You just take a look over there and pick out whatever you want, and old Papa Saul will pay for it tonight. Anyone who's willing to come out on a rainy night like this deserves to have a treat on the house."

"Oh, no you don't," protested Georgia. "She's my great-granddaughter, and I don't get to spoil her nearly enough. I'm paying for that candy bar, and I don't want to hear another word outta you, you old goat."

"It's good to see you too, Mrs. Davis," Saul said, with a twinkle in his eye. "Is there anything I can do for you tonight, or did you just come by to call me names?"

"Yes, as a matter of fact, there is something you can do for me. You can hold still for a few minutes and let me tell you about my Jesus."

"No, I don't believe I can do that right now. It's late, and I'm tired, and besides you came through the wrong door for that. The front door is for customers only. Peddlers all have to use the rear door. You know that, Georgia."

With that, Georgia let out a peal of laughter, not a ladylike chuckle, or a girlish giggle, but a deep belly laugh that came from the depths of her soul. She could be heard across the street above the sound of the traffic and the storm. She laughed loud and long, just for the sheer joy in it. Oh, how she loved this old man, and what joy she got out of just being in his presence. Somehow, with all his goodness and brotherly love, he just had to come to Christ. She just couldn't see God letting him slip away.

"*DON'TANYBODYMOVE!!*" came a shout from out of nowhere. Tony had just burst through the door with the double-barreled shotgun leveled squarely at Saul and Georgia. Right behind him sprang in Scott with his revolver held at arm's length. They were dressed in black leather, with ski masks and dark glasses covering their faces. They looked and sounded like they were deadly serious.

"Oh, my Sweet Jesus," Georgia whispered. "Tamika, come here to Grandma, right now!"

She needn't have bothered. Tamika had dropped the candy she held in her hand the instant Tony hollered, and was making a beeline for Georgia. On reaching her, she ducked in behind her and burrowed as deeply into the folds of her grandma's coat as she could.

"Now, just take it easy, young fella," Saul said as evenly as he was able. "Nobody here's a threat to you. We don't want no trouble. Just tell us what you want."

They had previously agreed that Tony would do the talking since Scott had been in the store the night before, and they didn't want to risk the owner recognizing his voice. Besides that, Tony couldn't wait to play the part of the cruel desperado. Scott gave him no argument about it either. He had expressed no desire to play such a part while they were outside in the car talking about it, and even less so now that they were actually inside the store. His job was to cover the hostages while Tony worked on the old man.

"You! You two. Get to the back of the store!" Tony growled at Georgia, as he motioned toward the rear with the barrels of his shotgun. As they began to move, Scott followed them, with his pistol pointed in their direction, although he couldn't actually bring himself to point the muzzle at either one of them.

"As for you, old man, you can get me all the money out of the cash drawer, and do it *NOW*!" Tony was really getting into it.

"Yeah, okay, take it easy, I'm goin,' I'm goin.' Just don't be shootin' at anybody, okay?"

"You just do what you're told, and nobody'll get hurt."

With that, Saul opened the cash drawer of the old register and pulled out all the bills and laid them on the counter.

"Now lift the tray and gimmy the bills underneath."

Papa Saul frowned. He had hoped the hoodlum wouldn't think to ask for those bills too. During the day, he had periodically put the larger bills beneath the tray just in case something like this might happen. Nonetheless, he complied with the demand. A few extra dollars weren't worth running the risk of somebody getting hurt, especially with Georgia and Tamika in the store.

"Now bag it, Pops," Tony demanded, again threatening Saul with the business end of his shotgun.

"Sure thing, sonny, will that be paper or plastic?" Saul shot right back, but immediately regretted his ill-timed sarcasm.

"Don't you get smart with me, old man!" Tony tried to sound as threatening as possible, but inside he wanted to laugh. "No wonder Aaron loves this old guy so much," he thought to himself. "He's staring down the barrels of a shotgun, and he's cracking jokes."

"But as long as you're asking, put it in a plastic bag. No, double that. It's rainin' outside, and I don't wanna get all those dead presidents wet."

In the back of the store, Scott was trying to act forceful and threatening, but perhaps the slight tremor in his gun hand, or something else about him had given him away. At any rate, Georgia wasn't buying any of it.

"Now, young man," she said calmly, "why don't you put that gun away? You know you don't plan on using it, and you're scaring the little girl with it."

"No way, the gun stays right where it is, lady. And don't think for a minute I won't use it if you try anything stupid."

"Ummm, you said a bad word," Tamika said scoldingly, poking her head around Georgia's sizable waist.

"Don't you worry about my language. You just get your head back around there and shut up, if you know what's good for you," he said menacingly, pointing the gun in her direction.

Her head disappeared behind her grandma like a shot, but he heard her say softly, "Ummm, you said another bad word."

"What the heck's going on around here?" he thought to himself. "I'm the mean, bad guy with the gun, and nobody's taking me seriously. The old lady is trying to talk me out of it, and now the kid is correcting my language."

"Sonny, I don't know why you're doin' this," Georgia said softly, "but I know, deep inside, you don't wanna be a-doin' it. I can tell by your voice you're a good boy. I don't know what kind a problem you've gotten yourself into, but guns ain't the way of solvin' it. I know. I've seen it in my son and my grandson. Jesus has the answer to all your troubles, if you'll only give them over to Him."

"You shut up with that Jesus stuff!" Scott practically shouted. "Good grief!" he thought to himself again. "It's not enough for Dr. Schumway to preach to me about Jesus, or for my parents to preach to me about Jesus, or for Candi to preach to me about Jesus, now this old lady I'm holding at gun point is preaching to me about Jesus too. This isn't the way this was supposed to happen."

Just then, the front door of the store swung open, and in walked Joseph and Aaron Muller. They had been talking intently about the contents of the lecture they had just heard, and had not even looked within the store until they were both inside and it was too late.

Tony spun around when he heard them come in, and he leveled the shotgun on them. "Get away from the door! Move it! Get to the back with the others!"

"Papa Saul, what's going on?" Aaron asked in shock and surprise.

"Dad, you okay?" Joseph added as they were being herded down the aisle.

Tony was dealing with a bit of shock and surprise himself. "What in the world is Aaron doing here?" he thought. "And this has to be his dad. He's seen me and Scott at swim meets lots of times, and Aaron sees us nearly everyday. But there's no way they'll be able to recognize us in these disguises, unless we do or say something stupid."

"I'm okay," Saul reassured his relatives. "These gentlemen just made a withdrawal from the cash box and were about to leave. Isn't that right, sir?"

"Not so fast there, pops," Tony responded, being careful to keep his voice disguised. "You haven't introduced us to your family yet. This must be your son and grandson. This adds a whole new wrinkle to things."

"Just take your money and go. You got what you came for. Just take it and leave us alone."

By this time, Scott had motioned Aaron and his father over to join his other hostages, and was holding a somewhat unsteady gun on all of them.

"No, I don't think we're ready to do that just yet," replied Tony as he went over to the door and stepped out briefly to check up and down the street. Seeing no one, he came back inside and approached Saul again, who was still standing behind the cash register. "No, we're not ready to leave until we find out what's inside that safe of yours first."

"Safe? What safe?" asked Saul, trying to sound mystified, but his voice betrayed his awareness.

"Oh, you know, the one under the counter over there, concealed behind some cosmetics or something."

"I don't know what you're talkin' about," said Saul, but his mind was racing. "How could this punk know about the safe?" he asked himself. "Nobody but my family knows anything about that safe. I never showed anybody, and I never even told anybody else about it."

"Oh, yes you do, and so do I. You have people work here, and they see things, and they talk. Now get over there and open it up, or somebody's gonna get hurt!"

"Even if I did have a safe, I wouldn't open it for the likes of you. You can do whatever you want to me, I'm not gonna budge. I'm not afraid of you punks."

"No, I really don't think you are, but what about those other people over there? Maybe they are. You gonna open that safe, or do I havta have Mac put a hole in one of them first?"

"Oh, for God's sake, Dad, open the safe!" pleaded Joseph Muller, obviously terrified by now. "They know it's there, and they won't give up until they get what's in it. It's only money, and it's not worth anybody getting shot over."

"Yeah, especially you, you big chicken!" thought Saul. "You've been trying to get me to sell this store for years, and now you're in cahoots with these thugs to starve me out."

"All right, all right, I'll open it, but you keep away from my family and friends, or so help me . . ."

"Take it easy, old timer," said Tony reassuringly. "We don't want to hurt nobody, but we *do* want the money."

Papa Saul grumbled and walked back to the far end of the counter and knelt down behind it. Tony picked up the money sack and followed him so he could keep an eye on him. He put one hand on the counter and then hopped up on it on his bottom. He swung his legs up and scooted over so he could see what was going on below.

Saul swung out a false front, complete with shelves stocked with perfume and cologne samples, and went to work on the combination. When he had opened the door, Tony hopped down beside the older man to make sure he pulled out all the money, and only money. This would not be a good time to be surprised by a hidden pistol or a concealed alarm button.

Tony handed Saul the bag, and watched as the older man put stacks of large bills inside it. Saul hated to do it, but it really wasn't all that much money, and now, at least, these punks would leave, and his loved ones would be safe.

Satisfied that all the money had been transferred into the bag, Tony took it from Saul and then escorted the older man around the far end of the counter and over to where the others were standing.

Scott had been about to go nuts, waiting for what seemed like forever. He endured Georgia's continuing pleas for him to turn to Jesus because he didn't want Aaron to hear his voice if he had tried to silence her. He had a feeling he wouldn't have been successful anyway. He kept his gun pointed in the direction of his four hostages, and spoke only when he felt he had to, but he was especially careful not to speak in his normal voice. He felt naked and exposed so close to his teammate in spite of the heavy disguise and the itchy ski mask. He was sweating and mildly hyperventilating and ready to bolt for the door just as soon as Tony gave the word.

"Now, how about the other safe?" Tony asked smugly. "You know, the one that's in the storeroom back there." He remembered vaguely that's where Aaron had said it was, but he tried to sound as though he knew all about it.

"Oh, no!" thought Scott. "What's wrong with you, Tony? We got the money from the cash register and the safe. That's gotta be enough. Aaron's standing right here, breathing down my neck. I don't know how much longer I can do this. Someone else could come in, or worse yet, maybe the old guy hit a silent alarm and the police are on their way here right now. Besides, *you promised!*" he could hear his own voice screaming inside his head.

But Tony was on another wavelength. He was having the time of his life. He felt invincible. It was true, they had a lot of money already, but he figured the other safe was probably really stuffed. Furthermore, with his son and grandson under the gun, the old man would gladly give away the whole store, and his own underwear too, if necessary to keep either of them from being hurt.

Carl Singleton picked up his pace. He wanted to get to the store and get at least one beer down before Georgia and Tamika showed up. He was frustrated because he had been forced to retrace his steps. He had been over halfway to The Corner Store when he realized he had forgotten to bring his wallet. He had to go back and get it, and make apologies to his hungry-for-oatmeal wife, and set out again. He was nearly there now, and he could almost taste the cold Bud sliding down his throat.

It was well after ten-thirty by now and he thought it strange he hadn't encountered his adopted daughter and her great-grandmother yet, but he knew how long those evening services could last over at the Antioch Baptist Church. He assumed they had just gotten a late start and would be showing up any minute—but not too soon, he hoped. He had his heart set on that beer.

He rounded the corner and was approaching the door, when he heard a muffled shout coming from deep in the store. It sounded like, "No way!" He froze. His body was hidden from view from inside the store by the magazine racks just on the other side of the plate glass. He poked his head around the edge of the last rack and peered inside the store. At first he didn't see anyone, then as he looked farther back in the store he saw a figure in black, wearing a knit cap over his head, holding what appeared to be a shotgun in his hands.

He jerked his head back as cold chills danced on his flesh. "What am I gonna do?" he said under his breath. "There's a robbery going on in there, that's for sure. I gotta get some help!"

He stepped back around the corner so he couldn't be seen or heard if someone inside came to check things out, and he called 911 on his cell phone. He identified himself to the operator when she came on the line and explained where he was and what was going on. She said she would send back up right away, and then asked if there were any hostages in the store.

"Oh, no!" he said, more to himself than to the operator. No wonder he hadn't seen Georgia or Tamika. They were probably in the store right now! "I don't know. You send out the cavalry and I'll go check and see who else is in there. I'll be back in a second."

Carl bent down and pulled his revolver from his ankle holster and checked to make sure it was fully loaded before going back around the corner. He went slowly down the storefront, looking for an opening he could see through. He stopped abruptly. Between two of the magazine racks was a slight gap, through which he glimpsed figures at the back of the store.

By pressing his face right up next to the glass, he could see several people clearly. There was Papa Saul, obviously agitated and angry. Beside him were two men Carl didn't recognize. One was quite young, and the other considerably older. On the other side of Saul, at the edge of his vision, was a large elderly black woman. That had to be Georgia. He didn't see Tamika, but he knew she had to be in there too if Georgia was.

He retreated back around the corner and told the operator that there were at least four hostages in the store besides the owner. She needed to send over a SWAT unit, and to make it quick. She confirmed his instructions, and asked if there was anything else he could add.

It was then he noticed the beige Toyota Corolla parked beside the curb. He thought it was right where he would have parked it if he were going to rob the store. Besides, it was unlocked, strange indeed for this neighborhood at night. If the thugs were somehow able to make their escape, it would be helpful for the police to have a description of their getaway car. He gave a detailed description of the vehicle and its license number, and did the same thing for the late model Cadillac parked in front of the store, but he told the operator his money was on the Corolla. The Caddy probably belonged to some of the hostages inside.

The operator read back the details to make sure she had everything down correctly, then told him to stay out of the way and on the line until the police got there.

"Not a chance! My daughter and her grandmother are in that store, and there's no way I'm gonna hide around the corner here as long as they're in danger. I know you've instructed to keep me on the line and all, but I'm gonna hang up now. I got work to do and I can't be talkin' on the phone. You just get the cops out here and I'll mind the store."

He heard her start to protest as he clicked off the cell phone and put it back in his pocket. He crept back around the building, wondering why he felt so terrified. He was a motorcycle cop. He was trained to handle crisis situations. Yet, he was trembling as he approached the door, trying to see what was going on inside, but desperate not to be seen by the robber, or robbers, lurking inside.

He poked his head around the end magazine rack and looked again to see if he could determine exactly what was going on in the back of the store. He spotted the dark figure with the shotgun he had seen before, and coming into view was another one, dressed in a similar fashion and wielding a handgun. He couldn't see the hostages from this viewpoint, but he could hear Papa Saul through the crack between the old door and the jam.

"I'm telling you, I don't have another safe, and even if I did I wouldn't open it for you!" the unmistakable voice boomed out. "You got your money, now take it and leave us alone!"

"Look," said Shotgun, "I'm losing my patience with you, old timer. I know you got another safe in there, and you're gonna open it for us, or I'm gonna have Mac here waste one of your friends. Now, you don't want that to happen, do you?"

"You're not gonna kill somebody over a few extra dollars that don't exist anyway," argued Saul. "You're both young men, not hardened criminals. So you need some money? Well, you got it right there in that bag. Take it while you still have a chance of getting away before the cops come."

"The cops ain't comin', and we ain't goin', not until you open that other safe," Shotgun growled. "And as far as shootin' goes, ole Mac here's gunned down four people already, and another one or two won't make any difference to him."

Carl was straining to hear the conversation inside the store, and growing more and more panic-stricken with every passing second. "Where are those cops?" he demanded to know. He didn't know what they would be able to do to dismantle the situation inside, but at least the monkey would be off his back.

Inside, Scott Graham was every bit as desperate as was Carl Singleton outside. He tried not to let it show, but he was about to lose control. He didn't care about the other safe, or the money inside it, but he did care about these innocent people he was holding at gunpoint, and he cared most of all about his own safety and well-being. They were at a stalemate here, and the longer they waited, the greater their chances grew of being discovered and apprehended. But he knew he dared not argue with Tony in front of their hostages. He just hoped his friend would come to his senses before it was too late.

But Tony was relentless. No old man was going to back him down, not when he knew that safe was back there, and it was full of cash. "Okay, Mac, shoot one of them!" he commanded. He knew Scott wouldn't do it, neither did he want him to, but he figured the threat would cause old Saul to crack.

"Which one?" Scott asked, trying to sound both able and willing, being neither.

"I don't care. I would suggest either Aunt Jemima there or the Jew Boy. Take your pick."

Outside, Carl heard those words and his mind struggled to comprehend them. Could it be that the hooded figure in there, who was now aiming his pistol at someone, would really go ahead and shoot? And if so, what if he did? What could he be expected to do about it? Sure he was a cop, and he did have a gun, but what could he really do? There were two of them in there and one of them had a shotgun. He had never fired his own weapon in the field, and he even had difficulty qualifying at the range with his regular service pistol, much less with this snub-nosed thing he now held in his hand.

But on the other hand, his daughter was in there, and the great-grandmother she adored. If he stood by and let something happen to either of them, how could he ever explain it to Sarah? How could he ever live with himself? "*WHERE ARE THOSE COPS?*"

As he stood there, with his ear pressed up against the crack by the door, he could feel a warm liquid spreading down his pant leg. "Well, what's it gonna be, Carl?" he asked himself. "Are you gonna stand here and pee your pants while they shoot Georgia or Tamika, or are you gonna do something about it?"

What happened next, took place in less than two seconds, but for all those involved, it seemed like a lifetime.

Tony D'Angelo was confident. Seeing the desperation on the old man's face, he knew he was about to cave in.

Saul Frieberg, indeed, was about to end the stand off. He still didn't think the gunman would actually shoot someone, but he couldn't take that chance, especially since he was now pointing his pistol squarely at Aaron's heart.

Scott Graham was about to crack, himself. He could see the .38 Special in the hand at the end of his arm, but both the gun and the hand seemed foreign, like neither one of them belonged to him. The hammer was pulled back on the gun, and the barrel was pointed unsteadily at the chest of one of his friends. His heart was pounding in his own chest and his nerves were at their breaking point.

Joseph Muller was in shock. He knew he should do something to protect his son, but he was paralyzed. He just stared at the shaking gun pointed at Aaron's chest, his mind incapable of rational thought.

Aaron Muller wasn't terrified, as he thought he ought to be. A strange sense of calm had come over him. He felt a presence he could not identify assuring him of his preservation, even as he stared down the muzzle of a gun held in the unsteady hand of the man who could well be about to shoot him.

Tamika Singleton was weeping softly into the fabric of her great-grandmother's coat as she hid behind her. She was praying Jesus would keep them safe, and she had never wanted her mother so badly in all her young life.

Georgia Davis was angry. No way was she going to let that frantic gunman shoot the nice young man standing by her side. This was Saul's grandson, of whom he was so proud, and of whom he had spoken so often. She couldn't overpower the adversary, but she wasn't going to just stand there and let it happen either. She began to take a step to her left to position herself between the gunman and his target. If he was indeed going to shoot someone, she was determined that she was going to take the bullet rather than Saul's grandson.

Just then, the front door banged open and Carl landed in the doorway, his feet spread apart, both outstretched hands firmly grasping his inadequate weapon. "*FREEZE! POLI . . .*" he started to shout.

But he never got a chance to finish the phrase. At the first sound of the door opening, Tony began to pivot to face whoever it was coming in the door.

Carl saw the gunman swinging the shotgun around toward him, and he knew he was outmatched. His only chance was to get off the first shot.

He aimed at the middle of the black figure, thankful that none of the hostages was visible behind him, and pulled the trigger.

There were over forty feet between Carl and his intended target, which resulted in a combination of good and bad news for the policeman. It was bad news in that it was just too far for him to shoot accurately with such a hurried shot. He missed his target and hit, instead, a number-ten sized can of tomato juice to the right of it, which exploded, splattering blood red liquid over everything in the vicinity.

On the other hand, the distance represented some good news, of sorts, for him. As Tony completed his turn and got the shotgun pointed toward

Carl, the gunshot and the exploding tomato juice can beside him prompted him to return fire. The distance allowed the load of number eight, quail shot, to expand, so Carl didn't have to take the full impact of the blast in a small area of his body. As it was, the pattern of shot expanded widely and struck him squarely over his entire chest and stomach area. His coat and sweatshirt underneath stopped much of the impact, and none of the small lead shot had enough force to penetrate into any vital organs, sparing his life. So much for the good news.

The rest of the bad news is that the blast hit him like the kick of a mule, knocking the breath out of him and sending him flying backwards through the plate glass of the door. He landed with a thud on his back, knocking himself unconscious as he struck his head on the wet concrete of the sidewalk outside. His coat was torn in shreds and blood from his multiple wounds began to seep through the holes. He looked as though he had just been blown to bits.

At the same instant, Scott jumped at the sound of the two gunshots going off almost simultaneously, and his muscles contracted involuntarily. His hand tightened its grip on the pistol, and his finger tightened its grip on its trigger. The gun seemed to explode in his hand, and he dropped it to the floor, at first not even aware of what had taken place. But as much as he had determined not to, and as much as he would hate himself for it afterwards, he had just fired his pistol, at point-blank range, into the body of another human being.

Georgia Davis had just stepped in front of Aaron Muller when the gun went off. The 158-grain bullet left the muzzle at a velocity of nearly 800 feet per second and tore through her body with 200 foot/pounds of energy. It punched a neat hole through her coat, her dress, her bra, and through her left breast, just to the left of her heart. It smashed its way through a rib and ripped through her left lung before it nicked another rib on its way out. The bullet was flattened out by the flesh and bone it had encountered as it passed through her body and it made a much larger hole as it exited. It carried with it blood and bits of flesh as it tore through the fabric of the back of her coat.

The bullet was slowed considerably by its path through Georgia's body, but it was not entirely spent. It shattered a button on the front of Aaron's coat and pierced the fabric of his clothing. It entered the center of his chest, boring through his sternum and penetrating his chest cavity. It finally came to rest against the pericardium, the protective sac, in which his uninjured heart continued to beat.

Saul Frieberg was stunned for at instant; everything had happened so quickly. But seeing both Georgia and Aaron fall to the floor shocked him into action. He turned to run past Tony and to hurry to their aid. Tony, pumped full of adrenaline, saw the movement out of the corner of his eye and interpreted it as a threat. He whirled and struck the older man in the forehead with the butt of his shotgun, sending him instantly unconscious to the floor. The blow opened a large gash in his forehead, and the blood began to flow freely from the wound onto the wooden floor and down into the cracks between the boards.

Scott Graham and Joseph Muller just stood there, neither one of them able to move. Both of them stared at the stricken bodies between them, neither able to comprehend what had transpired. They might have maintained their respective positions for some time had it not been for Tony.

He bent and grabbed up the money sack and the fallen .38 Special and then straightened and seized his paralyzed partner by the shoulder. "C'mon, Mac, we gotta get outta here!" he yelled as he forcefully guided Scott down the aisle.

Scott stopped and looked back, tears streaming down his cheeks. He turned and made a move to go back. He was devastated by the realization of what he had just done, and he wanted to go back and help if he could. But Tony grabbed him again and hissed under his breath, "Get a grip! There's nothing we can do for them now. We've gotta save our own butts. LET'S GO!"

Reality finally set in and Scott became aware of the gravity of their situation. Fear replaced pity in his eyes, and he bolted ahead of Tony and out the door. Tony took one last glance at those at the rear of the store. Tamika and Joseph were now bending over Georgia and Aaron, respectively, and no one was paying attention to them. He followed Scott through the shattered door, without bothering to open it, over the scattered glass and the motionless body of Carl Singleton, and out into the night and the rain.

Aaron moaned incoherently and semiconsciously as his father made an effort to stop the bleeding with a handkerchief. Tamika wept uncontrollably as she tried to solicit a response from her great-grandmother. Georgia's eyes stared blankly for some time, her mind and body in shock. After some seconds, she blinked and focused her eyes on the anxious face of her beloved Tamika. She reached up and pulled the child down to her bosom on her uninjured right side.

"Come here, sweet child," she said calmly, "Everything's gonna be alright. Don't cry, baby, they're gone now. Ain't nobody gonna hurt you."

"I don't care about me, Grandma," wept Tamika, as she hugged Georgia. "You're hurt, and I don't know what to do."

"Now, you don't be worrying about me, sweetheart. I'll be fine." She looked over at Aaron, lying next to her, and then at his father, bending over him. "How's he doin'?" she asked weakly.

"His breathing seems normal and he's got a strong pulse," Joseph said, somewhat amazed. "I think he's going to be alright."

Aaron lifted his head and opened his eyes. He looked at the older woman and smiled. "I'm okay. I don't think the bullet went in very far. You saved my life, ma'am."

"Oh, thank you, Jesus!" Georgia said with amazing energy, as she looked upward. "I'm ready to go now, if you're calling me, Master." Then she turned to Joseph and Aaron and winked and said, "I didn't want to die of old age and arthritis anyway."

Tamika held her tighter and cried, "No, Grandma, no! Please don't die! Please don't die!"

Georgia smiled and held her little body as it shook with sobs. "Now, don't you cry. I'm in Jesus' hands and I feel Him callin' me home." She coughed, but continued on weakly, "You got your mommy and daddy to take good care of you, and the angels are coming to take me to see your Grandma Tasha. We'll be waitin' for you over on the other side whenever it's your time to join us. Remember, Jesus loves you very much, child, and so do I. Don't ever forget that."

Georgia stopped talking, but continued to hold Tamika as she wept in her arms. She smiled as she looked upward as though she saw persons invisible to the others in the room. She took a few more breaths, coughed again softly, and then the smile relaxed from her face and her eyes became fixed. She was gone.

CHAPTER TEN

THE CHASE

Minutes after Scott and Tony had fled, police and emergency vehicles pulled up in front of The Corner Store. Immediately, the body of Carl Singleton became visible, lying prostrate on the sidewalk, and through the shattered door, the hostages could be seen moving unmolested. It was apparent they had arrived too late and the perpetrators had already fled the scene. An alert officer noticed the Toyota Corolla, which had been reported at the scene, was now missing, and he assumed the robbers had made their escape in it. He radioed in his observation and requested all units be put on the lookout for it.

After taking necessary precautions, entrance was gained into the store, and the paramedics began to attend to the fallen. Georgia Davis was given CPR and whisked off immediately to nearby St. Vincent's Hospital, but it was apparent to everyone that she had already expired. Surprisingly, none of the other victims seemed seriously injured.

Carl Singleton began to regain consciousness and was surprised to find himself alive. His body was like a human pincushion with little holes punctured across his entire midsection, and he had sustained a major concussion from striking his head so hard against the sidewalk, but basically, he was okay. He was in for a painful experience over the next two days as hundreds of tiny lead shot would have to be individually plucked from his chest and abdomen, but he had sustained no life-threatening injuries.

Saul Frieberg moaned, as he too regained consciousness. He also sustained a concussion from the blow he received from the butt of the shotgun, but his skull had not been fractured. The laceration was deep and ugly. It would require some twenty-seven stitches to close it, and it would leave a nasty scar, but it was only superficial, and he would be back on his feet in a couple of days.

Aaron Muller's condition caused the most amazement of all among the emergency personnel. He had obviously been shot with a large caliber handgun squarely in the heart, and yet he was breathing and alert and talking. His vital signs were completely normal, and he was insisting on standing up. This was not allowed, of course, and he also was sent to the emergency room with the highest of priorities, but it would soon be discovered that the bullet had not penetrated his heart at all. He would have to have the bullet removed and would need some time to recover, but he would have his health back, given time. When, and if, the police ever decided they no longer needed the bullet for evidence and released it, he would have it on a chain around his neck, reminding him that Georgia had clearly saved his life by sacrificing her own.

Little Tamika Singleton was devastated and confused. She had to be physically separated from the body of Georgia Davis by members of the SWAT team so the paramedics could attend to the older lady. Tamika wailed in protest when Georgia's body was placed in the ambulance and she was not allowed to accompany her. A young officer named Murphy, who had a daughter of his own about her age, held her and comforted her until she regained her composure, and after obtaining permission, he took her home and explained to her mother what had just taken place. Whereupon, Sarah Singleton immediately took Tamika and rushed to the hospital to learn the condition of her adopted grandmother and her stricken husband.

Joseph Muller, the only adult witness left uninjured, was being questioned by the police, but he wasn't being very cooperative. He was frantic to be with Aaron and to be assured that he was going to be all right. But the police were insistent. They needed descriptions of the robbers, of their vehicle, of the direction they went in it, and were not willing to let him go until they got some answers. He told them what he remembered, which wasn't very much; and wanted to leave, but they kept pressing him for more details. It was only when they heard over the police radio that the suspects' vehicle had been spotted and that an officer was in pursuit that they lost interest in him and many of them left to join the chase. Joseph left immediately to be with his son at the hospital.

For a few minutes, Tony thought he and Scott had made their getaway just in time. They had no sooner gotten into the car after fleeing the terribly botched robbery, and pulled out onto Alvarado Street, than they spotted flashing lights to the south headed their way. They took off their sunglasses and ski masks and leather jackets and tried to look as natural as possible.

Tony turned east on Wilshire, not wanting to meet the emergency squad head-on. In the rearview mirror he watched the procession of vehicles with flashing lights speed north across the intersection behind them, racing toward the scene of the crime. Farther back, he saw more of the same approaching on Wilshire from the west. "I'm glad I didn't turn right back there," he said to Scott. "That cop must have called in reinforcements before he jumped us back there. They're coming in from every direction." But Scott wasn't listening. He had been staring straight ahead ever since they had first gotten in the car, the image of his two fallen victims still indelibly etched across the canvas of his mind.

After Tony drove farther up the street without incident, he began to relax a little bit, beginning to feel they would soon be out of harm's way. He had wanted to flee the area as fast as the little car would take them, but he forced himself to drive carefully, and well within the speed limit. Just when it seemed they were home free, he saw a squad car, with lights ablaze, top a hill and approach them head on. "Play it cool," he told himself. "That guy's headed toward a crime scene, he's not looking for us."

Tony slowed down even more and pulled over to the right, just like you're supposed to do, to give the cruiser plenty of room to pass. He noticed the officer looking them over, but he was careful not to turn his head in that direction. He proceeded on carefully and approached the Harbor Freeway, but there was no access ramp, so he decided to follow Wilshire down into the downtown area. It would be a good place to get lost for a while, he thought, before they headed back to dump the Corolla and pick up Scott's Blazer.

Just then, in the rearview mirror, he saw the squad car do a 180 in the middle of the street behind them, and begin to accelerate rapidly toward them, lights still flashing, and now he could hear the sound of his siren. Somehow, the cop had identified them, and now he was in hot pursuit.

"Oh, my God, Scott. He's after us! What're we gonna do?" Tony yelled, suddenly in a panic.

That jolted Scott back to reality, and he was forced to focus his mind away from the grief in which he had been drowning. Quickly, he surveyed their situation and decided they definitely didn't want to get stuck in the downtown area. Neither one of them was very familiar with it, and it would be too easy to get trapped by the streetwise cops who patrolled it every day. "Take a right here!" he yelled, indicating the first cross street east of the freeway.

Tony slammed on the brakes and skidded around the corner and gunned the accelerator. "And another right!" Scott yelled as they approached Seventh Street almost immediately. Again Tony careened around the corner, and now they were headed west, back across the freeway again. No sooner had they crossed the freeway than they saw the squad car fly around the corner behind them and fishtail in their direction. He had made up much of the distance that had separated them and, at this rate; he would be on them in no time.

Scott sensed their only chance of escape was to get on the freeway and, hopefully, disappear into the traffic there. They would be dead meat for sure if they tried to shake this guy on the streets. "Take a left!" he yelled, indicating a narrow street that headed down a steep hill and toward the freeway that was angling to the west. Tony negotiated the turn pretty well, considering he was driving a strange car, way too fast, at night, and on wet pavement. He bounced over the curb and took out two parking meters and a trash can before he was able to get the car back onto the street and headed down the hill again.

The heavy police cruiser behind them took the corner faster and without incident and continued to make up the distance between them. At the bottom of the hill, their street intersected with Eighth Street, and a red light there signaled them to stop, which was completely out of the question. A series of flashing red lights behind them had been signaling them to stop for the past eight blocks, and they hadn't heeded them. They weren't about to stop for a single puny one in front of them now. Besides, they could see that beyond the intersection, their street became an onramp leading up to the southbound Harbor Freeway.

But all reason dictated that they definitely needed to slow down and proceed with caution. They were descending a steep hill, which ended abruptly at Eighth Street, and then the onramp shot up steeply on the other side. One could drive through that intersection at no more than twenty-five miles per hour without hitting bottom, and they were presently traveling at nearly sixty. Besides that, a car was coming from either direction on Eighth Street, but Tony gunned the accelerator anyway. The Corolla bottomed out badly and bounced through the intersection, barely missing both of the other cars, leaving its own severed muffler spinning in the middle of the street.

The drivers of the other vehicles instinctively slammed on their brakes when the Toyota flashed in front of them, instantly putting them both into a spin on the wet pavement. They sideswiped each other and wound up locked together on the side of the road, completely blocking the onramp to the freeway. The officer in the cruiser slammed on his own brakes to avoid a collision, but the wet street was unforgiving. His heavy vehicle too went into a spin and it half bounced, half slid, across Eighth Street and smashed sideways into both the other cars.

The police officer was shaken up, but unhurt. He looked over at the drivers of the other vehicles and they appeared to be all right as well. He had already radioed in that he was in pursuit of the suspect vehicle and had reported on his position. Now, he had to get back on the line and tell the dispatcher that he had been involved in a collision and was unable to continue the chase.

Ahead, Tony was driving erratically, weaving in and out of cars as he sped down the freeway. "Slow down, man," Scott warned. "We lost him back there in that pileup. We might just get out of this after all, but not if you keep driving like a maniac. Try to blend in with the traffic and maybe we can sneak off at Manchester without being noticed."

"Yeah, you're right. I gotta get my act together," Tony agreed as he backed off on the gas pedal and the Corolla slowed to about fifty-five. "I kinda lost it back there for a minute. Thanks for bailing me out. Say, how is it you were a basket case back there in the store, and you turn into Cool Hand Luke in a high-speed chase?"

"What, don't you get it, man? We just killed three or four people back there. We killed them, you and me. We ended their lives. I've never intentionally hurt anyone before in my life. I'm sorry, but I wasn't prepared to deal with that, and I never will be. But when I'm on the defensive, and somebody's trying to nail my bod . . . I can deal with that. There's a big difference between the two."

"Yeah, I know what you mean. Boy, it really got hairy back there in that store. I thought you were really going to freak out."

"Look, Tony, I know I lost it back there, but I wasn't prepared for any of that stuff. What were you thinking, anyway? If we had left when we got the money out of the first safe, we would have been fine. Why did you have to push it? You went against everything we agreed on."

"Now, hold on there, buddy boy," Tony said defensively. "I was following our plan to the letter. The money the old man pulled out of that safe didn't look nearly like no ten grand to me. But when we threatened to shoot somebody, he fell for our bluff just like we planned, and he would have opened that other safe too if that stupid cop, or whoever he was, hadn't broken through that door. If you wanna blame someone, blame him, not me. I saved your butt. If it hadn't been for me you'd probably have a bullet in you right now, or at least be sittin' in handcuffs in the back of some squad car up there."

"But at least those people back there would still be alive. I would gladly be in handcuffs right now if it would bring them back."

"Not me. What's done is done. It was just a tragic twist of fate. Our motives were good. We didn't intentionally hurt anybody. We just have to put it behind us and move on."

"I really don't get you, Tony. You acted like you were enjoying it while we were shooting people, and now you act as though it was no big deal. I just can't shrug it off that easily, okay?"

"Hey, don't get me wrong. I hate what happened up there as much as you. All I'm sayin' is we can't change what happened. Us fallin' apart or turnin' ourselves in or somethin' stupid like that won't make it any better. We gotta keep on lookin' out for ourselves."

"Speaking of looking out," Scott changed the subject, "that's the Manchester exit up ahead. You need to get over to the right."

"Yeah, you're right, thanks," Tony replied, as he began to slow and change lanes.

Just then, the entire car was flooded with light, and they heard an amplified voice coming from above them, *"This is the Los Angeles Police Department. Pull over to the side of the freeway and stop the car!"*

Scott bent forward and looked up through the curve in the windshield, but he saw nothing but a blinding light. He could hear the sound of the rotor blades now, and he knew there was a police helicopter hovering directly above them. To make matters worse, the freeway behind them began to be illuminated by flashing red and blue lights as four squad cars made their presence known.

"Oh, man, this is it, they got us good!" Tony practically cried. "I don't know what to do!"

"Keep going!" Scott commanded. "Step on it!" He had been so overcome with guilt earlier, he had actually thought about turning himself in, but he had wanted it to be on his own terms, not those of the police. He was not at all in favor of getting busted alongside the freeway and hauled off to jail in the back of a police cruiser with some rookie cop leering at him through the glass.

Tony obeyed instantly, stomping on the accelerator and pulling back into the mainstream of traffic. The irony of the situation never occurred to him. He had been in undisputed command back in the store, but now he was eager for Scott to take charge. He didn't have a clue what to do next.

"Just keep flying down the freeway," ordered Scott. "They won't try anything funny. There's too many other cars around us, and they won't run the risk of innocent motorists getting hurt."

"Okay, you're the boss, but how long are we gonna be able to keep going? We can't outrun 'em, and they sure as heck aren't gonna let us get away."

"I know, but it will buy us some time. I gotta think what to do."

"I don't know what you're gonna come up with. It looks like they got about half a dozen cruisers back there now, and with that chopper up there, about the only way we'd be able to ditch em' is to drive off into the ocean and make like a submarine."

"What did you just say?" demanded Scott, suddenly very interested.

"I was just makin' a joke, okay? I said the only way we're ever going to shake these guys is to drive off into the ocean."

"That's it, Tony, you're a genius. That's exactly what we'll do."

"Hey, I was just kiddin' around," Tony replied, taking his eyes off the road for an instant to look at Scott to see if he looked as serious as he sounded. "As spectacular as that might sound to you, I have no desire to commit suicide."

"Neither do I. And I am serious. If we pull this off right, it just might work."

"What the heck are you talking about?"

"You'll see soon enough, just keep drivin'. I gotta think this thing through. The San Diego Freeway is coming up here real soon. The cops will think we'll get off either north or south. They may even have a road-block on the off ramp to stop us when we try. They'll never expect us to keep going straight because this freeway dead-ends in San Pedro, but that's just what we're going to do."

"Okay, but we're just going to be driving right into a box canyon. When we get to San Pedro, it's the end of the line, and you're not really serious about driving off into the ocean are you?"

"I sure am, only not that way," Scott said, looking out the window as they prepared to pass under the San Diego Freeway. The Harbor freeway divided and cars preparing to go either north or south on the San Diego exited to the right and paralleled the freeway for about a quarter of a mile or so before actually reaching the interchange. "Wow, look at that, just like I thought! They've got the entire off ramp barricaded off. They must have half of the entire police force right down there. That's good. They can't have that many cars up ahead of us now."

"Okay, so we escaped disaster for the present moment," conceded Tony as he increased their speed even more. He had become used to how the Corolla handled and was weaving in and out of traffic with improving skill. "But, you gotta tell me where we're goin' and what we're gonna do when we get there."

"Okay, here's the plan," Scott said, even as he was formulating it in his own mind. "We keep going straight down the freeway until we get almost to the end, then we take Highway 47 east across the bridge and on over to Long Beach. We get off on Shoreline Drive and then you drive the car off the road and into the harbor where our boat is docked."

"Are you crazy? There's a guardrail there, and it's got to be at least a twenty-foot drop to the water. That alone could kill us!"

"Yeah, I know. That's what makes it such a good plan. The cop's will think we died in the crash, or at least drowned in the icy water afterward."

"So, what's going to prevent that from really happening? Or have you thought that far ahead?"

"Yeah, I think so. This car is equipped with two airbags. I just hope they're both still in working order. They should protect us in the crash, and then we can swim underwater over to the dock. From there we can get over to the boat, and once inside, we can hide out until the dust settles."

"What dust? We'll be drowned for sure. It has to be a hundred yards across that harbor from the sea wall to that dock. We could never make it."

"No, it isn't that far, and I figure if we're going fast enough, we can jump almost half the way. We won't have to swim much more than forty yards, fifty tops."

"And you think we can do that?"

"I don't know, but that's the beauty of it. Nobody out there will think we can. That chopper up there will keep his light on us all the way and they'll know for sure we haven't come to the surface. They'll think we drowned when we don't come up. But maybe . . . just maybe . . . we can make it. And if we do, we'll be home free."

"You know, you may have something there. Your average biker dude couldn't begin to make it, and hopefully that's what they think we are. Neither could most anyone else, for that matter. But you and me, we surf and dive all summer and we swim all winter. If anybody could do it, we should be able to."

"Exactly, and if we can't, we just come to the surface and get arrested. We won't be any worse off than we would have been if we had given ourselves up back at Manchester, maybe a little colder and wetter is all."

"Hey, let's give it a shot. At this point, we don't have much to lose."

The chase continued down the Harbor Freeway, past the Pacific Coast Highway exit. Both Tony and Scott noticed the sign and inwardly wished they had been in a position to simply exit the freeway and follow the familiar streets to the safety of their homes in Rancho Palos Verdes, but neither of them said anything. As the poem says, they had, "miles to go before they slept."

The half-dozen squad cars behind them had increased by two. They presented an overwhelming force, but they seemed to be content to stay well behind the Corolla, not trying to overtake or stop it. Experience had proven in such cases that the fugitive driver will almost always make a mistake and bring himself down if he is left alone. But, on the other hand, if a forceful takeover is attempted, violence is virtually inevitable, and innocent bystanders wind up getting hurt. So they were willing to follow, at least for now, and see how things would play themselves out.

The police helicopter continued to maintain its vigil, following a safe distance above and behind the speeding automobile, its floodlight bathing the area around the little car with a moving circle of light.

The brightly lit little caravan proceeded south, and just before it reached the end of the freeway, it veered to the right and then back again to the left, up over the freeway and off to the east on Highway 47. They crossed the high Vincent Thomas Bridge and descended down to, and across, Terminal Island. The chase continued past docks and ships and cranes and sea containers, but no one was paying any attention. The occupants of the little Toyota were intent on maintaining their lead, and everyone else was willing to let them have it, but determined not to let them get away.

They bridged another channel and the Los Angeles River and began their descent into the downtown area of Long Beach. They had the option of turning left and taking an access ramp that would lead them to the northbound Long Beach Freeway, and that is what all the law enforcement personnel expected them to do, because all other possible routes would lead to bottlenecks and certain capture. But instead, the Corolla went past the access ramp and down into the city. It ignored the traffic signal and careened around the corner, heading south on Shoreline Drive.

Shoreline curved gracefully to the left, with the aquarium and the convention center on the left side, and the waterfront on the right. The wide and relatively straight street allowed Tony the opportunity to accelerate. By the time he approached the overpass, the speedometer was registering over seventy miles per hour. The overpass was for pedestrians only, to convey them from the downtown area to the waterfront without having to cross the busy street between them. It ended at a round tower at the edge of the sea wall, separating the street level from the harbor below. People crossing the overpass had to descend the circular staircase inside the tower to reach the street level.

During the chase, Scott and Tony had managed to remove their boots, and planned to leave them in the car, along with their coats and the shotgun. They had thrown their sunglasses aside as well, having no further use for them. On the other hand, they had put their ski masks back on, not wanting to leave them to be found, since they would certainly have hairs in them that could be traced back to them. Scott had also had to make sure his father's pistol was securely tucked down the front of his pants. He could not allow it to be found and traced back to its owner. He had tied a knot firmly in the top of the plastic bags containing the money, and Tony had stuffed the bundle inside his shirt. He said he just wanted to carry his fair share, but Scott suspected he didn't want the money to get away from him should the two of them become separated. They had rolled down all the windows and tightened their seat belts. They had done all they could do to prepare for what lay immediately before them.

"Jump the curb up here, Tony, and drive just to the left of the tower," Scott shouted, "only not too close. There's an electric transformer box or something there, and we don't want to hit that. Make sure you drive between the posts holding up the guard rail, and STEP ON IT!!"

Tony responded without hesitation. Over the curb they went and out across a narrow mall area, made up of grass and concrete walks. They shot under the overpass and turned slightly to the right and straight toward the guardrail at the top of the sea wall. It looked formidable, and indeed the uprights were. They were made of solid four-inch steel I-beams, buried in concrete, and one would not want to drive into one of them; but they were set nine-feet apart, and Tony could easily drive between them. There were only two lightweight aluminum pipes connecting the uprights forming the horizontal rungs along the length of the rail, and they would offer little resistance at all.

Tony had his foot to the floor when they hit the guardrail and they were traveling in excess of seventy-five miles per hour. The aluminum pipes released their hold on the uprights without hesitation and shot like javelins out into the harbor. The Corolla didn't even slow down. Tony had a death grip on the steering wheel and held his breath as they shot out into space. Scott braced his hands against the dashboard and for lack of anything better to say, yelled, "GERONIMO!" as they became airborne.

The tide was going out and the water level was a good twenty feet below the top of the sea wall. The little car shot out into the harbor like it was launched from the deck of an aircraft carrier. It cleared a ten-foot wide dock next to the sea wall and a small craft moored to it with ease, and sailed well out into the harbor before it finally nosed down and plunged into the sea. There it bobbed for a few seconds, but quickly filled with water and sank unceremoniously out of sight.

The police vehicles in pursuit screeched to a halt, two of them right next to the guardrail. Their drivers stared in disbelief at the disappearing automobile before them, their spotlights trained on the scene. The helicopter stopped its forward motion and hovered above the small harbor, its powerful floodlight illuminating the entire area. Because of the lateness of the hour and the driving rain, no one else was privileged to witness what had to be one of the most spectacular demonstrations of reckless abandon ever staged in the Southland. Some of the officers had now gotten out of their vehicles and were standing at the guardrail, straining as they looked out into the water, trying perhaps to spot a survivor struggling to the surface.

Other cars were now arriving at the scene and out of one of them stepped Sergeant Kyle Witherspoon, a burly, no-nonsense man in his forties with a bulldog face and a body to match. He immediately took charge and ordered his men to spread out. Some were ordered to drive around to the south side of the harbor and come through the Shoreline Village and down onto the docks on the other side. They needed to surround the area so they could be there to render aid to an injured survivor; but even more importantly, they needed to be there to prevent anyone from swimming to the shore and slipping away in the darkness.

But that was becoming more and more unlikely. The car had been under the water for more than a minute now, and nothing and no one had come to the surface. "They're goners, Sarge," said one of his men. "They must have been on drugs or something to have done something like this."

"Yeah, you're probably right," replied Witherspoon, "but we're gonna wait right here until we know for sure. We're gonna assume they're still alive and well until they haul that car outta that water and we see their dead bodies in it. Now radio and get some support down here. We may be in for a long night."

Water is soft and yielding. It offers little resistance when you put your hand into a basin or step your foot into a bathtub full of it, but drive a car off a twenty-foot embankment at nearly eighty miles per hour into it, and it's a totally different story. The nose of the Corolla struck the surface of the salt water in the harbor like as though it had been driven into an embankment. It stopped almost immediately, with enough force to deploy both of the airbags. It plunged into the water, bobbled momentarily, and then, like a torpedoed ship, sank quickly without even putting up a fight.

Tony and Scott were held in place by their seat belts and protected by the airbags, but the jolt of the impact nearly knocked the wind out of both of them. The airbags deflated almost immediately and they were able to recover quickly enough to unfasten their seat belts and take several deep breaths before they were carried beneath the surface. The water temperature was in the low fifties, cold enough to provide a cruel shock, but not enough to pose any real threat. Besides, they were protected by their clothing, which, though wet, would retain some of their body heat.

They quickly pulled themselves out their respective windows, and pulled off their gloves. They didn't have to worry about leaving fingerprints any longer, and they could swim much better without them on. Being on the driver's side and thus closer to the dock off to their left, Tony started out in the lead, which was fine with Scott. Tony was the stronger swimmer and had an uncanny sense of direction under water. Scott's purpose was to stay right on his heels and hope he didn't run out of air before they reached the dock, nearly fifty yards away.

Light from the spotlights on the squad cars and the floodlight on the chopper enabled them to tell where the surface was and to maintain a safe distance beneath it, but at the same time, not to go too deep and use up precious energy in the process. Tony was swimming strong and fast. The breaststroke was his specialty, and he was holding nothing back. Scott had great difficulty keeping up, but a determination rose up within him that propelled him at a speed faster than his natural abilities would ever have allowed him to achieve.

Still, after what seemed an eternity, his strength was almost gone, his lungs were screaming for air, and there was still no sign of the floats that held up the dock. Tony had to be experiencing the same torment, but Scott couldn't tell it from his viewpoint. His friend's stroke never faltered and his pace never slowed. If Tony hadn't been in front of him, Scott would have given up and surfaced. He was exhausted and absolutely out of air. But Tony kept forging ahead, and that fact beckoned Scott to follow.

But after a short time, Scott noticed his vision beginning to narrow as dark borders began to spread in from the periphery. An alarm went off in his head telling him he was about to pass out. If that happened here, underwater, he would most assuredly drown. As much as he hated to give up the chase, he was going to have to surface. That meant he would be spotted and apprehended, and then, so would Tony. He hated to betray his friend, but not badly enough to sacrifice his life.

Just as he was about to push upward for the precious air his body was literally dying for, he detected a dark shape beginning to materialize in front of them. It was a black rectangle, about four feet long, just below the surface.

It took an instant for his oxygen-starved brain to identify the object, and then suddenly, it shouted at him, "It's the float, dummy, it's the float!"

Tony had already reached it and was about to surface on its far side. "He made it!" Scott marveled to himself, still struggling to deal with the reality of this unexpected turn of events. "I can't quit now. If he made it, I'll make it too . . . or die trying!" As he frantically pressed on, he realized he might very well do just exactly that.

The dark borders by now had all but robbed him of his sight, and he was struggling to maintain consciousness, as he approached the float. Through a narrow tunnel he saw himself pass beneath the dark shape of the float, and with the last vestige of strength he had, he propelled himself to the surface. As his head broke free, his lungs fairly exploded, and he gasped in the most precious air he had ever breathed.

He was still on the brink of unconsciousness, and Tony had to grab him to prevent him from slipping back underwater. Both of them labored loudly for air, not being nearly as inconspicuous as they had intended to be. Fortunately for them, no officer had yet reached the end of the dock to discover them. Besides, the roar of the helicopter overhead pretty well drowned out the sound of their struggles anyway.

After some time, their breathing and mental awareness returned nearly to normal. Tony grinned widely and gave Scott the thumbs up signal, which Scott could see only because his friend's hand was highlighted by the light being beamed down behind him in the harbor. At the same time, they could hear footsteps pounding toward them on the wooden planks on the dock above. They were certainly not out of danger yet.

They were beneath the end of the center, and by far the longest, dock in the little harbor. It was anchored by twenty large, concrete pillars firmly driven into the harbor bottom, forming two parallel rows, with ten pillars in each row. The pillars were about thirty feet apart, making the entire length of the dock around three hundred feet. The main dock was about ten feet wide and it was secured between the two rows of pillars. Midway between each of the pillars, smaller three-foot wide docks extended out on both sides, perpendicular from the main dock. These smaller docks were somewhere around thirty feet long, and it was to them that the many boats and yachts were moored. The entire dock system was held aloft by a series of large black polyethylene floats like the one the two young men now hid behind. This allowed the docks to rise and fall with the level of the tide.

However, the Graham yacht wasn't tied up to this central dock. It was moored on the far side of the much shorter dock to the east of them. To reach it, Scott and Tony would have to travel undetected under the longer dock, back toward the shore until they were about straight across from the yacht, then they would have to swim underwater again over to the other dock. Once there, they could negotiate around to the back of the craft and get aboard.

By now, the officer was standing on the dock directly above them, but he wasn't looking down between the cracks for them. He couldn't have seen them anyway in the darkness that concealed them. He was instead looking out into the waters of the harbor, straining to detect some sign of life or death out there.

Scott motioned to Tony with his hand, indicating with a downward movement that they should swim underwater again, rather than risk detection by moving under the dock on the surface. It probably wasn't necessary for them to do so, because the bottom of the dock sat so closely to the surface of the water, but having nearly died making it thus far, he didn't want to take any risk that would nullify their previous accomplishment. Besides, they could surface anytime they needed to come up for air.

Tony nodded his approval and, after taking several deep breaths apiece, they sank quietly beneath the surface. They swam about fifty feet before they came up for a brief breather, and then they dived again and swam about fifty more. This time Scott was in the lead, partly because he was more familiar with the dock area, and partly because he was more winded, and could surface whenever he felt he needed to.

At this point they were almost directly across from where the yacht was moored to the shorter dock to the east of them, so they swam the relatively short distance underwater to the end of the little dock that extended out perpendicular from the main one. This was as close as they could get before they had to cross open water again, so they rested for several minutes before attempting the swim. There was probably no one near where they were, but they dared not risk speaking out loud, so Scott tapped Tony on the shoulder when he was ready and gave him a little shove, indicating he should go first. Tony would be sure to find the little dock extending out from the main one to the east of them, and Scott wasn't at all sure he would be able to do so himself.

They again hyperventilated to prepare themselves for the swim, and pushed off for the dock, some ninety feet away. It wasn't nearly so far as had been their first lung-bursting feat, but it was no easy task either. They were more tired now and they had less adrenaline pumping through their veins. Besides that, there wasn't nearly as much light over here, which made finding their way more difficult. Tony had a little trouble locating his target, and both their heads were pounding and their lungs were screaming for relief by the time they surfaced again behind the float at the end of the little dock across the way.

Both of them were fairly exhausted, but they still had one more leg to go. After catching their breath again, they swam underwater to the center of the main dock, and then out to the end of the short dock on the other side. Finally, they were near the end of the *Pacific Pearl*, and all that remained was for them was to get onboard without being seen by anyone on the shore or on the docks. Fortunately for them, everyone's attention was focused farther out in the harbor, around the sight where the Toyota Corolla had gone down several minutes before. Also to their advantage was the fact that the aft deck of the yacht was low, not more than a foot or so above the surface of the water, making climbing aboard an easy task.

They looked around as much as their location would allow them to and saw no one who might spot them boarding the craft. On Scott's signal, they swam underwater to the back of the yacht and, together, pulled themselves up onto the aft deck and threw themselves over the back seating section and into the well in front of it where they were hidden from view. Scott crawled over to the port side and reached up and pulled down the cushion that contained the key. After unzipping it and retrieving the key, he zipped it back up and returned it to its place, and crawled back to where Tony was.

Continuing to lie down, Scott reached up with one hand and fumbled with the key until it finally fit into the lock on the sliding glass door. He unlocked it, removed the key, and then brought his hand back down. Before attempting to open the door, he poked his head up for a couple of seconds to look around. Still he saw no one looking their way, so he returned to the door and opened it just wide enough for Tony and him to crawl in. Scott went in last and immediately closed the door behind him. The curtain had been pulled across the doorway and Tony had just rolled under it. Before following him, Scott turned the dead bolt, making sure the door was locked behind him.

Once inside, behind the locked door and drawn curtain, for the first time since the chase had begun back on Wilshire Blvd., they began to feel again like they might actually get away. They waited silently, listening for the slightest sound of detection or pursuit, but heard nothing but the pounding of their own hearts. As they finally began to relax, both of them began to shiver uncontrollably. They were suffering from exhaustion and hypothermia, and their bodies were letting them know about it.

Scott whispered through chattering teeth, "We gotta get outta these wet clothes."

As quickly as they could, their trembling hands not obeying very well the instructions of their minds, they disrobed and left their wet clothes in a soggy pile by the door along with the pistol and the sack of money. In the dark, Scott made his way to the head and secured towels for them to dry off with, and then got warm clothes from the closet for them both. He was thankful his father was such a stickler for details. Bruce Graham insisted that they always keep extra clothing onboard just in case someone got drenched in bad weather or happened to go over the side.

After getting dressed, Scott gathered up the wet things by the door and put them in the bottom of the shower stall for the time being, removing their wallets from the pants pockets and drying them as best he could. He also put his dad's pistol and the plastic bag of money in with the clothing, not knowing what else to do with them. Then he and Tony took towels and mopped up the water from the tile entryway and stashed the wet towels in the shower stall as well.

With the exception of the wet things in the head, there was no evidence that they had just boarded the craft. The continuing rain masked the water they had left outside the cabin, the water in the entryway had been removed, and they were now dressed in dry clothing. Their continued shivering was the only thing that might have given them away if anyone were to have come aboard to question them. It would remain a mute question, however, because all continued to remain quiet outside and no one, to their knowledge, even approached the *Pacific Pearl* that night.

They were clothed and dry now, but they still weren't warm. They dared not turn on any light and there was nothing they could do in the dark, so they decided to go to bed and try to figure things out in the morning. Scott took the master cabin in the bow of the yacht and Tony found his way to the spare cabin across from the galley. Once in bed, even with their clothes on, it still took them thirty minutes to stop shivering. Even then, sleep didn't come easily. The events of the night were still racing through their minds, and the uncertainty of the future demanded their attention. But eventually sheer exhaustion settled in, and they fell into a troubled sleep around two o'clock.

CHAPTER ELEVEN

THE NEXT DAY

The rain had stopped sometime in the predawn hours of the morning and the sun's rays beamed through broken clouds as Scott awoke just before seven o'clock. A combination of the increasing light and the sound of voices outside on the dock aroused him out of a deep sleep. Scott called softly to wake Tony, but when he looked out the door of his cabin, he saw him already up, sitting at the galley table with piles of money spread out in front of him. He had been sitting there ever since it had been barely light enough to see.

"Mornin', Scott. I couldn't sleep, so I thought I might as well be doing something useful. You'll never believe how much money's here, man!"

Scott was angry. He was angry because he believed that stinking money had cost several people their lives, and Tony had no right to handle it with so much eager disregard. He was also angry that Tony was being so careless. From the sound coming through the walls of the yacht, things were already buzzing with activity outside. If the police were conducting a boat-to-boat search and were to knock on their door, they would never be able to conceal so much cash in time to avoid detection.

"Tony, how can you be so dumb?" he asked, not even trying to hide his emotions. "Don't you know the cops could bang on that door at any second? How are you gonna explain all that cash when they come bustin' in here?"

"Hey, calm down, already. Nobody's gonna come bustin' in here. Besides, I just had to know how much is here. Aren't you even curious?"

"I wish we'd never seen that money," Scott said, sitting down at the table beside Tony. His eyes saw the clean bills stacked neatly before him, but his mind saw them filthy and dripping in blood.

"Well, buddy boy, *I'm* glad we saw it, and I'm even gladder we've got it. This, my friend, represents the end of our problems. There's almost fifteen thousand dollars here!"

"What? That's far more than we needed. If you hadn't been so insistent on getting into that other safe, we could have had all the money we needed and nobody would have been hurt!"

"Wait a minute, Scott," Tony warned. "I had no idea there was this much money here last night. The bundles were so small. How was I to know they were full of so many hundred-dollar bills? Look, we gotta put last night behind us. What's done is done, and your moping around here ain't gonna bring those people back. Besides, we don't even know for sure any of them are dead."

"What! Are you kidding? I shot that old woman right in the chest, and I musta hit Aaron too. I saw them fall dead right in front of my eyes. And you practically blew that cop in half. Don't tell me he's not dead. And the old man . . . you bashed his skull in. How was he supposed to live through that?"

"Okay, okay, I got the picture. Maybe they are all gone, but we're not . . . and neither is this money. Their lives will have been lost for nothing if we don't keep this money and put it to good use. I think God, or whoever is up there, intended for us to have this money. Why else were we allowed to make the most bodacious escape in the history of the world last night?"

"I don't know, but I don't think God had anything to do with it. He would never have wanted innocent people to die just so we could get our greedy little hands on somebody else's money."

"Whatever you say. The point is, they're gone and we got the money. Now help me figure out how we're gonna keep it."

He was right, and Scott knew it. They couldn't change what had happened, and there was no sense in not keeping the money at this point, so he agreed to put together a plan. First, he insisted they bag the money back up, and he put it in the freezer compartment, behind a stack of empty ice cube trays. Then he convinced Tony that they would soon need to make an appearance topside to find out what was going on as other residents of the marina were doubtlessly doing. Not to do so would be to draw attention to themselves when their presence was detected later on, as it inevitably would be. But they needed to clean up first. They both needed a shave, Tony's hair was a tangled mess, and they both looked as though they had slept in their clothes, which of course, they had.

They took turns showering in the master bath, since the guest shower still contained the wet things from the night before. Scott shaved his beard and his head as he was accustomed to do each day to reduce resistance in competitive swim meets, but he still finished before Tony. Tony only had to shave his face, but he more than made up for the extra time with all the primping he did with his hair to get it back into acceptable condition.

Next they had to address their clothing. In the dark, Scott had grabbed whatever his hands had first encountered the night before, and neither one of them looked any too fashionable. Scott gave Tony the smallest clothes he could find in the closets, which still fit a bit loosely on him, but not noticeably so. The deck shoes were a little big as well, but he cinched them up tightly, and no one would be able to tell that he wasn't wearing his own clothing. Scott dressed in some of his own clothes he had kept in the yacht, and now, they at least looked as though their presence there was legitimate, even though it certainly was not.

Before they went out on the dock, they agreed on the story they would tell the police when they were questioned. Scott's parents were out of the country and he had asked Tony to spend the night with him on the yacht. They had dinner at Tony's house the evening before, they had done some shopping in the mall, had taken in a movie, and had arrived here at about eleven. They had gone right to bed and to sleep, and they hadn't heard or seen anything until this morning. Tony needed to leave because he had classes that morning, but Scott was going to stay and take the boat out later and do a little fishing. Tony was going to come back and pick him up later that afternoon, and they would return to their respective homes.

What they would not be telling the police is that Tony would be catching a bus in downtown Long Beach and making connections back to the Wal-Mart in Inglewood and to Scott's Blazer. In the meantime, Scott would be taking the boat out into deep water, where he would dump the wet clothing and his dad's .38 over the side. He hated to discard the expensive weapon, but he dared not keep it. If the police ever suspected them and checked the pistol against the slug taken from the crime scene, they would be held for trial for sure with an airtight case against them. Tony said it would be easy to find another gun just like it through some connections he had, and Bruce Graham would never know the difference. Besides, they had more money than they needed, and this would be a good way to spend some of it.

Just before they went out on deck, they removed all unnecessary paper from their wallets and flushed it down the head, keeping only plastic cards and currency. Their wallets were nearly dry and looked normal, but soggy paper in them would be a dead giveaway. Scott gave Tony the key to the

Blazer and they opened the door and went out into a stiff breeze and broken sunlight.

Once on the dock, they purposed to look as bewildered and inquisitive as possible. They immediately began to look for Eddie, who would inevitably be there. Sure enough, they spotted him right away over on the center dock in the presence of a burly looking police officer. Scott called to him and asked what was going on. Eddie waved and told them to come on over. They knew they would have to talk to the police sooner or later, so they had decided to initiate the conversation and appear to be eager to gain information rather than appearing eager to withhold it by trying to be evasive. They knew Eddie would vouch for them, and he appeared to be helping the officer conduct his investigation.

They walked the short distance down their dock to the one next to the sea wall and followed it around to the longer dock leading out to where Eddie and the officer were standing. As many as fifty other boat owners and policemen were standing about at various locations on the three docks, so Scott and Tony did not appear to be conspicuous. They waved at Eddie as they approached the older man.

"Hey Eddie, what's all the ruckus?" Scott asked, as nonchalantly as possible.

"What! Where you guys been? Don't tell me you missed all the excitement too."

"Do you know these men?" asked Sergeant Witherspoon, looking as though he had too much coffee and too little sleep, which was exactly the case. He had been up all night, spending the last half of it right there at that little harbor. The question was entirely unnecessary since it was obvious that Eddie knew them, but it was the kind of question policemen are expected to ask, so he asked it.

"Of course I know them. Do you think I talk this way to strangers? This is Scott Graham and his friend Tony D'Angelo. The Grahams own that fancy white yacht over there," Eddie said as he pointed out the two young men respectively and then the vessel where they had spent the night.

Witherspoon wasn't accustomed to being talked down to by those assisting him, but this Eddie character was a civilian, and he was proving himself to be very valuable in identifying the people emerging from the various boats; so he let the comment pass.

Eddie continued, "The Grahams have kept a boat here for years, and I see them all the time. These two were just here on Saturday to do some fishin'. They took the yacht out and brought in a nice catch of bottom fish. Say, Scott, I didn't see you come in yesterday. You must have gotten here after I went home."

Scott rehearsed before Eddie the story he and Tony had agreed on earlier; about the dinner at Tony's, the movie, and the late arrival; but he was more interested in Witherspoon hearing it than he was the older man. While he was talking, he kept looking at all the activity taking place around them and acted much more interested in it than in the matter-of-fact stuff he was sharing.

"So what did happen here? Why are the police crawling all over the place?" He directed his questions as much to the officer as he did to Eddie.

"Hey you really don't know, do you? It's all over the news. Two thugs knocked over a convenience store up in LA last night and got in a gunfight with an off duty cop. They killed a lady customer and wounded three others, including the cop and the owner, and then the darndest thing-they led the cops on a high-speed chase down the freeway in the rain and then ended up here in Long Beach. Would you believe it, they ran their car right off that wall up there, through the guardrail, and made like Evel Knievel, right out into the harbor here!" His voice was ever rising and his presentation was full of animation and gestures, then he slowed down and said with obvious disappointment, "And I missed it all. It happened long after I'd gone home." Then he picked it back up again, "Boy, would I have loved to have seen that car go over that wall!"

"So, what happened to 'em?" Tony asked, with convincing interest.

"That's the crazy thing. Nobody knows. They never came up. The cops have had divers down there for hours and they haven't found 'em. They found the car and some clothes an' stuff, but no sign of those two guys. The tide was goin' out and I think they drowned trying to make a getaway and the tide carried 'em out to sea; but the good sergeant here thinks they made it to the docks here and are hiding out somewhere."

"That's only one of the possibilities we're considering," Witherspoon interjected. "It's a long shot, but it just might be possible for two experienced swimmers to make it to the end of the dock out there. But then, where would they go? We've had the entire area secured ever since it happened, and they didn't get away, they're not in the water, and they're not on the docks or on any of the boats we've checked so far. If we don't find them inside one of the remaining boats, I'll have to agree with Eddie here. They must have drowned and their bodies got carried away in the tide."

"So, you're going to search all the boats here?" Scott asked, trying not to sound as anxious as he felt.

"Yeah, we've already started over there," Witherspoon said, pointing to the short dock to the west of them. I would appreciate it if one of you would stick around until we have a chance to go through your boat a little later on."

"Sure, I can stay," Scott said. "Tony has some classes he really ought to attend, but I can hang around, and maybe I can still take the boat out and get in a little fishing later on."

"I'm afraid that won't be possible, son," the sergeant said, liking the sound of the authority he heard in his own voice. "Nothing goes in or out of here until we've finished our investigation."

"Sure, okay, that makes sense. I'll just stick around until you're through searching the yacht, and Tony can come back and pick me up after his last class."

"O'Neal, come here and get the information on these two," Witherspoon called to one of his men carrying a clipboard. Then he turned to Scott and Tony and said, "After the officer takes your statement, you're free to go about your business."

"Thanks officer. See ya, Eddie," said Scott as he and Tony turned and walked over to the young policeman with the clipboard.

"Stick around, Scotty," called Eddie over his shoulder as he and Sergeant Witherspoon were walking over to talk with an elderly couple who were just emerging from a sailboat tied up nearby. "They're gonna bring in a big crane and fish the car out of the harbor pretty soon. I'm at least gonna get to see that."

"Okay, I'll watch for it."

After Tony and Scott had given their drivers' licenses to Officer O'Neal and identified the Graham yacht and told him of their whereabouts the previous night, he gave them back their licenses and thanked them matter of factly. O'Neal went on to interview the next person waiting to identify himself, and they walked casually back to the yacht. But inside, they were struggling with an unforeseen challenge. How were they going to get rid of the stuff still in the shower before the police got there to search the yacht?

Scott told Tony he would take care of it, and that Tony needed to go ahead and leave as they had said he was about to. There was no sense drawing the cops' attention by him continuing to hang around. But Scott instructed Tony to walk well down the waterfront to the east before he turned north to catch a bus downtown. The police must not see him walking up the street instead of driving the vehicle in which they supposedly had arrived the night before. He dared not take a taxi either, because the drivers are required to keep a record of all their fares, and such things could easily be traced later on.

Scott went back into the yacht and tried to figure out what to do with the stuff in the shower. Together, it was all quite bulky, and there weren't many good hiding places in the relatively small cabin area. A thorough search would surely uncover everything and he and Tony would be going away for a long, long time. He decided, as risky as it would be, he would have to stash it all overboard.

He found a heavy cotton laundry bag in the master cabin closet and stuffed everything inside it: the wet clothes, the towels, his father's gun, the plastic-wrapped money and all. He also put in the bag a couple of small hand weights his mother kept onboard to exercise with to give the bag more weight. Then he tied a cord securely around the top of the bag. That was the easy part. Now he had to get it out the door and over the side without being seen.

The police divers had covered the entire area already, and it was unlikely they would soon be returning to these murky waters so far from the Toyota's original point of impact. So, once he got the bag down there, it should be safe for the time being. But he just couldn't drop it over the side and hope that no one would see him do it. There were cops everywhere, not to mention the other boat owners. Besides that, curiosity seekers had begun to gather around the perimeter of the harbor to check things out having heard on the news of the bizarre incidents that took place there the night before. The chances were very good indeed that he would be readily seen by any number of people just as soon as he made his move.

The police search teams were working their way in his direction, and Scott figured he had less than half an hour before they would be knocking at his door. He had to do something, and he had to do it quickly. Just when he had about decided to take the bag outside and drop it over the side and hope for the best, he heard the sound of a big diesel engine firing up and a cheer from the crowd. He left the bag inside and went out on the aft deck to see what all the noise was about. He looked up across the harbor to the top of the sea wall where their car had broken through the guardrail the night before, and there, behind the rows of yellow police tape stretched across the gap in the rail, was a large crane.

"Of course!" Scott thought to himself. "Just what I needed. A diversion. While everyone is watching the crane, nobody will be looking at me."

Sure enough, when the operator swung the big boom out over the harbor, nearly every eye in the vicinity was fixed on it. Scott went back inside and retrieved the bag of contraband and brought it out through the door and set it down in the well in front of the seating section, hidden from anyone looking from the shore. He waited until the divers under the water had run the heavy webbed belt through the open windows of the Corolla and attached it securely to the end of the crane's cable and had surfaced to signal the operator to lift away. Then he lifted the bag up onto the seat next to the side of the yacht, and waited for just the right moment.

The huge diesel engine roared, the cable snapped to attention, the big pulleys began to turn, and the little car began to rise from the bottom of the harbor. Just as the roof of the car broke through the surface and the water began to pour out of the windows, the crowd cheered loudly, drowning out the sound of the splash made by Scott's laundry bag going over the side. It sank almost immediately. As the car was going up, the bag was going down, and everyone but Scott watched the former. His eyes alone saw the bag sink beneath the surface of the water.

He went back on the dock again to watch with the rest of the onlookers as the crane raised the Toyota up over the sea wall and onto the back of a waiting tow truck. They all watched together as the car was secured to the truck and the crane boom was lowered back in place. At about the same time, the tow truck and the heavy crane fired up their engines and left the area. That seemed to be the cue for the crowd as well, and people began to drift away.

The search of the boats continued, and soon Scott had the privilege of showing the investigating officers through the *Pacific Pearl*. They were very thorough, and Scott was convinced they would have found the contraband, no matter where he might have hidden it. Even the freezer failed to escape their investigation. Their search completed, the officers thanked him and went on to examine the sailboat moored nearby. Scott went back inside and, for the first time in almost twelve hours, he began to relax and feel somewhat at ease.

He remembered Eddie's words from their previous conversation. The older man had said that only the woman had been killed. He was still sickened by the thought of having caused her death, but he was overjoyed to have learned that Aaron hadn't died, neither had his grandfather, nor the policeman. He turned on the radio at ten o'clock and listened to the news, which confirmed Eddie's synopsis. All three survivors were listed in good condition at St. Vincent's Hospital. The gunmen had not been located and were presumed to have drowned, although an investigation was still being conducted. Scott began to believe that maybe, just maybe, they might actually get away with this thing after all.

Shortly after noon, the police had concluded their investigation in the harbor, and had found nothing more. They had recovered one heavily damaged beige Toyota Corolla, two coats, four boots, two gloves, one pair of sunglasses, and one sawed-off shotgun. But still considered missing were two gloves, another pair of sunglasses, a handgun, two gunmen, and a big bagful of money. They would continue to send divers down farther out in the main channel, and to drag for the bodies, but they wouldn't be very optimistic. There was a big ocean out there, and it was filled with lots of hungry scavengers. If their bodies were still out there, they wouldn't be for long.

Tony showed up just before one in the afternoon in Scott's Blazer. He had ditched the duffel bags in Scott's garage before returning just in case the cops might check out the vehicle when he drove up. They didn't. They had all but left the area, leaving only a few officers to keep an eye on things. Even Sergeant Witherspoon had filed his report and gone home to get some much needed sleep.

They were both exhausted, having slept very little the night before, and they still needed to take care of the clothes in the duffel bags before a gardener or deliveryman or someone else discovered them. So they decided to skip swim practice that afternoon. It was usually a light one on Monday anyway.

On the way home, Scott told Tony what he had done with the laundry bag. Though Tony was visibly upset with the fact that the money was still not in their possession, he agreed it was a smart and gutsy move on Scott's part to dispose of it in that fashion. They agreed that they would have to go back and retrieve it the next afternoon since Scott had to replace the gold coins before his parents returned on Wednesday.

Later that night, home alone with his own thoughts, Scott experienced a number of conflicting emotions. First and foremost, he felt a tremendous sense of relief. He was safe and sound in his own home, with no guns or violence, nobody chasing him, and no life-or-death escape maneuvers. It had all been so totally foreign to anything he had experienced previously, that now it seemed almost as though it hadn't happened at all. It was like some bizarre dream from which he had finally awakened. He felt such an overwhelming sense of relief now that it was all but over.

But it wasn't over. He was haunted still by the memory of that sweet black lady's face as the bullet from his gun tore through her chest. How had she been able to face death with such courage and peace? She had been so strong in her faith, so committed to her Jesus, and yet He had let her die. What kind of God was that? If a faithful servant like her were allowed to die such a violent death, what would be in store for the likes of him, the thieving punk who gunned her down? The answer frightened him so much he forced himself not to think about it.

But think about it or not, he could not escape the deep sense of loneliness that gripped him. He was twenty-one years old and longing to get out from under the domination of his parents, but right then, he wanted his mom and dad. They had always been there for him in the past and he knew he could draw from their strength, but they weren't there. He could call Tony up and talk to him, but somehow that held no interest for him. Tony seemed absorbed only with getting the money and getting away with the robbery. He seemed to be immune to the guilt and doubts that plagued Scott. No, Tony couldn't help him.

He longed for warmth and comfort and understanding. He thought of Candi. Oh, how he needed to be with her, to pour out his heart to her, to tell her everything, and to feel her love and acceptance. But what gave him the idea he could expect those things from her now? She hadn't accepted him before, when he was a clean-cut college athlete, how was she ever going to accept him now that he was a fugitive, guilty of robbery and murder?

Maybe, he thought, what he really needed was to get right with God. He had been told by practically everyone: his parents, his pastor, his girlfriend, even the woman he had just killed, that coming to God through Jesus Christ was the only real answer to the really tough problems he faced in life. But how could he come to God now? He hadn't been able to do it when he was doing his best to be a good person, how could he possibly do it now, now that he was convinced of his sin and deep depravity? No, he had gone too far. God would surely reject him now, even if he did cry out to Him, so he decided to dismiss the idea altogether.

With these jumbled thoughts running through his mind, he wandered around the empty house for awhile, prepared another one of his mother's microwaved delights, and sat down in front of the TV to eat it. The news rehashed again the strange account of the violent robbery and the spectacular escape attempt. Scott watched with detached interest, almost as though he had played no part in it at all. What was wrong with him? Was he losing his mind? He watched the rest of the newscast and part of the program that followed it, but he comprehended little of either one of them, so deeply absorbed was he in his own world of loneliness and grief.

Finally, mercifully, exhaustion from the events of the past few days settled deeply into every crevice of his body, and he fell asleep on the couch with his meal half eaten and the TV still playing. At about three, he woke up long enough to turn off the TV, rolled over, and went back to sleep.

That Monday had been a depressing day for Candace Mercer as well. She had been thinking about Scott and was strangely worried about him. She didn't know why, but she was convinced he was in some sort of danger or trouble. She had a troubled, anxious feeling concerning him ever since their tearful parting the previous Thursday. She wanted to call him and talk with him, but she had left him with an ultimatum, and she didn't feel like she could go running back to him so soon. She had been praying that God would be working in his heart, and she didn't want to get in the way, yet she couldn't escape the haunting suspicion that he was in trouble and he needed her.

She had looked for him at church the day before, but he wasn't there.

He had left a message on her answering machine the night before, and that would have given her a ready excuse to call him that afternoon, but still she didn't feel comfortable about it, so she didn't call. She stayed in her room that night to be sure to be there if he called again, but she heard nothing from him. She fell asleep late at night praying for him with a terrible sense of dread on his behalf.

Monday morning she waited for him outside one of his classes, but he didn't come. She stopped by the pool to see him at practice but he wasn't there either. That was so unlike Scott. He had never been one to cut classes, and he had always been faithful to make it to all his practices. Where was he, and what had he been up to?

That afternoon, she called his home, but no one answered and she hung up without leaving a message when the answering machine came on. She had heard about the terrible shooting up in LA the night before and that Aaron Muller, one of Scott's teammates had been wounded. Perhaps Scott had cut class and practice to see about the welfare of his friend. This thought made her feel better about him, but something deep inside her told her that it just wasn't the case. But where else could he be?

She decided to give him one more day. If she didn't hear from him by Tuesday, she was going to track him down. She loved him, and whether he was yet saved or not, she felt he needed her, and she was going to be there for him.

Things were buzzing at St. Vincent's Hospital that Monday. All four victims of a shooting at a nearby grocery store had been brought into their emergency room the night before. The staff regretted the death of the elderly lady, but she had been dead before the paramedics had brought her in, so there was no real sense of loss on their part. What had them so excited was the fact that the other three had made such amazing recoveries.

The off-duty policeman, who looked as though he had been blown in half when they first brought him in, was completely out of danger. He was complaining loudly as a multitude of tiny birdshot was being painfully extracted from his upper torso, but he appeared overjoyed to be alive. He didn't want his pregnant wife and little daughter to leave his side, and he kept telling them how much he loved them and what a different kind of man he was going to be now that God had given him a second chance.

The elderly gentleman who looked as though his head had been caved in, had been stitched up and was recovering nicely, surrounded by a room full of devoted family members. His biggest concern seemed to be about who was going to run his store until he was well enough to take care of it himself again.

But what amazed the hospital staff most of all was the condition of the old man's grandson. The young man was brought in with a bullet hole squarely in the center of his chest, directly in line with his heart, and yet he was alert and active. In emergency surgery the bullet was removed, revealing that it had penetrated his chest cavity, but had not entered the heart itself. He had literally come a fraction of an inch from death.

The boy's father came in with him after the shooting and explained to the surgical team that the elderly lady had stepped in front of his son just before the gunman fired, and the bullet passed through her body before striking him. The word quickly spread throughout the hospital, and everyone from surgeons to orderlies wanted to come in and see the young man whose life had been so wondrously spared.

Not only that, people from the press got word of the situation and were clamoring to be the first to get a personal interview with the young man who had so narrowly cheated death. They, in turn, were run off by the homicide investigators, who needed to get a firsthand statement from him about the incidents of the night before. All in all, it was quite a show. Finally, the police themselves posted a man outside his room to keep out all but family and authorized personnel.

Among those authorized personnel were two officers from the Homicide Division of the Los Angeles Police Department: Sergeant Myron Spangler and Detective Theo Farley, who had been assigned to the case to investigate the death of Georgia Davis. It appeared to them at first to be rather routine. An off-duty cop interrupted an ongoing robbery, and got himself and two other people shot by two hardened criminals in the process. It was tragic, but that sort of thing happened all too frequently in the LA area. But as they interviewed several of the witnesses, facts started coming to the surface that made this case start to take on a special significance.

Saul Frieberg, the proprietor, told them the robbers had been young and nervous, not the hardened, biker type, which was interesting; but what really got their attention was what he said about the safes. The assailants had known about the existence and the location of both his hidden safes. Nobody but a few of Saul's immediate family members had known he kept a sizable amount of money in those safes. How those two had known about those safes was a complete mystery to him.

Joseph Muller added more to the puzzling details of the crime. The one who had held the gun on him and the other hostages had been extremely nervous and apparently inexperienced with guns. Muller was convinced that the young man had not intended to fire the pistol. He dropped it to the floor the instant it went off, and just stood there after he had done so. He even made an apparent attempt to come back and help, rather than flee, before his partner literally pulled him out the door.

Muller told them he had known about the safes and had tried repeatedly to talk his father-in-law out of keeping his money in them. But he also assured them that he had told no one about their existence. He remembered that his son Aaron also knew about the safes, but he was sure that he had not divulged that information to anyone either. That was the question Spangler and Farley wanted to ask of him personally.

After coming into the young man's hospital room and asking all visitors and hospital staff to leave, Spangler introduced himself and Farley to Aaron Muller. Spangler was a tall thin man with an angular face, about forty-five years of age. He had thinning brown hair and wide set, piercing eyes. Farley was good looking, with sandy colored hair and a freckled face. He was younger and shorter than Spangler, but equally thin. Aaron wasn't able to keep from wondering how they might fare if they were ever to get into a fight trying to apprehend some really big bruisers sometime.

After some routine preliminary questions, Spangler asked Aaron if he could recall ever telling anyone about the existence of the safes in his grandfather's store. At first Aaron said no; but after thinking about it, he said he thought he might have told some of the guys on his swim team. When asked the identity of those team members, he gave them several names; among them were the names of Scott Graham and Tony D'Angelo.

These names were then dutifully recorded by Farley, and each of the young men were to be thoroughly investigated. This information provided them with their most promising clues so far. Aaron reconfirmed what his father had told the officers earlier about the gunman who shot him. He also was convinced the shooting itself had been accidental, an act committed by an unwilling assailant. If that were so, it would have fit in well with the possibility that the gunmen had been some of his teammates; put onto the crime by the tantalizing information he had casually shared with them.

Another visitor that day at St. Vincent's Hospital was the Reverend Robert Davis. Pastor Bobby, as his parishioners called him, had actually come the night before. Sarah Singleton called Tamika's grandfather from the hospital after she learned of Georgia's death. He got dressed and drove right over. It was about 1:00 A.M. when he arrived, and he hadn't left since.

On the way over, driving in the rain, he was alone with his thoughts. Could it be true that his mother was dead? He had seen her only a few hours before, and she had been so radiant and full of life. Oh, how he loved that woman! He wasn't able to remember: had he told her he loved her when he put her and Tamika on that bus to ride across town? Why had he ever let them do such a foolish thing? If he had driven them over like he had wanted to, she would be alive right now. In a way, he bore the responsibility of his mother's death.

Along with his sorrow and guilt, he experienced a sense of almost uncontrollable anger. What kind of animal would gun down a defenseless old woman with a little girl? Thank God Sarah had said Tamika was okay. Right then, if he could have gotten his powerful hands on the lowlife who had gunned down his mother, preacher or no preacher, he thought he would have beaten that scum to death.

Upon arriving at the hospital, he was greeted by a weeping Sarah and a sleeping Tamika. The ordeal of the previous hours had caught up with the eight-year-old, and she had cried herself to sleep in her mother's arms. After learning that Carl and the others were going to be all right, he was led to the room where his mother's body was being kept.

There, alone with her, he wept unashamedly for a long time. He asked her forgiveness for allowing her to go off alone at night, and for every other time he could think of where he had also failed her. He told her repeatedly how much he loved her and how much she meant to him. He pledged he would not rest until those who had taken her life were brought to justice. He thanked her for her unceasing prayers in his behalf, and promised to continue on in the right path and to make her proud of him. He knew she was not there, and did not need to hear his words, but he needed to say them.

Some time later, some officials came to take the body to the morgue, and it was an excruciating experience for Bobby. After they had taken her, he returned to find Sarah and Tamika. He insisted Sarah take her daughter home and both of them get some rest. He would stay at the hospital and let her know if there were any need for her to return. He wanted to see Carl, but he was told he had been sedated and would be out till morning. Again alone with his thoughts, he walked the halls. He wept, he cursed, he prayed, he argued with himself and with God. Finally, he too gave in to exhaustion and fell asleep sitting up in a chair in the waiting room.

Early in the morning, Bobby went into Carl Singleton's room and found him awake and alert. They wept together over Georgia's death and Bobby wanted to hug the younger man, but Carl was in no condition for it, so he simply put his hand on his shoulder instead.

"Bobby, I thought I was going to die, for sure," Carl said after they had both regained their composure. "I saw that shotgun pointed at me, and I actually saw the blast. The last thing I remember thinking is that I knew I was going to die and I didn't know for sure where I was going."

"Praise God, Carl, you didn't die. But you sure could have, and you need to know where you're going when you do. My mother's in heaven with her Savior right now. She never expected to die last night either, but she was ready. She knew where she was going, and I know she's there right now."

"Of course she's in heaven," Carl had agreed. "I've never known such a godly woman. If anybody ever went to heaven, it would have to be Georgia Davis."

"Nonsense, Carl," Bobby scolded him. "Mama's in heaven today, not because she was such a godly woman, but because she was a sinner who had enough sense to admit it, and enough faith to believe God would forgive her and save her anyway; and He can do the same thing for you too. People don't go to heaven by being good; they go to heaven by being saved."

"But, Bobby, what about my sin? Does God just forget about it when I ask him to save me? Does He just sweep it under the carpet, do I have to pay for it in purgatory, or does He allow me to take my sin into heaven with me?"

"None of the above," Bobby said. "He condemns your sin and demands death be paid as its penalty. That's why he sent His Son Jesus Christ to earth to die on the cross for your sin so you won't have to."

Just then an idea entered Bobby's mind that he thought must have come from God Himself. "Listen, Carl, there's a young man in a room down the hall who's alive this morning because my mother died in his place. As I understand it, the gunman had the pistol pointed right at his heart, and Mama stepped in front of him and took the bullet herself. She died that he might live. That's what Jesus did for you when He died the death you should have died on the cross so you won't ever have to face that horrible judgment yourself."

"You mean I'm already saved, because of what Jesus did for me back then?"

"No, Jesus died to pay for your sin and He rose again to establish life and righteousness as a free gift, but like any gift, it has to be personally received. It's available to you, Carl, but it's not yours until you accept it."

"Is it really that easy? How do you go about accepting it?"

"Well, Carl, as you know, several years ago now, I was rotting in prison, guilty of robbing, stealing, dealing drugs, you name it. I was going to hell, and I knew it, but my cellmate told me what I'm telling you right now. He was always singing and praying and preaching all the time, and nearly drove me crazy, but he was different from all the other cons. His life backed up what he was saying, and I started listening. About that time, my wife got sick and both she and Mama got saved. They started telling me the same thing old Benny in the joint had been telling me all along.

"A few months after that my wife died. She died of AIDS, Carl, and I gave it to her. I'm HIV positive, but I haven't gotten sick yet. The guilt of knowing I had killed my wife was almost too much for me. But at the funeral, old Brother Wilcox told me the same thing I'd been hearing from everybody else. Tasha went to heaven because she had trusted Jesus Christ and had been born-again.

"Well, I didn't do anything right then. I was still too stupid and proud, I guess, but a couple of months later I couldn't stand it any longer. The guilt and shame were just too great. So I got down on my knees with old Benny in our cell and confessed my sin to God and asked Jesus Christ to come into my life and forgive me. And you know what? He did exactly that. I got saved that night, and I haven't been the same since."

Big tears welled up in Carl's eyes as he reached out painfully and took Bobby's hand. "Do I have to get down on my knees, or can I do it lying here on my back?"

"You just go right ahead right where you are, brother. God looks at your heart anyway, not your posture." Bobby had difficulty getting the words out. He too had become overwhelmed with emotion.

Carl closed his eyes and squeezed Bobby's hand tightly and said, "God, I'm a sinner, and I know it and I don't deserve to go to heaven, but thank

You for sparing my life so I could understand Your plan of salvation. I don't know why, but You loved me and You sent Your Son to die for me so I could receive the gift of salvation. Right now, I receive Him as my own Savior. Come into my life and forgive my sin and help me to live the rest of my life like Bobby's doing, serving You in whatever way You want me to. And please help me to be a better husband and father. Well, I guess that's about it, God. Thank you. Amen."

Bobby laughed and wept and shouted and carried on for some time with Carl, until a nurse came in and told Bobby he would have to leave. Carl had a lot of mending to do and they needed to get started on his treatment. Bobby told Carl he needed to tell Sarah and Tamika what he had done, which he gladly consented to do, and the preacher left, praising God.

He visited the other two injured men and asked if he might pray with them. The older man, Mr. Frieberg, thanked him, but said that he was Jewish and didn't want to hear anything about Jesus Christ. His good friend Georgia Davis had trusted in him as her Savior, and look what good it had done her. Bobby tried to share the gospel with him, but he politely cut him off and asked him if he wouldn't please excuse him so he could get some rest.

His grandson Aaron Muller, on the other hand, was eager to talk with Bobby. He was apologetic about being spared at the expense of the life of the pastor's mother, but thrilled to be alive. He was convinced that God had spared his life for some future purpose and calling. He was not willing to consider the claims of Jesus Christ, but said he was fully committed to help usher in the coming of Israel's Messiah. He respectfully allowed Bobby to pray for him, but he was apparently unmoved by the poorly disguised gospel presentation Bobby slipped into the prayer.

Aaron promised Bobby that he would be at the funeral for his mother whenever it would be held, but he wasn't sure about his grandfather. He was already talking about getting back to the store and opening up for business just as quickly as possible.

Bobby spent most of the morning at the hospital, especially rejoicing with Carl and his family over his newfound faith and his new lease on life. Sarah and Tamika were thrilled to have him, not only alive and healing physically, but to have him now a possessor of eternal life as well. Sarah admitted she had suspected that his profession earlier hadn't been truly genuine, but she had no doubts now. It was evident to all that Carl was now truly a changed man.

Bobby also spent several hours that afternoon at a funeral home, making arrangements for the funeral that they agreed on for that Friday at 10:00 A.M. at the Antioch Baptist Church. He had been totally unprepared for such an assignment, and found it very disturbing. He tried to reach both Jamal and Marcus during the day, but he was unsuccessful, so he had to make all the difficult decisions by himself. As he left there and started for home, he silently prayed that the Lord would come before he had to go through that experience again for another loved one.

As he drove down the familiar street leading to his home, he found it strange that his mother wouldn't be there to greet him with one of her big hugs and a sumptuous meal. It would take a lot of getting used to, facing life without her. She had always been there for him. He was still not reconciled to the fact of her death, but already one soul had been saved as a result of her homegoing. Maybe God was still in control after all.

Little did he know how great a role his mother's death was going to play in the lives of many others, and indeed, in God's great plan for the ages.

CHAPTER TWELVE

THE CLOSE CALL

If the robbery and shooting had taken place in a smaller community, it would, no doubt, have received front-page coverage. The radio stations would have been buzzing with the news and it would have been all over the TV as well. But with about thirteen million people living in the Los Angeles area, such events took place virtually every day. Yes, they did get reported in some fashion, but it was a rare occasion indeed when much attention was paid and much interest generated. This was one of those occasions.

The fact that an elderly black woman had stepped in front of a young Jewish man to take the bullet intended for him, and saved his life by sacrificing her own, was news indeed. Everyone in the media was talking about it, and each of the networks was trying to get a leg up on the others. The events of the gunfire and bloodshed were in all the papers and on all the stations all over the Southland. What made it all the more amazing was that neither Jamal nor Marcus Davis knew anything about it until Tuesday morning.

Jamal had slept in late Monday morning and got up just in time to get dressed and across campus for his first class. He went directly to practice after a full day of classes, and had an extra hard workout, as did all the other players. Coach Barnes had not been pleased with their performance on Friday night, and wanted to exorcise whatever demon had possessed them by working their buns off. Jamal went to dinner and then straight to the library after practice to do research on a term paper due the next week in his political science class. He did not return to his room until late, and then went to bed, neglecting to check for messages on his answering machine.

Now he sat on his bed, staring at his phone. He had just got up and punched the play button on the answering machine to catch up on his messages. The first one revealed the voice of his father, telling him there had been a robbery and a shooting and his grandmother had been killed. His dad was going to St. Vincent's Hospital and Jamal could contact him there. Jamal never heard the other two messages. He just sat there and stared at the phone for the longest time.

Later, after the realization of what he had heard finally registered, he called his father and woke him up. He apologized for his delay in getting back to his dad and explained what had happened, and Bobby confirmed that his grandmother had indeed been killed. Jamal was not normally an emotional person, but he broke down on the phone and found no words to express his feelings to his father. He managed to get out that he was coming over, and he hung up the phone.

Marcus Davis went the whole day Monday without hearing about Georgia's death, either. The reason is that he spent the whole day doing something he hadn't done in years. He worked all day.

He had known that he was going to have to do something. He had hocked or sold everything of value he had so he could bet it on the Houston game, and he had, of course, lost it all. He had no car, no phone, no TV, no nothing . . . and he had bills coming due. He thought about selling some drugs or committing some sort of robbery, but that was before Jamal had talked him into going to church with him on Sunday.

At the Antioch Baptist Church, he ran into an old friend of his, Gilbert Matthews. Gil had run with Marcus years before when they were both gang bangers. He was as short and round as Marcus was tall and lean, and the two of them had made an odd-looking team on the streets back then. But Gil was off the streets now, married to a lovely wife, and the father of two little girls. He also ran an auto salvage business in the city of Vernon. They were talking about how busy he was and how he needed some help when Gil asked Marcus if he could use some work. Marcus jumped at the suggestion and agreed to show up bright and early Monday morning.

About the only thing he hadn't hocked was his alarm clock, and that was only because he didn't think he could get anything for it. It rattled him awake at 6:00, and after catching a bus, Marcus arrived at the Empire Auto Dismantlers at 7:00.

He worked until seven that night, stopping only long enough to borrow some money from Gil and grab some lunch from a catering truck at noon. The day went quickly, and he enjoyed learning the auto salvage business. He even made friends with Killer, Gil's pit bulldog. He found him to be a big lovable cream puff after he managed to get past his initial display of hostility. Marcus decided that everything he had heard about junkyard dogs hadn't been necessarily so. Neither, he also decided, had been all the things he had heard about the evils of working for a living.

Gil must have sensed the severity of Marcus' financial situation, because he gave him his earnings in cash at the end of the day and told him he had the job permanently if he wanted it. Marcus took the money gladly and thanked him and said he would see him in the morning. He had a good feeling about himself for the first time in as long as he could remember. He stopped by a Chinese restaurant on the way home for dinner and then returned to his nearly empty apartment with no means of communication with the outside world. He was tired and went to bed early.

It was not until Tuesday morning that he too learned of his grandmother's death, and that was only when Jamal drove into the wrecking yard and told him. He had told Jamal about the job Gil had offered him at dinner Sunday afternoon, and his younger brother had been able to talk to some mutual friends and track him down.

He received the news of Georgia Davis' death numbly, the reality of it not really sinking in. Gil offered his condolences and told Marcus to take the rest of the day off and go be with his family. As he got in the car with Jamal, Marcus felt as though the world, as he had known it, had been systematically dismantled since the previous Friday, not unlike the hulks in the wrecking yard that had once been automobiles. As they drove off to the awkward, and inevitably painful reunion with their father, Marcus wondered when, and if, his world would ever be put back together again.

Scott Graham woke early Tuesday morning with a stiff neck from sleeping on the couch in an awkward position. He had a bad taste in his mouth, and he felt anything but rested. He began to feel more like a human being after he had shaved, showered, and put on some clean clothes. As he was fixing himself some breakfast, the phone rang. He practically ran to pick up the receiver hoping it would be Candi, but the familiar voice of his mother greeted him on the other end instead.

She informed him that they had just completed their last day in Jerusalem and would be boarding the plane first thing in the morning for their return flight home. They expected to be arriving at LAX at about one and should be at home by three that afternoon. They had a wonderful time and couldn't wait to show him all the footage they had taken on video. He lied and said he was anxious to see it. She asked if everything had been going well for him while they were gone. He lied even more profoundly this time and said everything had been fine. She asked why he had never been home when she had called. This time he told the truth and said he and Tony had been really busy and had gone out to a ball game and a movie and had spent a couple of days on the yacht. And, oh yes, they had knocked over a convenience store in their spare time.

She laughed and said she couldn't wait to see him. By now, he was into telling half-truths when he said he was anxious to see them too. He did want to see them because he felt so terribly alone; but on the other hand, he didn't want to see them because of how guilty he felt about all the rotten things he had done in their absence. She told him she loved him, and he almost choked up when he responded from the depths of his heart that he loved her too. Then he said goodbye and hung up the phone.

Scott faced another busy day. He felt he had to attend his classes and swim practice, having cut everything the day before. He had to see Candi. He wasn't sure what he was going to say or do, but he knew he had to see her. He had to get together with Tony and tie up the loose ends they had left at the marina, and he had to buy back some double eagles to replace those he had stolen from his father's safe. He wasn't at all sure how he was going to get it all done, but he was going to have to do it, nonetheless. He was running out of time.

After a hurried breakfast of the remains of his dinner from the night before, nuked and nasty, but also quick and easy, he headed off for class. The morning dragged by and he may well have skipped those classes too, as he had the ones the day before, for all the knowledge he gleaned from them. Try as he might, he just couldn't bring himself to concentrate on the boring lectures being served up to him. His mind was swimming with the details of all the other items that were clamoring for his attention.

After his third hour class, he hurried to the spot in the mall where he had often met Candi, and was delighted to see her waiting there for him. He practically ran to her, dropped his books, and picked her off the ground with a big hug. She hugged him right back, and both of them began to lose it emotionally. He just held her in his arms until he regained his composure, then he held her out at arm's length and just looked at her. Both of them had tears in their eyes.

"It seems like a year since I saw you," he said. "I've missed you so much, and you look soooo good."

"I wish I could say the same for you," she responded. "You look awful. Have you been sick, or what?"

"No, I've been okay. Just been real busy, that's all."

"Come off it, Scott. I know better than that. You look like you've been carrying the weight of the world on your shoulders. I've sensed something's been wrong. What is it?"

"Oh, just a lot of things piling up, I guess. You telling me to take a hike last week didn't help, and then Aaron Muller got shot Sunday night in a holdup."

"Yes, I heard about it on the news. It was awful. What kind of person would shoot Aaron and a defenseless old woman like that? And I didn't tell you to take a hike. I just felt like my heart was getting way ahead of my mind, and I thought we needed to slow down until we were on the same wavelength spiritually."

"How do you slow down from stop?" Scott asked a bit sarcastically, perhaps taking offense at what Candi had said about the shooter; but he regretted saying it almost immediately. "What I meant to say is I don't think we are getting too involved. Good night, we haven't even kissed yet, not that I wouldn't like to. And maybe we're not as far apart spiritually as you may think."

"Oh, Scott, have you . . . ?" she started to ask.

But Scott realized what he had led her to conclude, and cut her off, "No, Candi, I haven't received Christ, as you call it, but I have been doing some very serious thinking these past few days, and I really want to look into it more. That's one of the things I wanted to talk to you about."

"What things?"

"Oh, about life and death, and heaven and hell, and things like that. Aaron very nearly got killed *'by me'* (he thought, but didn't say) and it could have happened to me or Tony or any one of us. It just really got my attention, and I want to find out more about that kind of stuff."

"Great, we're starting a study on the book of Revelation in our college group at church next Sunday night. Why don't you go to it with me?"

"Yeah, okay, I'd like that, but right now I want you to promise to go someplace with me."

"Where?"

"To the funeral of the lady that got killed saving Aaron's life."

"Why do you want to go to her funeral? Did you know her?"

"No, but Aaron's a good friend, and he's alive today because of her. I can't explain it, but I just feel like I gotta go . . . to show my appreciation or something, I don't know."

"When is it?"

"I don't know yet, but I'm going to see Aaron in the hospital tonight and I'll call you when I find out."

"Sure, Scott, if it's that important to you, I'll be glad to go with you. And I think it's really sweet of you to do that."

"If you really knew why I have to go to her funeral, you wouldn't think it was so sweet. You'd hate me and never want to see me again," Scott thought to himself, but didn't say. He did say, "Thanks, Candi, I knew I could count on you."

Candi wanted to talk further and find out more about what was bothering Scott and where he'd been the past three days, but he said he had to go to his next class. He would be busy all afternoon with something he couldn't get out of, and then he had swim practice and a hospital visit scheduled for the evening. He said he would call her later that night and tell her about the funeral, and he promised to answer all her questions real soon. He lied about the last part. He had no present intention of ever telling her about the events of the past three days.

He left her and went to his last class of the day, at least feeling better about the possibility of their relationship continuing. But he still had some tracks to cover before he was out of the woods. He met Tony on the way to a philosophy class they attended together and arranged to go to the marina right after it was over.

Again, they took Scott's Blazer so they could park it in the owners' lot, and made their way down to the docks. They saw no sign of the police this time. Even the broken guardrail had been repaired, and the yellow caution tape had been removed. They saw Eddie right away, and he was eager to share with them the latest on the great escape.

The police divers had found the missing pair of sunglasses about a hundred yards down the harbor from the point of impact, and a glove that matched one they already had, clear out in the main channel. They had concluded the two fugitives had tried to make their escape by swimming underwater, but had drowned before reaching safety and the current and tide had carried their bodies out to sea. They had quit searching for them. They figured the bodies might wash up down the beach somewhere, sometime, but as far as the local police were concerned, the case was closed.

That was good news to the ears of Scott and Tony. They told Eddie they had come down after class to do the fishing the cops hadn't let them do the day before. That seemed to satisfy the older man and he was off to see what or whom he might find of interest elsewhere.

After boarding the *Pacific Pearl,* Tony went below and put on a wet suit he had taken from one of the storage compartments, while Scott made preparations to cast off. When he untied the bowline, he purposefully allowed the end of the rope to dangle into the water rather than securing it as he was supposed to do. Tony casually dropped off the aft deck into the water, making some comment about checking out the props just in case anyone might find his actions curious.

But instead of looking at the props or anything else on the craft, he headed straight for the bottom; under the spot where Scott said he had dropped the laundry bag the day before. He turned on the waterproof flashlight he had brought with him and began to search for the bag. It was not where he thought it ought to be, so he began to make ever-widening circles, straining his eyes in the murky darkness, trying to locate his prize.

He could not find it, and was about to run out of air. He was beginning to panic, thinking it had been carried away by the tide, or worse yet, had been found by someone else, and others now had their money. But just as he felt he had to resurface to get some more air, he spotted something settled in the mud below and to his right. He swam quickly to the spot and, sure enough, there was the bag, all tied up and waiting for him.

He didn't bother picking it up. He left it where it was and rose straight up to the surface. He came up about fifteen feet closer to the front of the boat than from the point where Scott had said he had dropped it. How it had moved, he couldn't imagine. The current and tide did funny things sometimes. No matter. Its movement would make it that much easier for him to accomplish his mission.

He caught his breath and then dived again, this time going directly to the submerged bag. He picked it up and swam the rest of the way to the front of the craft, where he found the bowline suspended before him. He tied the end of the line securely around the top of the bag and let it drop. The bag hung suspended from the line beneath the bow of the boat. Before resurfacing, Tony pulled hard on the bag, but the line held it fast. Convinced his treasure was secure, he swam underwater back near the rear of the yacht and surfaced, flashing Scott a grin and a thumbs up sign.

They took the sleek yacht out into the bay without incident. No one could possibly have known what they were towing beneath them. Once out beyond the breakwater, Scott piloted her out into the open ocean. About a mile out, he turned off the engines and let her drift. No other craft could be seen anywhere near them, so they felt it safe to haul their prize onboard. Tony hoisted the bag over the bow of the yacht, noticing how much heavier it was out of the water. It took him several minutes to untie both the bowline and the cord tied around the top of the bag. Both of them had been tied to stay that way. But he was highly motivated and persistent, and in time, both knots yielded to his determination.

He rummaged inside the bag, sorting through the soggy clothes and metal objects until he found what he was looking for. He pulled out the bundle of cash, still tightly knotted inside the plastic bags and just as dry as it had been inside The Corner Store two days before. He held it up and gave it a big kiss and then tossed it over to Scott. He was about to tie the cord once again around the top of the laundry bag when Scott told him to wait. Scott dug inside the ice chest and pulled out the two good-sized rocks he had put there that morning and carried them over to the bag. He knelt down and felt inside it until he found the two hand weights he had put there to cause it to sink quickly. He retrieved them and replaced them with the two rocks. He would return the weights to their proper place below, determined not to arouse any more suspicion than absolutely necessary. Once the rocks were in place, he retied the bag and unceremoniously dropped it back over the side and secured the bowline.

The two of them fished for a couple of hours, not because they wanted to, but to justify their being out there in the first place. They filleted their catch and headed back to the marina. On the way, Tony put the money, still securely wrapped in plastic, in the bottom of the ice chest, covered it completely with ice, and then put the filleted fish on top of that. No one would have guessed that their ice chest was in truth a treasure chest.

Once back on the docks, having properly secured the yacht, they made their compulsory stop to show Eddie their catch. Having gained his approval, they carried the ice chest back to the Blazer, and Scott drove them back to the campus. On the way, Tony divided the money, keeping an extra share for himself, so he could pay for the .38 Special he had located to replace the one now at the bottom of the ocean. They had no time to allow Scott to stop and buy back the gold coins that day. They were going to be late for practice as it was. Somehow, Scott was going to have to do that the next day and get them back in place before his parents got home that afternoon.

Jamal and Marcus arrived at their father's home late Tuesday morning to find him in his study. He was trying to put his thoughts down on paper to form the basis of a message he hoped he would have the composure to deliver at his mother's funeral on Friday. His phone had been buzzing all morning, not to mention the dozen or so messages that had been left on his machine from the day before while he had been gone. Mostly, they were from people in the church and the community, calling to offer their condolences and to offer any assistance they could. People were bringing over food, and a committee had already been organized to handle everything at the church for the service there Friday and the dinner that would follow.

Bobby Davis jumped up from his desk when his sons came through the door, and though he thought he had absolutely cried out his last tear already, he broke down again as he hugged them both. They joined in with him as they too lost their composure, and they had a good cry together as they stood there in the middle of the room with their arms around each other. They were big men, all of them 6'5" or better, but right then they were weak and vulnerable and needed each other's support.

After a few minutes, they had regained control over their emotions, and each took a seat in the study. The boys apologized again for not being there for him the day before and Marcus explained where he had been. Bobby understood, and assured them not to worry about it. He was especially pleased to hear that Marcus had landed a job at the wrecking yard. He knew Gilbert Matthews personally and found him to be a young man of faith and character. He and his family were always at church, his wife sang in the choir, and his tithe check was always in the collection plate the first Sunday of every month.

Marcus welcomed his father's approval, trying to remember how long it had been since he had done anything that had pleased both him and his dad. He enjoyed the feeling, and decided he would try to keep headed in that direction. He still had a lot of monkeys on his back that would try to lead him astray, but right at that moment, he had them well under control.

The three of them talked for about an hour about their family, the good times they could all remember, but mostly they talked about Georgia Davis. They let the answering machine field the several calls that came in during the time so they wouldn't be constantly interrupted. They agreed Georgia was about as fine a woman as God ever placed on this earth, and they each owed a great deal to her. Bobby told his sons that he would like for them to act as pallbearers, along with him, at the funeral, and they readily agreed. He said he needed a couple of other strong bodies because his mother was a big woman and the other three pallbearers were suspect, to say the least.

Bobby hadn't been too surprised when Carl Singleton asked if he might serve in that capacity. He would be out of the hospital by then and he was sure he would be able to carry his share of the weight. He had just trusted in Christ, and it was Georgia's death that had brought him to the point of making that decision, and Bobby wasn't about to turn him down. But what really floored him was when Aaron Muller called him from the hospital that morning and asked if he and his grandfather might be considered for that responsibility as well.

Aaron said that Papa Saul was going home from the hospital that afternoon and he would be released on Wednesday. Saul considered Georgia a very good friend and she had died in his presence, in his store. He would consider it a great privilege if he were to be allowed to render this small service in her behalf. As far as Aaron was concerned, he would not be alive today if it were not for her. He knew he was not a friend or a member of the family, but because of the unique circumstances, he would be honored if he could be allowed to serve in this capacity. Bobby told him he would be pleased to have them both serve as pallbearers.

Bobby felt better about the prospects of carrying the heavy casket now. With Jamal on one side and Marcus and himself on the other, at least he felt confident that they would not drop the thing, even with three unsteady, injured men assisting them. They all laughed when he expressed his relief, and Marcus said he was sure Grandma would have gotten a chuckle out of their predicament as well.

Bobby took his sons out to lunch at a nice restaurant and savored their company much more than the food. They all agreed they would have to do this more often. Afterward, Bobby had to get back to his study, Jamal had to hurry to make it to practice, and strangely enough, Marcus was anxious to get back to work. Bobby led them in a short prayer before they parted and they agreed they probably wouldn't see each other until the morning of the funeral.

Coach Englehart was especially tough on Tony and Scott during their swim practice that evening. They had a tough meet against Loyola Marymount the next day and, as far as he knew, they hadn't swum at all since the past Friday. He didn't know that they had experienced the most demanding swim of their young lives late Sunday night, and they weren't in any position to tell him about it either, so they just had to endure the grueling workout.

When it was over, Tony left to buy the gun he had waiting for him at a special price. One thousand dollars would buy him a like-new Colt .38 Special that was identical to the one Scott had taken from his dad's nightstand. It was a lot of money, but it was a small price to pay for the protection it could well afford them. Tony promised to get it to Scott first thing in the morning, as he had a date that night with Heather from the travel agency, and he would be getting home much too late to make any transfer.

Scott didn't like the idea of getting the gun so late, but he said it would be all right. Tony was doing him a big favor by purchasing the gun for him on the black market in the first place. He couldn't be too fussy about when he took delivery. He wouldn't even know where to begin to obtain such a weapon himself. He said goodbye to his friend, and got in his Blazer and headed off toward Los Angeles and St. Vincent's Hospital.

In the hallway outside Aaron's room in the hospital, Scott had difficulty mustering enough courage to go in and face the friend whom he had just shot in the chest. He didn't really have to be there at all, the practical side of his personality reminded him, but something else deep within him demanded his presence. So, he cleared his throat, put the most casual expression he could manage on his face, and strode through the open door into the already crowded room.

Two pretty young nurses were tending to Aaron at the time. One was checking his blood pressure and the other was taking his temperature. One nurse could have handled both tasks easily enough, but Aaron was a handsome fellow, and it wasn't every day they got a chance to attend to someone so good-looking, especially one who had been shot in the chest and lived.

Besides the nurses in the room were Aaron's family: his parents, Joseph and Miriam Muller, and his younger sister, Rachel, all of whom Scott had seen at a distance at swim meets, but had not actually met. In addition to them were four more people he had never seen before. They turned out to be an uncle and an aunt and their two teenaged sons, who had just stopped in to lend their support. Papa Saul had been in earlier as well, but he had been discharged and had gone home to the store to make preparations, so determined was he to open for business in the morning.

Scott almost turned around to leave, but Aaron spotted him and insisted he come in and meet everyone. His parents were ordinary looking professional people in their mid-forties, but his younger sister was a striking brunette with fascinating eyes and a beautiful smile. Scott realized he must really be in love with Candi because though he noticed Rachel's beauty right off, he found himself not attracted to her in the least.

Aaron insisted on telling him everything that happened Sunday night at Papa Saul's store. Scott didn't want to hear it. He had played it over and over again in his mind, and it always came out the same terrible way. He would have given anything if he could have forgotten all about it, but as Aaron told the story again in graphic detail, he had to live every agonizing moment over again.

He tried to listen with detached interest, but as Aaron led up to the shooting itself, Scott's hands began to tremble and his palms became moist with perspiration. He stuffed his hands in his pockets and gritted his teeth. He willed the condemning monologue to cease, but Aaron proceeded to carry it out to its inevitable conclusion, leaving out nothing. When he was finally through, everyone in the room was impressed and amazed, that is, everyone except Scott. He was depressed and overwhelmed with guilt. He tried to conceal his emotions and joined in with the others in their comments about how lucky Aaron and the others were to be alive, and how brave that poor woman was who got killed.

Aaron surprised them all when he said it had nothing to do with luck. He had known throughout the entire ordeal that he would be spared. He didn't know how, and he was sad that it had cost Mrs. Davis her life, but he knew that he was not going to die. He didn't know what it was yet, but he knew God had spared him for some divine purpose. He admitted that it sounded crazy, but God was, and had been for some time, preparing him for something special in the future.

Everyone agreed that it must have been so, only no one actually believed it, with the possible exception of Scott Graham. He knew things had gone on in that store that night that had no earthly explanation. For the past two days, he had wrestled with the haunting impression that God was trying to impact his soul through all the horrifying events of that night, but he had tried to dismiss it. But now, with Aaron saying almost the same thing, he felt cold chills of confirmation running down his spine.

Aaron changed the subject and told them all that Pastor Davis, the slain woman's son, had agreed to allow him and Papa Saul to serve as pallbearers at the funeral. He personally really wanted to serve in that capacity because the lady had literally died to save him, but Papa Saul certainly surprised him when he asked if he might be included as well. At any rate, they were both going to be there, perhaps the only Caucasians in an all black service.

Scott said he thought he might also like to attend the funeral. He had been interested in what he'd heard, and he thought he might like to learn more. He asked for and received information about where and when the funeral was to be held, and told Aaron that he and a friend would probably see him there. He also commented that he suspected there would be a lot of other "white folk" making an appearance there. This was the kind of story that people of all shapes and colors would find fascinating.

Scott left the hospital and drove home via the same freeway he and Tony had flown down only two days before, accompanied by a police escort. As he drove, he wondered how all this was going to end. Somehow he knew it was far from over.

When he arrived home, he called Candi and told her the particulars about the funeral and confirmed that they would be going together. They talked for a long time and Scott felt more at ease with her than perhaps he ever had before. He found that strange, because his life was more tangled up right now than it had ever been. He hoped that through all this he could wind up with her. He didn't much care what else happened to him. But how could she ever want him if she found out what he had done, and how could he keep it from her the rest of his life? Even right then, he wanted to pour out his very soul to her. He had been walking a tightrope for about a week now. How long could he keep it up before he lost his balance and fell?

The next day was fairly routine for almost all those whose lives had been impacted by the events of the past week. Bobby was busy with ministry and in preparing for the upcoming funeral. Jamal's ankle was back to nearly full strength and he was looking forward to playing against the Bruins' cross-town rival that night at USC. Marcus was working long hours at the auto salvage yard and thoroughly enjoying himself. Aaron was checking out of the hospital that morning and would be moving in temporarily with Papa Saul. He needed some time to sort things out, and his grandfather needed some help in the store. Carl would need one more day in the hospital, on antibiotics, to make sure his multiple wounds did not become infected, but he was healing nicely and would soon be as good as new. Spiritually, he was already brand new. Candi was optimistic and hopeful about Scott's new interest in spiritual things and was eager to see what might happen at the funeral. Tony was reveling in his newly acquired cash and the lovely thing on whom he had been able to spend a good chunk of it the previous night. He was home free, and didn't have a care in the world.

The only one whose life was still very much up in the air was Scott Graham. He had to get to school and obtain the gun from Tony and hide it somewhere in his Blazer. He had to go to his classes till 1:00, convinced he couldn't afford to skip any that day because he had missed them all on Monday, and he would miss some more on Friday because of the funeral. He had to buy back his father's gold coins and get them, and the gun, back in their rightful places before his parents got home at three. He had to spend time with his parents and lie to them about how well things had gone in their absence, and then he had to beat it back to school to go with his team to Loyola Marymount for their swim meet that night. It was doable, but it was going to be another one of those days with little margin for error.

All went according to plan until early afternoon. Scott met Tony in the parking lot before his first class and took the pistol, wrapped in a paper bag and, without even looking at it, stuffed it under the driver's seat in his Blazer. Tony told him he had taken the liberty of loading the gun so Scott would have one less thing to worry about. He thanked his friend. Loading the gun was something he hadn't even thought about.

He then attended all of his classes, and even managed to pay attention most of the time. Afterwards, he noticed that he had just about enough time to drive downtown and purchase the coins and get home before his parents got there. He was just walking out of his last class, when he heard someone call out, "Excuse me, are you Scott Graham?" He turned and saw two men in suits whom he had never seen before standing to the side, obviously comparing his appearance with that of a picture the taller one held in his hand.

"Yes I am. What can I do for you?" Scott answered, somewhat surprised.

"It will only take a few minutes," the taller one said. He was older and it was obvious that he was the one in charge. "Is there someplace where we can talk?"

"Well, I'm really busy right now, could we make it another time?" Scott knew they had to be police detectives by the way they looked. He knew they would be coming around sooner or later because Aaron would surely have informed them of the names of the people whom he had told about the existence of the safes; and they would have to check out all the leads. He and Tony had even rehearsed the things they would say to them so their stories would not contradict each other. But he never expected them to confront him so soon.

By this time, the other students had cleared the area and the tall one felt he could talk more freely. "We're Los Angeles homicide detectives," he said as both he and the shorter one flipped out impressive looking badges. "I'm Sergeant Spangler and this is Detective Farley. We got this picture of you and your class schedule from the administrative office. It's important that we ask you a few questions, and like I said, it will only take a few minutes."

Scott had mentally prepared for this confrontation, and though he was surprised by their sudden appearance, he wasn't panic-stricken. Actually, he surprised himself by how composed he felt. He might want to give himself up voluntarily some day, but his competitive nature resisted strongly the idea of caving in under pressure. He bent and examined the shields because he thought that was something an unsuspecting, innocent person would do, and then he extended his hand and said, "I'm pleased to meet you both. I'm headed out to the parking lot; could we just talk on the way? What's this all about, if you don't mind me asking?"

It was clear that the detectives were not accustomed to shaking hands with those whom they interrogated, but they took Scott's hand in turn, and Spangler, again taking the lead, said, "That would be fine. We just have a few routine questions in connection with a case we're working on. Do you mind if we record your answers?"

Yes he did mind. He minded even being asked the questions, especially at this particular time. Like the saying goes, he had places to go, things to do, and people to see. But he lied and said, "No problem at all. What do you want to know?" He was lying a lot lately, and he had a suspicion that he wouldn't be in a position to stop anytime soon.

Farley took a small tape recorder out of his pocket and pushed a button on it and pointed it toward Scott. As they began walking on the wide sidewalk toward the parking lot, Spangler said, "State your full name and address for the record please."

Scott did so, and then Spangler asked, "Do you know a certain Aaron Muller?"

"Sure, he's on our swim team. He got shot in a robbery the other day, and I just visited him in the hospital last night."

"Then you're aware of the fact that a woman was killed in the robbery?"

"Yes, Aaron told me all about it. He said she saved his life by stepping in front of him just as the gunman pulled the trigger. She was a very brave woman, and he was one lucky customer."

"Yes, so it seems. Did he also tell you how the gunmen forced the owner to open a hidden safe and took the money out of it?"

"Yeah, he sure did, and he said they were trying to force his grandfather to open another one in the storage room when all the shooting started."

"Had Aaron ever mentioned the existence of those safes to you before last night?"

This was the big question. Scott had known it was coming, and he was prepared to give the answer on which he and Tony had previously agreed, "No sir, I don't think so, not that I recall."

"You don't recall him telling you and some other teammates on a trip to a swim meet about how concerned he was about his grandfather because he didn't trust banks, and that he kept so much money in those safes at his store?"

"Oh, yeah, now that you mention it, it does sound familiar. I had forgotten all about it. Yeah, we were all talking about our parents and how tight they are with their money, and Aaron said something about how eccentric his grandfather was."

"Did he happen to mention where his grandfather's store was located?"

"That I don't remember. I believe it was in the LA area, but I don't think he ever said exactly where it was. I guess from what Aaron said last night, it was up in the MacArthur Park area."

"Yes, and the gunmen knew right where it was and where those safes were too. Only a few family members knew about their existence and what they contained, and they apparently told very few people about them. That's why we're here. We're questioning everyone on the list."

"Yeah, that makes sense. Is there anything else I can do for you, officers?" Scott asked, obviously wanting to conclude the conversation. They were getting close to his vehicle now, and he just remembered about the gun under the seat. If they got suspicious and searched the Blazer, he would be a goner. Not only would they find the gun, but they would also find somewhat over six thousand dollars in a bundle locked in the glove box. He had no excuse for possessing either one of them.

"No, I think that will about do it for now, but we may need to talk to you again in the future. You don't have any plans for leaving the area, do you?"

"Not except for swim meets. Sometimes we go out of town, even out of state, for a meet, but it's only for a day or so at a time."

"That should not present a problem. You may be hearing from us again."

With that, Farley clicked off the tape recorder and put it back in his pocket, they both thanked him and said goodbye, and they turned and walked off in the opposite direction.

Scott breathed a sigh of relief, but he knew it was a long way from being over. As soon as they learned about the Graham yacht at the location where the chase ended, and of Scott and Tony's presence there the next morning (and they were bound to learn about it soon), they would be back with a vengeance.

Scott had even planned to work it into the initial conversation himself so as to disarm them by volunteering the information, thereby appearing innocent, rather than to have them dig it up later and then nail him with it. But such a disclosure would be mind-boggling to the police, and the interview would be greatly prolonged, maybe even transferred down to headquarters, and he just flat didn't have the time for such a delay.

Thus already delayed, Scott was frantic for time. He wanted to screech his tires and drive like Tony had last Sunday night, but he knew he dared not act out of the ordinary with the distinct possibility that Spangler and Farley were still watching him. So he walked calmly to his vehicle and drove casually out of the lot. Even when he got away from the campus, he didn't speed. He could not afford to be pulled over at a time like this.

He made it to Pine Street and to the precious metals dealership with only a minimum of delays. He could still make it home in time if everything went like clockwork. But the clock seemed to stand still when he got inside. There were several people in front of him and he had to take a seat and wait for the next available agent. It was only about ten minutes, but it seemed like hours to Scott when he was finally shown into the tiny office of an agent named Mary Mascarenas by her nameplate on her desk. Scott was glad Silas would not be waiting on him this time. The man would surely have been suspicious of him returning so soon to buy back the coins he had just sold a few days before. Scott had even wanted to go to a different establishment, but he could locate none close enough, and again, he just didn't have time to go elsewhere.

Mary was middle-aged and methodical. She calculated the cost of thirteen American Double Eagles, and rechecked her figures. Then she added in the commission charge, and rechecked the total. Next she filled out several forms and checked them carefully for accuracy. By the time she was ready for Scott to sign, he was ready to explode. She asked him to recheck her figures, but he couldn't have cared less. He signed and counted out fifty-nine one hundred-dollar bills and drummed his fingers on the desk, waiting for her to give him the coins so he could go, but she was not to be rushed.

She excused herself, and after what seemed like another hour, returned with the coins, his change, and a receipt. She insisted on counting out the $38.27 in his presence and had him sign a receipt for it before she would give him the coins. Scott had tried to be patient and pleasant, but that was all gone by this time. He grabbed the container with the coins in it and walked quickly out of her office, barely acknowledging her perfunctory, "Thank you, have a nice day."

It was 2:42 when he glanced at his digital watch. It was another twenty-minute drive to get home, and his parents were due there by three. There just weren't enough minutes left to make it, especially if they happened to be a little early. If they should happen to beat him home, he was all but dead. The first thing Bruce Graham was likely to do would be to check on the presence and condition of his pistol, and he would be sure to check the contents of his safe long before Scott would have a chance to replace the coins. He just simply had to beat them home.

Cops or no cops, he had to make up for lost time. He drove well above the speed limit, weaving in and out of cars on the surface streets, went through one intersection after the light had already turned red, and generally made a menace of himself to all other motorists. He managed to make it to the Long Beach Freeway without hitting anyone or anything, incurring only several long horn blasts and uplifted fists, some with extended middle fingers.

He shot north on the freeway, looking for openings in the traffic and police cars at the same time. Finding several of the former and none of the latter, he made good time for the relatively short distance to the Pacific Coast Highway turnoff.

Having exited the freeway and barreling west on PCH, he was startled by an abrupt ringing in his ears. At first he thought it was a police siren, but then he realized it was his cell phone. It startled him because he hardly ever used it and it almost never rang. It was for emergencies only, and his father would deduct from his allowance any charges on it over the small minimum allowed each month. He hadn't even given out the number to anyone he could think of.

"Oh no," he thought. It had to be his parents. They had beaten him home and not found him there and were trying to track him down. He was sure he was a dead man, but he continued to carry on the ruse. He picked up the phone, pushed a button, and said in a casual voice, "Hello."

"Scott, where are you?" It was his mother. "I called the house and you didn't answer. I was worried about you."

So they weren't home yet. He still had a chance. "I'm on my way home. I got held up at school. Where are you guys?"

"We're on the Harbor Freeway, and we just passed the San Diego. Your father is right behind me, and it looks like we should be home in about ten minutes."

"I'm way ahead of you. I should be home in less than five. I'll be waiting at the door to welcome you home."

Actually, he was more than ten minutes away himself, and the only way he was going to beat them was to pull out all the stops. He said goodbye and hung up the phone and stomped down on the accelerator. The Blazer responded enthusiastically and Scott passed the car in front of him by driving into the lane of oncoming traffic. The car headed right toward him swerved to get out of his way, nearly causing an accident. They narrowly missed each other as they passed, and Scott glanced over at the ashen face of an elderly lady who would probably need her pacemaker readjusted at her next doctor's visit. He swerved back onto his side of the street and didn't look back.

The rest of the drive home was much the same: accelerating, braking, honking, swerving, swearing, sweating, and even a little praying. It must have worked, because he made it through to his turnoff without either crashing or being reined in by the police. He slowed down somewhat as he drove up the familiar streets in Rancho Palos Verdes. Neighbors knew him there, and he didn't need to attract that kind of attention. Police investigators might be talking to some of them soon, and he didn't need them reporting him driving like a maniac the same afternoon they first questioned him.

As he pulled up to the Graham residence, all looked quiet. Scott pulled to the left of the garage under a big cypress tree where he usually parked, leaving the garage for his parents. He grabbed the coins in one hand and the gun from under the seat with the other. He slammed the door shut with his arm and sprinted for the front door. He clamped the gun between his legs and fumbled with his keys, trying to find the right one for the door. Finally, he identified it and managed to get it in the lock and turned the heavy deadbolt.

Once inside, he slammed the door with his foot and, not bothering to lock it again, he ran for his parents' room. He dropped the coins by the door of his father's study and took the gun out of the paper bag as he rounded the corner into their bedroom. He jumped over the corner of the bed and opened the nightstand drawer in one fluid movement. He placed the substitute gun in the same position he remembered the other one being in, and he slammed the drawer shut. As he left the room, he only hoped his dad hadn't memorized the serial number on the gun or its exact location in the drawer, neither of which would have surprised him.

Sweat was now running down his face as Scott snatched up the parcel of coins and burst into his father's study. He pulled open the drawer and retrieved a pen to write down the combination, and then dropped to the carpet under the desk. From the bottom of the drawer, he copied the combination onto the palm of his left hand, pushed the drawer shut, and rolled over to the closet. He slid open the door, pulled back the carpet, lifted the metal cover from the top of the safe, and went to work on the combination.

Just then he heard the muffled sound of the garage door opening. His parents were home and he still had his hand in the cookie jar!

Scott dialed in the remaining two numbers and tried the lever. Mercifully, it turned and the door swung open. He lifted everything straight out and then retrieved the box of coins in the bottom. He opened the box and put the thirteen new coins along with the two he hadn't sold originally in with their fellows, hoping Bruce Graham would not be able to tell the difference. He heard engines shutting down and car doors opening and closing as he replaced everything in the safe. He had no time to make sure it was exactly as it had been before. Maybe all the wonders of the Holy Land had so filled his dad's mind that some of it had crowded out the exact memory of the contents of his safe. Scott certainly hoped so as he closed the lid and spun the dial. He replaced the other things as they were and closed the closet door just as he heard the door from the garage open into the house.

His mother's voice called out, "Yoo hoo, Scott, we're home. Where are you, honey?"

Scott closed the door to his dad's study quietly, thankful that, here in the hall, he was around the corner from the entryway and hidden from his parents' view. Quickly he walked down a few steps and into the hall bathroom. He reached over and flushed the toilet, ran some water and tried to wash the combination numbers off his hand, grabbed a towel for his hands and the sweat on his face, and headed for the front of the house.

"Here I am. I'm afraid you caught me with my pants down," he responded, realizing how true that almost was. He ran around the corner and picked his mother off the floor with a big bear hug. "Welcome home, Mom, I've sure missed you." Florence Graham was an easy woman to pick up. She was almost 5'10", but she weighed less than 130 pounds. She was an attractive lady, with a stylish salt-and-pepper hairdo and a slender face to go along with her figure. After the customary kiss and hug from his mother, he put her down and turned to his father. "You too, Dad. It's good to have you back," he said, extending his hand. There would be no easy picking up of his father, even if Scott had been so inclined, which he wasn't. Bruce Graham was at least two inches taller than Scott and a good fifty pounds heavier. His stern look and his massive shock of prematurely silver hair made him an imposing figure in the family room as well as in the courtroom.

The large attorney took his youngest son's hand and used it to pull him in. He gave him a big hug and patted him several times firmly on his back. Scott was always getting hugs from his mother, but he couldn't remember the last time his ever-proper father had enthusiastically hugged him.

"Boy, it's good to see you, Son," Bruce said as he held Scott out at arm's length to look him over. "Hey, what's that writing on your hand there?" he laughed. "You been cheating on your tests again?"

CHAPTER THIRTEEN

THE SHAKEDOWN

Scott laughed too and said no, someone had swiped his lock from his locker in the gym and he had to replace it. He wrote the new combination on his hand and had left it there for a couple of days till he had it memorized so he wouldn't have to keep looking it up.

That seemed to satisfy his dad, who changed the subject, and they all talked about a dozen different topics over the next few minutes. There were so many other things more deserving of discussion; the matter of a lock combination written on his son's hand was apparently dismissed by the brilliant attorney. On a different day, he would have checked it out thoroughly, probably wanting to write the combination down in his own planner just in case he might ever need to open Scott's locker. That's just the way Bruce Graham's mind worked, but not on this particular occasion, thankfully.

Scott kept his hand turned away from his father's line of sight and breathed a sigh of relief. He had dodged another bullet. He had dodged a lot of bullets lately. He wondered, as he helped carry luggage into his parents' room, how many more he would be able to avoid before one of them nailed him right between the eyes.

As he set a big suitcase down, he noticed his dad reach over and open the drawer to the nightstand and check his handgun. It only took about ten seconds, and it was soon dismissed, as there were many other things to attend to; but had it not been there, Scott knew everything would have started to unravel.

However, he had no time to relax, for in a few minutes, his dad took their passports and some other documents from his travel bag and took them into his study. Without being too obvious, Scott lingered out in the hall to see if he could detect anything out of the ordinary. But his concern was unnecessary. Bruce Graham must have found everything to his satisfaction, because in a couple of minutes, he came out showing no particular interest or concern on his face.

Two more bullets dodged, but that was cutting things much too close for comfort. Scott wondered if things would ever get back to normal where he didn't have to live right on the edge, and his stomach wasn't constantly tied up in knots.

The rest of the evening went without serious incident for Scott and, indeed, for all those involved in the events of the past week. Scott and Tony and their teammates won their meet against Loyola Marymount, but barely so. Aaron's presence was seriously missed. Tony was his usual brilliant self, and Scott more than did his part, but a better team would have beaten them, and they were to face several better teams before the season was over. Coach Englehart was obviously concerned about it, but what could he do? It was hard to expect a kid to swim with a hole in his chest. He feared Aaron might not even be able to return to the team in time for the national meet.

Things looked much more promising for the UCLA basketball team. They dismantled the USC Trojans on their home court. Gone were the demons that had plagued them against Houston the week before, and they played together like a well-oiled machine. Jamal's ankle, taped even tighter by a determined Fred Baker, seemed to give him little difficulty, if any, and he led both teams in scoring, rebounding, and blocked shots. The Kid beat him by two, or he would have had the most assists as well. He played with passion, determined to put the purposefully inferior game as far behind him as possible. The only thing that bothered him was the knowledge that the mob was going to call his number again sometime, and he still couldn't bring himself to accept the idea of throwing another game.

Candi watched Scott's meet, and wanted to go out with him afterwards and find out what had been troubling him so much lately, but she deferred to his parents who hadn't seen him in two weeks, and were not about to share him with her or anyone else that night. She went home by herself, but they did have a good talk on the phone late that night, and she was hopeful again about things working out between them.

Marcus sat in the front row at the USC game, as usual; only this time he thoroughly enjoyed himself. He was working now and feeling better about himself than he had in he couldn't remember when. Jamal was playing like a man possessed, and obviously feeling better about himself too. The difference between this game and the one played last week was so astronomical that it made Marcus think that honesty might indeed be the best policy after all, even if there wasn't any easy money in it.

Aaron checked out of the hospital and moved in with Papa Saul above The Corner Store. The family was beside themselves that Saul would not finally hang up his apron, even after he had been robbed and beaten by thugs, and friends had been shot and killed in the process. Much to their relief, he did agree to empty the sizable contents of the remaining safe and put it in the bank. That was the first thing he and Aaron did together when Aaron got out.

Not only was Aaron going to have to give up his swimming, he had decided to drop out of school altogether, at least until he could figure out what was going on in his life. He had such a sense of divine calling that he couldn't even think of continuing his studies until he settled that issue first. The family disapproved of his actions about as much as they did of Papa Saul's, so the two took solace in one another's company. Aaron added a strong factor of help and security for his grandfather, and Saul's wisdom and simple acceptance provided comfort for his searching grandson.

Bobby didn't attend Jamal's game. He went as often as he could, but that night Bobby had the regular prayer meeting and Bible study at the church. Even if he hadn't, it was doubtful he would have gone to the game. He was still searching his heart about his mother's death and was struggling with how he was going to express his feelings at the funeral on Friday.

Thursday turned out to be an ordinary day for everyone involved, that is, with the exception of Scott and Tony. It seemed Scott, especially, was through having ordinary days. It had been so long since he had one, he couldn't remember what it had felt like.

The day started out ordinarily enough, but halfway through the second hour, both Scott and Tony were called out of their respective classes and told to report to the administrative office. Once there, they were directed to a conference room where detectives Spangler and Farley were waiting for them; only this time, they didn't have that look of casual politeness. Rather, they had the look of two fat cats that had just sprung a trap on a couple of rats.

They had talked to Tony the previous afternoon as well, along with most of the other members of the swim team. They found his story the same as Scott's, and took no particular interest in any of the testimonies. That morning, they were to have scheduled interviews with the dozen or so other people who might have been told by some other family member about the existence of the, by now, infamous safes. That was until Detective Farley came across a piece of information that changed the whole course of their investigation.

Sergeant Spangler was in the captain's office at police headquarters, talking about the Davis case, and about how important it was that they move quickly on it. The media had picked up on the story of the courageous black woman who had sacrificed her life to save a young Jewish man whom she had never met before, and the public was demanding swift and sure justice. While Spangler was assuring Captain Dibbel that they were moving on it with great thoroughness and dispatch, Farley was occupying his time by going over the police report filed by Sergeant Kyle Witherspoon Monday afternoon. Farley saw nothing particularly noteworthy until something caught his attention, and then just jumped right out and grabbed him.

There, on the list of those questioned at the Pacific Terrace Harbor, were names he recognized from another list he had in his briefcase. He quickly retrieved the latter list and compared the two. Sure enough, there they were. The names of Scott Graham and Anthony D'Angelo were on both the lists. They were members of the CSULB swim team, to whom Aaron Muller had told about his concern over the large amount of money kept in his grandfather's safes; and they were also among those questioned at the harbor the morning after the robbery. This was far more than a coincidence. This was something he had to share with his superiors immediately.

Farley interrupted the meeting between Spangler and Captain Dibbel, and received stern looks from both of them until he showed them the duplicate names on the two lists. His superiors were ecstatic, and Dibbel ordered them to get out to the university and put the squeeze on those two punks immediately. Perhaps they would be able to wrap this thing up in time to ensure justice be done, and to elevate the LAPD in the eyes of the public at the same time.

So here they were, looking smug and confident, as Scott and Tony walked cautiously into the room. They were seated and didn't bother to get up or to shake hands with the two young men. "Please take a seat," Spangler said as he motioned to two chairs on the side of the table opposite the detectives.

The friends sat down and gave each other that knowing look, as if to say, "Well, here it comes. Let's see if we can bluff our way out of this mess like we thought we could when we planned it last week."

Spangler continued, "We called you here because we've discovered some very interesting information, and we wanted to give you the chance to explain if you can."

"We'll be happy to help out in any way we can, officer," Tony said.

"Well, you can start by explaining why you two happened to be at the marina on the morning after two gunmen, who fit your general description, drove their getaway car into the Pacific Terrace Harbor last Sunday night; the same gunmen who robbed a grocery store in Los Angeles and killed one woman and severely injured three men; the same gunmen who knew about the existence and location of two hidden safes containing a great deal of money; the same safes that you both admitted hearing Aaron Muller tell about on the way to a swim meet."

Scott spoke up first, "I see how this must appear to you detectives, but I assure you, there is logical explanation. My family has rented a slip at that marina for years. We go down and take our small yacht out quite often. My parents have been out of the country for the past two weeks, and Tony and I have taken the boat out several times while they've been gone. We took her out last Saturday, and we were going to go again on Monday, but the police wouldn't let us because of their investigation. So we went down on Tuesday afternoon and went out for some fishing then. The fact that we were there after the fugitives drove their car into the harbor is not so phenomenal. We're actually there quite a lot."

"Why didn't either of you tell us about your being there yesterday when we questioned you then?"

"Well, you didn't ask, for one thing," Tony answered, a little sarcastically. "I didn't even think about it at the time. You were asking about the safes in Aaron's grandfather's store. How was I supposed to connect that store with a ship in a harbor thirty miles away?"

"You're a college boy, you should be able to figure it out," Farley entered into the conversation for the first time. "The gunmen were young and tall and athletic, like you two. They appeared inexperienced and nervous, like you would have been. The taller one (he looked squarely at Scott) dropped his gun and almost messed his pants when he shot the old lady. I bet that was real traumatic, don't you (still looking straight at Scott)? Then, when they were pursued, they drove straight to the harbor where your boat is docked and dumped their car in the water almost next to it. The gunmen were never seen again, nor was the stolen money, but you two expert swimmers show up on the dock bright and early the next morning. Are you following me okay so far?"

"I know you think you've solved your case here, officers," responded Scott, surprising himself by how much self-control he displayed, especially considering how nervous he felt inside. "But, before you read us our rights and haul us away in handcuffs, I think there's something you ought to be aware of. My father is a prominent defense attorney and I'm a pre-law major myself, so I know a little bit about how all this works; and you have nothing on us. You're trying to scare us into making a confession, but it's not going to happen."

"Oh, I wouldn't call it nothing," Farley shot back. "We have you with the knowledge about the safes, you fit the description of the gunmen to a T, and we have you at the scene of the aborted escape. I wouldn't call that nothing."

"No, you're right it's not nothing, but it's real close. It's true; we did have the opportunity to commit such a crime, but what about a motive? We don't need the money. Our families are wealthy. What possible reason would we have for robbing an old man, killing an old woman, and shooting one of our best friends? And how about some real evidence? Where're the eyewitnesses that can place us at the scene of the crime? Where's the murder weapon? Where's the stolen money? Where're the fingerprints and the blood and hair samples? Where's anything that can link us to this stupid crime, anyway?

"Oh, by the way," Scott thought to add, "have you seen how far it is from where that car went down to the end of the dock down there at the marina? They told us the whole place was lit up by floodlights and crawling with cops that night. You explain to us how we were supposed to have swum all the way from the car to our boat without being seen, and maybe you flatfoots might have the beginning of a case."

"Now don't you get haughty with us, young man," said Spangler, stepping in to calm Scott down, and to rescue Farley from any further embarrassment.

"I'm not the one that started with this haughty crap. You guys were coming in here, accusing us of this gruesome crime with nothing to go on. Check your records. Those cops on the docks checked us out and searched my dad's yacht from top to bottom and didn't find any wet clothes, any guns, or any stolen money. The only things we're guilty of is hearing some information we never solicited about some safes we have no interest in, and being near the spot where the real criminals dumped their getaway vehicle. There's not a court in the land that would dare try us on that so-called evidence. You'd get laughed out of the DA's office if you even tried to get them to consider it, and you know it."

"I suppose you can account for your whereabouts last Sunday night at the time of the robbery?" Spangler asked, trying to change the subject, obviously not making much progress in their present approach.

"Yes, we can," Tony butted in, not wanting to miss out on the fun. "I spent the night with Scott since his folks were out of town, and we went to a movie late that night. I think I still have the ticket stub in my other jacket pocket. We talked to a couple of girls who worked there who I think will remember us. Check it out; we went to that big theater complex over at the Long Beach Mall. Then we drove down to the marina to spend the night on the yacht so we could go fishin' first thing in the morning. We got there around eleven, I guess, and went right to bed. Slept like a rock too. I didn't hear anything until morning."

"Oh, I'll bet you did," said Farley, sarcastically. "By the way, what movie did you see?"

"*Desert Planet*. But it wasn't much good," Tony replied. Then he went on to explain the basic plot of the film.

"That's fine, we don't need a movie review here," Spangler butted in, wanting to end the disastrous interview before any more damage was done. "We'll check out your alibi and examine all the evidence very carefully before we talk again. But believe me, we *will* talk again. Everything we've seen so far points to you two, and if you did do it, we'll find out soon enough. Rookie criminals always screw up somewhere, especially in a botched job like this one. Sooner or later, we'll talk again, and we'll be better prepared next time. And you better have your lawyer daddy standing by, because I've got a feeling you're gonna need him."

The interview ended abruptly, with Spangler dismissing the young men with another warning not to even think about leaving town except to participate in scheduled swim meets. On the way back to class, Scott and Tony agreed they had to talk about what they were going to do next. They couldn't do it right then because there could be someone watching them, so they agreed to meet that afternoon at Starbucks before practice.

Later that morning, Scott met Candi at their usual spot to make plans to attend the funeral together the next day. He had gotten directions to the Antioch Baptist Church in Compton, and he figured it would take only about thirty minutes to get there, but he expected a big crowd to show up, so he suggested they leave before 9:00. She agreed that it would be wise to get there early, so they arranged for Scott to pick her up in front of her dorm at 8:45.

Before they had to go to their next class, Scott told her briefly about the session he and Tony had just had with the two detectives and about the accusations they had made against them. Candi was flabbergasted to think anyone could think such a thing and talked of lodging an official protest or something, but Scott told her about the safes and the marina, and she began to see the problem.

"But you didn't do it!"

"Of course, we didn't do it," Scott lied. But he almost choked on the words. He had lied convincingly to his parents without a problem. He had lied passionately to the police and actually enjoyed it. He had lied so much to others and to himself that he had almost convinced himself that he really hadn't done anything wrong after all. With all that, why was it now so hard to tell a simple lie to Candi? Could it be that he still had hopes of building an open and honest relationship with her?

"They have absolutely no evidence to actually connect us to the crime at all," he continued. "We just happened to hear the wrong information at one time, and to be in the wrong location at another; and since they still haven't located the actual gunmen, they are going after us because of all the pressure on them to solve the case. They'll hound us for a while, but they have no case, and sooner or later, they'll have to leave us alone."

"Is this what's been bothering you over the past week? I've known something was wrong."

"That's part of it, I guess, along with all the other things I told you about. I suppose after awhile it begins to add up. I didn't realize it showed so much."

"Well it does, and it concerns me. I care a lot about you, you big oaf. Seriously, Scott, did you ever think that God might be allowing all these things to happen to get your attention? You know, I mean, to consider your own eternal destiny and all?"

"Believe me, I've thought a lot about that. That's one of the reasons I want to go to that funeral tomorrow. I want to see how this woman's death impacts the lives of those who call themselves born-again Christians. I want to hear what her preacher son has to say about it. If what everybody has been telling me is true, then I should be able to see a real difference in how they handle this as compared to how ordinary people would. Do you know what I'm talking about?"

"Yes I do, and I will be praying God really speaks to your heart through all those people there tomorrow."

After his last class, Scott knew what he must do. Those two detectives were on to them, and they wouldn't leave a stone unturned, as the old saying goes. He and Tony had covered their tracks pretty well, but there was still something that could trip them up if he didn't correct it. The police divers had recovered the shotgun, but that would do them no good because Tony had ground off the serial numbers, and he had wiped it free of any fingerprints after he put his gloves on that fateful night. But they obviously hadn't found the handgun because it was at the bottom of the ocean by now, so they would keep looking for it.

Now that they suspected him and Tony, Scott felt that the police might figure one of them may have used his own gun, or that of his father, in the crime; which was exactly the case. Their next step, he thought, would be for them to check with Bruce Graham and Michael D'Angelo to see if either of them knew of the existence of a Colt .38 Special in their respective households. Scott knew his father would invite the detectives to examine his gun immediately, and to fire it, so he could establish once and for all that it was not, and could not have been, the murder weapon.

That part was all well and good. The ballistics would prove that it was not the gun that had killed Georgia Davis and had wounded Aaron Muller. But Bruce Graham kept meticulous records, and on the registration paper for the pistol, the serial number would not match the one on the gun itself. Those two detectives would most certainly spot the discrepancy, and there would be no rational explanation for it. That would probably not be enough evidence to indict them, but it would confirm their suspicions of them, and they would continue to hound them forever.

Even if the detectives never asked to check the receipt, Scott knew his father would, and when he discovered the discrepancy, he would become suspicious and start snooping around, and no telling what he might find. He might realize it really wasn't his gun after all. He might also notice the missing clothes from Matt's old room, the sunglasses from the junk drawer, and that things were not exactly as they should have been in his floor safe. Scott couldn't afford to let that happen, so it left him little choice. He would have to find that certificate of registration and change the serial number to match the one on the new gun. How he was going to do that, he wasn't quite sure.

He did know, whatever he did, he better do it quickly. Spanky and Fosdick, or whatever their names were, weren't going to waste any time in turning over all the stones they could, especially after the way he and Tony had embarrassed them that morning. Scott knew his father would be at work that afternoon. After being gone two weeks, he would be champing at the bit to get back up to speed at the office. Also, Thursday was the afternoon his mother always went to her Bible study at the church. There was no way she would miss this opportunity to share all her Holy Land experiences with all the other women who hadn't been able to afford the trip. The house would be empty, and that might be his only chance.

As he arrived home, he had time to put his plan together. He first confirmed that his parents were both gone, and then he broke into his father's safe again and looked for the registration for the gun. It wasn't there, so he put everything back just as he had found it, and closed it again. Next, he started going through the large filing cabinet in the corner. Thankfully, it wasn't locked and he didn't have to waste time looking for a hidden key someplace. It still took him a good fifteen minutes to locate the certificate. He finally found it in the third drawer, in a file labeled *home security*.

The certificate itself was printed on an ordinary looking legal sized piece of paper, and fortunately, it was a copy and not the original. Bruce

Graham's office was well equipped, complete with a computer, a printer, a copier, a typewriter, a fax machine, and you name it. Scott figured he had all he needed right there. First, he whited out the serial numbers on the certificate and then made a copy of it on his father's machine. He compared the two documents and decided they were close enough to fool anyone except the most discriminating observer. Then he typed in the serial numbers, which he had jotted down from the new gun in his father's nightstand, in the now blank space on the new copy. Then he made yet another copy of the new document so the typed numbers wouldn't show up as having been added after the fact.

Scott was satisfied with the results. He folded and unfolded it several times to give it the appearance of age. Then he put on some cotton gloves and wiped the paper off with a tissue to remove his fingerprints from it. Unfortunately, he wouldn't be able to add any of his father's, but he figured his dad would put plenty of them on it anyway when he retrieved it from the file later on. The police probably wouldn't check for them anyway, but Scott was determined to be as thorough as possible.

Having finished, he replaced the new copy in the file, and the file in the cabinet, being careful to wipe down everything as he went. He wiped off all the machines he had used as well, and just to be sure, he reopened the safe and wiped off everything he had touched in there too. With everything as print-free as possible, he left the office and went into the bedroom and wiped down the gun, the shells, the shell box, and everything else in and on the nightstand he might have touched.

He retrieved the two pair of cheap sunglasses from his book bag that he had purchased on his way home and replaced them in the junk drawer. Then he sat down on the family room couch to think of what else he could do to eliminate any further suspicion, or worse yet, incrimination. The only thing he could think of was the clothes and boots missing from Matt's room. Now he wished he had never taken them in the first place, but it had seemed so logical at the time. There had been no reason to buy the stuff he needed for a biker outfit when he could simply borrow it for a day, and then put it right back. That, of course, had been before the botched robbery, the car chase, the midnight swim, and the deep-six burial at sea of all Matt's clothes.

Scott got up and went out into the garage and brought in some flattened storage boxes. He assembled them and put all the remaining things from Matt's room in them. Then he carried the boxes out to the old stable/storage shed, and stacked them alongside his mother's boxes of Christmas decorations. He went back in the house and moved a bunch of his summer clothes into the now-vacant room. His closet really had been overcrowded, and he would simply tell his mom he had made the switch to give him more room for his clothes. By the time Matt ever came to get his stuff, if he ever did, this present incident would have been long forgotten.

With that done, Scott sat again and tried to think if he had overlooked anything. Finally he decided he had done about all he could do. It seemed funny, having so much time to think and take action. Up to this point, he had been forced to make split-second decisions with either people chasing him, watching him, questioning him, or about to burst in on him. Hopefully, those days were behind him now, but he couldn't shake the feeling that this was only a temporary lull in the storm.

Later that afternoon at Starbucks on the Pacific Coast Highway, Scott told Tony of the precautions he had taken, and asked his friend to think if there was anything else they were overlooking.

"Scott, you're amazing," Tony said. "I never would have thought of all that stuff, let alone come up with anything else. And the way you tore into those cops was classic. I was about to panic, but you handled them like a pro. They'll think twice before they call us in again. You stick with that pre-law major, kiddo, you're a natural-born defense attorney."

"Thanks, Tony, maybe I will. Those guys made me mad. They had every reason to suspect us, but they were so rude and cocky and condescending about the way they thought they had us dead to rights, I just felt like I needed to sorta let the air out of their sails. But they're not going to go away. We're the only game in town. No bodies are going to wash up on the beach, and no one else is going to turn himself in, so you can bet that they will do everything they can to pin this thing on us."

"Yeah, I know. What do you think we should do now?"

"Well, we need to tell as many people as we can what's happening, starting with our parents. They'll find out soon enough anyway, and they need to hear it from us rather than when the police show up at our front doors. We need to act as casual about it as we can, like we can't believe the cops actually think we may have had something to do with it. Let's tell them that we heard about the safes and that we were at the marina and everything; well, everything we *can* tell them anyway, so it will seem like we have nothing to hide."

"Yeah, I guess you're right, but my old man is gonna hit the ceiling."

"So's mine, at first anyway, but if we do this right, we'll come out looking like the innocent victims of police harassment rather than the guilty lowlifes that we really are. I've already told Candi, and she bought my story completely. I think my parents will too. I know my mom will, right away; but my dad may be a little harder to convince. He never really stops being an attorney."

"Yeah, I know what you mean. My old man never stops figuring. It doesn't matter whether he's at work or at home. And he's going to have to figure this thing out completely, but in the end, there just isn't any real evidence out there to say we did it. I'm sure he'll come around."

"There's just one other thing maybe I ought to let you know about."

"What's that?" Tony said, skeptically, not liking the tone of Scott's voice.

"Well, Candi and I are going to go to the lady's funeral tomorrow, and I thought you ought to know about it."

"Hey, I don't think that's such a good idea, Scott. You know what they say about a killer always returning to the scene of the crime. Well, this is almost the same thing. I heard that cops always hang around the funerals of victims to see if they can spot some suspicious character that just might be the killer coming to check up on his work or something. That's the last place I'm gonna be tomorrow."

"Yeah, I know, but it's not like I've got no business there. Aaron is a good friend, and he got shot with the same bullet that killed that Mrs. Davis. He told me he's going to be one of her pallbearers, and he thought it was great when I told him I was planning to go to the funeral."

"Okay, but it could wind up being your funeral too, or should I say, *our funeral*. Remember, if one of us screws up, he takes the other one down with him. We're kinda joined at the hip on this deal."

"I hear you, man. I'll be careful. But look at it this way. If those two cops are there, they'll see that I'm not intimidated by them. If a guilty guy were to be shaken down by the cops over a murder, he would never dare show up at the funeral the next day. My presence there may cause those two to have second thoughts about our guilt."

CHAPTER FOURTEEN

THE FUNERAL

The sun rose on Friday morning to be greeted by a flock of sheep-like clouds being herded in from the west, almost as though they were running ahead of the front to keep from getting wet in the storm that would surely follow. Bobby Davis looked up at the sky as he walked out of his house for the short drive to the church. "I hope the rain holds off until after the funeral," he said to himself as he got into the car.

Jamal made arrangements to be gone all day, but he told his coach he might be back in time for practice that evening. Coach Barnes encouraged him to make it if he could because they had an important game against UNLV the next night, and there were some things he really wanted the team to work on that afternoon. But he told him to be there for his family, and if he couldn't make it back, not to worry about it.

Marcus didn't even need to ask for the day off. Gil closed down the whole yard till afternoon so everybody could go to the funeral. He even offered Marcus a ride if he needed one, but he declined graciously, saying Jamal was going to stop by his apartment and take him to the church.

Papa Saul, uncharacteristically for him, closed up shop too. He hung a sign on the door, and he and Aaron got in Saul's Chevy panel truck that he used to deliver groceries in forty years before, and headed out for the funeral. Normally, Aaron would have driven, but his chest was still too sore. Saul had to take Advil quite often to quiet his throbbing head, but even with that, he was in better shape than his grandson. It would take them longer because he refused to drive on the freeways, but he knew the truck like an old friend, and they were getting an early start.

Carl Singleton was feeling remarkably well for a fellow who had just gotten out of the hospital. He too was really sore, but everything worked, and he was thrilled to be alive. Sarah helped steady him down the stairs, and Tamika held the door as his wife helped him ease into the passenger seat of their new Honda Accord. Tamika hopped in the back, and Sarah drove them to the Antioch Baptist Church in Compton. It would be strange going to that familiar place without seeing Grandma Georgia's face smiling back at them from her place in the choir.

The church had already begun to fill when Scott and Candi walked in the front door at 9:25. They had to park down the street because the church lot was already full when they got there. They took a little commemorative folder from an usher as they came in, and found their seats about two-thirds of the way back on the left side. A large black lady with a beautiful countenance was playing the organ, and folks were talking quietly and greeting one another as they filed into the church. The casket was already positioned just in front of the pulpit. It was closed and a large floral spray covered the top of it. Literally dozens of other flower arrangements and potted plants surrounded the casket on either side.

By 9:45, every seat was taken except for a small section in the very front that had been roped off. Ushers were setting up extra chairs down the aisles and across the back. Many people had to stand in the back and out into the foyer, and some latecomers were not able to get into the building at all. Sergeant Spangler and Detective Farley were among those standing in the back. There were other police officers in attendance as well, along with several members of the press and representatives from city hall. The sanctuary was designed to seat 300 people, but there were well over 500 there that morning. The fire marshal would not have liked it, but no one was about to ask anyone to leave.

Right at ten o'clock, the outer doors were closed and no one else was allowed in. The organist began to play *Amazing Grace,* and the pallbearers and the rest of the family were escorted in by one of the employees of the funeral home, and they took their seats in the section up front that had been reserved for them. The last one in was Pastor Bobby Davis, dressed in his best navy blue suit, the one his mother had bought for him a couple of years before just for occasions such as this. He walked up onto the platform and took his place in his customary seat to the right of and behind the pulpit.

As the song ended, he walked to the pulpit and welcomed everyone. He asked that the members of the press not take flash pictures or walk about during the service. Then he read Psalm 90, in which Moses reminds the faithful how brief their lives really are, and tells them, among other things, to number their days, and to apply their hearts unto wisdom. Then he prayed a simple, but eloquent and heartfelt prayer, thanking God, the giver and sustainer of life, for loaning Georgia Davis to them for more than the three-score and ten years, which was the length of time Moses had said we might expect to live. He thanked God that her journey on earth was over now and she had gone home to be with her blessed Savior. He concluded his prayer by asking God to open the eyes of all those present to the great truth of His word and the glory of His presence. Then he thanked Him in Jesus' name, and sat down.

Next, Zelma Parsons, the dear woman who first invited Georgia to church, came to the pulpit and began to sing. She made no introductory remarks, and had no musical accompaniment. She just began to sing, in that deep rich, Mahalia Jackson/Ethel Waters kind of voice that cannot be taught or learned, the kind of voice God imparts to certain African-American women for the sole purpose of glorifying His name. She began softly to sing about *Sweet Beulah Land;* that blessed place of rest and comfort waiting for the weary pilgrim at the end of his journey.

I'm kind of homesick for a country, to which I've never been before;
No sad goodbyes will there be spoken, for time won't matter anymore.

She took her time, holding the notes, pouring emotion and conviction into every word. Gradually she began to increase, not the tempo, but the intensity, until one would believe she were actually standing in His presence in spiritual ecstasy. There wasn't a person in attendance that remained unmoved. Many were openly weeping, and even street-hardened policemen fought to hold back the tears. There was something very real about the hope Zelma conveyed as she sang, almost as though she had already seen heaven and longed to return.

Beulah Land, I'm longing for you, and someday on thee I'll stand;
Where my home shall be eternal—Beulah Land, sweet Beulah Land.

When she finished, she looked down at the casket before her and smiled, nodding knowingly, and then she stepped down from the platform and took her seat on the front row. It took Pastor Bobby some time to regain his own composure before he once again came to the pulpit. He thanked Zelma and commented on how much his mother loved her and how much her friendship had meant to her. Then he began to share the story of the life of Georgia Davis.

That part of a funeral was normally called the obituary, but Bobby's version would hardly qualify. An obituary was usually a lengthy list of statistics, delivered in a routine fashion, often by someone who didn't even know the deceased personally. But Bobby shared the life of his mother with the congregation in an intimate and personal way. He relived with them her struggles and her strengths, her trials and her triumphs, those whom she had loved and subsequently lost, and especially, what had led to her spiritual conversion and the dramatic transformation that had taken place in her life.

During his presentation, the people alternately laughed and cried and nodded their heads in recognition and confirmation and, as is characteristic of most black congregations, many people voiced their assent audibly. Phrases like, "Amen," "That's right," "Preach it," "C'mon," and an assortment of various others, could be heard circulating freely throughout the sanctuary.

When Bobby had finished his personalized version of the obituary, he sat down again, and selected members of the choir filed in through a side door and took their places on the platform. Brother Andrews, their director, stepped up to lead them, and as he did, others also took their places at the piano and organ, while still others picked up various other musical instruments. What followed was a very lively and very customized version of *When We All Get To Heaven*.

People in the audience began to tap their feet and clap their hands. Many stood and raised their hands and swayed back and forth. Visitors, not accustomed to this type of worship, were stunned. Most thought such a display of enthusiasm and unabashed joy to be totally out of place at a funeral. And, indeed, the contrast between the two songs couldn't have been greater, but they were both received naturally by the congregation, and with equal acceptance and sincerity. The combination of sadness and joy seemed to them to be both fitting and welcome.

When the choir finished, the congregation broke into spontaneous applause and shouts of "Glory!" and "Hallelujah!" It took some time for the singers and musicians to clear the platform area and for the congregation to settle down and resume their seats. Bobby came again to the pulpit and thanked the choir for their performance and encouraged the people to let the joy of the Lord be their strength. This was followed by still more applause and shouts of praise and thanksgiving.

When order was again restored, Bobby opened the service up for those in attendance to share from their own experiences the special ways in which Georgia Davis had impacted their lives. Two ushers carried wireless microphones up and down the aisles to assist those who spoke so everyone could hear their testimonies. One after another stood and told of incidents in their memories where Georgia had blessed them, helped them, amused them, and inspired them. The congregation again affirmed the accounts with audible expressions of confirmation and praise. The last two to speak had the most profound impact of all.

The first of the two came from Carl Singleton, who stood and fought back tears as he told of what she had meant to him. Though not related officially, she had accepted him and treated him as though he were her own grandson. He had seen Christ modeled in her life, and being around her had brought him to the conclusion that what he had wasn't genuine Christianity. He had been wounded in the same holdup that had resulted in her death, and he had been sure that he was going to die. When his life was spared, he realized he had been given a second chance. He was determined to find the kind of faith she had modeled, and one that would equip him to face death confidently when it did actually come. Pastor Bobby had shared the gospel with him in the hospital and he had accepted Jesus Christ as his own personal Savior. Now he knew he would go to heaven when he died, and he owed a great debt of gratitude to Georgia Davis for helping him to come to salvation.

The last testimonial of the morning came from an unexpected source. Aaron Muller stood and took the microphone from Carl and turned to face the congregation. He confessed that he hadn't known Georgia Davis at all; he had only met her minutes before she died; yet he owed more to her than to anyone else in the world, with the possible exception of his mother. His mother had given him life originally through the suffering of labor and the pain of delivery; but Georgia had given his life back to him through sacrificing her own life for his. For in that store, the gunman had his pistol aimed squarely at Aaron's heart; but at the last instant, Georgia stepped between the two of them. When the shooting started elsewhere, the gun went off, he thought involuntarily, and the bullet tore through her body before it got to his. But by then, it was nearly spent, and it lodged in his chest, coming to rest up against his own heart.

At this point, Aaron choked up and had to pause until he could regain his composure. A hush fell over the audience, and not a sound could be heard, with the exception of an occasional sniffing or blowing of a nose. Aaron concluded by saying he didn't know why she had done what she did. He was much younger than she and of a different gender. He was of a different race and a different religion. They were perfect strangers, with almost nothing in common, yet she had laid down her life for him. Perhaps he would never understand it, but he stood alive before them that day as the result of the sovereign will of God and the unselfish act of one of his servants. Fighting to hold back the tears, he thanked God, he thanked the family, and looking at the flower draped casket, he thanked Georgia Davis.

Then he broke into tears, handed the microphone back to the usher, and sat down.

Virtually no one in attendance was left unmoved. Most of them were also in tears by that time. Papa Saul, himself visibly moved and shaken, put his arm around his grandson's shoulder and gave him a gentle hug. Jamal, who was sitting on the other side of Aaron, reached over and took his hand and squeezed it hard. Through his own tears, he smiled and thanked him for what he had said. He wanted to pick him up and hug him, but he thought it probably wouldn't be appropriate at that time. Besides, with a gunshot wound in his chest, Aaron probably wouldn't have appreciated it much either.

Eighteen rows back, Scott Graham had lost complete control. He had wept more in the past week than he had in the previous ten years. He had his head buried in his hands and his shoulders shook with his sobs. His tears came from a combination of emotions that normally couldn't occur simultaneously: sadness, joy, guilt, and amazement . . . all at the same time.

Candi was also moved by what Carl, and especially by what Aaron, had said, but not to the extent that Scott was. She had never seen him like this, and just for an instant, the thought of his possible involvement in the robbery started to creep into her consciousness, but she quickly drove it away. But it didn't really go away. It just ducked below the level of conscious thought, to await a more opportune time to resurface and file a petition to be heard.

His behavior did not go unnoticed by Myron Spangler and Theo Farley either. From their vantage point in the back of the room, the two detectives had spotted Scott earlier, and they had been watching him carefully throughout the service. They paid particular notice to his present reaction to Aaron's testimony about the shooting of himself and Mrs. Davis. To them, Scott's behavior had guilt written all over it.

Rev. Bobby Davis stepped once again to the pulpit. This was the time when he was expected to tie things together, to put everything into proper perspective. This was his unique opportunity to tell hundreds of people what single thing had made the difference in his mother's life, the unique ingredient that had transformed her life and set her apart from so many others present in the building. He was nervous, but not intimidated. He had prayed for the wisdom to know what to say and for the strength with which to say it, and he felt God's Spirit enabling him in both areas.

Even as Bobby opened his Bible and prepared to deliver his message, Saul Frieberg quietly reached inside his suit pocket and placed some tiny earphones in his ears. Then he reached back inside his pocket and located the switch that turned on the small transistor radio he had placed there. He had pre-tuned it to a classical music station and had turned the volume up about as loud as it would go. He knew what was coming and he wanted no part of it. He had loved that old woman and he wanted to be there to honor her, but he had never allowed her to preach at him while she was alive, and he wasn't about to allow her son to do so after she was gone. He had been born and raised a devout Jew and he planned to die as one. He didn't want any passionate Baptist preacher placing any erroneous thoughts in his head. He smiled and looked attentive enough, but heard not a single word that followed.

Bobby cleared his throat and began, "Thank you all for your kind words of appreciation and tribute. If my mother had been present to hear all the nice things you said, she would probably have asked me who it was everybody was talking about." That brought a laugh and eased some of the tension and emotion that had been building up. He continued, "Georgia Davis never thought of herself as a great woman, or even a particularly good woman. She was well aware of her faults and shortcomings. I'm confident she's in heaven this morning, but not because she spent a lifetime doing all the good things you folks here have been talking about. She's in heaven today because she had a personal encounter with Jesus Christ less than ten years ago that transformed her life here on earth and changed her eternal destiny."

Bobby picked up his well-worn King James Version of the Bible and said, "Let me share with you a passage that was one of my mother's favorites. It's found in 1 John 5:11–13." Then he began to read:

> *And this is the record, that God hath given to us eternal life; and this life is in his Son. He that hath the Son hath life; and he that hath not the Son of God hath not life. These things have I written unto you that believe on the name of the Son of God; that ye may know that ye have eternal life.*

Bobby used the KJV, not because it was the easiest to understand, because it wasn't. In fact, it had been hard for him at first to decipher its archaic language. But it had been the version Rev. Wilcox had used for over forty years at the Antioch Baptist Church, and his people weren't comfortable with anything else. So Bobby always used it in the pulpit, and he thought it fitting. He didn't think reading from God's sacred book should necessarily sound like it was coming from the *Reader's Digest* or this week's issue of the *TV Guide*. However, he did have a couple of other versions in his office, to which he often referred as he studied.

"Georgia Davis," Bobby continued, "was baptized, joined the church, sang in the choir, paid her tithes and offerings, read her Bible and prayed daily, and did all sorts of good deeds, but that's not why she has eternal life. You see folks, good people don't go to heaven. Oh, I suppose they would, if there really were any good people. But Paul tells us in Romans that, '*For all have sinned and come short of the glory of God.*' The only ones who do go to heaven are the ones who admit that they are sinners and who accept God's free gift of eternal life.

"Don't ask me why He chose to love us undeserving sinners, but He did. And He sent His Son to die on the cross to pay for those sins so we wouldn't have to. Then He raised Him from the dead to provide life and righteousness as a free gift for all those who would humble themselves and accept it by faith. John tells us that, '*As many as received Him, to them gave He power to become the sons of God, even to them that believe on His name.*'

"Now going to heaven isn't a matter of being good enough. It's simply a matter of admitting you can never be good enough by yourself, and accepting by faith God's gift of righteousness, which He makes available to those undeserving sinners who put their total trust in His Son. Paul puts it this way in the Book of Romans, '*But to him that worketh not, but believeth on him that justifieth the ungodly, his faith is counted for righteousness.*'"

As Bobby continued to zero in on the fact that everyone was a sinner, that Jesus had died to pay the penalty for their sin, and that people needed to accept Him personally in order to be saved, he encountered mixed reactions. Most of the people were members or friends of the church and were in complete agreement with him. They expressed their agreement vocally and encouraged their pastor to tell them more. But for others who were not of his persuasion, the atmosphere was becoming tense. Some were coming under conviction of their own sin and their resulting estrangement from God, while others were becoming resentful that the pastor would use this sensitive occasion to try to foist his religion on them.

Both Jamal Davis and Scott Graham were genuinely moved by the clear presentation of the gospel, and were becoming more and more convinced of their need to do something about it. Aaron Muller and Marcus Davis were among those who were becoming uncomfortable and upset. Aaron knew what Rev. Davis was saying couldn't be true because Jesus wasn't the Messiah, nor was he the Son of God. He could not possibly be the Savior of the world. Marcus was becoming resentful because he wasn't ready to deal with his selfish, indulgent lifestyle, and he didn't want anyone, even his father, bringing the subject up.

Bobby began to wrap up his message by, once again, concentrating on the effect the gospel message had made in the life of his mother. "Life had not been easy for my mother. After very short marriages, she lost both her husbands in death. She had to work hard to make ends meet, and I didn't help matters. I turned to the streets and to a life of crime, bringing shame and reproach upon her gallant efforts to establish a decent life for the two of us. My wife's fatal illness brought my mother to the point where she had no answers and desperately needed help. She was directed to the church and to God, and both she and my dear Tasha trusted Jesus Christ as their own personal Lord and Savior. That alone is what transformed both of their lives and guaranteed them a place in heaven when they died. I can only imagine the great reunion they're having up there right now.

"I was a profane, thieving, drug dealing criminal, doing time in prison when they came to Christ, and it was their testimony to me and their prayers in my behalf that broke down the barriers in my own heart, and eventually brought about my own conversion. I stand before you today, a different man, because the Jesus my Mama shared with me has changed my life. He laid down His life for me, that my life and soul might be spared. John's gospel tells us that, *'Greater love hath no man than this, that a man lay down his life for his friends.'* Christ demonstrated his love for me when he laid down His life for me on the Cross.

"There's a young man here this morning who is alive today because Georgia Davis laid down her life for him. She did not hesitate to do so because his life was deemed more precious to her than her own. She was just simply following in her Savior's footsteps. She took a bullet that was intended for someone else. Jesus took God's wrath that was intended for all of us. She became the savior of one man's physical life. Jesus became the Savior of the spiritual life of all who will believe on Him.

"My mother would not have wanted her sacrifice to have been in vain. Young man, realize the gift you have been given, and live a life worthy of the sacrifice that has been made in your behalf. People, Jesus does not want His sacrifice to be in vain either. Again John's gospel tells us, *'He came unto his own, but his own received him not. But to as many as received him, to them gave he the power to become the sons of God, even to them that believe on his name.'* Don't be like those unbelieving Jews who rejected His love and crucified Him. Instead, be one of those who receives Him and believes on Him to the saving of your soul. He will forgive all your sins, adopt you into His family, impart all of Christ's life and righteousness to you, and prepare a place for you in heaven when you die.

"You may be out there right now wishing I would get this over with so you can get back to whatever you would normally be doing this Friday morning. You figure you have plenty of time to consider spiritual things later on, right now you just want to get on with your lives. Well, I'm asking you to consider this one fact, and then I'm through. Last Sunday morning the most pressing items on the mind of Georgia Davis were: what could she take to ease her arthritis pain, and what was she going to plan for dinner that afternoon. She had no inkling that she would be called to stand before God before the day was over. Friends, none of us knows when his number might come up. We do know this, however. The Bible says, '*It is appointed unto man once to die, but after this the judgment.*' Where would you spend eternity if today were to be that appointed day for you?

"Now, I know what some of you are thinking. You're thinking you're young and healthy and careful. Your odds of living are overwhelmingly greater than your odds of dying anytime soon, so you're willing to take your chances. Well, consider this. Jesus could come for His church any day now. The temple is nearly completed in Jerusalem right now. The United States of Europe has become the world's greatest superpower. And their laser implanted identification number is all set to replace credit cards entirely. If you know Bible prophecy at all, you know these signs and others all point to the imminent return of Jesus Christ. If you are one of His children when that happens, He will take you home to be with Him in heaven, but if you're not, you will be left here to go through hell on earth during the coming tribulation period. And if you don't accept Him now, you'll most surely perish during those terrible days to come."

As Pastor Bobby wrapped up his message and prepared to offer his closing prayer, his son Jamal was in tears. His father had systematically dismantled every excuse he had ever held for not receiving Christ as his own personal Savior. He felt an overwhelming force drawing him to abandon all excuses and cry out to God for mercy and grace, and to place his confidence once and for all in the one who had loved him and had given Himself for him.

Scott Graham felt a similar conviction, but he fought against it. There was no way he could profess to become a Christian now. He was a thief and a killer. He didn't believe God could forgive him today, and he was positive that the Davis family never would be able to. No, he couldn't possibly make that decision now, and he wasn't really very hopeful about ever being able to do so.

As Bobby was praying to God in closing, he paused to address those in the building. He encouraged them to join with him and pray silently as he led them in a prayer of faith. He then proceeded to confess sin and to ask God for forgiveness. He led them to receive Jesus Christ into their hearts and lives and to accept the free gift of eternal life through faith in His death, burial, and resurrection in their behalf.

Virtually everyone gathered there, saved and unsaved alike, repeated, almost automatically, the words in their minds as Bobby slowly spoke them audibly. But before He said amen, Bobby paused and asked those who had been serious about their commitment to keep their heads bowed and their eyes closed, but to raise their hands so that he could see them. He lost all the compliant participants right there. To follow along silently in a sympathetic prayer was one thing, but to publicly profess faith in Christ was quite another. Nevertheless, many hands were raised. The first hand up, and unmistakably visible in the front row, was that of Jamal Davis. He sat with his head raised and his gaze fixed on the face of his father, with a smile on his face and tears in his eyes. He was through playing games. His mind was made up. He had chosen that day whom he would serve for the rest of his life.

Scott Graham had repeated the words of Bobby's prayer in his mind and wanted them to be serious, but he could not bring himself to raise his hand. He had much too much garbage still in his life to be taking that stand right then. Candi would almost surely notice if he were to do so, and she would begin to respond to him as a true believer. He would be delighted to receive her unqualified love and affection, but he could not accept it under such false pretenses. He knew he had not made a complete commitment to Christ, and he couldn't allow her to think that he had.

What could even be worse was the fact that the pastor would surely see his hand as well, and he might even come up to him afterward and congratulate him on his decision. How would he ever be able to respond to such an overture? "Oh, yes, Pastor, I received your Jesus and killed your mother all in the same week, praise the Lord." Somehow that just didn't ring with authenticity.

Aaron wasn't about to raise his hand. No way was he going to trust in someone who was obviously an impostor, but he was fascinated with what Bobby had said about the signs of the end of the age and the coming of the Messiah. This preacher was obviously misguided about the identity of the Messiah, but he might be right on as to the proximity of His coming. Papa Saul wasn't inclined to raise his hand either, primarily because he hadn't heard a word of Bobby's message, and had no idea what was being asked of the congregation.

Marcus folded his arms tightly to keep them from betraying him by one of them raising itself involuntarily. He knew if he were ever to make such a commitment, it would be an unconditional one, and he wasn't anywhere near ready to give up his accustomed lifestyle and to start living the life of a committed Christian.

Bobby finished his prayer and said amen. He encouraged those who had prayed to receive Christ to tell someone right away what they had done, and to find a good church where they could begin to grow as Christians. He then thanked everyone for coming, and invited them to proceed to the cemetery for the graveside service, which would follow immediately.

As he stepped down from the platform to join the rest of the pallbearers in the front row, representatives from the funeral home came forward to open the casket and to direct the people to file by in front of it to pay their last respects.

Jamal moved forward to meet his father as he approached and gave him a big bear hug. "I've been playing games with you and with the Lord," he said through his tears, "but not anymore. I'm dead serious, Dad. I received Christ as my Savior just now, and I plan to live for Him for the rest of my life. I want you and Grandma to be proud of me for the right reasons."

Bobby hugged his younger son tightly, and he too was choked up with emotion. He told Jamal that he was never more proud of him anytime in his life, and he figured his mother and grandmother were turning handsprings in their brand new bodies in heaven, right then.

Marcus witnessed the exchange between his father and his brother, but he purposefully looked back toward the front of the church. He pretended to be watching the crowd file by the casket, but he was wrestling with his emotions inside. On the one hand, he was happy for Jamal. He had been a bad influence in his younger brother's life, and he was relieved that Jamal had gotten saved before it was too late. On the other hand, he had been convinced that it was already too late for him, and witnessing his brother's conversion only made him feel that much more guilty about his own hopeless condition. He couldn't wait for the building to clear so he could get away from the present heat of conviction he was feeling.

Aaron and his grandfather were, for the most part, unmoved. Aaron felt sympathy for the family, but he was still firm in his conviction that they were all misinformed about the person of this Jesus of Nazareth, and that their faith, though sincere, was clearly misplaced. Papa Saul had just now turned off his radio and removed the earphones from his ears and was trying to make the transition from Mozart to memorial service without appearing too conspicuous.

Candace Mercer was watching the face of Scott Graham closely to see if she could read what was going on inside him. He had obviously been moved with emotion throughout the service. One would have thought he must have had a connection with the family closer than that of a friend of the young man who had been wounded at the time of Mrs. Davis' death. Candi had peeked and seen that Scott hadn't raised his hand at the invitation of Pastor Davis, but she sensed that he had wanted too. So, what was going on inside the heart of this young man she had grown to love, but had miserably failed to understand?

As the crowd finally cleared the building, the attendants from the funeral home closed the casket, cleared the flowers and had them transported to the gravesite, and directed the pallbearers to transport the casket from the cart, down the steps, and into the back of the waiting hearse. This they were able to do with a minimum of difficulty, in spite of the fact that three of their number were still in a weakened condition, recovering from their recent injuries.

Most of the crowd had already begun to find their way back to their respective homes or jobs, but a good number retreated to their automobiles and proceeded to follow the funeral home vehicles to the nearby cemetery. Among them were the people from the media, looking for a special observation or photo shot that would give their particular story an edge that none of the others would be able to capture. Also present were Detectives Spangler and Farley. They, like the media people, had forced themselves not to pay any serious heed to Pastor Davis' message, feeling the necessity of maintaining their objectivity. They were at the gravesite for one purpose only. They wanted to see if they could read guilt written across the face of Scott Graham. They had already decided that he and the D'Angelo boy were guilty, but they were going to need all the help they could get in gathering any hard evidence against them.

Scott and Candi were there, having driven pretty much in silence from the church. Scott said he wanted to speak to Aaron and to Pastor Davis personally, and hadn't had the opportunity to do so after the congested church service. In reality, Scott had been fascinated by what the pastor had said in the previous service, and didn't want to miss out on anything he might say at the gravesite that might help bring some clarity to his troubled mind.

The sky was overcast by now, and a stiff breeze from the west was assisting a few remaining dry leaves as they played tag across the manicured lawns of the cemetery. Rain could not be far behind. The crowd gathering under and around the green canopy covering the prepared gravesite near the back of the cemetery was much smaller than the one that had been packed inside the church earlier. The weather was not cold, in the true sense of the word, but the chill in the air and the threat of rain gave everyone the sense of needing to expedite matters. There would be no song singing or long eulogizing at this service.

The pallbearers placed the casket on the metal stand over the open grave and, with the exception of Pastor Bobby, took their seats in the first row of chairs set up under the canopy. Bobby took his place with his open Bible at the head of the casket. Elderly ladies from the church sat in the only other row behind the pallbearers, and the rest of the mourners gathered around them in a semicircle. At the very outside of the gathering stood the people from the media, the police detectives, and Scott and Candi.

Scott couldn't help thinking how the funeral people had gone to such great lengths to mask the reality of death. The grave had been lined with a concrete vault and the mouth of it had been covered with a green draped stand, on which the casket had been placed. The grave itself had been completely camouflaged. Even the mound of earth, freshly dug from it, was covered with what looked like green carpeting. The casket was constructed of an attractive polished bronze metal and, once again, covered with the beautiful floral spray. Everything was neat and clean and proper. But the body inside was still just as dead as it would have been had it been resting in a pine box, ready to be lowered into a naked grave and covered over by loved ones, manning the shovels themselves. Somehow, Scott thought, funerals in the old days were more honest. But then, how could he criticize others for their lack of candor? Here he was, pretending to be nothing more than a concerned loved one of the deceased, when all the time he was her killer, the one who had, alone, caused the whole bloody mess in the first place.

Bobby wasted no time. As soon as everyone had gathered around, he began by thanking them again for coming and reminding them of why they were there. They were going to commit the body of his mother into the grave, a cold and dark and inhospitable place. But they were doing so without the hopeless despair experienced by others in similar circumstances. He reminded them that the Bible gave them every reason to have confidence, even at a time such as this. He began to read from the passage in 1 Thessalonians 4:13–18 that he had previously selected. This time, he read from a more modern version because it was so much easier to understand.

The passage spoke words of comfort to the saints whose loved ones had died. Bobby then went on to explain that the apostle Paul's words clearly taught that Georgia Davis was already with the Lord and they were only placing her discarded shell into the grave. When the Lord returned, her body would be resurrected and glorified and she would be reunited with it in the air. He also said those who were believers and alive on the earth at the time of the Lord's glorious return would be instantly transformed. They would then be caught up into the air to be united with the Lord and with all the saints who had gone on before. This was commonly called "the rapture of the church."

He concluded by saying once again that all the evidence of biblical prophecy and current events pointed to an imminent return of the Lord. This cataclysmic event could well take place in the very near future. He challenged them all to examine their own hearts and make sure they were indeed saved, and that they would be ready to go to be with the Lord when he called His children home. He said as far as he was concerned, his mother had just laid down for a good night's rest, and he would look forward to seeing her in the morning, that great resurrection morning.

In conclusion, he led the people once again in prayer, thanking God for His promises of resurrection and life, and committing the body of his mother to the grave to await the sure and soon return of her Lord and Savior Jesus Christ. He thanked Him in Jesus' name and said amen. He again expressed his appreciation to all the people for their attendance and for their prayers for himself and his sons. They were all invited back to the church social hall for lunch prepared by the good ladies of the congregation.

With the service concluded, people were inclined to tarry and visit with the family and with one another, but it was as though God had approved of everything His servant had said and done, and He pronounced the final benediction Himself. A bolt of lightning split the leaden sky, and a clap of thunder shook the barren trees. Almost instantly, drops of rain began to rattle off the metal roof of the canopy and to dance on the asphalt of the pavement. People were sent scurrying to their cars and, much more abruptly than anyone on earth had planned, the funeral was over.

CHAPTER FIFTEEN

THE BIBLE STUDY

The social hall at the Antioch Baptist church was buzzing with activity. There were over 150 people sitting around tables in a room that could not comfortably accommodate them. No one was able to go out in the patio area because of the rain, so they just had to make do. Tables were set up in the center of the room, with as many chairs around them as space would allow. These chairs were all occupied by happy people, eating and talking loudly as though they were enjoying a potluck social on the Fourth of July. In addition, folding chairs were set up all around the perimeter. Nearly all of them were occupied as well; only in this case, the people sitting on them ate from paper plates balanced on their laps. It made for awkward eating, to say the least, but no one seemed to mind. There was such a festive mood, no one would have guessed they had all come from a funeral.

The food was all provided by the women of the church and the surrounding community, and there was no limit to either the volume or the variety of it. Several self-appointed ladies were walking among the tables, pouring coffee and iced tea, and bussing any spot vacated by someone who had finished eating, making way for those still coming in.

Any media people, city officials, and policemen who had gone to the graveside service had taken the rain as their cue to head back to the office, or to stop off at a restaurant for lunch. At any rate, they had not come back to the church to eat. Those gathered in the social hall were almost all those who had been friends and neighbors of Georgia Davis, that is, with the exception of four unlikely guests sitting at a table near the patio door. They were sitting with the remaining members of the Davis family, but they were neither black, nor were they friends of any of the family.

Of the four, two were Saul Frieberg and his grandson Aaron Muller. Saul had not wanted to attend. He accurately pointed out that the dinner was prepared for Georgia's family and friends, and they didn't really qualify. He felt they had fulfilled any obligation they might have had by serving as pallbearers at both of the services. They really ought to be getting back to the store. But Aaron insisted that he wanted to talk with Pastor Bobby, and pestered his grandfather until he finally gave in. They felt awkward as they came into the building, but Bobby spotted them almost immediately and insisted they join him at his table. Aaron was delighted at the prospect of getting to talk with Pastor Davis, and Papa Saul was relieved to see people he recognized; for also sitting at the table were Carl and Sarah Singleton and their daughter Tamika, who were regular customers at his store.

No sooner were they seated, than in walked Scott Graham and Candace Mercer. She too had not wanted to come. She didn't know any of those people and neither did Scott, but he had insisted that he wanted to talk to the pastor, and the sudden rain had prevented him from doing so at the cemetery. He promised they would only stay for a few minutes, so she reluctantly agreed to accompany him. Since she didn't want to sit out in his Blazer in the rain to wait for him, she consented to come inside if he would promise her that they wouldn't impose on these good people by staying for lunch. He readily agreed. He said he was indeed hungry, but not for physical food.

Aaron saw them as they came through the door, and were just standing there awkwardly looking around. He was surprised, but pleased to see them, and he asked the pastor if he might invite them to join their table. Bobby quickly agreed and Aaron fetched them over. As they sat there, they felt out of place, especially Candi. Had this meeting not been so important to Scott, she would have excused herself and found her way back to more familiar surroundings.

Scott was nervous as well, because seated at the other end of the table was Saul Frieberg. The old man had seen him at his store on the Saturday night prior to the robbery, and Scott was afraid he might remember him. But he'd had his coat collar turned up and his hat pulled down, and had purposefully avoided direct eye contact that night. Those precautions had apparently paid off, because Saul only looked at him casually at present, and there was no hint of recognition in his eyes. Scott was sure it was because of the different context in which they now saw each other. He was confident that if he were to walk into The Corner Store, Papa Saul would remember him almost instantly.

There was someone else at the table who felt even more out of place than Candi, and more apprehensive than Scott. Marcus Davis squirmed in his seat, trying to come up with some excuse that would allow him to graciously leave the table. He hadn't wanted to come for the meal, but he was with Jamal, and his younger brother simply refused to take him anywhere other than to the church. He was hungry, but he could have eaten elsewhere. He had received his fill of conviction for one day already. He didn't want to sit at the table and listen to more talk about God and the Bible and about salvation and heaven, which only made him feel more nervous. But they hadn't even eaten yet, and he knew he was obligated to stay, at least for the meal.

The thing that made him even more anxious was the fact that Carl and Sarah and Tamika were sitting directly across the table from him. Sarah was just as pretty as he had remembered her. But he had dated her, seduced her, gotten her pregnant, and then deserted her. That was over nine years ago, and he hadn't talked to her since. What must she be thinking about him right now? Their daughter Tamika was a beautiful little girl, although he certainly didn't even qualify to be called her father. He had only seen her on a few occasions, and that was when he stopped by his father's house when she had been visiting there. He had never spent any time with her before, and now there she was, sitting across the table from him, checking him out thoroughly. Then there was Carl, a tough policeman who was very much aware of Marcus' shortcomings, sizing him up as well. He had stood in several police lineups before, but he never felt more vulnerable than he did right at that moment.

After everyone had been properly introduced, Bobby broke the tension by suggesting they all go through the line and get something to eat. All four of the uninvited guests began to protest loudly, but he would hear none of it. At his insistence, eventually everyone agreed and followed him to the makeshift buffet line constructed out of folding tables at the other end of the building. Candi shot Scott a killer glance as they joined the others, as if to say, "You promised me, and now look what you've gotten me into!" But there was so much food, and it all looked so good, she soon forgot her inhibitions, and her plate was nearly as full as anyone else's when she returned to the table. When Scott looked at her plate and then at her, she just smiled and shrugged, as if to say, "Don't ask. I'm a woman. I changed my mind."

Bobby asked Jamal to bless the food, and though he was a bit surprised and embarrassed, he complied without protest. He bowed his head and thanked God for his grandmother and for the fact that they all knew she was in heaven. Then he thanked Him for saving his own soul so he could go there too someday. He was about to find a stopping place when he realized he hadn't said anything about the food, so he tacked on a thank you for it and for those who had prepared it, and said amen. Bobby reached over and squeezed his son's shoulder and smiled, pleased that Jamal had confessed his newfound faith so willingly, so soon, and in front of so many witnesses.

They all enjoyed the good food and made only small talk for some time as they ate. Several of the men even went back for more, including Scott. Candi had thoroughly enjoyed the meal and wanted to go back for seconds herself, but her pride wouldn't allow her. She had made such a fuss about not eating in the first place, she was sure she would totally destroy her already damaged credibility if she went back the second time. She did accept a piece of apple pie, offered to her by one of the ladies who were bringing desserts around to the tables, and justified her actions by the fact that she had not actually gone after it herself.

As they were finishing up, many of the people came by the table to offer their final condolences and to say goodbye as they began to leave for their various homes and places of employment. After several minutes, their table was the only one left occupied. Some of the ladies were packaging up the remaining food at the other end of the room and were cleaning the kitchen, but apart from them, the building had been vacated.

Marcus was feeling a certain measure of relief. Not only had he enjoyed an excellent meal, he had been let off the hook by the Singleton family. Sarah talked openly and easily to him. She said that she had been bitter against him for several years after he dumped her, but she had become a Christian through her relationship with Georgia and Pastor Bobby, and God had taken all the resentment away. She even thanked him for giving her such a wonderful daughter. Her life had become complete when Carl told her of his own salvation experience and she was at peace with the world. Tamika was young and resilient and showed no animosity toward him, and even Carl was cordial. He did mention to Marcus how much difference getting saved had made in the way he felt about him. That part made him feel uneasy, but he readily accepted it. Compared to how they all might well have reacted toward him, he considered himself to be fortunate indeed to have gotten off with only a few guilt feelings.

It appeared that it was about time for everyone to be going, when Aaron changed the subject and expressed his fascination with what Pastor Bobby had said about the evidences for the coming of the Messiah. He had been studying the same subject for months and didn't realize that Christians were interested in it as well. He would be very interested in talking further about these matters.

At that point, Scott voiced his agreement. He had been wrestling with the claims of evangelical Christianity for many months himself and, he too, had been fascinated with what the pastor said about the proximity of the return of Christ. He felt that if it were really to happen, he would be convinced of the validity of the gospel and would himself become a convert.

Others picked up on the conversation and it was generally agreed that the coming of Christ and personal salvation were closely linked together. Christ's coming would be either a means of bringing salvation to those who were not yet decided, or a great confirmation for those who had already placed their trust in Him. Someone suggested that it would be great if they could all talk about it together and have Pastor Bobby lead them. Everyone except Papa Saul agreed, and they asked the pastor if he would consent to lead such a study.

Bobby was already a busy pastor and really didn't have the time to accept another responsibility, but he saw this as an opportunity to accomplish two goals at the same time. There were at least three young people and an old man around the table who were not yet saved, and this Bible study would give him an opportunity to clearly present them with the claims of Christ. Besides that, at least two of the others were brand-new Christians, and the study would provide him the chance to disciple them and help them get grounded in their newfound faith. He said he would agree to lead such a study if they would all agree to four conditions.

They indicated they would be willing to do anything reasonable. What were his conditions?

He said first, they all had to agree to come consistently. He didn't want to waste his time if they were going to be inconsistent in their attendance. Next, he said they had to contribute to the discussion. They all had to agree to study anything assigned to them and to participate in the resulting discussion about it. Then, he said they would all have to be open and honest about their feelings. He didn't want anybody playing games and refusing to deal with the issues they would discuss. Finally, they all had to agree to hold in strictest confidence anything of a sensitive or personal nature someone might reveal to the rest of the group.

It was Aaron's analytical mind that seized what Bobby had just said, and he summarized it for the rest of them. "If we all agree to the four C's, we have a deal: to come, to contribute, to be candid and confidential. I'll agree to that. How about the rest of you guys?"

All but two voiced their agreement. Even Tamika was game, but her parents said they would have to talk about it later. Papa Saul was cordial, but he flatly refused to participate in any such study. He used the excuse of his age and how tied down he was with the store, but the truth was, he would never study Christian doctrine and, frankly, he didn't want Aaron to either.

The other dissenter was Marcus who said he felt out of place. He had been living a life on the streets and just didn't fit in with a bunch of intellectual college types. But they all voted him down. They insisted they wanted him in the study. In fact, if he didn't agree to participate, they weren't going to either. He was hesitant, but they persisted, and finally he agreed. In reality, he wasn't that hard to convince. He too thought it would be interesting to find out more about the possible return of Christ. It might act as an incentive to help motivate him to clean up his act. Also, never on the streets had he sensed the type of sincerity and concern these people naturally showed him. Perhaps there was something to this Christianity after all. Besides, if he agreed to attend the Bible study, that should count as church attendance, and he wouldn't be expected to attend any of the other services. He was sure a casual Bible study would be a lot easier to handle than the convicting fires his dad served up on Sunday mornings.

Then it was agreed, everyone at the table, with the exception of a determined Saul and a disappointed Tamika, was committed to attend the makeshift Bible study on the soon coming of Jesus Christ. Next, they needed to decide on how often, and when and where they were going to meet. They all agreed that they should meet once each week for about two hours, but because of the erratic schedule of swim meets and basketball games, the only day they all knew they would have free, and be in town for, was Sunday. So it was agreed, they would meet in the church conference room every Sunday afternoon, from four till six o'clock, just before the church's evening service.

As they were preparing to leave, Scott asked if it would be all right if he invited a friend of his to join them. He mentioned that he and Tony D'Angelo had read some of the *Left Behind* books, and that his friend might be interested in joining a discussion about future events predicted in the Bible. Aaron voiced his approval, saying he knew Tony and that he would like to have him aboard. No one objected, so Bobby agreed to have Scott invite Tony to join the study, and asked if anyone else would like to invite a friend.

Aaron reminded them that he wasn't a believer in Jesus Christ, and didn't expect to become one, but he was fascinated with the prophecies concerning the coming of Israel's Messiah. He very much wanted to be a part of the study and would like to invite his friend Anna to join them. She was also Jewish, and he didn't know if she would be interested, but he would like their permission to ask her. Again, no one objected, and it was agreed that she would be welcome. Bobby then asked them not to invite anyone else. The conference room wasn't all that big, and a dozen people were about all that could comfortably fit around the table in it. Everyone agreed, and they all seemed genuinely excited about meeting for the first time that coming Sunday.

Before leaving, Bobby asked them all to study the passage in 1 Thessalonians 4:13–18, which he had read at the graveside service. He told them it was one of the clearest passages in the Bible teaching about the coming of the Lord. Aaron confessed he didn't have a New Testament, so Bobby gave him an inexpensive Bible from the lost and found closet, which had no name in it and had gone unclaimed for months. He assured Aaron they would be studying Old Testament passages as well, along with current events, so it wouldn't be just a Christian assault on his Jewish heritage.

It was nearly 1:30 when they left the church. The rain had slacked off, but it was still coming down steadily. As they found their vehicles and drove away, they all had things to do. Marcus asked Jamal to take him home so he could change and go back to work for a few hours. He would catch a bus over to UCLA later to watch Jamal's home game against UNLV. Papa Saul couldn't wait for him and Aaron to get back and open the store and work a few hours as well before they closed at 6:00. for the Sabbath. Sarah was anxious to get Carl back home and into bed. He was exhausted and his pain medication was beginning to wear off. Bobby headed home to work on his Sunday sermon for a few hours before he too would go to watch Jamal play. He decided he would go by Marcus' apartment and see if his older son wanted to go with him.

On the way home Scott drove in silence for a time, until Candi couldn't stand it any longer. "What was that all about?" she demanded.

"What was what all about?" he replied, trying to act innocent and unaware.

"You know very well what I'm talking about. What has this whole day been about? You have me come with you to a funeral for a woman neither of us even knew. There you carry on like she was your own mother, and then you insist on going to the graveside service, even though it was mainly for family and close friends. If that weren't enough, you drag me back to the church to eat with perfect strangers, and then you get us signed up for a weekly Bible study at a church neither of us has ever attended before. Is it just me, or does that sound a little weird to you too?"

"Yeah, I see what you mean. I know it sounds crazy, but it just seems I was drawn to do all those things. You know how I've been struggling for months with the kind of Christianity you and my parents have been trying to get me to accept. It all seemed so confusing before, but what Pastor Davis said today really opened my eyes. I can't wait to find out more of what he has to say. For an uneducated ex-con, he sure can communicate the Bible."

"Well, I have to admit, I'm looking forward to it myself. To be honest, I only went along with this funeral business because I care about you so much, and I was willing to do about anything to help you come to Christ. But I never expected to get caught up in any of it personally. And I really like those people, all of them. It won't be like any Bible study I've ever been in before, but I think it's going to be a kick."

"And what about Aaron?" Scott added. "He's as Jewish as Moses and yet he's going to study with us. And Marcus, he's a gangbanger if I ever saw one, yet he's coming too. Then there's Jamal. He just happens to be about the hottest thing going in college basketball in the whole country, and yet he's going to be sitting down to study the Bible along with the rest of us. I never believed in things being predestined before, but it looks to me like God could be putting together a select group here. He just might have a special plan He's going to be working through us."

"Oh, Scott, I can't believe you're talking this way. You're all excited about studying the Bible and what God is going to do through it, and you're not even saved yet."

"Hey, I'm gettin' closer. I've got a few questions I need answered, and a few things I've still got to work out in my own life before I can make that commitment, but I'm more intrigued with the possibility than I ever was before."

"That's encouraging," Candi responded as she reached out and took his hand in hers. "Only, don't wait too long. God doesn't play games. He expects you to respond when He calls you."

At that same moment Sergeant Myron Spangler sat at his desk at police headquarters, looking through an open folder. Detective Theo Farley stood beside him, looking over his shoulder. Both of them were frustrated, but Spangler was especially agitated.

"They're as guilty as sin," he growled, and then he swore to punctuate his frustration. "But for the past three days we've collected all the evidence I think we're gonna get, and we can't prove a thing."

"But Sarge," interjected Farley, "we've got a lot on them." He called his partner by his title, not his name. No one dared call him Myron, not even his wife. He even signed his name M. Wade Spangler. Farley thought it safer to stay away from names altogether, and stick with the safer "Sarge."

Spangler scowled and insisted again that they really had nothing. Oh, sure, the two college boys fit the general description of the gunmen, and they had prior knowledge of the existence of the safes in the grocery store. It was true they could be placed at the scene of the splashdown at the end of the car chase, but none of that would hold up in a court of law. What they really needed was an eyewitness that could place them at the scene of the crime, but none could be found. The security camera at the store had turned out to be a dummy, so they didn't even have any footage to look at.

Farley protested that the bodies of the shooters had never been found, and that no persons had been reported missing. If other perpetrators had ever really existed, they had to have family and friends somewhere, and those people would have notified the authorities by this time when the gunmen failed to show up. It had to be those two college punks.

Of course it was, Spangler agreed, but they couldn't prove a thing. They had interviewed employees at the movie complex, and the alibi the two had given them checked out. Two attractive young women distinctly remembered the two of them being there at the theater during the time of the robbery. Sure, they could have staged their being there, but such a thing could never be proved.

The two detectives had gone over and over Sergeant Witherspoon's report, and there was simply no evidence that Graham and D'Angelo had done anything other than spend the night on the yacht, and there was no crime in that. Their fingerprints weren't found anywhere near the crime scene, and no evidence was found that would indicate that either of the young men ever had in their possession any of the clothing, the weapons, or the money associated with the robbery.

Spangler even commissioned professional divers to try to duplicate the underwater swim from the site of the car's impact to the end of the dock, which the two would have had to accomplish to have escaped undetected. Not one of them was able to get any closer than about twenty feet. One of the divers said he thought perhaps he could have made it if it just had depended on it, but he wasn't willing to risk his life to try to prove the point.

The day before, they thought they had hit on something when they discovered that Bruce Graham, one of the suspect's father, was the registered owner of a .38 Special. That was the caliber of bullet that had killed Mrs. Davis and had wounded the Muller kid. The senior Graham had been very cooperative, apparently anxious to prove that his son had nothing to do with the crime. They compared the serial number on his pistol with that on the certificate of registration, and they were the same. When they checked everything for prints, they found only Bruce Graham's; his son's prints weren't found on anything that might remotely be connected to the gun. And after they fired the pistol and compared the ballistics with those of the slug from the murder weapon, they weren't even close. This too turned out to be a wild goose chase. The college boys were either innocent, or else they were very clever. He was convinced of the latter.

Why else would that Graham kid show up at the funeral and fall apart when the preacher started talking about how his mother died? Graham wasn't even supposed to have known the woman. Oh, they were guilty all right, but he didn't see any way they were going to be able to prove it. They would keep digging, but they were going to need some help. Perhaps they would stumble onto some incriminating evidence, or perhaps the two suspects might just do something stupid and give themselves away. At any rate, Spangler wasn't about to let them off the hook. He prided himself in never being outsmarted, and he wasn't about to let these two spoiled little rich kids be the first.

Later that evening, the front passed on to the east and the rain gave way to cold wind and broken clouds. After swim practice, at Starbucks once again, Scott told Tony what had happened at the funeral and about the planned Bible study.

"What, you gotta be crazy, Scott!" Tony blurted out. "We need to stay as far away from those people as we can. I can't believe you did that."

"No, you're wrong, man," Scott corrected him. "It's the smartest thing we could have done. You know those two cops are watching us. The last place in the world they would expect a couple of guilty dudes to show up is at a Bible study, especially one taught by the victim's son. They would never expect us to become friends with Mrs. Davis' two grandsons, and pal around with the guy I shot in the store. Guilty people just don't do things like that."

"What do you mean, we, Lone Ranger?" Tony asked. "Surely you don't expect me to join in on this hokey Bible study do you?"

"Yes I do, if for no other reason than to throw off those detectives. But more than that, Candi and I really enjoyed getting to know those people, and Pastor Davis made more sense when he talked about spiritual things than anyone I've ever heard. I'm sure we can learn a lot from this man."

"Who says I want to learn about spiritual things from him, or from any other preacher, for that matter?"

"Look, Tony, it's only a couple of hours a week on Sunday afternoon, and it will help throw the cops off our trail. You're always coming up with trivial facts you dug up somewhere, and you're bound to learn some real juicy ones about biblical prophecy; and besides, Candi and I would really like to have you there."

"Okay, okay, I'll give it a try. Not because I give a flip about Bible prophecy, but I would love to throw a monkey wrench into the machinery of those two detectives. But most of all, I would welcome a chance to be around Candi more often. Maybe it will give her a chance to see what she's been missing all the time she's been hanging around with you."

Scott laughed. Even though Tony's motives weren't what they ought to be, he felt relief knowing that his friend was going to be sitting under the teaching of Pastor Bobby. Funny, here he was concerned about the spiritual welfare of his friend when he was a long way from being out of the woods himself. He didn't understand why, and he certainly wouldn't have been able to explain it, but he felt certain that this Bible study somehow held the key to their future, and for the first time in a week, he actually began to look forward to what lay ahead.

At home that night, Scott was grilled thoroughly by his father, as only a trial lawyer knows how. Attorney Bruce Graham wanted to know everything Scott and Tony had done on and around the date of the robbery when that black woman had been killed.

Although he had told his parents earlier about being questioned by the police, this time Scott told his dad the same detailed story he and Tony had told the police about what happened the past Sunday night. Basically, what he told him was true. They had eaten dinner at the D'Angelos, they had gone shopping, they had gone to a movie, and they had driven down to the marina, and had spent the night on the yacht. What he didn't tell his father is that only Tony had done any shopping, and that it was for a disguise and a shotgun and a car to steal. He also didn't tell him that they had seen the movie prior to the time he said they had, and that their drive to the marina had ended up in the middle of the harbor, instead of in the parking lot. So much for telling the truth, the whole truth, and nothing but the truth.

His father wanted to know if he had anything to corroborate his story. After pretending to think about it, Scott said he thought he could come up with a few things. Of course, Mrs. D'Angelo could verify their presence at dinner that night, and he was sure a couple of the attendants at the movie complex would be able to remember them being there because Tony had been flirting with them. He even thought the ticket stub might still be in the pocket of the jacket he had worn that night.

That sparked the interest of the attorney in his father, and Scott was asked to produce the stub. Scott went to his room and came back with the jacket and pulled the stub out of the pocket. He could have simply brought back the stub, but he thought the presence of the jacket would make it more convincing.

It seemed to work because his father grabbed the stub from him without hesitation and was delighted when he confirmed the time of the showing. If they were in the movie at that time, there was no way they could have committed the robbery and the shooting clear up in LA.

Scott couldn't think of anyone who could verify their presence in the shopping mall. They had just walked around for a long time and hadn't bought anything. Neither could he come up with anyone who could testify of their arrival at the marina. It had been late when they got there, and they had gone straight to the yacht, without talking to anyone.

Bruce Graham seemed to be satisfied with his son's answers, but he wasn't through yet. He wanted to press on and cover every minute detail, but his wife objected and called for a recess. She had been away from her son for nearly two weeks, and she had hardly talked to him since she got home. The cross-examination would have to wait for some other time. Bruce reluctantly agreed, and Scott was delighted.

The rest of the evening was spent talking about family interests. Scott told his parents about his classes, his swim meets, and his fishing expeditions, and they told him about their trip to the Holy Land. Florence had gotten about a dozen rolls of film developed and she provided a running commentary as Scott looked at the pictures. He was particularly interested in the shots of the new Jewish temple nearing completion. It was a massive and beautiful structure, located just to the north of the Dome of the Rock. Numerous guards, armed with automatic weapons, could be seen in every picture. Tension was high, but so was the security to deal with it.

The Grahams both commented on how excited the whole nation seemed to be about the upcoming dedication ceremony when it was completed. Even Constantine Augustus, the president of the U.S.E. and the newly elected Secretary General of the World Federation of Nations, was scheduled to be there to make a speech and offer his congratulations.

Scott found the shots of the temple fascinating perhaps because of what he had recently heard about it being one of the signs of the soon return of the Lord. He asked if he might borrow some of those pictures to show his friend Aaron Muller who was a devout Jew and completely hung up on the rebuilding of the temple. His mother said it would be okay if he would be sure to return them to her.

Later, as Scott lay in bed, he had trouble falling asleep. He was amazed once again how he had been able to avoid detection even by his dad, the ever-vigilant lawyer. This apparent triumph spawned many questions in his mind. Was he becoming that proficient as a liar? Why was God protecting him and aiding him in concealing a long series of sinful acts? Did he really think he would be able to carry on this charade indefinitely? How could he seriously contemplate pursuing knowledge of spiritual things and consider committing his life to Christ while all the time he was living a gross lie?

As he lay there, it became apparent to him that he would not be able to continue to straddle the fence. He would have to make a choice between the two opposing alternatives. Either he was going to have to continue to pursue his life of deception and self-preservation and forget about any thought of spiritual new birth, or else he was going to have to come clean with everyone else if he ever hoped to come clean with God. But as he thought about it, neither alternative was acceptable.

If he continued to lie and protect himself, he would certainly lose Candi in the long run, and worse yet, he would lose the wonderful spiritual contact he had recently experienced with God, and maybe even lose his own soul. But, on the other hand, if he went all the way with a commitment to God and told the truth about everything else, he would undoubtedly feel better spiritually, but he would most surely lose his freedom, and almost certainly lose Candi as well. She wouldn't want to join her life to a criminal who was going to spend the rest of his life in prison. He would also lose all the people he had just met and so admired. They would want nothing to do with the one who had brought so much pain and suffering into their lives.

There was no answer, but for some reason, he was not desperate or depressed. He didn't have a clue how, but something seemed to reassure him that things were going to all work out in the end. With that thin thread of hope, he said a little prayer, asking God for wisdom to make the right decisions. Then he rolled over and, amazingly, drifted off to sleep.

CHAPTER SIXTEEN

THE RAPTURE QUESTION

After a week of action, tragedy, and suspense, the next two days went by without serious incident. Jamal and his team won handily over UNLV on Friday night. Jamal had a great game athletically, but that was to be expected. The unusual thing about him was the easy and enthusiastic way in which he shared with his coach and teammates his newfound faith in Jesus Christ. Samuel Clayton revealed that he was a Christian too, but had failed to tell anybody on the team about it. The rest of the team didn't really understand what the two were talking about, but they had so much respect for Jamal they were happy for him anyway.

On Saturday, Marcus finished his first full week of work in years. And for the first time in an even longer time than that, he finished a week without getting drunk, doing drugs, gambling, or breaking the law. Gilbert Matthews was so pleased with his work at the salvage yard that he gave him the use of an old Plymouth Duster that he had reconstructed from several junked cars from his lot. With his first paycheck he got a phone, a used TV, and a clock radio. With a steady job, a set of wheels, and a few bare necessities, he felt almost human again. He even enjoyed going to Jamal's ball game with his dad, and the three of them hanging out afterwards. To top it off, he went to church Sunday morning without being bribed or even asked.

The Singletons' lives were practically back to normal. Carl was still off work on medical leave, but he was healing rapidly. They spent Saturday afternoon at MacArthur Park, having a picnic and flying a kite in the stiff breeze that followed Friday's storm. They drove to Compton Sunday morning to go to church at Antioch Baptist, and they spent the afternoon with Pastor Bobby and his sons, all of them looking forward to the Bible study at four. During the time of the study, they had made arrangements for Tamika to stay with a family they knew who lived near the church and who had a daughter just Tamika's age.

Aaron helped Papa Saul get the store back in good condition while they were closed on Saturday. New glass was installed in the front door to replace the plywood that had been put in it temporarily, and the shelves were all cleaned and stocked. They broke the Sabbath a little, but they both agreed the circumstances were unusual and they were sure God would understand. They spent a lot of time talking about religion and about what God was doing in the nation Israel. They agreed on almost everything except the Bible study on Sunday afternoon. Aaron was insistent upon going and pressured his grandfather to go with him. Papa Saul flatly refused and tried to talk Aaron out of going himself. Finally they reached a compromise. Aaron would go and Saul would stay, and neither one would try to coerce the other.

Anna Berger had visited Aaron a couple of times in the hospital after his injury, and came by once to see him at the store after he was released. Their conversation was pleasant, and both of them were encouraged. But when Aaron called her and explained about the Bible study he was going to be attending and invited her to join him, she became almost as indignant as Papa Saul. She made it clear in no uncertain terms that she was not interested in becoming involved in his messianic obsession, especially not in a Bible study taught by a Baptist preacher. She told him the bullet that missed his heart must have lodged in his brain.

Tony was feeling great. He had a date on both Friday and Saturday nights with two different, but equally beautiful, co-eds, and had plenty of money from his share of the loot to spend on them. He and Scott swam well and their team was able to narrowly defeat Pepperdine in a swim meet on Saturday afternoon. He slept in late on Sunday and went out to eat with his parents at 1:00 P.M. He looked forward to seeing Candace Mercer at the Bible study later that afternoon.

Scott spent much of the day Saturday trying to get caught up on his studies. He had neglected his classes badly over the past week and he really needed to hit the books. His heart wasn't in it, but he did manage to repair some of the damage that had been done. After the swim meet, he and Candi went out to eat at a Burger King on the closest thing to a date they had ever had. They read the passage together in 1 Thessalonians that Pastor Bobby had assigned to them and discussed it. Scott found it stimulating and couldn't wait to learn more about it from Pastor Bobby. On Sunday, he went to church with his parents, but sat with Candi. He didn't really get much out of Dr. Schumway's message, and wondered what the service was like over at Antioch Baptist Church that morning.

Pastor Bobby Davis looked out at the small congregation gathered in the conference room at his church. It was shortly after four, and the last person had just arrived. It was Marcus, and his tardiness didn't surprise his father. Bobby was pleased, and a little surprised, that he made it at all. He was also surprised when Tony D'Angelo showed up as well. He came in with Scott and Candi, just ahead of Marcus. Bobby had never met him before, nor had most of the others in the room, yet he was there, looking nervous and uncomfortable, but there nonetheless.

The primary cause of Tony's nervousness stemmed from the fact that the first face he saw when he entered the room belonged to Carl Singleton, the same Carl Singleton he had shot in the chest with a sawed-off shotgun just one week before. Scott had neglected to mention that Carl and his wife would also be in attendance at the Bible study. Tony's first impression was to turn around and leave the building and never return, but Scott had hold of Tony's elbow, and tightened his grip when he felt his friend stiffen. On second thought, Tony decided he would stay after all. There was no way the guy would be able to identify him, and besides, the fact that he was studying the Bible with the man he was supposed to have gunned down would drive those two detectives nuts.

Bobby took the initiative and greeted everyone warmly and introduced himself to Tony. He then introduced him to the others and told everyone to help themselves to the refreshments set up on the counter in front of the window. There was a large dispenser of hot water and an assortment of individual packages of coffee, tea, and hot chocolate. To go along with the drinks was a box of assorted doughnuts. This proved to be a welcomed icebreaker, and they all began to help themselves and then to find their seats around the table.

The conference room at the Antioch Baptist Church was not particularly impressive. It was about 16 by 20 feet in size and contained only the counter along one wall, a large wooden table in the center of the room, and a chalkboard on the wall at one end. There were about a dozen chairs arranged around the table to accommodate the deacon and staff meetings held there, and the small adult Bible class that met there during Sunday School.

As Bobby looked around the table, he thought to himself that this had to be about the most diverse group he had ever attempted to teach. Of the eight people seated around him, there were six men and two women, four blacks and four whites, four Christians and four unbelievers; some Baptists, one Jew, one apparent Catholic, one pagan, and he wasn't sure what else. The only thing they all had in common, as far as he knew, was that they were all young and full of life.

Bobby admitted it was corny, but he produced some stick-on nametags and several felt tipped pens and asked everyone to fill them out and wear them, just this one time. It would help them to learn one another's names and facilitate their conversation. He also requested, since it was their first meeting, that they go around the room and tell a little about themselves and what they expected to derive from their Bible study together.

As they went around the room, sharing some of their background and why they happened to be present at the study, Bobby noticed that they unwittingly divided themselves into four distinct pairs. Aaron and Scott were eagerly anticipating learning more of what Bobby thought the Bible had to say about the coming of the Messiah. Though neither was a believer, they both had serious questions they wanted to ask, and they had important decisions pending on what the answers to those questions might be. Carl and Jamal were brand-new converts, and they were looking forward to learning more about their newfound faith and what the future had in store for them. Sarah and Candi were more mature in the Lord, and were there primarily in support of someone else, but they both expressed interest in what they might learn for themselves as well. Marcus and Tony both admitted that they weren't really sure why they were there. Neither was particularly interested in religion or the future, but both had been pressured to attend by a friend or family member, and were there primarily out of compliance and curiosity.

When it came his turn, Bobby told them briefly of his own experience; of his dissipated youth, his conversion in prison, his independent study of the Bible until his release, and his ministry at the church since then. He readily admitted that he wasn't an educated Bible scholar who had studied under the great theologians of his day, and he made no apology for it. He was primarily self-taught, but he had studied a great deal while he was in prison and had continued to do so since his release. He felt he might be able to shed some fresh insight into certain passages of Scripture whose interpretations had been pretty much stereotyped by the so-called experts in the field.

Everyone seemed to be completely comfortable with Bobby's qualifications to lead the study and someone suggested they begin. Bobby agreed and started the meeting with a brief prayer, asking God for His wisdom as they studied His Word, and for openness on their part to accept what He had in it for them. He looked around the table to make sure everyone had a Bible, and then asked them all to turn to 1 Thessalonians, chapter four. While some of them were still turning pages, he began to explain the context of the passage he was about to read.

He told them the apostle Paul, an early church missionary, had previously been in the Macedonian city of Thessalonica for very short period of time, during which he had won many of the residents to Christ and had started a church there. Pressure from the unbelieving Jews had forced Paul and his companions to leave the city and to travel south into Greece, but he had maintained contact with the church through letters. In one of their letters, the Thessalonian believers had asked Paul concerning the fate of the saints who had died since he had left their city. Paul had told them the Lord was going to come back soon and they were to look for His return, but they wondered what had happened to those who wouldn't be alive to welcome Him back. Bobby told his class that Paul had written this particular passage in the letter he sent back to the church to answer that question.

Once he was sure everyone had found his place, Bobby read aloud from his New American Standard Bible the same verses 13–18 he had read at the graveside on Friday:

> *Brothers, we do not want you to be ignorant about those who fall asleep, or to grieve like the rest of men, who have no hope. We believe that Jesus died and rose again and so we believe that God will bring with Jesus those who have fallen asleep in Him. According to the Lord's own word, we tell you that we who are still alive, who are left till the coming of the Lord, will certainly not precede those who have fallen asleep. For the Lord Himself will come down from heaven with a loud command, with the voice of the archangel and with the trumpet call of God, and the dead in Christ will rise first. After that, we who are still alive and are left will be caught up together with them in the clouds to meet the Lord in the air. And so we will be with the Lord forever. Therefore encourage one another with these words.*

When he finished reading, he noticed several puzzled faces around the table, so he began to explain what was just said.

He explained that when Paul used the term *sleep,* he was a referring to those who had died. He said Paul assured the church that the spirits of those who had died had gone on to be with the Lord, and only their bodies slept in the grave. To confirm this, he pointed out that those saints would be accompanying the Lord when He came back. At the sound of the trumpet blast and the angel's shout, the bodies of the saints would be resurrected and reunited with their spirits, and that the living believers would be instantly transformed and they would all meet the Lord in the air. This catching up of dead and living saints was what was referred to as the rapture. He concluded by saying the rapture was the next thing that was going to happen on the prophetic calendar, and that Christians all over the world were looking forward to it occurring at any moment.

Just then, Aaron pointed out that the author included himself among those who were going to be alive and remaining at the time of the so-called rapture. Since Paul had obviously been dead for nearly two thousand years, didn't that prove that he was in error and guilty of giving them a false prophecy? Tony and Marcus agreed, and they were ready to discredit the passage altogether.

Bobby commended them on their perception, but told them Paul had been absolutely correct concerning the doctrine of the rapture, he had just been disappointed in his personal hope of living to see it occur. Actually, none of the first century writers had any idea that the return of the Lord would be delayed for so many centuries. They all looked forward to it happening during their own lifetimes.

Well then, Scott responded, if it had been delayed for all this time, what reason did Christians have for expecting it to occur at any time? Couldn't it be delayed for another two thousand years just as easily?

Bobby commended him for his insight as well, but he assured him that the Bible describes certain conditions that would exist on the earth at the time of the coming of the Lord. He said they could determine the proximity of the rapture by comparing those biblical descriptions with actual developments taking place in the world around them. He had decided that they would look at those comparisons during their study the following week because, as far as he was concerned, for the first time in history, there was currently a nearly perfect match between them.

Several around the table urged Bobby to discuss those comparisons right then, but he declined. He wanted them to do some reading on their own before they discussed the matter as a group. He said their assignment for the next week would be to read Matthew 24:1–14, 2 Thessalonians 2:1–4, and Revelation, chapters 13 and 17. But before they left their current passage, there was something he wanted each of them to see.

Bobby pointed out that not everyone was going to go to be with the Lord when He came again. Throughout the passage, Paul always prefaced his remarks about those going at the time of the rapture as being those who were *in Jesus* or *in Christ*. Notice, Bobby confirmed, that Paul never mentioned those who were good, or moral, or church members, or baptized, or anything else that had to do with their own merit. He identified those who would be taken simply as those who were intimately identified in the person of Jesus Christ.

He spent the rest of their time together pointing out passage after passage that confirmed that one's salvation depended entirely on the finished work of Jesus Christ and one's personal faith and identification in it. He concentrated on the writings of the apostles Paul and John in the New Testament, but for Aaron's sake, he also included Psalm 22 and Isaiah 53 in the Old Testament. The former of the two passages described, in graphic detail, the crucifixion of Christ, even though David wrote of it hundreds of years before the Romans ever invented that excruciating form of capital punishment. In the latter passage, Isaiah told how Israel's Messiah suffered and died for the sins of His people, and how He was able to justify them through His resurrection and exaltation.

Aaron was fascinated by what he was learning, but he was not convinced. Jamal and Carl shared his fascination, but they needed no convincing. They marveled at the abundance of Scripture that taught about salvation exclusively through Jesus Christ, and the clarity with which they taught it. They kept asking over and over again how they could have been so blind that they hadn't been able to see it before. Candi and Sarah were patiently polite. They had both learned all those things years before, and found a review of them less than captivating, but they knew how important they were for the others, so they didn't protest the amount of time spent going over the elementary doctrine of salvation. Marcus and Tony were clearly uncomfortable. They had obviously not accepted Christ and had no present inclination to do so, and they resented Bobby's unveiled attempt to change their minds. Their relief was apparent when he finally wrapped things up at 5:45. Had it not been for their interest in the things Bobby said they were going to discuss the next week, neither one of them would have agreed to come again.

Scott was troubled by what he had read and heard. It all made perfect sense to him, and he wanted to believe every word of it, and to do whatever was necessary for him to be forgiven and to become one of those *in Christ*. But the events of the previous week haunted him, and he somehow knew that he could not be freed from his sins before God until he was willing to deal with them openly before men. But how could he? There wasn't a person there he would not offend and alienate if he even breathed of what he and Tony had done. So he said nothing, and made no decision. Surely, if he kept coming and kept learning, a solution would become apparent. God knew he wanted to come to Him. He would surely make a way for him to do so without it being so hard. It just didn't seem right that this free gift should wind up costing him absolutely everything.

The next week went by quickly and without serious incident. UCLA won two more basketball games and Jamal easily maintained his lead in the national NCAA scoring competition. What was more important, he also maintained his testimony before his teammates and the players on the opposing teams. God had given him a new control over his anger and over his formerly profane tongue. He was having the time of his life, but he was plagued by the knowledge that he still owed the underworld a game sometime in the future. How was he ever going to be able to throw another game? It had been nearly impossible for him to do it before he was a Christian. He didn't see any way under heaven he would ever be able to do it now that he had become one. He prayed God would cause them to change their minds and not make any further demands on him, but he had a nagging feeling they knew they had him hooked, and they were just waiting for the right moment to reel him in. He studied his assigned Scriptures, but they didn't contain any answers to his problem that he could see.

The swim team at CSULB was not so fortunate. They lost both of their meets by narrow margins. Tony swam as brilliantly as ever, but Scott was unable to match the performance of his friend. In both meets, his times were slightly slower than they had been in previous outings. Somehow, his heart just wasn't in it like it had been before. Then, of course, Aaron wasn't swimming at all, and the team sorely missed the points he would normally have contributed. Unless they were able to win the rest of their meets, they would not win the conference championship, and would probably miss a shot at the nationals in Saint Louis. That fact was driving Tony nuts, but it didn't seem to be that big of a deal to Scott.

In fact, Scott was having a difficult time even concentrating on his studies. He was spending most of his free time reading in his Bible and making notes and jotting down questions to ask at the Bible study on Sunday. There were many things he didn't understand in the passages he had been assigned to read, but it wasn't because he hadn't studied them. The passages in the book of Revelation were especially confusing to him. He couldn't wait for the light he was sure Bobby would be able to shed on them when next they all got together.

Aaron also spent a lot of time pouring over the Scriptures. Try as he would, he could not explain away the things Pastor Bobby had taught on Sunday. Psalm 22 and Isaiah 53 were especially troubling to him. He even made an appointment with his rabbi and talked with him about them, but the explanation he received was hardly satisfactory. Rabbi Roth told him the suffering one spoken of in both passages referred not to an individual, but to the godly remnant of Israel, which had suffered for the sins of the rest of the rebellious nation. The fact that Aaron didn't buy Roth's answer was obvious, and it only served to make his rabbi angry, who promptly forbade him to attend the Gentile gathering in the future. That only galvanized Aaron's resolve to continue in the study and to find the answers on his own. The passages Bobby had assigned the class might as well have been written in a foreign language for all the help they were to him. He had no background in the New Testament and understood practically nothing of what he read. So, he too, was looking forward to getting some help from the pastor on Sunday.

Marcus surprised even himself as he also read the assigned passages. He was reading on his lunch break one day and Gil commented on how unusual it was to see the Snowball getting into the word. He reminded Marcus about the only other time he had seen him with a Bible. It had been years before when they had both been running with a gang, and Marcus had taken a big Bible and cut out the inside of the pages, leaving only the outer edges intact. The surgery left the outside of the Bible looking normal, but there was a nice big cavity inside to carry undetected the stash of drugs he always had on him. Gil laughed and said he hoped Snowball got more good out of the Bible this time as he read it, than he did before when he used to shred it.

The week was a frustrating one for Detectives Spangler and Farley. They searched through everything they could get their hands on to come up with some evidence to link Scott and Tony to the robbery and murder case they were working on. They were both convinced that the two college boys were guilty, but the frustrating part was that they still could come up with absolutely no hard evidence against them.

The detectives would keep the case open, but unless something just fell into their laps soon, they saw it eventually going into the large file of unsolved cases. It was too bad, Spangler thought, that the law wouldn't allow them to haul the two punks in and beat a confession out of them.

The next Sunday found Scott and Candi in the morning service at the Antioch Baptist Church in Compton. It was Scott's idea, but Candi was a willing participant. They had both been impressed with Pastor Bobby's knowledge of the Bible and his ability to express it to others. They were not the only Anglos in the service, yet they still felt conspicuous at first, but the people were so warm and hospitable that they soon felt at ease. The style of worship was different from what they were familiar with, yet they had gotten a taste of it at the funeral, and were prepared for the change.

They didn't particularly like the style of music they sang, but they thoroughly enjoyed the exuberance and sincerity of those doing the singing. They didn't particularly like the style of the pastor's preaching either, yet again; they thrilled to his passion and the content of his message.

Scott told Candi afterward on their way home that he wanted to continue worshipping there, at least until he was able to make it through the spiritual dilemma he was facing. Candi agreed to accompany him, and it didn't take that much convincing. She sensed that Scott was close to making a decision, and she wanted to do whatever she could to help facilitate it. Besides, she had never been in a church before where people seemed so genuine in their love, and so committed to their faith. She felt her own walk with the Lord could only benefit from her association with these good people.

CHAPTER SEVENTEEN

THE CERTAIN SIGNS

At the Bible study that afternoon, Pastor Bobby wasted little time. He greeted everyone and they all spent a few minutes in small talk, but he soon had them turning in their Bibles to Matthew, chapter 24. He began by telling them they were going to be looking at seven different conditions, which the Bible indicates would exist on the earth at the time of Christ's return. He said there were many passages of Scripture that depict these conditions, but they were going to restrict themselves to the four he had assigned them to read.

He began by telling them that the twenty-fourth chapter of Matthew marked the beginning of what is called the Olivet Discourse. There, he told them, Jesus explained to His disciples the conditions that would characterize the end of the present age and those that described the age of tribulation that would follow. They read the first twelve verses together and then he went around the room and asked his students to list the conditions Jesus said would prevail during this present age. As they did, the list began to grow: the emergence of false messiahs, wars and rumors of wars, increasing natural disasters, severe persecution of the faithful, defection on the part of some, false prophets and deceivers, and a general state of apostasy. Bobby was careful to show them that Jesus told them that it did not constitute the end of the age, and that it was, as the King James Version puts it, "*the beginning of sorrows.*"

They each agreed that all of the things Christ had predicted had certainly been present in the world since the first century, and that they had increased in both frequency and intensity in the past few decades. But

Aaron insisted that alone didn't prove anything. Bobby agreed with him, but told him to be patient, there was much more to come. This was just the first sign that they were approaching the end of the age.

Then he directed their attention to verse fourteen, which read, "*And this gospel of the kingdom will be preached in all the world as a witness to all the nations, and then the end will come.*" He reminded them that the Lord had given His followers what is called the Great Commission: to preach the gospel to all the nations of the world. That commission had been given early in the first century, but it was just now being fulfilled, in the twenty-first century. Just in the last year, Christian leaders had announced that they had finally been able to get the gospel message to every people group in the world, and to get at least portions of the Bible translated into all their various languages.

Bobby pointed out that in the very next verse, the tribulation period was described as beginning, with what the prophet Daniel called the "Abomination of Desolation" standing in the Holy Place. He promised to explain what that meant in a moment, but insisted that the unprecedented phenomenon of the universal preaching of the gospel constituted the second sign that the end of the age was near, and the tribulation was just around the corner.

For his third comparison, he had them turn to 2 Thessalonians 2:3–4, where he said Paul explained what Daniel's Abomination of Desolation would be. He told them that it would occur when the antichrist presented himself as God in the temple in Jerusalem. But he pointed out no such thing could have happened during the past two thousand years since the temple of Christ's day was destroyed by the Romans in 70 A.D., just as Jesus said it would be. For nearly two millennia there had been no temple in Jerusalem.

"That's right," Scott blurted out, "but there's one there now. My parents just returned from Israel and I've got some of the pictures they took of the new temple right here." He took out the pictures he had placed inside the cover of his Bible and passed them around for the others to see. "And it's almost completed," he continued. "The Jews should be dedicating it in just a few weeks from now."

Bobby agreed. He said he couldn't help but believe that the appearance of the temple now, after so many centuries, must surely mark the soon return of the Lord.

Next, he had them turn to Revelation, chapter thirteen where, in the first ten verses, they read about a certain beast that came out of the sea, having seven heads and ten horns. Bobby had to take several minutes to explain that John was using symbolic language to describe a world leader who would rule over the seventh major empire in the history of the world, and that he would have the leaders of ten nations in alliance with him. Bobby had them compare the Revelation passage to similar ones in Daniel, chapters two and seven. It became apparent after awhile to all of them that the Bible indeed did prophesy about a powerful world leader who would rule an empire formed out of the remnants of the old empire ruled by the ancient Roman Caesars.

They all agreed that there had never been such a ruler since the fall of Rome, but they were all fascinated by the suggested possibility that such a ruler just might have come on the scene in the past few years.

Constantine Augustus, the new president of the United States of Europe, had experienced a meteoric rise to power and had led the U.S.E. to become the most formidable superpower on the planet, rivaling even the dominance of ancient Rome. It was Aaron who pointed out that Augustus was also the new head of the World Federation of Nations, which had exactly ten voting members. Everyone present generally agreed that those ten nations could very well represent the ten horns on the beast.

The passage in Revelation 13 went on to describe the coming beast as one who would be empowered by the devil himself, and that he would apparently be killed and then raised back to life again. Bobby said those things would be realized after the rapture, but he was convinced that Augustus was the only person in the past two thousand years who could very easily fulfill those prophecies because of his widespread power and charismatic personality.

Next, the pastor informed them that the last half of Revelation 13 contained the fifth sign that the earth was rapidly moving toward the end of this present age. Bobby had Candi read from verse thirteen to the end of the chapter, and then he explained its strange contents.

It spoke of a second beast whom, he said, most scholars called the false prophet. He would be able to perform miracles and to make an image of the first beast, which could both think and speak on its own. It would force everyone to receive a 666 mark on their right hand or on their forehead, without which they could neither buy nor sell anything.

"Wow, that's scary," Scott exclaimed. "I know it's symbolic language, but if I understand it correctly, that stuff is already available today. They have created an artificial intelligence through computer science, so creating a robot that thinks and talks is entirely possible today. And as far as that mark is concerned, they're already experimenting with something like that in Europe right now. We discussed in one of my classes at State that Augustus wants to do away with cash, checks, and even credit cards altogether. I saw him on the news the other night, and he was saying they have the technology in place to affix a laser-tattooed number on people's hands or foreheads that will do away with the need for all other forms of identification.

"If I remember correctly, the number is invisible to the naked eye, but can be read by special scanners. The number is actually eighteen digits long, arranged into three groups of six digits each. The first group identifies the person's country and specific area within it; the second identifies his birth day, month, and year; and the third group represents his own personal six-digit identification number. With that combination of numbers, every person on the earth could be immediately identified."

"Yeah, I saw something about that too," Jamal interjected. "They've already tested it, and it supposedly works perfectly. It's all on a voluntary basis right now, but I guess thousands of people are standing in line to get their numbers already. Augustus claims that when the program is fully operational, it will help the world economy tremendously. It will do away with all paperwork completely, and we'll never have to worry about anything ever being lost, stolen, or counterfeited again. It sounded like a great idea when I first heard about it, but suddenly I've begun to smell a rat."

"Yeah, me too," agreed Marcus, "and the rat's name is Constantine."

"Even if it isn't him, and it may not be," cautioned Bobby, "it will be somebody like him. The point is; the technology is in place to pull off something like this today when it couldn't have happened even a few years ago. But I think this next passage will provide us with the sixth sign of the Lord's coming and will help tie all this together even better."

Bobby had them turn to Revelation, chapter seventeen. Marcus hadn't entered into the conversation much up to this point, so Bobby asked him to read verses one through six. Marcus appreciated being included, and although he didn't have much of a formal education, he was naturally intelligent and was an avid reader. He welcomed the opportunity to show these college kids he wasn't totally illiterate. He began reading fluently and with no apparent effort, although he had no comprehension whatsoever of anything he was saying. But then, no one other than the preacher did either.

After Marcus had finished, Bobby explained that the woman described in the passage called, *"BABYLON THE GREAT, THE MOTHER OF HARLOTS,"* who was riding on the back of the beast, was a symbol of all the corrupt and heretical religions of the world. She was seen as incredibly wealthy, but also incredibly wicked, guilty of spiritual fornication and drunk with the blood of God's people.

Bobby informed them that false religion began back in Babylon in Genesis 11 and spread throughout the world from there. Bible scholars believe that during the tribulation, all false religions will be united under one head and will be endorsed and supported by the antichrist, at least in the beginning.

He went on to say the churches of the world had never been united before, but that was all changing. Augustus had publicly proclaimed he wanted to unite the peoples of the world economically, politically, socially, and spiritually. He sponsored the religious union between the Catholics, Muslims, and Jews the previous year, calling it the World Church of Humanity. Its main headquarters was established in Vatican City in Rome, but it also had a strong presence in Jerusalem, a city held to be sacred by all three religions. Augustus gained great popularity for his cause by financing the building of St. Mary's Basilica there, along with the rebuilding of the Jewish temple and the repair of the Muslim Dome of the Rock. Most of the other religions of the world were also eager to join the alliance in an effort to form one big happy family.

"Not everyone is happy, and not everyone is joining either," said Aaron defiantly. "It's true, most of the liberal and secular Jews have embraced the World Church of Humanity, but every true son of Abraham has rejected it as an alliance with the devil himself. I hate what's happening over there. We orthodox Jews believe the only answer for Israel is not to unite with the other religions of the world, but for our Messiah to come and destroy the ungodly works of the World Church and set up His own kingdom of righteousness."

Bobby said that the Messiah wouldn't have to destroy the World Church. According to the latter part of Revelation 17, those rulers loyal to the beast would actually destroy the Mother of Harlots themselves, not willing to let anyone or anything share in the glory they felt belonged only to the antichrist.

Their time was nearly gone, but Bobby told them he wanted to show them one more interesting phenomenon revealed in the Book of Revelation that could be realized only at that present time. He showed them several passages that stated the whole world would witness a coming event. Whether it was the marvels of the beast in chapter thirteen, or the death of the two witnesses in chapter eleven, or the future coming of Christ revealed in chapter one; the point made was, all the world would witness it at the same time. With satellites circling the earth to relay the signals and the universal presence of televisions to capture them, it was entirely possible for people all over the world to witness the same events simultaneously. But that could not have been true in previous generations before the advent of global satellite telecommunications.

Bobby then briefly reviewed all the things they had discussed that indicated the rapture of the church was near. He reminded his students of the many conditions that existed on the earth that had not been extant, or even possible, until their present day. Those were the same conditions, he insisted, that were listed in the Bible, describing almost exactly the world of the coming tribulation. When he had finished he asked them what their impression was of all they had studied that afternoon.

Without exception they all agreed the similarities were uncanny. They also agreed that John, writing so long ago, could not have foreseen such things if they had not been revealed to him through some supernatural means. Scott wanted to know if that meant that the rapture would of necessity take place in the immediate future, and if so, could they know when it might be.

"That's a great question, Scott," answered Bobby. "The answer is no. The rapture doesn't necessarily have to happen immediately. Many Bible scholars in the past had been sure the rapture was going to take place in their generation, but they were mistaken. It's possible that we could be mistaken too. The Lord could delay His coming for many years, but everything is in place as never before for Him to come without delay. Personally, I expect His coming to be very soon. Yet even if I'm right, we can't know exactly when. It could be in the immediate future, or it could be a year or two from now, or even longer; but I just don't see how it could be postponed for very long.

"That brings me to the question I've been wanting to ask many of you for a couple of weeks now," Bobby continued. "Four of you have indicated you have not yet accepted Jesus Christ as your own personal Savior. With the probability of the rapture so near, and the tribulation sure to follow, wouldn't you like to accept Him right now so you'll be ready when it does happen?"

An embarrassing silence followed as those seated around the table nervously looked at each other. After what seemed a long time, Tony was the first to speak up. "I have to admit, you've pointed out a lot of stuff I never knew was in the Bible, and I really don't have an answer for it. I can't speak for the others, but even though it's pretty convincing, I'm not ready to commit my entire life to someone I'm just now learning about. But I'll tell you what. If the rapture really does take place, and you dudes are all gone, I'll be the first to believe the gospel, and I'll get saved in a New York minute."

That answer seemed to trigger a common response from the others. Marcus said he was going to take the same wait-and-see approach. He figured he had plenty of time to make up his mind before he died or the Lord came back, and even if he missed the rapture, he could be like Tony and get saved afterwards.

Scott agreed that if the rapture were to take place, it would certainly galvanize him into action, but he wasn't necessarily determined to wait until it happened. He said he was considering making his decision for

Christ without waiting for something that cataclysmic to occur, but he said he still had some things he had to resolve before he could make that commitment. However, it was Aaron's answer that surprised Bobby the most.

He said he was more convinced now than ever that Israel's Messiah was soon to come, but he could not bring himself to believe that Jesus Christ was the one promised by the prophets. Jesus had already lived in the past, but He had failed to destroy wickedness, establish righteousness, and restore the kingdom of David to Israel like the Messiah was prophesied to do. If He couldn't do it the first time He came, why should anyone believe He would be able to do it even if He were able to somehow come again?

Bobby didn't know how to answer him in a way that would change his mind. He knew from the first time he met Aaron in the hospital that he was a very different young man. He was a deeply spiritual person and unconditionally committed to God. He was possessed of a strong conviction that he was destined to serve the Lord in some special capacity, but he was not then, nor yet now, inclined toward biblical Christianity. Bobby could only encourage him to continue to attend the study in hope that God Himself would open his eyes.

Before Bobby closed the study, he asked how many had read any of the *Left Behind* series of apocalyptic novels about the tribulation period. He was not surprised to see that over half of them had. Both Candi and Sarah had read all twelve books in the series, and Scott and Tony and Carl had each read one or two of the volumes. Bobby suspected the rationale behind their postponing their decision to receive Christ might stem from some assumptions they had made after reading the books. He produced several used paperback copies of *Left Behind*[1], the first book in the series, and passed them out to all those who didn't already have a copy at home. He asked them all to read, or reread, as much of the book as they could before their meeting the next week.

Sarah spoke up and apologized for delaying things, but Bobby's mention of the *Left Behind* books reminded her of a question she had wanted to ask about the signs of the end times. "What about the big invasion from Russia?" she asked. "Doesn't it have to take place before the rapture can happen?"

"What invasion?" her husband wanted to know.

"You know, in the first book of the series, there had supposedly been a huge invasion of Israel by the Russian armies, and they had been miraculously defeated by divine intervention. That had apparently already hap-

[1] Tim Lahaye and Jerry B. Jenkins, *Left Behind* (Wheaton Ill.: Tyndale House, 1995).

pened as the book began, and the rapture took place afterwards. Pastor Bobby, doesn't that invasion also have to take place before we can realistically look for the Lord's return?"

"No, I really don't think so," Bobby replied, "but that's an excellent question. You see, the authors, like so many other Bible scholars, want to place that Russian invasion either right before the tribulation, or during it sometime. But I think it's real clear from Scripture that it can't happen until after the tribulation is all over."

He had them open their Bibles to Ezekiel chapter 37. Then he showed them that from that point on, clear to the end of the book, some eleven chapters in all, the whole context was about the great messianic kingdom to come, not about the present age or that of the tribulation period. The whole context describes Israel as dwelling peacefully in the land without any defenses at all at the time of the invasion from the north. He asked the group if anyone else besides him saw anything funny about trying to place that into present-day context.

"Yeah, I do," Aaron said confidently. "Israel is armed to the teeth right now, and it has been ever since it became a nation back in 1948. It has had to fight many wars with its Arab neighbors just to keep from being driven into the Mediterranean Sea. Her existence has always been precarious. Never has she dwelled in peace and safety, and she certainly won't be doing it during the horrible tribulation that's coming. No, this invasion has to take place after the Messiah comes and sets up His kingdom on earth. Only then will there be peace and safety in Israel."

"Bravo, Aaron!" Bobby almost shouted. "I couldn't have said it better myself."

"Then the battle must be at the end of the millennium, where Revelation, chapter twenty also talks about the invasion of Gog and Magog, right?" Candi asked.

"Some scholars think so, but that really doesn't add up either," Bobby replied. "In Ezekiel 39, after God destroys the invaders, the prophet goes on to describe many more details about the kingdom, as he does throughout the rest of the book. But the invasion in Revelation occurs at the end of the millennium and then right after that, the heavens and earth are destroyed and new ones are created.

"No, I personally believe it will take place during a transition period after Christ comes at the end of the tribulation, but before His millennial kingdom is actually fully established.[2] But that's another study for another day, and we don't have time to get into it now. However, I do think we've

[2] See Appendix One for a more detailed examination of the invasion of Ezekiel 38-39.

shown that we don't have to wait until there's some invasion of Israel from the north before the rapture can take place."

That seemed to satisfy everyone and it was time to go. Even Tony and Marcus had been keenly interested in what they had covered, and everyone expressed an eagerness to continue the study the next week.

As they all left the church that Sunday evening early in February, darkness had already settled over the city. A shiver snaked its way down Marcus' back as he made his way to his old Duster. How long, he wondered, would it be before the gloomy night of the coming tribulation would begin to shroud the entire world in darkness? If it happened before he got around to making his decision for Christ, he would surely be able to get right with God afterward, wouldn't he? His mind told him he would, but something much deeper inside him told him he better not count on it. The thought made him feel uncomfortable, so he did what he always had done in such situations in the past. He tried not to think about it. Yet, as he drove away into the darkness, the nagging thoughts refused to be dislodged from his mind.

On the following Wednesday, Marcus was driving the forklift at the salvage yard, moving what remained of a Pontiac Grand Am from one side of the back lot to the other, when Gil called him on the loudspeaker. He needed to shut things down for a minute and come to the front. Someone was there to see him. That was strange. Nobody ever came by to see him at work. He stopped the forklift and lowered the crumpled body of the car to the ground. After shutting off the engine, he hopped down from the lift and walked to the office.

As soon as he entered the back door, he spotted the hulk of Sal Whatshisname, pacing impatiently back and forth in front of the small office. Marcus didn't know him personally. He didn't even know his last name. But he knew he worked for Mr. Apparicio, and he knew he wasn't there to buy a part for his car.

"He says it important," said Gil, motioning to the large figure out front.

Marcus thanked his boss, who was also in the process of becoming one of his best friends, and walked outside to find out what Sal wanted from him. He knew it couldn't be anything good.

"Hey, Snowball, what's happenin'?" boomed Sal, with an insincere attempt at being friendly.

"Nuthin' much," replied Marcus warily. "What can I do for ya?"

"Just a little social call. Mr. Apparicio asked me to stop by and remind you and that celebrity brother of yours that we still got a deal. UCLA's got a game comin' up with Stanford in a coupla weeks, and Mr. "A" expects the Cardinals to upset the Bruins, if you know what I mean."

"No way, man!" Marcus protested. "Stanford's got a sorry team this year. No way could they beat UCLA, not on their best day. Jamal could play on *their* team, and they still couldn't win the game."

"That's not the way Mr. Apparicio sees it. They knocked off Arizona a coupla weeks ago, and the Wildcats were ranked in the top twenty at the time. Stanford is gonna have a great game at home, and UCLA is gonna be off. Your brother is gonna see to that. Stanford will win the game. Capeesh?"

"And what if Jamal can't pull it off?"

"Look kid, my boss and his people lost a lotta money on the Houston game last month. They stand to win that back, and a lot more, with this Stanford deal. But they won't stand for another foul-up. If either of you expect to be around for the championship tournament in March, you better convince your brother to play ball with us. Cause if he don't, you're both gonna be playin' in that big coliseum in the sky. You know what I mean?"

"Yeah, I understand."

"Good. Now you make sure your brother does as well. Mr. "A" says there'll be a coupla grand in this for you personal if everything goes down as planned. So it's in your own best interest to see that it does. We'll be in touch."

With that, the big man patted Marcus on the back and walked away, lighting a cigarette as he went. Marcus stood and watched him go, and when he was far enough away not to detect it, he spat on the asphalt in his direction.

When he went back inside, he lied to Gil and told him the guy was trying to set a drug deal, and that he had turned him down. Once back on the forklift, Marcus cursed his bad luck. Somehow, he would have to convince Jamal to throw the game, but he knew it wouldn't be easy. Since his brother had accepted Christ, he was a different person. He hadn't even been able to get him to run a stop sign since his conversion at the funeral. How was he going to get him to do something as rotten as this? He would just have to figure out a way. He simply had to . . .

Jamal continued to play his spectacular brand of basketball, but he had become even more concerned about winning at the game of life. He witnessed to his teammates on a regular basis and volunteered to lead the team in prayer before their games. Sammy Clayton followed his captain's example and became bold in his own witness. Most of the players were suspicious about this sudden change in their behavior, but some of them were interested and impressed. Especially so was Russell Thomas. But The Kid would probably have shaved his head and started wearing sandals if Jamal had joined the Hare Krishnas, so enamored was he with his hero. Therefore, Jamal didn't know how personal and sincere his interest really was. But he was pleased when The Kid asked if he could go with him and Sammy to church the next Sunday. He began to pray that the young man would soon be genuinely saved. The thought of that gave him a bigger thrill than the thought of winning the national championship again.

Tony continued to eat well, sleep well, swim well, and party well. He was young and healthy, athletic and handsome, and his life was filled with pleasure and the promise of fame and fortune. He had no desire to make any spiritual decision that might jeopardize the future he had planned, especially after he reread a couple of chapters in the *Left Behind* book. He would just continue to live his life as he pleased, and worry about getting right with God only if and when all of his Christian friends were to suddenly disappear.

His chief concern was the precarious position their team was in regarding the national standings. They managed to win their meet on Wednesday and remained in contention for an invitation to the national tournament, but their situation was tentative. They had to keep winning so they would have a chance to compete in the nationals. He had no illusions about their team winning the title, but he wanted to swim against the nation's best so he could get the attention and recognition he felt he deserved. He put a lot of pressure on his teammates to excel, especially on Scott. It bothered him that his friend was apparently so caught up in religion that he was neglecting the really important matters of life, like winning swim meets, going to the Olympics, and getting all the bucks and babes that go along with being a celebrity.

He considered a little religion to be a good thing, just so long as you don't become a fanatic about it. And he was afraid Scott was about to do just that. Candi was one beautiful girl, and he could see why his friend was taken with her, but she wasn't worth giving up all the really good things in life over. His personal philosophy was, if a chick doesn't straighten up and fly right, set her free. There're always lots of other birds in the flock to choose from.

Scott, on the other hand, had all but lost interest in swimming altogether. He hadn't shaved his head since the time of the robbery. His hair was nearly half an inch long by now, and he planned to let it just keep right on growing. It wasn't an act of conscious rebellion. It was just an outward manifestation of what was going on inside him. He still continued to swim well, but it ceased to be of any great importance to him. The dream of making the upcoming Olympic team held little attraction for him. He tried hard not to disappoint Tony and the rest of his teammates, but his heart just wasn't in swimming any longer.

He tried to stay up on his studies, and he did manage to keep his grades from falling off noticeably, but again, he had no heart for academics either. He even thought about dropping out of school altogether for awhile like Aaron had done, but he would never be able to justify it to his parents, and it would only make him look all the more guilty to those two detectives who just wouldn't go away. The whole problem with that was the simple fact that he was guilty . . . as guilty as sin . . . and his conscience wouldn't let him forget about it.

What he really wanted to do was to receive Jesus Christ as his personal Savior and be born again and become a brand-new creature like Pastor Bobby talked about. He wanted to marry Candi if she would have him, and then he wanted to spend the rest of his life loving her and serving the Lord together with her. But his sin kept hanging over his head like a heavy cloud, releasing an acid rain of judgment down upon him.

He seriously tried to pray about his situation. At night he lay in bed before falling asleep, asking God to take away the guilt and set him free . . . if it didn't cost him too much in the process. He still wasn't willing to lose Candi or go to prison for the rest of his life, but surely God could work out something in between. Wasn't salvation supposed to be a free gift? Why couldn't he just confess his sin privately to God and be saved while continuing to conceal his crimes before men? Wasn't that what some people said O. J. Simpson had supposedly done back in the nineties? But whenever he tried to pray and make things right with God, the guilt clouds opened up again and he was forced to quit lest he drown in the flood of his own hypocrisy and self-condemnation.

Candi was struggling too, but under totally different circumstances. First of all, she was angry with herself. She was hopelessly in love with Scott by now. The more time she spent with him, the more deeply she fell. She had promised herself that she would never fall for a guy who was not a Christian, and yet here she was. Scott had still not accepted Christ, and she wasn't sure he was ever going to, but she couldn't imagine living her life without him. She knew he wanted to marry her after they graduated the following year, and she could think of nothing she wanted more, except perhaps his salvation. She prayed earnestly every day that he would receive the Lord so she wouldn't ever have to choose between her Christian convictions and being with the man she loved.

The other thing that nagged at her was the robbery of Papa Saul's store a few weeks before, and the fatal shooting of Bobby's mother. Scott and Tony were still the primary suspects in the crime, although a few biker types had been hauled in and grilled by the police. Scott never brought up the subject, and he became visibly nervous whenever anyone else did. She had gotten to know him quite well by now, and she was convinced he would never purposefully harm anyone. But could he have gotten mixed up in that crime some way? Could that be the obstacle keeping him from accepting Christ? She had the uneasy feeling that there wasn't a lot of time left to sort all those things out. She prayed that God would reveal to her how she could help her friend slay the dragons he faced and find his way out of his darkened maze and into the light of Jesus Christ.

Perhaps most confused of all was Aaron Muller. He found himself drawn ever closer to the God of Abraham, Isaac, and Jacob; and his zeal for the nation Israel was at its zenith. But he could not reconcile what he was learning at the Sunday Bible Study with everything he had been taught before. That would not have been a problem if he could simply dismiss what Pastor Bobby was teaching him, but he found he couldn't do it. The New Testament prophecies he learned were being amazingly fulfilled in current events around the world and what was worse; they seemed to agree with the Old Testament passages he knew so well. But they couldn't be true. That would mean Jesus Christ really was the Messiah of Israel and he would be compelled to accept Him as his own personal redeemer as well. And he just could not possibly consider doing that.

He was an Orthodox Jew, and he was not about to convert to Christianity. Why then did he feel so compelled to attend the Bible study and to read the damnable heresies that contradicted his faith? It was as though God wanted him to know and understand the Christian faith, but not to accept it. Perhaps that was it. God wanted him to know it thoroughly so he would be able to refute it convincingly.

But, if that was the plan, it wasn't working very well. The more he studied, the less sure of himself he became, the more questions he came up with, and the fewer answers he was able to discover.

He had ceased trying to discuss the matter with any of his family or religious leaders. They didn't have any answers for him anyway, and all they did was get mad at him for exposing himself to the cunningly devised lies of the Gentile subversives. However, he never even thought about dropping out of the Bible study. As confusing as all this was to him, that was one thing he was sure he was supposed to do. He would see it through to the end, learn as much as he could, and trust God to reveal the divine purpose behind all it in His own sovereign time.

CHAPTER EIGHTEEN

THE ENIGMA

At the Bible study the next Sunday afternoon, they were supposed to discuss the *Left Behind* books and see what light they might shed on the rapture question and the timing of salvation in relationship to it. But Jamal surprised everyone by interrupting right after the prayer and asking if he might pursue another subject for a moment. He said it wouldn't take long and he would burst if he tried to hold it in any longer. Bobby was a bit annoyed because he had his lesson all planned out and he was sure he would need all the time he could get to make it through all the material. But he was pleased his son was so excited about his newfound faith, and he didn't want to discourage him, so he agreed to let him go ahead if he would try to be brief.

Jamal was obviously excited and eager to share with the others, but he was having trouble finding the right words to express what was on his heart. After a couple of false starts he said triumphantly, "Me and Sammy saved The Kid today!"

"What you talkin' about, Jamal?" asked Marcus. "You saved him from what?"

"I mean, God saved him . . . but we helped," beamed Jamal. "The Kid came with Sammy and me to church this morning, and afterward we stopped at a Kentucky Fried Chicken place for lunch on the way home. While we were there, The Kid started askin' questions about Dad's message and what it meant to be a born-again Christian. Well, we told him as best we could and showed him some Scriptures we've been learning, and he said he wanted to do it right there."

"You've gotta be kidding," said Carl. "Whaddya do?"

"Well, we didn't really know what to do. We thought about bringing him back here and trying to find Dad, but we decided we could handle it ourselves. I just told him about what I said when I prayed to receive Christ, and told him to say that to the Lord. He said he didn't know quite how to do it, so I just told him what to say, and he repeated after me. I know I didn't get all the words right, but right there, over a plate of fried chicken and coleslaw, The Kid asked Jesus to come into his heart and save him. I think it took too, cause I've never seen him so excited about anything else before."

"That's wonderful, Jamal," said Candi. "Isn't that just great, everyone?"

Exactly half of them agreed enthusiastically with her. The other four would just as soon Jamal had kept the news to himself. They hadn't made that decision, they weren't ready to make that decision, and the news of someone else making it only served to make them more nervous and self-conscious about it all. They mumbled something and smiled, but they clearly weren't as excited about the good news as the others were.

"That's great, Jamal," Bobby agreed. "Now that you've brought a new baby into the world, you're responsible to see that he gets off to a good start."

Bobby got up from the table and went over to the counter, where he bent and retrieved some booklets out of one of the drawers. He came back and sat down and handed them to Jamal. "Take these back to the dorm with you. You and Sammy need to start a Bible study of your own there. Invite The Kid and anyone else who's interested and go through these books. They cover all the basic doctrines a new believer needs to learn. One of them's a leader's guide, and it will tell you how to conduct the class. It will be good for The Kid, and good for you too. I always get more out of teaching a class than any of my students ever do."

Jamal gratefully received the booklets and agreed to start the Bible study that week. He already had in mind several people he was going to invite.

Now, Bobby was eager to get right into his own Bible study, but Marcus interrupted and asked if he might bring up something himself. He had been reading in the Book of Revelation, and he thought he'd discovered something, but he wanted to bounce it off the others to see what they thought.

Bobby really didn't want to delay any longer. He was sure the observation would add little, if anything, to the conversation, but he was thrilled that Marcus was studying on his own and asking questions, so he pretended he was interested and encouraged his son to proceed.

First of all, he said he had to ask Aaron a question. Everything else he had to say depended on his answer. Aaron was fascinated to know what this tall black man, whom he hardly knew, had to inquire of him. He readily gave his permission.

"Are you a virgin?"

"Snowball!" shouted Jamal. "That's not funny, man."

"Marcus, I'm ashamed of you," Bobby scolded. "This is a serious conversation. If that was an attempt at humor, it failed. You have no right to ask Aaron, or anyone else, a question so personal. It's none of your business, and it has nothing to do with what we're studying. I insist you apologize right now!"

"Hey, I'm sorry, man," Marcus quickly replied. "I didn't mean to embarrass you or nothin', but I'm really serious. I know it's none of my business, but it's not a stupid question. If you don't want to answer, it's okay; but there's a couple of chapters in this book that really got me goin', and your answer will help straighten things out for me."

"You're right, it's none of your business," agreed Aaron. "But it's not embarrassing to me. I have committed my life completely to God. I have no time or, for that matter, any interest in romance. Yes, I'm a virgin, and I plan to stay that way. But I'm dying to know why you asked."

"Me too," said Tony. "I can't say I understand the man's answer, and I sure can't agree with his chosen lifestyle, but I sure wanna know why you had the gall to ask him that question."

"Well, Tony," replied Marcus, "I guess an explanation is in order. I just had to know to help me figure him out. Everybody else I got down pretty good. You and me, we're just alike. We like our freedom and we like our fun, and we don't want to give it up in order to get saved. Mr. Scott over there, on the other hand, I think he wants to get saved, but he's strugglin' with something that's keepin' him from it right now. The two ladies are good as gold, fine Christian women, here to stand by their men. Jamal and Carl here are blossoming young Christians, growing like weeds, but Aaron over there, he had me buffaloed. He's been what I think they call an enigma. But now, I think I've got him figured out too."

"Oh, yeah?" Tony came back. "Besides being a Boy Scout, what do you know about him?"

"Well, I could be wrong," admitted Marcus, "but unless I miss my guess, he's gonna be one of those 144,000 Jewish dudes in the Bible."

"How in the world did you come up with that conclusion?" asked Bobby.

"Well I got my first clue here in Revelation, the seventh chapter. Here let me read it to you, beginning with the first verse."

He opened the New American Standard Bible he had borrowed from his dad and began to read where he had marked the place:

After this I saw four angels standing at the four corners of the earth, holding back the four winds of the earth, so that no wind should blow on the earth or on the sea or on any tree. And I saw another angel ascending from the rising of the sun, having the seal of the living God; and he cried out with a loud voice to the four angels to whom it was granted to harm the earth and the sea, saying, "Do not harm the earth or the sea or the trees, until we have sealed the bondservants of our God on their foreheads." And I heard the number of those who were sealed, one hundred and forty-four thousand sealed from every tribe of the sons of Israel.

"Now if I understand this correctly, these dudes are sealed at the very beginning of the tribulation, before any harm comes to anybody or anything, right?"

"Yes, I believe so," said Bobby. "But what makes you think Aaron could be one of them? Sure, he's Jewish, but so are about a hundred million other people on this planet."

"Yeah, I know, but what really got me goin' was what I read at the beginning of the fourteenth chapter. Here let me read it to you."

He flipped over a few pages and read aloud:

And I looked, and behold, the Lamb was standing on Mount Zion, and with him one hundred and forty-four thousand, having His name and the name of His Father written on their foreheads. And I heard a voice from heaven, like the sound of many waters and like the sound of loud thunder, and the voice which I heard was like the sound of harpists playing on their harps. And they sang a new song before the throne and before the four living creatures and the elders; and no one could learn the song except the one hundred and forty-four thousand who had been purchased from the earth. These are the ones who have not been defiled with women, for they have kept themselves chaste. These are the ones who follow the Lamb wherever He goes. These have been purchased from among men as first fruits to God and to the Lamb. And no lie was found in their mouth; they are blameless.

"Now, unless I got this all wrong," continued Marcus, "these are the same 144,000 guys as before, only now they're at the end of the tribulation, standing on the mountain with the Lord when He comes back to the earth."

"Now I see where you're coming from," interjected Candi. "The 144,000 are described as being virgins and above reproach. I've got to admit, I don't know of anyone who is more moral or more committed to his religion than Aaron, but there's a problem with your theory there, Marcus. The 144,000 are totally committed to the Lamb, and Aaron hasn't even accepted Jesus as his Savior yet, and he says he's not going to. He can't be one of the followers of the Lamb."

"Of course not," responded Marcus, "not yet, anyway. If he accepted Jesus now, he'd become part of the Church, and he'd be taken out of here at the rapture. He's got to stay committed to God and to Israel and to morality, but he can't get saved yet. Then, after the rapture takes all you Christian types outta here, God will zap him and 139,999 others just like him, and they will carry on the Lord's work during the tribulation after y'all are gone."

"Marcus, where did you come up with that idea?" asked Bobby. "As crazy as it sounded at first, it's beginning to make sense. That would explain Aaron's almost fanatical commitment to spiritual things, but also his absolute resolve not to accept Christ at this time.

"But, Aaron," he continued, turning his attention to the young man sitting quietly at the other end of the table, "we're all sitting here speculating about your future, and we haven't even asked you what you think. The possibility of you being identified with the 144,000 sounds intriguing, but we could argue back and forth about it all day and be no closer to the truth than we are right now. The only really important question is, 'What do you think about all this?' Do you think you could be one of them?"

Aaron had been quiet through all the previous conversation. He found it almost amusing that Marcus had come up with the outlandish idea in the first place, but Marcus was pretty outlandish himself, so it wasn't too surprising. What really amazed him was the way the rest of them seemed to buy into it so quickly. "Not a chance," he said. "There's no way I could ever be one of those 144,000. I'd never even heard of them before today. There're two good reasons I can think of right now that would make it impossible for me ever to be one."

"Yeah, what are they?" asked Scott, having become very interested in the conversation. He had struggled to define his own reasons for not being included in God's family. He was eager to hear someone who seemed to have no ambiguity at all; who knew exactly where he stood and why.

"Well, for one thing," responded Aaron, "God would have to hit me over the head with a two-by-four to get me to place my trust in Jesus Christ. No offense, but I just don't buy your claim that He is the Messiah of Israel. These 144,000 are supposed to follow the Lamb wherever He goes. Well, I can't see myself ever doing that. They're supposed to have His name branded on their foreheads. I would rather have my head cut off than to have it branded with the name of one I consider to be a false Messiah."

"You sound just like Saul of Tarsus, in the Book of Acts," Bobby said. "He heard the gospel preached by Stephen and others, but he rejected it completely. He considered the preaching of Jesus Christ to be the devil's assault on his beloved Judaism. He went about opposing Christianity with all that was in him until God hit him over the head with a two-by-four when he was on the road to Damascus in Acts, chapter nine. Christ appeared to him personally and changed him instantly from being His greatest enemy into being His greatest advocate. That sort of thing could happen to you too if you happen to be one of His chosen vessels like Paul was."

"Well, it would have to be against my will," said Aaron, "and I don't believe God would ever make me do something against my own free will. Besides, even if He did, I couldn't be one of your 144,000 anyway."

"Why not?" Scott wanted to know, but he asked for everyone else in the room as well. This wasn't the subject scheduled for discussion for that afternoon, but it certainly had everyone's attention.

"Because I don't qualify, that's why," he answered. "Sure I'm a zealous Jew, and I happen to be a virgin, but I'm certainly not blameless like those 144,000 are supposed to be."

"Why, what terrible things have you done?" kidded Tony. "Have you snuck a peek at a girly book, or talked back to your mommy, or what?"

Aaron didn't laugh. He became very serious, and glanced at Carl Singleton as he spoke, "No, Tony, I wish it were something as simple as that. I've never talked about this before with anyone, especially with a policeman sitting in on the conversation, but I guess now's as good a time as any. I could never qualify as being blameless, because I'm guilty of massive destruction of property and, quite possibly, the taking of human lives."

"What are you talking about?" demanded Scott. "You gotta tell us!" He was intrigued to hear about what skeletons might hang in Aaron's closet. He thought he was the only one who was plagued by ghosts from the past. Tony showed no sign of conviction at all over what he had done, and Scott was beginning to feel that something was wrong with him because he was struggling so much with his own conscience. It was refreshing to hear that someone else might also be struggling with the same sort of thing.

"Alright, I will . . . under two conditions," responded Aaron. "First of all, if it's alright with you, Pastor Bobby. I know you had something else planned for today's study, and this could take awhile."

"That's okay, son. You go right ahead," replied Bobby. He had planned a different lesson, but now he was just as intrigued as the others to hear what Aaron had to say. And besides, this might lead to a breakthrough with him that could result eventually in his salvation.

"The other thing," said Aaron, "is your confidence. You all gotta promise not to repeat what I say. I have no desire to go prison for the rest of my life. Will that be a problem for any of you, especially you, Carl, being a peace officer and all?"

Carl looked puzzled for a moment as he sorted through the information he had just received. After a moment, he said, "I don't know if I can make that promise absolutely. If you committed a major crime right under my nose, I don't think I could just look the other way, but if it was out of my jurisdiction and had no lasting impact, I see no reason I would have to say or do anything about it. Is that commitment enough for you?"

"Yes, that'll do just fine," Aaron said. "Not only was it not in your jurisdiction, it wasn't even in your country. It all happened last summer when I went to Israel to attend the groundbreaking ceremony for the new temple in Jerusalem. I went only as a tourist, to attend what I considered to be the greatest event in the history of Israel in the past two thousand years. I never intended to become a terrorist."

So, with the ground rules established and the schedule cleared, Aaron revealed his story. With few interruptions, the eight other people in the room sat spellbound for the next hour as he told of his exploits in the Holy Land.

He went to Israel by himself; other friends and family quite content to watch the proceedings on TV from the comfort of their own living rooms. But he felt compelled to be there in person. He used money from his own savings account to pay for the trip, which he considered to be a worthwhile and, indeed, a necessary investment. When he arrived there, he found the whole country awash in young men just like himself who had come from all over the world, tens of thousands of them. They too had felt compelled to come, to be there for the rebirth of their sacred temple. After all, what was Israel without its ceremonies and sacrifices, and what were they without the temple? For nearly two thousand years, Israel had been spiritually handicapped, but that was all about to end.

The hotels were soon filled beyond capacity, and the young men were camping out in fields and parks in and around the city. There were rallies and meetings every day. Their preaching and singing and praying was filled with enthusiasm and optimism, that is, until the day before the scheduled groundbreaking ceremony. A Palestinian suicide-bomber disguised himself as a Jew and blew himself up inside the Great Synagogue in western Jerusalem, killing himself and dozens of innocent people. The Muslim extremists claimed responsibility and threatened to continue even more violent acts of terrorism unless Israel agreed to abandon its plans to rebuild the temple.

The rebuilding of the temple had long been sought after by the Jews, but the Muslims, who controlled the temple mount, had absolutely refused to consider it even after Israel regained control of that part of Jerusalem in

1967. It wasn't until Constantine Augustus negotiated an agreement between Israel and the PLO that it became a possibility. Israel agreed to give up land to the Palestinians and to Syria in exchange for the guarantee of peace, and for permission to rebuild the temple on its original site. A wall was constructed just north of the Dome of the Rock, dividing the temple mount between the Muslim sector to the south, and the Jewish sector on the north. The temple was to be built directly west of the walled-up Eastern Gate, which is believed by most scholars to be the exact location of the former temple.

Most of the Muslim Arabs accepted the fact that the temple was to be rebuilt, just as long as it didn't infringe upon their exclusive sovereignty over the southern half of the mount. But certain radical factions swore to do whatever was necessary to prevent the building of the cursed Jewish temple; hence the suicide bombing and the threat of even worse to come.

After the bombing of the Great Synagogue, several Jewish men got together to decide what they were going to do about it. Aaron felt privileged to be asked to attend the meeting. The room was filled with young men, all in their early twenties. One particularly zealous man, by the name of Joseph, seemed to be in charge. The meeting went long and was heated and emotional at times, but in the end, they did come to a conclusion. They must retaliate, and they must do it quickly.

It was decided that the Dome of the Rock must be attacked to show the Muslims that the Jews could not be intimidated, and that they could fight fire with fire. It was revealed that a hand-held rocket launcher with its missile had been hidden in one of the tombs on the Mount of Olives some months before just in case it would be needed in such a time as this. All that was lacking were two volunteers who were willing to risk their lives by firing the missile. About fifty hands shot into the air.

Joseph told them that since the Muslims had that area so heavily guarded, the only ones who would even be permitted on the Mount of Olives would have to be those from another country without a Jewish sounding name. That eliminated everyone except Aaron and a young man from Philadelphia by the name of Mark Robertson. He was a handsome medical student of average height and build, with sandy colored hair and blue eyes. Both he and Aaron were devout Jews, but they had the looks and the passports of American citizens, and they had inherited Gentile last names from male ancestors somewhere in the past.

It was agreed they would join a sightseeing tour, scheduled to tour the Mount of Olives the next day. They would separate themselves from the group and hide out until after dark, at which time they would locate and remove the missile hardware from its hiding place. They would be given training on how to operate the rocket launcher so they would be able to fire it, even in the dark. Their mission was to fire the missile across the Kidron Valley and into the side of the Mosque of Omar, otherwise known as the Dome of the Rock. The missile wasn't armed with a huge warhead, so it shouldn't destroy the entire building, but it would cause considerable damage, and it would definitely make their point.

After some training on how to fire the rocket launcher and some instructions on how to carry out their mission and make their escape, Aaron and Mark tried to get some sleep.

In the morning they went to the King David Hotel as instructed, and located the large tour group from the U.S. that Joseph had told them about. The group was comprised of nearly eighty excited charismatics from a huge church in Denver. They were in the process of boarding two large luxury buses in front of the hotel. Aaron and Mark identified the obvious tour leader who was directing the loading operation and counting heads. They introduced themselves to a harried little man everyone called Brother Larry, and handed him a hastily forged letter from the senior pastor back in Denver, identifying them as two of the church's college students who had decided at the last minute to go to the Holy Land. In it, the pastor requested they be added to the tour. Brother Larry accepted the letter, and them, with a hearty, "Praise the Lord, thank You Jesus," and they were introduced to the other, much older, pilgrims on the tour.

They were to spend the day on a walking tour in the old city of Jerusalem. The buses took them to the Dung Gate at the southern end of the walled city, and dropped them off there. They all walked through the narrow streets to the site where the ancient Jewish temple had once stood. There, they visited the Western Wall, also called the Wailing Wall, which had been part of the two thousand-year-old foundation of the temple mount. There they prayed and put little bits of paper in the cracks between the massive stones of the wall. On the papers they wrote prayers calling on God for the rebuilding of the temple and the coming of the Messiah. Both Aaron and Mark thrilled to actually be praying at such a sacred place.

Next they visited the Muslim sector of the temple mount, which neither of them enjoyed at all. They made excuses and neither of them even entered the Dome of the Rock. They felt that it would have been an act of sacrilege to do so. They were not allowed to visit the northern Jewish sector of the Mount. Nothing was there yet anyway, and preparations were being made for the groundbreaking ceremony, which had been temporarily postponed, because of the terrorist bombing.

The rest of the morning was spent following the path of Christ's journey to the cross, down what is called the *Via Delorosa,* or the Way of

Sorrows. Again, this was not pleasant for either of them, so filled was it with Christian tradition. But they pretended to be enjoying themselves, taking notes and photographs at appropriate places. After lunch at a sidewalk café, their group visited the Church of the Holy Sepulcher where Jesus was supposedly crucified and buried, which they found crowded and unimpressive. Then, in the mid-afternoon, they all went to the site of the Garden Tomb, just outside the Damascus Gate. They found this enclosed park-like setting beautiful, restful, and relatively quiet. But it was operated by a group of evangelical Christians from England who tried to indoctrinate them with evidence of the empty tomb and the resurrection of Jesus Christ. They were immensely uncomfortable all the while they were there, and were greatly relieved when it was finally time to go.

At last, toward evening, their entire group was loaded onto their two buses and transported east of the city to the Mount of Olives. When they entered the Arab sector, the buses were stopped and armed guards entered to check everyone's passport. Aaron and Mark were cleared, along with everyone else on the tour. The buses stopped near the top of the hill and everyone exited to face the ever-present horde of peddlers who preyed on the occupants of the endless caravan of sightseers. Some of the tourists purchased souvenirs, others paid for short camel rides, while still others busied themselves taking various pictures of the Old City across the valley with the rays of the setting sun reflecting off the golden dome of the Mosque of Omar.

A group picture was arranged and everyone was instructed to assemble along a stone guardrail with the city, draped in twilight, in the background. Aaron and Mark managed to slip away unnoticed. The last thing they wanted was to have their pictures taken at the scene of the crime.

The final event scheduled for the day was a walk down the steep and narrow Palm Sunday Road to the Church of all Nations, located at the bottom of the Kidron Valley and next to the Garden of Gethsemane. After visiting the church and then praying at the darkened garden, just as Jesus had done so long ago, the buses would pick them up out front and take them back to their hotel for dinner.

Aaron and Mark told Brother Larry they had to get back to their hotel right away, so if it was all right with him, they would catch a taxi back, and they would join the group early in the morning for the next day's trip to Jericho and the Dead Sea. Larry was so tired from riding herd over scores of senior citizens all day that he would have been agreeable to just about anything. He made a notation in his planner and blessed them as he hurried off to assist some of the more feeble folk down the steep descent to the valley below while there was still enough light to see.

Once Brother Larry was well out of sight, Aaron and Mark started down the road behind the others, but they ducked into an alcove and waited there until they were sure everyone else had gone on down the hill. Then they climbed the stone wall behind them and waited in the enclosed cemetery for the hours to pass.

Sometime near midnight, when that area of the hillside had long been deserted, they felt it safe to move about. They located the tomb in the corner of the little cemetery, just as they had been instructed, and slid the heavy stone slab from off the opening and located the rocket launcher inside it. They put on cotton gloves, so as not to leave any fingerprints, and retrieved the heavy launcher and its missile from the tomb. They replaced the slab and carried their equipment to the wall. Aaron climbed the wall first and Mark handed the materials over to him before he scaled the wall himself. Once they fired the missile, they were going to have to make their escape immediately. They didn't need a wall in their path while dozens of Palestinian soldiers were descending upon them.

That part of the western slope of the Mount of Olives was covered with thousands of Jewish graves. They would have to make their escape down the hill, through the graveyards, and into the Kidron Valley below. Moving under the cover of darkness, they crossed the road into the adjoining cemetery, thankful that the moon had not yet risen and it was quite dark. Also, the Jewish graves were built above ground, from stone or concrete vaults covered by stone slabs. The would-be terrorists were able to sit down and hide among the raised monuments.

Aaron turned on a small flashlight and checked to see that the missile was loaded properly into the launcher, and then he activated them both. He had never fired anything like it before, but he had done some bird hunting with his father, so he had volunteered to be the shooter since Mark had never even touched any sort of a weapon in his entire life.

They both looked around the area carefully, trying to spot any sign of life or movement. Satisfied they were alone on the hillside, Aaron stood up and shouldered the heavy weapon. He put his finger on the trigger mechanism and looked through the sight until he located the lighted dome of the sacred mosque. He had been told the missile would adjust its own course in flight so he wouldn't have to calculate for a curving trajectory. It would fly straight and true until it ran out of fuel. So he just aimed it at the base of the golden dome and began to squeeze the trigger. He wondered why he wasn't more nervous. He felt measured and confident, as he imagined King David must have felt before he entered into battle with the hated Philistines. He was God's man fighting a holy war against the enemies of Israel.

Suddenly the missile shot from the muzzle of the rocket launcher with lightning speed. There was no recoil, but the light from the exhaust was blinding. The mosque was less than a thousand yards away, and the rocket covered the distance almost instantly. The following explosion was as brilliant as it was thunderous. Had their situation not been so desperate, it would have been a marvelous sight for them to drink in and savor.

As it was, they didn't get to see the collapsing dome, crumbling walls, and devouring fire. All they saw at first was a big red spot in the center of their vision, as though a camera had just flashed in their faces. Fighting to regain their night vision, they stumbled to find their way down the hillside before they themselves became the target of enemy fire.

Almost immediately they heard the sound of angry shouts and engines roaring to life on the hill above them. Beacons of light soon began to dance over the graveyard as searchlights sought to locate the desecrators of the sacred shrine.

Aaron and Mark had left the rocket launcher right where it landed when Aaron dropped it after the shot. They now crawled on their bellies down the hill, snaking their way between the raised monuments of the graves, trying desperately not to be seen. They could hear the sound of voices and running footsteps up the hill, and they knew they would soon be having company.

Gradually, the spots began to fade from their eyes and they were able to see somewhat where they were going. Mark whispered they were going to have to make a run for it. If they continued as they were, they would be overtaken before they made it to the bottom of the hill, and neither of them even wanted to think about what might happen to them if they were taken captive. Aaron agreed and, on a signal, they sprang to their feet and began running headlong down the hill.

Their silhouettes were picked up almost immediately in the beam of one of the searchlights, and the sound of human voices was drowned out quickly by the staccato of automatic gunfire. Bullets rained down upon the graveyard as the two young men raced down its steep incline. The projectiles smashed into the rocky ground around their feet, and ricocheted by their heads off the stone monuments next to them. But neither were they struck by any bullets or by chunks of stone dislodged by them, nor did they stumble or fall as they sprinted down the hill. It was as though God had sent His angels to escort them safely out of harm's way.

At last they reached the bottom of the hill, vaulted a wall, and turned left, running down the road at the bottom of the Kidron Valley. They were temporarily out of sight from the guns at the top of the hill, but they were by no means out of danger. Soon those pursuing them would also scale the wall and open fire again, and armed vehicles would soon overtake them on the road on which they now ran. They could hear their engines backfiring and, over their shoulders, they could see the headlights making their way down the hill. The two fugitives had but one chance of escape, and it was a slim one at best.

They sprinted down the middle of the road, amazed at the speed and stamina they possessed, and equally amazed at the fact that no one and nothing appeared to impede their retreat. Just before they were bathed in the light of the headlamps of the pursuing vehicles, they jumped off the road to the right and ran between two structures and down some stairs, only to be met by a metal gate secured in place by a sturdy chain and padlock. Not only that, they found themselves standing in water above their knees. But rather than curse their bad luck, they rejoiced over the fact that they had been able to reach their desired destination so quickly, and in the dark.

They ducked down as several vehicles passed on the nearby road, shining their spotlights to the right and left. When the Jeeps had passed, the two fugitives jumped to work, knowing they had little time before those on foot would be combing every inch of the entire area. With his little flashlight, Aaron located the bolt cutters and padlock stashed above a ledge by some of Joseph's men. As Mark held the light, Aaron used the bolt cutters to sever the old lock so they could remove the chain and open the heavy steel gate. They went through the gate and closed it behind them and then put the chain back in place and used the new lock to secure it as before. They dropped the old lock in the water inside the gate and, carrying the bolt cutters, they started wading down the narrow tunnel that led westward into the side of the hill.

They hurried around the corner as the tunnel made a bend to the left and angled toward the south. There, they stopped and turned off their flashlight. They waited in the total darkness for a few seconds before they heard voices and saw a beam of light being shown down the tunnel after them. The foot soldiers had arrived at the gate and were trying to gain entrance, but the chain and lock were keeping them out. After banging at the gate for a while, apparently the soldiers became satisfied that the fugitives had not been able to gain entrance either, and they left to pursue them elsewhere.

After waiting a short time to make sure their pursuers were indeed gone, Mark and Aaron turned on their flashlight and resumed their trek down the narrow tunnel, deeper into the side of the hill. They were wading in the water from the Gihon Spring, which had flowed from that spot for thousands of years. The tunnel they were in had been chiseled out of solid rock over twenty-six hundred years earlier by order of King Hezekiah of Judah. The Gihon Spring in that day, as it is today, was on the outside of the city walls and unavailable to the inhabitants of the city in time of siege. So Hezekiah had ordered workmen to start at either side of the hill, which separated the spring from the city, and tunnel toward each other. Amazingly, they were able to meet almost straight on, in the middle of the small mountain. The water began to flow from the spring, under the hill, under the city wall, and into the Pool of Siloam, located in the midst of the ancient City of David, almost half a mile away. And twenty-six centuries later, it continued to flow.

It was through that ancient tunnel that Aaron and Mark slowly made their way, sometimes having to stoop to keep from banging their heads, and sometimes wading in water almost up to their waists. The tunnel was maintained as an attraction for the more adventurous tourists, but it was always locked up at night for security reasons. As it was, it made an excellent getaway device for the two amateur terrorists, just as Joseph had thought it would.

After some time, the tunnel made a gentle turn to the right, and the two soon arrived at the western end of the tunnel. They again cut through the lock at the gate and made their exit. And again, they found another lock placed previously on a ledge above their heads, with which they secured the gate behind them. As they waded out of the pool, a car came roaring up from out of the shadows, the door was flung open, and the familiar voice of Joseph beckoned them to get inside. They threw the bolt cutters and the ruined lock inside and jumped in after them as the car sped off into the night.

They made it back to where they were camped without incident, and were never questioned by the authorities about the terrorist bombing. Constantine brought in U.S.E. troops to quell the rioting between the Jews and the Muslims, and declared a state of martial law. After securing the peace and making promises to both sides, the groundbreaking for the temple took place a week late, simultaneous with the ceremony to commence the restoration of the Dome of the Rock. The day after the missile attack, Aaron was on an El Al 747 on his way back to LAX. He had never told anyone anything about what had happened in Israel until now.

"So you see," said Aaron, "I couldn't be one of your 144,000. I willingly took part in a terrorist attack on a religious shrine, and destroyed a priceless monument from antiquity. The Muslims said a caretaker and two guards were killed in the attack, although no bodies were ever produced. So I may be guilty of murder as well. I'm certainly not blameless like you say those guys in the future are supposed to be."

"Wow, you are some kinda bad dude, alright," Marcus agreed. "But I don't know. Does that mean you couldn't be one of the 144,000? Dad, it seems to me what they did was pretty righteous. What do you think?"

"I'm afraid I agree with Marcus, Aaron," answered Bobby. "The amazing story you've just shared with us makes me more inclined to believe you might be one of the 144,000, rather than convincing me that you couldn't be."

"How can that be?" Aaron asked, dumbfounded.

"Well, for one thing, there were so many young men just like yourself over there at the same time. Were they all as committed and zealous as you and that Mark fellow were?"

"Yeah, now that you mention it, I think every one of them would have done what Mark and I did if they had been given the opportunity. I've never been around men with whom I've had so much in common."

"Well, there you go," Scott cut in. "It sounds like you're all part of one huge, exclusive fraternity to me. Besides that, how do you account for how you and Mark were able to pull that off without any military training whatsoever? Two college-boy tourists could never have blown up that mosque and then got away from that army. You should have been caught, or shot, or both, a dozen times over. The only answer I can come up with is that God was watchin' your backsides while you were exposing them to every trigger-happy Palestinian in Jerusalem with a gun."

"And even though what you did was violent and destructive," added Bobby, "it doesn't necessarily disqualify you from being one of the 144,000. Like I said before, Saul of Tarsus was a zealous Jew who hated Christians and inflicted much suffering on them in his own pre-Christian days. But he did it in ignorance, and God called him anyway, and he went on to become the apostle Paul, perhaps the greatest of all Christian leaders of the early church."

"And didn't Jesus Himself get rather physical and even destructive when he drove the moneychangers out of the temple?" asked Sarah.

"You're right," said Bobby. "He took some whips and drove them out. He turned over their money tables and turned their animals loose. John's gospel in the old King James Version tells us that He said, *'The zeal of thine house hath eaten me up.'*"

"I bet if He'd had a Stinger missile back then, he'd have used it on them moneychangers, just like you boys did on them Muslims," Marcus added.

"I don't know about that," Bobby broke in, "but He certainly was protective of His Father's temple, even as you and Mark were of yours. No, I can't be positive, of course, but perhaps the two of you, and maybe all those young men back there as well, are being set aside as God's special instruments for His use during the coming tribulation period."

"I don't know if I agree with all this stuff or not," said Tony, "but I gotta tell you, I find it really exciting. That's why I'm gonna wait and see how it all pans out before I make any decision for Christ. If nothin' ever happens, then I'll go on livin' the good life. But if what you're saying really takes place, then I'm gonna get saved along with Aaron here, and join him and his gang and fight the devil's bunch."

"Me too," agreed Marcus. "I read in that *Left Behind* book how a bunch of dudes got saved after the rapture and then whipped up on that Nicholae character, big time. They seemed to outsmart him on every turn. I want to get in on some of that action."

"Now hold on there," Aaron objected. "I don't plan on accepting Christianity at any time, before or after the rapture. I am not, nor will I ever be, part of your 144,000. I'm sold out for Judaism, and I always will be. And as far as all that excitement and adventure goes, I hope I never get involved in anything like that missile attack again as long as I live. I'm sorry, but you've got the wrong guy."

"I think you may all be wrong," observed Bobby. "Aaron, if God has chosen you as one of His special witnesses, and it looks like He may well have, He will change your stubborn heart when the time is right. Never say never when it comes to God and His will.

"As for you two," he said, as he looked at Tony and Marcus, "I know for sure your reasoning is dead wrong. In our study next week, we'll see just how foolish it is to think it's a good idea to put off getting saved until after the rapture. I wanted to talk about it today, but the Lord seemed to have other plans. And what He had us learn will better prepare us for what He has for us next week anyway."

With that, Bobby wrapped up the study. He assigned them to read about Daniel's seventy weeks, in Daniel 9:24–27, before their meeting the next Sunday. He wanted them to compare what the prophet said there with what they had already studied in the Bible, and with what they found implied in the *Left Behind* series. Bobby said he was confident they would change their minds after next week's study about wanting to wait till after the rapture to come to Christ.

As they all left that evening, Aaron lingered behind. He wanted to talk to the pastor alone. He had been bothered by something Bobby had said, and he wanted to get it clarified if he could. Bobby agreed to meet with him for a few minutes, but he said he would have to leave before six to get ready for the evening service.

"Do you really think God could convert someone against their will?" Aaron asked, when they were alone in the conference room together.

"No, certainly not," answered Bobby. "Throughout the Bible, the invitation is given out to, '*Whosoever will.*' God would never force anyone to do anything against his own will, but sometimes He works in people's hearts to bring about a change in their wills. That's what happened to the apostle Paul, and lots of others like him since then. But I wouldn't wait till it happens if I were you. The rapture may still be a long way off, and you may not be one of the chosen 144,000 after all. You could die before any of that ever takes place. You need to accept Christ right now if you feel the Lord tugging at your heart."

"That's the crazy part about it, Pastor," said Aaron. "I find all these things we've been studying fascinating, but I feel no compulsion to convert to Christianity at all. If I prayed to receive Christ right now, my heart wouldn't be in it, and it would be to no avail, right?"

"That's right," admitted Bobby. "Don't do it unless you're sincere. Hell is full of people who made empty professions of faith. But don't harden your heart either. I really believe God has placed His hand on you, son. He's got some great things planned for you. Just keep listening, and respond to Him when He speaks to your heart. Okay?"

"Okay, but don't hold your breath. It would take a real miracle to get me to change my mind."

Aaron thanked Bobby and left by the back door, even as people were starting to come in the front one. The evening service would be starting soon. But before he went in to greet the faithful, Bobby knelt beside the table in the conference room and prayed earnestly for the miracle Aaron had talked about. "Whatever it takes, dear Lord," he prayed, "bring that young man to Yourself."

CHAPTER NINETEEN

THE SEVENTIETH WEEK

The week had nearly passed and still Marcus had not talked to Jamal about his conversation with Sal. It was Friday, and the game with Stanford was just two weeks away. It was to be the last scheduled game of the season before the beginning of March Madness, the NCAA tournament for the national championship. Sal had come by the wrecking yard again, looking for confirmation, and Marcus had assured him everything was set with Jamal, lying through his teeth.

The problem was, he just didn't have the heart to confront his younger brother about the mob's demands. Jamal was playing great basketball, but that was to be expected. The thing that really had him excited was his Bible studies. He enjoyed the one at the church each Sunday afternoon, and he was learning a lot, but the one in the dorm at school was absolutely thrilling to him. About ten of his friends and teammates had attended the first meeting on Monday night and things had gone great. The Kid gave his testimony about receiving Christ, and everyone seemed to enjoy the discussion Jamal led. Afterwards, Sky King stayed and talked with Jamal and Sammy for a long time. Before he left, he too bowed his head and prayed and gave his life to the Lord.

Marcus had tried to talk to Jamal about the Stanford game after UCLA's victory over Arizona State on Thursday night, but he couldn't get a word in edgewise. His brother was so filled with praises to the Lord and thanksgiving for the salvation of another one of his teammates, Marcus just didn't have the heart to break in and bring up the subject. He figured he would have a better opportunity to drop the bomb when Jamal wasn't so excited about spiritual things. But seeing the way his brother had been acting over the past several weeks, he wasn't at all sure when that opportunity might present itself.

Scott and Candi continued to see one another regularly. They weren't technically dating, but it was close. They spent most of their free time together, and there was no denying their deep love for each other. Still, Candi resisted getting involved romantically. Scott didn't even try to embrace or kiss her, even though he desperately wanted to. She insisted she was not ready for that stage in their relationship. She no longer brought up the fact that she was keeping her distance until such a time as Scott came to Christ, but they both knew that was the reason, and it didn't need to be discussed any further.

Most of their discussions were about spiritual things anyway. After Aaron's revelation of his involvement in the terrorist bombing of the Dome of the Rock, they continued to speculate as to whether he might be destined as one of God's chosen 144,000. They agreed that if the rapture were to occur soon, then he probably was, but they also agreed that it would be foolish for Aaron to put off accepting Christ with the hope of being transformed supernaturally by God after the rapture. They also agreed there was something tragically wrong with the wait-and-see plan Tony and Marcus had adopted. Somehow it just didn't seem prudent to presume upon God's grace.

The more they talked, the greater became Scott's own conviction. How could he be critical of his friends' procrastination when he couldn't bring himself to make a commitment either? He promised Candi, and himself, that he would make his own decision soon. He wasn't going to keep postponing it indefinitely. He was determined that by the time they had finished the study with Pastor Bobby, he would have either washed his hands of Christianity altogether, or he would have made an irrevocable commitment to Jesus Christ.

On Thursday, the swim team at Cal State Long Beach lost its meet with Cal State Bakersfield, which had a surprisingly strong team. Nevertheless, Tony D'Angelo was furious. He knew his team should have won the meet, but his teammates just didn't put out like they could have. The loss meant they would most likely be eliminated from any invitation to the national champion meet. He was especially critical of Scott Graham. His friend seemed to be so wrapped up in his relationship with Candi and with that Bible study that he didn't have the time or the heart for swimming that Tony had.

Aaron immersed himself in his work at The Corner Store. He rose early in the morning to prepare for the business of the day and stayed long after closing time, cleaning up and stocking shelves. Papa Saul scolded him for working too hard. His grandfather tried to get him to take some time off and go see his family, or ask Anna out on a date or something, but to no avail. Aaron was not interested in pursuing a social life, or any other sort of life, for that matter. He worked at the store so enthusiastically, only because it gave him something to do to keep from going crazy.

He could not get out of his head the haunting accusation that Marcus had made that he was going to be one of the 144,000 chosen men of Israel to proclaim the gospel of Jesus Christ during the coming tribulation period. He didn't even believe in Christ, much less could he ever see himself being one of His evangelists. Yet, he had no answers for what those at the Bible study had said. Why were all those zealous young Jewish men gathered together at Jerusalem last summer, and why were they so united in their determination to rebuild and protect their temple? Why had he and Mark Robertson blown up the Dome of the Rock, and how had they been able to escape unharmed against all odds? Why was he so fascinated with biblical prophecy and the claims of Jesus of Nazareth when he had always believed Him to be a false prophet?

Questions like those, and others, prompted him to call back to Philadelphia and talk to Mark on the telephone. They had exchanged numbers before they left Jerusalem, but they hadn't talked in over six months. When Aaron identified himself, Mark was flabbergasted. He had been about to call Aaron. Things were happening in his life that he couldn't understand, much less explain. He had dropped out of medical school and had started attending night classes at the Philadelphia School of the Bible. He spent most of his time studying biblical prophecy and the Christian claims concerning the return of Jesus Christ and the coming tribulation period.

"Have you converted to Christianity yet?" was Aaron's question.

"Of course not," Mark replied, "and I don't plan too, but why am I drawn to these things? I was wondering if you had experienced anything like this?"

"You're not gonna believe this," said Aaron, and he commenced to tell Mark what was going on in his own life: from his narrow escape with death and the dropping out of school, to his participation in the Sunday afternoon Bible study. He went on to tell him of his friends' claim that he was being prepared by God to take his place among the 144,000 after the rapture of the church.

Mark said he hadn't considered that possibility, but he intended to check it out. They promised to keep in touch and to support each other in their Jewish faith in order to prevent either one of them from falling for the convincing lies of the Christian false teachers.

Bobby Davis rose from his knees in his office Sunday afternoon. He had been praying for the past hour for the souls of the four young men in his Bible study who still hadn't accepted Jesus Christ. He had long since given up questioning God about the death of his mother. She was freed from her arthritis pain and was present with the Lord, and dozens of people had come to Christ as a result of her death, including two members of his own family. A small revival had broken out in his church. He had never before seen so many of his people committed wholeheartedly to the things of Christ, nor had he seen so many visitors at church and so many new professions of faith. But he had been leading the Sunday afternoon Bible study since the end of January, and the four members who were unsaved at the beginning of the study were unsaved still.

He knew there was nothing he could do to cause any of them to come to faith, but he was a strong believer in the power of the Holy Spirit and the power of prayer. He had prayed fervently that the Spirit of God would take His Word and impress it on their hearts and that He would open their eyes to the truth of the gospel. He prayed for each one of them individually, and claimed their salvation before the Lord.

The water in the coffeepot was hot, and the bagels were fresh (a little something he had added on Aaron's behalf), and the ladies of the church had brought in some other goodies as well. He had his whole church praying for all the young people in the study, and the ladies had taken it upon themselves to keep them well supplied with refreshments. If a spoonful of sugar helps the medicine go down, they figured a plateful of sugar cookies ought to do the same thing with the gospel.

All was in readiness. He felt a shiver of nervous anticipation as he awaited the arrival of his guests.

Everyone arrived on time. So interested had they all become in the study that no one had been late at all since the first week. After a short time of small talk and refreshments, they all took their seats and opened their Bibles to the ninth chapter of Daniel.

Bobby began with prayer and then asked Aaron to read verses twenty-four through twenty-seven.

Aaron was familiar with the passage. He had studied it many times, but he was not at all sure what it meant. He was eager to hear what Bobby thought about it. He borrowed Marcus' New American Standard Bible because his Hebrew interlinear version was so difficult to understand, and began reading at verse twenty-four:

> *Seventy weeks have been decreed for your people and your holy city, to finish the transgression, to make an end of sin, to make atonement for iniquity, to bring in everlasting righteousness, to seal up vision and prophecy, and to anoint the most holy place. So you are to know and discern that from the issuing of a decree to restore and rebuild Jerusalem until Messiah the Prince there will be seven weeks and sixty-two weeks; it will be built again, with plaza and moat, even in times of distress. Then after the sixty-two weeks the Messiah will be cut off and have nothing, and the people of the prince who is to come will destroy the city and the sanctuary. And its end will come with a flood; even to the end there will be war; desolations are determined. And he will make a firm covenant with the many for one week, but in the middle of the week he will put a stop to sacrifice and grain offering; and on the wing of abominations will come one who makes desolate, even until a complete destruction, one that is decreed, is poured out on the one who makes desolate.*

When Aaron finished reading, he looked up at Bobby and said, "What was that all about? I know it refers to the future, because it speaks of the coming of the Messiah, but what is that stuff about seventy weeks, seven weeks, and sixty-two weeks all about?"

"I think I can help you with that," said Bobby, "but first I want you all to know that this passage forms the basis for all prophecy about the coming of Christ and the coming tribulation period. This is about the only place in the Bible that actually gives us specific dates we can work with. If we can understand what Daniel is telling us here, we can pretty well put the whole puzzle of biblical prophecy together. Let me explain it to you the way almost all the prophetic commentators understand it, and then we'll consider some other possibilities."

Bobby took the next several minutes to explain that virtually all Bible scholars agree that the seventy weeks Daniel mentioned were weeks of years, not weeks of days. Therefore, the entire period in question would have been 490 years. Most scholars agree that the seventy weeks began back in the fifth century B.C., when a decree was issued to rebuild the walls of Jerusalem. They also believe that sixty-nine weeks later, or after 483 years, the Messiah was cut off. That of course was when Jesus was crucified and later raised from the dead. After that, Christ inaugurated His church, thereby stopping the prophetic clock, so to speak, leaving the seventieth week yet to be fulfilled in the future after the church is taken out of the way at the rapture. The scholars believe the antichrist will be the *prince who is to come,* whom Daniel talks about in verse twenty-six, and he will be the one to actually start the seventieth week.

Then Bobby asked if anyone could explain how the antichrist would start the week and how it would play itself out.

"I think I can," said Tony. "I read a couple of those *Left Behind* books and I think I got it figured out pretty good. The antichrist fella is gonna negotiate a peace treaty between Israel and its Arab neighbors for a period of seven years. That'll be the beginning of the seventieth week. The first half will be a time of false peace, and things won't be too bad, but I guess in the middle of the week, he will break the treaty, and during the last three-and-a-half years, all hell will break out on the earth. I don't know for sure, cause I didn't read all the books, but I figure at the end of that time, the Lord will return and destroy the antichrist, and we'll all live happily ever after."

"Well, that's a bit of a simplification," Bobby said, "but that's more or less what the authors of that series would lead us to believe, and most other Bible scholars pretty much agree with them. Assuming the experts are right, how does that make you feel about entering into that seventieth week?"

"I want no part of it," interjected Candi. "I'm so thankful Jesus saved me a long time ago, and He's going to come and take me to heaven at the rapture, and I won't have to be here during that terrible time."

Carl and Sarah heartily agreed with Candi, as did Jamal. Carl and Jamal were both brand-new Christians, but they already had a sincere longing for heaven and a desire to escape the pollution of this world. Nothing about the coming tribulation period held any attraction for them at all.

Scott said he didn't want to experience it either, but if the rapture were to occur that night and he were to be left behind, he would get saved immediately, so at least, he would have the Lord with him during the next seven years of suffering.

Aaron said he didn't have to think about it, because he didn't believe the rapture was going to take place and nobody was going anywhere. He didn't expect to be left behind at all.

"But what if you're wrong, Aaron?" Scott asked. "What if you wake up tomorrow and find out all the Christians are outta here. What would you do then?"

"I have no idea," he admitted frankly. "I guess I'd be inclined to believe at that point. Just like if a space ship were to land out there in the church parking lot and little green men stepped out of it, I would be inclined to believe in alien life forms. But it's never happened yet and I don't believe it's going to. I believe this rapture stuff is the same kind of a deal."

"Oh, I don't think it would be so bad if it did happen," said Tony. "In those books I read, the people left behind fared pretty well. They got saved and formed that *Tribulation Force* and outsmarted that Nicholae character at about every turn. They built a safe house he couldn't find, they established a universal internet system he couldn't crack, they used high-powered cell phones he couldn't trace, and they traveled all over the world without him ever stopping them. Besides that, they bugged his plane, his office, and his home, I think. They had their own people planted in all his agencies, and they knew what he was going to do long before he ever did it. They had plenty of money and equipment and other resources to see them through the entire tribulation period."

"Yeah," Marcus readily agreed, "besides that, they had these little crosses on their foreheads that identified them as Christians, which Nicholae's bunch couldn't see. They could tell the good guys from the bad guys and could readily spot an impostor, but the bad guys were totally in the dark. Besides that, they were protected from all the plagues and demon attacks. Only the bad guys got stung and bit and torched. I would definitely want to be part of that *Tribulation Force* during that time. We could kick some serious butt."

"Yeah, Snowball, I can just see you and Tony and Scott and Aaron forming your own anti-antichrist group," chided Jamal, "but there's just one difference. You ain't got no money, no airplanes, no safe house, no internet, no connections, no nothin'. You're just an ex-con and three college boys, without a clue. What are you gonna call yourselves . . . *The Tribulation Farce*?"

Marcus' curse words directed at his brother were drowned out by howls of laughter. Even Bobby couldn't help himself. The tension that had been building inside him was released in loud guffaws. He quickly regained his composure and tried to restore order to the Bible study. He gave the thumbs up sign to one of his deacons who had heard the uproar and poked his head inside the door to check and see if everything was okay.

"Jamal," he said, "that was totally out of line. I would insist you apologize immediately, if I didn't agree so much with your assessment. I wouldn't have put it in just those words, but I have to admit, anyone who thinks it's a good idea to put off getting saved until after the rapture is either ignorant or a fool. And since I know none of you is a fool, I must assume you're all ignorant of what the Bible really says about that terrible time of tribulation. Let me share with you some of the things the authors failed to point out in their books.

"In the first place, the Bible never mentions anywhere, anything about any three-and-a-half-year period of false peace at the beginning of the tribulation. That period of relative tranquility, where those who're left behind can get saved and can fortify themselves against the antichrist, is purely the figment of their imagination, and the imagination of many others. I know I'm just an ex-con who's never been to Bible college, but I've read the Good Book plenty, and hundreds of other books written about it, and there just ain't no such period of peace described anywhere in it.

"Also, the Bible never divides the tribulation into two halves at all. It's divided by three different series of judgments, and again by three distinct "Woes", but it's never divided into halves at all. Scholars assume it's divided because the seventieth week of Daniel is divided in half, and they assume the tribulation and that seventieth week are synonymous. But the Bible never says they are, and the New Testament never even hints that there are two different periods in the tribulation."

These statements created a barrage of questions and even accusations, so Pastor Bobby spent the next thirty minutes going into great detail explaining his theory about Daniel's prophecy. He showed them that according to his investigations, the sixty-nine weeks ended at the beginning of Christ's ministry, not at the end of it, and that the first half of the seventieth week was fulfilled during His three-and-a-half-year earthly ministry. Christ was crucified halfway through the seventieth week, not before it began, thus leaving only the last half of the week to be fulfilled during the tribulation.

He used a great deal of Scripture and supported it with logic and historical data, and in the end he had convinced virtually all of his students that the coming tribulation would only be three-and-a-half years long, not seven as nearly all the scholars believed.[3]

"Okay, I give up, Dad," Marcus said, waving a Kleenex in the air like a white flag of surrender. "I didn't understand everything you said, but you've convinced me that the tribulation won't be seven years long. It looks like it'll only be the second half of Daniel's seventieth week. But, so what if it's only gonna be three-and-a-half years long, what difference does it really make, anyway?"

The rest of those sitting around the table voiced similar feelings. Jamal added, "You've had us studying this stuff for over an hour now. It must be pretty important to you. Tell us how the difference in its duration will affect the nature of the tribulation, and why is it so important that we understand it."

"Excellent point, Son. I tell you what. Let's take about a ten-minute break here. I've got to go powder my nose, and I think we could all use a little breather. Hold that thought, and we'll pick up on it right where we left off, at about a quarter after five."

[3] See Appendix Two for a more detailed examination of Daniel's Seventy Weeks prophecy.

CHAPTER TWENTY

THE TRIBULATION

Everyone was up from the table except Aaron. Some had gone to the restrooms. Others had stepped outside to enjoy the warmth of the late afternoon sun. Marcus and Tony had stayed in the room and were checking out the refreshments on the counter. Strangely, they had become friends over the past few weeks. About the only thing they had in common was their unbelief, but they had found camaraderie in supporting one another in their infidelity. They were talking quietly over a cup of coffee and a doughnut. But Aaron wasn't interested in their conversation, nor in anything else that might have been occupying the rest of the group at the moment. He just sat at the table, staring down at the ninth chapter of Daniel, reading and rereading verses 24–27.

What was he going to do? Intellectually, he no longer had a leg to stand on. Pastor Davis had thoroughly dismantled any confidence he had in his traditional beliefs. Not only did the passages in the New Testament they had studied support what Bobby had been saying, but the Old Testament confirmed it as well. Jesus of Nazareth was not the impostor he had always believed Him to be. Aaron could not deny that Jesus fit the biblical portrait of the Messiah to a T, and intellectually, he was ready to accept Him as such, but his will would not allow it.

There was a barrier there he just could not understand. He no longer felt any hostility toward Christianity, nor toward any of the Christians he had come to know and care about, but there was nothing in his soul that drew him in that direction either. He could profess an intellectual decision to accept Jesus as his own personal Messiah, but he knew it would not be a genuine commitment. He loathed hypocrites and he vowed he would never profess anything he did not sincerely believe.

He had prayed before that God would show him the errors in all the false teachings of Christianity so he could refute and reject it once and for all, but instead, he had become convinced that those teachings were supported both by Scripture and by the unfolding of history. Now he found himself ready to accept it all with his mind, but he found no faith in his heart with which to do it. What kind of game was God playing here anyway? He prayed silently as he sat there that God would reveal some answers soon, before he lost his mind.

Little tributaries of sweat seeped down his forehead, collecting at his brow. Tugged by gravity, they joined together and made their way carefully down the bridge of his nose until they had no place else to go. In spite of their efforts to stay together, gravity pulled them apart, one lingering drop at a time. The drops of salty perspiration splashed, one after another, into an expanding puddle on the tabletop in front of him, but Aaron was oblivious to its existence, so absorbed was he in the thoughts that were troubling him.

"Hey, Aaron, you alright?" Tony called out, noticing Aaron's blank stare and his sweaty brow.

"What? Oh, yeah, sure," Aaron stuttered, waking to reality. "I guess it's hotter in here than I thought."

He got up and went to the counter, where he splashed water from the faucet on his face and dried it with some paper towels. Then he used them to wipe up the puddle he had left on the table. He tossed the towels in a wastebasket and headed for the door.

"I think I'll go outside for a minute and get some fresh air," he said, a bit sheepishly.

"Hey, I know how you're feeling, dude," Marcus called after him. "My dad, the preacher man, has got me and Tony here sweatin' it out too."

Five minutes later, everyone was back in his place around the table. Bobby found it interesting that since the very first session, everyone always sat in the same spot each week. He also found it interesting that the believers sat closest to him and those unsaved found their places farthest away. Bobby sat at one end of the table, opposite the door and closest to the chalkboard, with Jamal next to him on his left. Next to him sat Candi and Scott, in that order. At the other end of the table Aaron sat, looking directly down the table at his teacher/tormentor. To Aaron's left sat Tony and Marcus, far away from Bobby and closest to the refreshments. Rounding out the table were Carl and Sarah, with Sarah sitting at Bobby's immediate right.

He got their attention and checked his watch. The break had lasted longer than he had planned, and they only had about thirty minutes left before they would have to adjourn. He reminded them their time was limited and asked them to hold their questions until the end, and he would try to leave some time to answer them then.

"Now let's get right into it," he said gleefully, rubbing his hands together in an exaggerated gesture of happy anticipation. "I believe the first half of Daniel's seventieth week was fulfilled during the three-and-a-half-year ministry of Jesus Christ in the first century. The week was interrupted at the halfway point when Jesus was betrayed and put to death. After His resurrection and ascension, God established the New Testament Church to replace Israel as His chosen instrument on this earth. Daniel's seventy weeks have been put on hold, and will stay that way as long as the church remains here on earth. The second half of the week will begin as soon as the church is raptured out of here and the antichrist sets himself up in the temple, proclaiming himself to be God.

"By the way, it looks like that could be happening sooner than you might think. I was watching on the news last night and I saw that the temple has been completed in Jerusalem now, and they've set the date for its dedication for a week from next Friday. It also just so happens to be the thirtieth birthday of Constantine Augustus, who plans to be there to moderate the ceremony himself. Unless I miss my guess, he's the antichrist, and I can't think of a better time for him to make his move than when all the world will be watching."

"But won't all the other prophecy buffs be expecting him to do it at that time as well?" interrupted Marcus. "I thought Jesus was supposed to come suddenly, at a time when the world was not expecting Him."

"That's right, Son," Bobby replied, "and the truth is, not many are expecting Him to come just yet. You see, most everybody is expecting the tribulation to start when the antichrist orchestrates a seven-year peace treaty between Israel and its Arab neighbors, not with him proclaiming himself to be God in the temple. They don't expect him to do that until three-and-a-half years later. No such treaty has been signed, no peace talks are being held at this time, and there isn't even any mention of any such treaty being considered. So, most scholars are thinking the rapture of the church and the start of the tribulation are still a ways off. If the rapture were to occur at the time of the temple dedication, it would take most people by surprise.

"But just for fun, let's say what I've been telling you is true, and the Lord does rapture His church soon, and Constantine does proclaim himself to be God at the time of the temple dedication, then what?"

"Please tell us, oh Enlightened One," Marcus said playfully, bowing and pretending to pay homage to his father.

Bobby just frowned and shook his head as others in the room laughed at Marcus' antics. "Okay, wise guy," he said, "I'll do just that. I expect the whole dedication scene to be electrified with fear and apprehension. If the rapture precedes it, and I think it could, the whole world will be in a state of chaos and panic. You see, if all the Christians are to be taken out instantly all over the world; their cars, buses, planes, and trains will crash because the drivers and pilots will have suddenly disappeared. Just think of all the mass destruction and devastation that will occur when all those Christians manning crucial machinery and equipment vanish instantly. Constantine will profess that he has an explanation and a solution for all the chaos, and virtually everybody in the world will be watching him for some answers.

"At the time of the dedication, he could give some lame excuse that the great 'World Soul,' or the 'Cosmic Consciousness,' or whatever he chooses to call it, has removed the evangelical Christians because they were hindering the movement toward global religious unity. He could tell everyone that there is nothing standing in their way now to prevent them from realizing the full spiritual potential of mankind. He could also tell them that this full potential can only be realized when they all recognize and accept their one true God. Him, of course."

"Do you think he'd be able to pull it off?" asked Jamal. "Could everybody really be that gullible?"

"No, not initially," answered Bobby. "I expect there would be great opposition to his declaration at first. Unless I'm wrong, some zealot would even rise up against him and kill him because of his blasphemies."

"You're kidding, right?" questioned Scott. "How could he be the antichrist throughout the tribulation if someone knocked him off before it ever got started?"

"Remember a couple of weeks ago, how we saw in Revelation 13 that the beast will be put to death, and then be raised back to life? Well, I think it could happen almost immediately. The devil is such a counterfeiter, he would probably leave him dead for three days, and then he will gloriously raise him back to life. Constantine would have all sorts of miraculous powers, and he would convince almost the whole world that he really was God in the flesh. The frightened and confused masses would flock to worship the miracle worker who promised to guide and protect them."

"But not everybody would follow him, right?" asked Jamal.

"Right. Ten national leaders would join him immediately, probably the heads of the World Federation countries, and he would appear to be invincible. But he would have his opposition as well. The 144,000 Jewish young men would be converted by then, and they would raise up a powerful spiritual force against him. Multitudes of both Jews and Gentiles would be saved as a result of their testimony, and they would refuse to fall for his lies. Besides that, some national leaders would oppose him, and even three of the ten who were with him at first would turn against him as things heated up. No, he wouldn't have the whole world eating out of his hand, by any means."

"So, how do you see the tribulation playing out, Pastor?" Aaron asked, looking across the table at Bobby, with a hint of agreement registering in his eyes.[4]

"Well, Aaron, I don't see any three-and-a-half years of false peace, allowing anybody any time to do anything. I see the tribulation just like Jesus described it in Matthew, chapter twenty-four. He said just as soon as the enemy brings his abomination into the temple of God, everyone better head for the hills, because all hell's about to break loose on the earth. In verse twenty-one, he says, *'For then there will be great tribulation, such as has not been since the beginning of the world until this time, nor ever shall be.'*"

"Yes, but Pastor Bobby," Candi interrupted, "don't most of the Bible scholars agree that the passage relates to the second half of the tribulation? Don't they say the antichrist will go about building his power base for three-and-a-half years before he ever steps into the temple to make his claim of deity?"

"Yes, you're right. They do make that claim, but it's just not consistent with what we see in the rest of Scripture. Let's all turn to Revelation, chapter six, and let's see how it describes the beginning of the tribulation. All the scholars agree that the first five chapters of Revelation are preliminary to the tribulation. It doesn't actually begin until chapter six. So, for those who believe in a seven-year tribulation, this chapter must be describing what takes place during the first three-and-a-half years. But just listen to how the apostle John describes it.

"It starts out in verse two with the introduction of the antichrist, just as I've already told you, but we don't see him as the author of any kind of peace. He's on a white horse, pretending to be the good guy, but in his hand is not an olive branch, or a turtledove, but a war bow. He isn't there to bring peace, but the Bible says, *'He went out conquering, and to conquer.'* He comes with a crown on his head, and he goes forth to make himself king of the world by force.

"The second horse is red, the color of blood, and the rider is commanded to take peace from the earth, not to establish it in any form. It goes on to say that he is given a great sword, and people on the earth go about

[4] See Appendix Four for a more detailed examination of the tribulation period.

killing one another. That doesn't sound like any kind of period of peace or stability to me. But it sounds exactly like what you would expect after the antichrist unleashes his fury on all those who oppose him.

"Then take a look at the third horseman, in verses five and six. He's riding on a black horse and he has a pair of scales in his hand. He introduces famine to the earth, where a quart of wheat will cost an entire day's wage. With the world engulfed in war, very little farming will go on, and what little is raised won't be allowed to be distributed. People will be suffering from hunger all over the world. So much for our boy creating the illusion of peace and prosperity.

"The fourth horseman is perhaps the worst of all. He rides in on a sickly lookin' horse and his very name is Death. Verse eight ends with the words, *'And Hades followed with him. And power was given to them over a fourth of the earth, to kill with sword, with hunger, with death, and by the beasts of the earth.'* Between these four horsemen, one out of every four people on the earth will be killed. That's nearly two billion people! What kind of peace is that?"

"Chill out, Dad," Marcus chided his emotional father. "We get your point. If what you've just described to us is three-and-a-half years of peace, then my name is Asser Arafat."

"Hey, I'm just getting started," Bobby added with a grin. "Look at verses nine through eleven. Here, we get a picture of a huge multitude of people who are in heaven, who have been killed for their faithfulness to the word of God. They are comforted and told to wait until the rest of their brothers should be killed as well."

"Whoa. I know you asked us not to interrupt, but we've been doing it all along anyway, and I gotta do it again," Jamal said apologetically. "I've been reading those *Left Behind* books and they don't sound anything like this. Nobody gets hassled for his religion in the first few books, much less put to death. That Nicholae character lets everybody have freedom of religion. He even lets people publish articles criticizing him and his program. What's up with that?"

"That's exactly what I'd like to ask the authors myself," said Bobby. "They don't really explain the sixth chapter of the Book of Revelation . . . or the seventh either, for that matter. If you look at 7:9–16, you'll see an even greater multitude of saints in heaven who had gotten saved, and then martyred for their faith during the tribulation. And remember, according to those authors, this all takes place early in the first half of the tribulation. According to them, the second half doesn't even start until after the eleventh chapter."

"So, exactly what are you saying here, Pastor?" Tony asked, his anxiety showing in his voice.

"Just this, Tony. You and your friends, who plan on waiting until after the rapture to make your decision for Christ, had better consider what you'd really be getting into. There will be no three-and-a-half-year period of relative peace, allowing you to get saved at your leisure, and then to prepare for the bad times to come. The tribulation will start out horrible, and then it will get worse. Even if you did accept Christ, you would face almost certain death. You would have no opportunity to outwit the antichrist. In Daniel 7:21 it says the antichrist, '*was waging war with the saints and overcoming them.*' In Revelation 13:7 it says, '*it was given to him to make war with the saints and to overcome them.*'"

"Are you sure the tribulation will be that bad?" Tony asked. "Surely the really bad stuff happens at the end, right?"

"I'm sorry to disappoint you, Tony, but it's all really bad, and then grows increasingly horrible. Take a look at verses twelve through seventeen, and you'll see what I mean. Remember, according to the books you've read, this is supposed to describe what happens about in the middle of the first half of the tribulation." He began to read:

> *I looked when he opened the sixth seal, and behold, there was a great earthquake; and the sun became black as sackcloth of hair, and the moon became like blood; and the stars of the heaven fell to the earth, as a fig tree drops its late figs when it is shaken by a mighty wind. Then the sky receded as a scroll when it is rolled up; and every mountain and island was moved out of its place. And the kings of the earth, the rich men, the commanders, and the mighty men, every slave and every free man, hid themselves in the caves and among the rocks of the mountains, and said to the mountains and the rocks, "Fall on us and hide us from the face of Him who sits on the throne and from the wrath of the Lamb! For the great day of His wrath has come, and who is able to stand?"*

"Now, I don't know about everyone else," Bobby said a bit sarcastically, "but I wouldn't want any part of conditions like that. Would you, Tony?"

"No, of course not," Tony agreed, "but that's not how the *Left Behind* books describe it at all. Those guys are Bible scholars, with doctor's degrees. How come they interpret the Bible so differently than you do?"

"I'm not sure how to answer that question, Tony. They, and other scholars like them, have a much better education than I do, and they're probably a lot smarter than me too, but I still believe they're wrong about the tribulation. In all fairness to them, though, we need to remember they were writing a novel, not a theological textbook. The scenario they created made for some very exciting stories, but it didn't necessarily square very well with the scriptural account of the tribulation at all. I think the primary result they were shooting for was drama, not doctrine."

"Yeah, Dad, but you even admitted that the rest of Bible scholars agree with them more than they agree with you," Marcus said. "Can they all be wrong?"

"That's funny, Marcus," Bobby replied with a smile. "A little while ago you said you were convinced that what I had shared with you was true. Now you're ready to reject it all. If you ask me, you guys want to reject my conclusions now, not because they're contrary to what the Bible says, but because they're contrary to what you want to believe. You don't want the tribulation to be horrible from the beginning. You want it to start out easy and non-threatening so you can justify putting off accepting Christ until after the rapture. Don't make the mistake so many others have made by tailoring your beliefs to conform to convenience rather than conviction."

"Well, I can't speak for the others," said Marcus, "but I'm willing to take that chance. I'll just hope that the other scholars are right and you're wrong. But even if you're right, I'll still have a chance. If I see the tribulation startin' out like hell on earth, I'll just accept Christ and try to hide out and make it through. If I can survive on the streets of Compton, I ought to be able to survive anywhere. But even if I die, I'll go to heaven with all those other dudes, and I'll wait till Aaron and his buddies whip up on the antichrist and his gang."

"Amen, brother, preach it," agreed Tony. "And if all of you are wrong, and no rapture occurs at all, me and Snowball here will live out our lives in pleasure and freedom while all you guys devote yourselves to serving a God who isn't even coming. You'll spend the rest of your lives all dressed up, with no place to go."

Scott and Aaron, the other two unbelievers in the room, failed to chime in, voicing their agreement. Instead, both of them just lowered their heads and stared at the top of the table. The reasoning of their two friends seemed rational enough to their natural minds, but something inside them told them it was dead wrong.

Bobby was obviously saddened by the response of Marcus and Tony, not because he had lost a debate, but because he feared he was about to lose his own son and a promising new friend. He said, "You're both free to make that choice, but before you do, we need to meet together one more time."

"Why's that?" Marcus asked. "I think we've heard about all we need to about when the rapture's coming and what the tribulation's going to be like."

"What I want to share with you isn't more of what we've already been studying. It's true, I could give you lots more Scripture to prove my point, but I don't think it would convince either of you. No, what I want you to see is on a different subject altogether. I'm afraid you're making the same mistake countless others have made down through the years. You think you can decide to reject Christ time after time, and yet still be in the position to receive Him whenever it suits your fancy."

"Yeah, so, what's wrong with that?" Marcus asked, genuinely surprised that his father would even question such reasoning.

"Just that the Bible condemns that sort of thinking, and those that think it. Next week I want us to look at what Scripture teaches about the destiny of those who know the truth and consciously reject it before the rapture. Will they be just as free to accept it afterwards?"

"Well, of course we will!" Tony almost shouted. "Why wouldn't we?"

"That's what I want us to find out about next week. In preparation for the class, I want you all to read 2 Thessalonians 2:1–12. And if you get real ambitious, you can read Romans, chapters nine through eleven as well. In the meantime, I want you all to stay alive, especially you four," Bobby said, looking directly at the four unbelievers seated at the other end of the table. "You've already failed to respond to so much truth. It would be a fearful thing indeed to have to stand before the Lord and try to explain to Him why you still haven't accepted it."

He had pricked their curiosity, and many of those in the room expressed their desire to continue the discussion. But they were out of time, and besides, Bobby wanted to leave them with a tantalizing question that would prompt them to read about it, and cause them to want to return the next week and discuss it. So, he declined their requests and dismissed them with a brief prayer.

As he watched them file out, Bobby prayed that the Lord would do whatever was necessary to break down the barriers that had been keeping the four young men from expressing their faith in his blessed Savior. Had he known what the near future had in store, perhaps he would have been more thoughtful before he uttered that prayer.

Although they had been studying the Bible and discussing spiritual things for nearly two hours, most of those in the study group stayed to attend the evening service at the Antioch Baptist Church. Jamal and the Singletons were in the habit of doing so each week, but on this occasion, they were joined by Scott and Candi. Out of curiosity, even Aaron decided to stay and find out what a Protestant Christian church service was all about. Only Marcus and Tony were absent. They left together, having made plans during the break for a night of entertainment, which certainly didn't include going to a church service.

The music that evening was happy and spirited. After about twenty minutes of singing, several testimonies were given by members of the congregation about what God was doing in their lives. Their words were powerful and convicting. Then, after Zelma Parsons sang a special solo number about God's love and faithfulness toward his people, Pastor Bobby got up and preached a message about the necessity of responding to the call of God. His message prompted a continuing chorus of approving remarks from the enthusiastic congregation, but it twisted the knife of conviction deep in the hearts of Scott and Aaron.

Aaron got up and left about halfway through the sermon, partly because he was so uncomfortable, but also because he had promised to get back and help Papa Saul close up after another busy Sunday night at The Corner Store. Ever since the robbery and shooting there the month before, Aaron had made it a point not to leave his grandfather there alone during the late hours of the night.

Scott sat through the entire service, his soul being torn in opposite directions all the while. Part of him wanted to join in worship with the others and praise the Lord for His greatness, but the other part of him wanted to run out the back door and never return. In response, he did neither. Instead he sat quietly and listened, showing little outward reaction of any sort. He felt himself being definitely drawn to Christ, but he dared not respond to that call, not yet anyway. He had hoped that the dilemma he faced would somehow have resolved itself with the passing of time, but it still stared him squarely in the face. As he sat there listening to Bobby pour out his heart, he felt the preacher was speaking directly to him. He knew he would have to make his decision soon. He sensed the door of opportunity rapidly closing before him.

CHAPTER TWENTY-ONE

THE PLOY

The alarm's loud and obnoxious buzzing forced Marcus into a state of semi-consciousness at 7:30 on Monday morning. He reached over to turn it off, and promptly fell out of bed. He had purposefully moved the nightstand away from his bed the night before because he knew himself all too well. He had been out late partying with Tony the night before, and he had way too much to drink. He knew if he had left the alarm within reach, he would have subconsciously turned it off and gone right back to sleep. As it was, he was rudely jarred awake as his lanky body sprawled on the floor beside the bed.

He had been at his job at the wrecking yard for a month now, longer than he had ever worked anywhere in his life. During that time, he had missed work only one day, to attend his grandmother's funeral, and he hadn't been late at all. He was proud of his record, and he didn't want to break it. So, as miserable and hungover as he felt, he still forced himself to get up and go into the bathroom and get ready to face the day. He even felt a twinge of guilt for his rowdy behavior the night before.

"That's strange," he thought to himself, as he looked at his puffy-faced reflection in the smudged mirror. "I've done a whole lot worse things before than I did last night, and I've never even given it a second thought, but now I'm feeling guilty about a few beers and a few babes. Maybe all this Bible study is starting to rub off on me. I'm working a steady job, I'm staying off the drugs, I'm going to church and Bible study, and now I'm feeling conviction over a little nightlife. What's next, a full-blown conversion?

"Nah," he told himself, "this is just a phase I'm goin' through. Things will start gettin' back to normal when we finish that Bible study next week, and I quit hangin' out with all them Christians. There is definitely such a thing as being exposed to too much religion."

Marcus shrugged it off and busied himself with his simple preparations for work. He shaved, dressed, picked up a slice of cold pizza from a cardboard container left on the table from Sunday afternoon, and padded down the stairs of his rundown apartment building. His throbbing head protested loudly with every step of his descent, but he knew from experience that after a few cups of coffee and a couple of hours on the job, his hangover would gradually go away. So, with determination, he pushed himself out the door and into the bright sunlight of the early morning.

The bright light only aggravated his discomfort, and he closed his eyes and turned his head away from the direction of the sun. Thus handicapped, he walked directly into a large body positioned in his path. He recognized immediately the one with whom he had collided, without even seeing him. The sunlight was still too painful on his eyes for him to open them, but it was the rancid smell of garlic, tobacco, body odor, and booze that gave away the other man's identity.

Sal grabbed Marcus by his shirt collar and backed him up against the side of the dirty brick building. He got right up in his face and spoke loudly, "The big game's comin' up a week from Friday, boy. You sure that celebrity brother of yours is set to throw that Stanford game?"

"Yeah, sure, don't worry about it, man. I've taken care of it."

"You better reconfirm it," Sal growled. "Mr. Apparicio ain't gonna accept no foul-ups this time. You get with your brother right away, and have him call me and tell me personal-like that he's for sure gonna throw that game. My number's on this card. And you better make it quick, cause Mr. Apparicio don't like no loose ends. You know what I mean?"

With that, he stuffed the card into Marcus' shirt pocket and released his grip on his collar. "You and Jamal do what you're told and we'll all be fine. You cross us this time, and neither one of you will live to see who wins the national championship this year. Am I making myself understood?"

"Yeah, I understand," moaned Marcus. "I'll have him call you by Wednesday."

"Make sure you do," Sal grunted as he turned and walked down the street.

The combination of the stale pizza and the hangover and the sunlight, coupled with Sal's stench and the fear he instilled in Marcus, were just too much for the latter's stomach. Waves of nausea seized him, and Marcus was barely able to stagger to the curb before he was doubled over with convulsions. The hastily chewed pizza and the remainder of the foul contents of his stomach were soon added to the already filthy gutter.

The practice Monday afternoon had been grueling. Coach Englehart had been especially hard on his swim team. His athletes had failed to live up to their potential, and to his expectations. At the beginning of the season, he had thought they might have had a good shot at the national championship. He had three potential all-Americans on the squad in Tony D'Angelo, Scott Graham, and Aaron Muller, and a strong supporting cast to back them up. But things hadn't worked out as he had hoped. Aaron had gotten shot and had understandably quit the team. And Scott had become distracted somehow and lost his competitive edge. The rest of the team seemed to sense their overall weakened condition and slacked off in their performance as well. Everyone, that is, with the exception of Tony. He continued to swim like a man obsessed. He was a cinch to make all-American and to be selected for the upcoming Olympic team. But he couldn't carry the rest of the team all by himself. The hopes for a national championship had long since been surrendered. In fact, it seemed doubtful they would even be invited to the national meet at the end of March.

The truth was, Coach Englehart feared for his own job. His superiors had voiced their disappointment over the team's less than sensational season, and had questioned his ability to lead them to excel. He was determined to end the season on a high note for his own sake more than that of the team. So, he pushed them relentlessly, demanding that extra effort that could make the determining difference in the few meets remaining before the nationals.

After practice, Scott was walking to his car, exhausted and discouraged. He was understandably tired from the demanding practice session, but it was the weight of his spiritual burdens that had really sapped his strength.

"Hey, Scott, wait up!" rang Tony's familiar voice.

"Oh, hi, Tony. What's up?" Scott replied, trying to sound upbeat.

"I need to talk to you a minute, man," his friend said, hurrying to catch up.

"What about? I'm kinda in a hurry."

"What is it this time, Scott? You can't wait to get home and study your Bible? Or is it Candi? You're obviously obsessed with her. I know it can't have anything to do with swimming."

"What are you talking about, Tony?" Scott said, becoming defensive.

"Oh, just that you're letting your swimming career go down the tubes, and you're carrying the rest of the team down with you. That's all."

"Look, I'm doing the best I can," Scott said, knowing it wasn't altogether true.

"Oh, no you're not!" Tony shot back, and then ended his sentence with a string of profanity.

"Look, Tony, I don't want to talk about it. The coach has been on my back all afternoon, I don't need you cussing me out too."

"Okay, I'm sorry, man," Tony apologized. "It's just that I wanted that national title so bad I could taste it, and I'm still not ready to give up. But you just don't seem to care whether we ever win another meet or not. What's with you, anyway?"

"I can't believe you can even ask me that, Tony. You may be able to put everything behind you and go on with your life as though nothing ever happened, but I can't. A little over a month ago, we robbed an old man of his life savings. You bashed in his head and shot Carl full of buckshot. I blew away a saintly old woman, and nearly killed one of my best friends. Since then, we've been studying about the coming of Jesus Christ and what's going to happen to those of us who are still in our sins when He gets here. I feel so guilty and bummed out I'm about to lose my mind; and you, of all people, have the gall to ask me what's wrong. You're a real piece of work, man."

"Look, all that's history now, Scott," Tony said, trying to be reassuring. "I feel bad about all that stuff too, but we can't do anything about it now. We've got to put it behind us and get on with our lives. And you're taking all that religious stuff way too seriously."

"What do you mean? How can I not take it seriously? What Bobby has been teaching us is all right out of the Bible. I believe what he says. Jesus could come for His church any day now, and you and I will be standing here with our pants down. What good's a national championship going to do us when we are thrown headlong into the tribulation without knowing the Lord?"

"Whoa, you really are taking that stuff seriously aren't you?" Tony said, with genuine surprise in his voice. "Look, Scott, all that stuff is only hypothetical. Oh, I admit, Bobby's pretty smart for a black, illiterate ex-con, but he even said the real Bible scholars don't agree with him. I just look at his theory as a remote possibility. There's no way I'm going to throw away my life, and my future, based on the pipe dreams of one bodacious African . . . no matter how sincere and persuasive he might be. And I don't want you to either, my friend."

"I just can't see things the way you do, Tony. I feel I'm at a crossroads, and I've got to make a choice. I can't just cruise along and ignore God's warnings and all the other stuff we've been studying."

"Well, why don't you just pray and receive Jesus Christ as your Savior, like they all want you to, and quit torturing yourself? I know Candi wants you to. If you do the deed, she will be all over you in a minute, man. Then you can get on with your life. You really can have your cake and eat it too."

"Do you really believe that tripe, Tony?" Scott asked, in genuine amazement. "There's no way I could do that. If and when I accept Christ, it's gonna have to be total surrender. I'd have to confess all my sin and do my best to make it right. When the others in the Bible study found out what I'd done, they'd all hate me. Candi would dump me, all the Davis family would want to kill me, and Carl would slap his handcuffs on me and haul me off to jail before I could holler 'police brutality.' But I can't just fake a conversion and pretend everything's fine. God knows my heart. I can't fool Him, and it wouldn't do any good to try to fool others."

"Look," scolded Tony, "you're Scott Graham, not Billy Graham. You don't have to become a world evangelist in order to become a Christian. Bobby said salvation was a gift. Just accept it and become Christian Graham, marry your Honey Graham, and raise a bunch of little Graham Crackers if you want to, but you don't have to throw your life away in the process, not to mention mine."

"What do you mean?" asked Scott. "This isn't about you. How would I be throwing away your life if I give mine to God?"

"Well, buddy boy, if you go confessing your sin, how long do you think it would take folks to figure out who it was that was sinnin' alongside you? Don't even think about going there, Scott," Tony warned, his eyes narrowing. "I won't allow you to dump my life in the toilet just because you're having a guilt and pity party and feel the need to fess up."

"How can you be so glib about all this, Tony? You're in the same situation as I am."

"I know, but I'm just not as melodramatic as you are. I'm going to live my life to the fullest. Like they say, 'You only go round once in life. Grab all the gusto you can get.' I'm going to have a ball and not worry about all this doom and gloom stuff Pastor Bobby has been talking about. I doubt anything will ever come of it anyway. But if it does, I can always repent at that time and get on God's side before it's too late. You'll do the same thing, if you really know what's good for you."

"I'll think about it," Scott lied, knowing there was no way his conscience would ever let him seriously adopt such a philosophy. "But, right now, I gotta be goin'."

"Okay, but really do think about what I said," Tony said as he turned and started to move in the direction of his Mustang. "Concentrate on swimmin', not sinnin'. And don't even think about telling anybody about what happened at that store. I *will not* take a fall on account of you. Do you understand what I'm sayin'?"

"Yeah, I do," Scott answered after him. "And thanks for the warning."

As Scott got in his Blazer and prepared to leave the parking lot, he thought to himself how convenient it would be if he could just look at life the way Tony did. But then he felt cold chills all over his body. He knew deep within that to adopt such a philosophy would be to commit spiritual suicide. But at least it would be simple and carefree for the moment, not riddled with complications and demands for sacrifice like his was.

It was starting to rain as Jamal left the gym after basketball practice Tuesday evening, but it would have taken a lot more than that to dampen the spirits of the tall athlete on this occasion. He had just had prayer with several players on his team, and he was thrilled with what God was doing in so many of their lives. Three more of them had made decisions for Christ during the past week, even though he had led only one of them to the Lord, personally. Sammy and The Kid had each brought their first converts into the kingdom over the past week, and Jamal had won Jared Andersen to Christ just the night before at the Bible study he led in his dorm room. Now all five members of the starting team were believers and excited about the things of God. Jamal was overwhelmed with the grace and power of God being manifested through him and his new Christian brothers.

Their team was still undefeated and ranked number one in the country. They had only three more games left in the season and none of them against a nationally ranked team. They were playing the best basketball in the country, which pleased them, but what really got them excited was their new life in the Lord. Jamal had a big grin on his face as he walked across the street, not even trying to avoid the rain. He lifted his face toward the heavens and let the cooling drizzle embrace him.

"Thank You, Lord," he said softly, and he actually skipped a couple of times as he approached his car. "It just doesn't get any better than this," he proclaimed at full volume, not caring whether or not anyone might overhear him.

"I wouldn't be so sure about that if I was you," spoke a disembodied voice from out of the shadows.

Startled, Jamal jumped and turned to face the one who had intruded into his private conversation with the Lord. In the next instant, his mind recognized the voice and his eyes picked up the unmistakable image of his brother in the dim illumination of the streetlight.

"Snowball, don't be sneakin' up on me like that," he gasped. "You 'bout scared the life outta me."

"Sorry, Jamal, I didn't mean to scare you. I thought you saw me. Who else were you talkin' to?"

"Oh, that? I was just talkin' with the Lord. You oughta try it sometime."

"Believe me, I have been," Marcus responded, "but it doesn't seem like it's doin' any good."

"Why, what's the matter?" Jamal asked, sensing the urgency in his brother's voice.

"Hey, man, we got a real problem. Remember those hoods in Vegas? Well they're back, and they want that game you owe them."

"Oh, no!" moaned Jamal. In his exuberance over what God was doing in his life and the lives of his friends, he had temporarily forgotten about the millstone the mob had hung around his neck. "Why can't they just leave us alone?"

"Money, my friend, lots of money," Marcus sighed. "With them, that's what everything is all about. And by the way, they promised us some of it after you guys lose to Stanford next week."

"No way, man!" Jamal almost shouted. "I'm not throwing another game, especially not to Stanford. I'm not interested in their filthy money. You can just tell them to forget about it!"

"Wait a minute there, baby brother," Marcus said, trying to calm Jamal down. "You act like this is all new to you. You knew all along they were going to collect on what you owe them. The season's almost over. You shouldn't be surprised to learn they've decided to come callin'."

"Well, a lot of things have changed since I agreed to throw that Houston game back in January. I didn't want to do it then, but I did. It wasn't my fault it didn't work out the way we planned, but I did my part. I never promised them I'd do it again, and I'm just flat not gonna do it."

"Whoa!" Marcus cried in genuine alarm. "You may not have signed a contract or nothin' but you agreed over the phone, and it's the same thing.

They're not askin', they're tellin', and unless you do it, we're both gonna wind up as statistics in the obituary section of the newspaper real soon."

"Maybe so, maybe not," Jamal surmised. "Marcus, I'm a Christian now, and that changes everything. I've won several members of my team to Christ, and there's no way I'm gonna trash my testimony with them by throwing that game. My God is bigger'n the mob. If I do what is right by Him, I believe I can trust Him to do what is right by me. The answer is no. I'm sorry if this puts you in a tight spot, but I just can't do it!"

"Yeah, it puts me in a tight spot . . . about as tight as a coffin . . . and you too! These guys don't mess around. Look, if you wanna be a Christian, I think that's fine, but don't let it control your life. You gotta look out for yourself here. So you lose a game, and maybe your teammates get bummed out at you. So what? You're still alive and healthy, you still go on to win the national championship, and you still get drafted into the pros and make millions. What's so hard about that?"

"What's so hard about it is that it isn't moral, it isn't ethical, and it isn't legal."

"So, what's your point?" Marcus said sarcastically. "You do what you gotta do to survive, and you don't sweat the small stuff."

"Well, I do," Jamal came back. "The Bible says everything we do, we're to do as unto the Lord. And you were wrong, Marcus, when you said it was okay for me to become a Christian, just so long as I didn't let it control my life. The whole point in becoming a Christian was to let the Lord control my life. Like you said, you do what you think you gotta do; but as for me, I *will not* throw that game. I won't do it for money, or for my career, or for my safety, not even for you. I love you, and I don't want anything to happen to you, but my mind's made up. There's no sense trying to convince me otherwise."

"Okay, bro," Marcus conceded. "I can see you need a little time to think about this. I'll get back to you a little later. I'm sure you'll come to your senses. Convictions or no convictions, when it comes right down to it, we all do what we gotta do to stay alive. And this is something we simply gotta do."

With that, he turned and walked back into the darkness. Jamal called after him not to waste his time because he wasn't going to change his mind, but Marcus didn't answer. As Jamal got into his car, he prayed that God would give him strength to do the right thing, and that the Lord would protect both him and his brother. Then he added, "But whatever happens, Lord, may Your will be done; and please, Lord, bring Marcus to a saving knowledge of Your Son before it's too late."

The green burrito from the catering truck had to have been made several days before, and it was hard from having been reheated so many times. Marcus tossed the remaining two-thirds of it in the trash can. Had it been fresh and delicious, he probably wouldn't have been able to eat it anyway. His stomach was churning in sympathy with the conflict going on in his mind.

It was Wednesday and he had promised to have Jamal call and confirm with Sal that he was indeed going to throw the Stanford game as he had been instructed. But his brother had made it unmistakably clear the night before that he had no intention of doing any such thing. It was noon already, and Marcus was beginning to panic. He knew it would do no good to appeal to the mercy of the mob. They maintained control through their ruthlessness. They kept their underlings in line through intimidation, and they dared not show any sign of softness, lest others begin to get any ideas.

He had entertained thoughts of leaving town and trying to disappear, but he knew they had ways of finding him. Besides, Jamal would still be there, and so would the rest of his family. He knew also that the mob would take out on them whatever vengeance they deemed his offenses might deserve. So, he had to stay, but what was he going to do? He couldn't just sit around and wait for Mr. Apparicio's henchmen to rub him out.

Suddenly, a thought came to him. Maybe he could call Sal and convince him that he was Jamal. Sal didn't strike him as being too intelligent, and he figured that to the big Italian, one black man would sound pretty much the same as the next one.

Marcus turned off the radio in his old Duster where he had been sitting, trying to eat his lunch. He picked up the cell phone Gil had installed in the vehicle and pulled the card with Sal's number on it out of his shirt pocket. Gil had placed the phone in the car so he could get in touch with Marcus when he needed to talk to him when he was away from the yard, and Marcus was thankful it was there. This way he could call discreetly, and besides, the voice on the cell phone wouldn't be as clear as it would have been on a regular one. The slightly distorted voice, hopefully, would help confuse Sal and convince him that he was talking with Jamal. He punched in the numbers on the card and actually prayed that God would help him pull it off.

"Yeah," the thick voice answered on the second ring.

"Excuse me, is this Sal LaMata?" Marcus asked, trying to sound as much like Jamal as he could.

"Who wants to know?" came the reply.

"This is Jamal Davis. My brother told me I was supposed to call this number and ask for Sal."

"Yeah, kid, this is Sal," the voice sounded pleased in response. "I been waitin' for you to call."

"Please, Mr. LaMata, is there any way I can get out of throwing that game. I don't want to let my teammates and the fans down," Marcus added what he knew would be a futile plea to add to his credibility with the gangster.

"Sorry kid, I don't make the rules, I just carry 'em out. The rules say you gotta throw that game or I gotta throw you. So what's it gonna be?"

"Okay, I'll do it, but you gotta promise not to hurt me or anyone in my family," Marcus added for effect.

"Look, kid, we're business people, not crooks, like in the movies," the voice came back. "You do what you're told, and nobody gets hurt. But you screw up this time, and even your own mother won't recognize you. You understand what I'm sayin'?"

"Yes sir, I'll do what you say, but this is the last time, okay?"

"Sure, kid. You pull this off, and it squares you with my people once and for all. Oh by the way, I'm pullin' for you guys to win the national title again next month."

"Thank you," Marcus replied, not knowing what else to say.

He heard a click, and the line went dead. Marcus breathed a sigh of relief, but not a deep one. He had succeeded in fooling a fool, but all he had actually done was to buy himself a little time. Somehow, he still had to convince his brother to agree to throw the game or he would be in deeper trouble than ever before. But how in the world was he ever going to get Jamal to actually comply with what he had sworn he would never do?

That would indeed take some finagling on Marcus' part. He had always seemed to be able to figure a way out of every mess he had gotten himself into in the past, but he wasn't at all sure how he was going to get out of this one. Fortunately, he still had over a week to get Jamal to change his mind. Surely he'd be able to think of something by then. But if that was so, why did he still have such a feeling of impending doom deep within his soul?

CHAPTER TWENTY-TWO

THE HARDENED HEART

The rest of the week passed without significant incident. The UCLA basketball team won its games and the CSULB swim team won its meets, so the athletes were pleased with their accomplishments. Detectives Spangler and Farley were completely frustrated in their efforts to build a case against Tony and Scott and had all but given up on ever being able to do so, so the perpetrators were pleased with their continued freedom. The Lord was blessing the church, the Bible studies, and the soul winning efforts of the saints; so all the Christians were pleased with God's willingness to manifest Himself in their lives and to use them for His glory. But there were still a few who weren't so pleased.

Jamal wasn't pleased with the pressure Marcus was putting on him to throw the Stanford game, and Marcus wasn't a bit pleased with Jamal's continued refusal to do so. Aaron wasn't pleased with the conflict he continued to experience in his heart. He had a greater love for God than ever before, and an unwavering commitment to serve Him. He had an overwhelming desire to believe on, and to receive personally, Israel's Messiah, but he could muster no faith at all to accept this Jesus of Nazareth, whom, his mind told him, was indeed the Promised One. Scott wasn't pleased with the dilemma he faced either, having a great desire to be saved, but having also a corresponding reluctance to pay the price. And Candi wasn't pleased with much of anything.

She wasn't pleased with Scott's refusal to commit his life to Christ, nor with his growing irritability and unwillingness to talk about it. She wasn't pleased with the gnawing suspicion that the man she loved was indeed involved with the robbery and shooting incident back in January. She wasn't pleased with herself either. She was disgusted that she hadn't been able to win Scott to the Lord, and yet she hadn't been willing to break up with him either because of his persistent unbelief. In fact, she was more than a little displeased with the Lord Himself because He hadn't stepped in and made all things right. If He truly was the all-loving, all-powerful God He claimed to be, why was He dragging His feet here when it would have been so easy for Him to fix it?

When Sunday afternoon finally rolled around and the members of the Bible study group began to file in and take their familiar places around the table in the conference room at the Antioch Baptist Church, there was an air of expectancy and anticipation among them. Many of them were facing a crisis in their lives and it was as though they were coming with the determination to find some answers. Some of them were near the breaking point and they were running out of time. No more gathering of superfluous Bible facts; they had decisions to make, and they were soon going to have to make them. The previous weeks had been like classroom study and preparation. Today, they sensed, would be their final exam.

Pastor Bobby Davis sensed the intensity in the room as he took his place at the far end of the table. He greeted them all, but did not enter into his usual practice of encouraging small talk about the past week's sporting events and items of personal interest. Instead he opened his Bible and began reading from Matthew 7:7–11:

> *Ask, and it shall be given to you; seek, and you will find; knock, and it will be opened to you. For everyone who asks receives, and he who seeks finds, and to him who knocks it will be opened. Or what man is there among you who, if his son asks for bread, will give him a stone? Or if he asks for a fish, will he give him a serpent? If you then, being evil, know how to give good gifts to your children, how much more will your Father who is in heaven give good things to those who ask Him?*

When he finished reading, he bowed his head and began to pray, his voice full of emotion, "Father, I'm your son, unworthy and undeserving of my position in Your family, and I thank you for accepting me, nonetheless. But, Master, there's something I just don't understand. You promise here to answer Your children's prayers, to give us what we ask for, but I've been askin', and seekin', and knockin' for so long, and I haven't heard a peep from You. And I haven't been askin' for a bigger salary, or better health, or denominational recognition, or anything else for myself. I've just been askin' You for the salvation of these four young men sittin' at the other end of this table. You know I love them and would give my own life for any one of them, and I've taught them about everything I know about why they should trust You, but none of them has budged.

"Father, I'm not sure why, but I feel like if they don't make that decision today, they probably never will. So, Lord, don't let their hearts be hardened. Open their eyes so they can see the truth of Your word. Don't let them slip away. I'm askin', and seekin', and knockin' one more time. Dear Father, hear me . . . ."

At that point, his voice broke and he was forced to stop speaking lest he completely break down, but it was obvious to the others in the room that he hadn't stopped praying at all. He continued for some time with his head down, rocking slowly back and forth, teardrops beginning to form an irregular pattern on the table in front of him, a low moaning sound coming from deep within him. His mouth moved as it formed his unspoken words, and his shoulders shook as he tried to keep from breaking down altogether.

The believers in the room were praying with him. Both Candi and Sarah were weeping quietly as they poured out their hearts on behalf of the young men seated around them. Even Jamal and Carl were all but overcome with emotion. Low sounds could be heard coming from all four of them intermittently as they subconsciously gave voice to some of their deeper supplications.

As for the four seated at the opposite end of the table, those few minutes seemed like endless hours. Conviction poured like rain, hammering at the heart of each of them individually, and each of them responded differently to its showers.

Tony was perhaps the least visibly moved of the four, but he was having a major struggle within. He felt embarrassed and uncomfortable, yet he was determined not to be swayed by their emotional pleas on his behalf. He could tell that they were sincere in their travail over his soul, but he resisted any desire he felt within him to respond to the strange conviction he was experiencing. He just sat there with his head down, waiting and hoping that it would all be over soon. It was not unlike holding his breath underwater, knowing that if he held out long enough he would eventually surface and be able to breathe again. But he dared not give in now and inhale the strange spirit that was seeking entrance into his soul lest he surely drown and his self-will and freedom perish forever.

Marcus was obviously the most agitated. He squirmed and fidgeted and even looked around, perhaps trying to discover some means of escape. He felt trapped, and he wanted out. He had been under conviction before, but he had developed a resistance to it. He had learned to shrug off strong biblical arguments and even loud and impassioned preaching, but he wasn't equipped to handle this. These people genuinely loved him and were pouring out their hearts to God that he might be saved. Part of him wanted to surrender to their pleas and cry out to God for His mercy, but another part of him held him back and refused to let him give in. Thus, the intense struggle going on inside his soul manifested itself in the exaggerated activity of his body.

Scott was not as agitated as Marcus was, but the conviction he was experiencing was even greater. The battle inside his mind and conscience wasn't between one force that wanted to accept Christ and another one that wanted to reject Him. The battle was between his spirit and his flesh. His spirit soared uncontested within him, reaching toward the heavens, reaching out to seize forgiveness and eternal life; but his flesh dug in its heels and screamed out for self-preservation. It reminded him if he ever hoped to enjoy life, love, and happiness, he had best not believe. If he allowed his spirit to obtain acceptance and peace with God in heaven, he could expect nothing but rejection, isolation, and suffering from people on earth.

He had his own Bible open to the same passage Pastor Bobby had read. He had his head bowed, but his eyes were wide open. He stared at the verses through tear-filled eyes as the Holy Spirit burned the truth of them into his conscience. All he had to do was ask in faith believing and he could receive the gift of eternal life. But the price was so very high. As he gripped his Bible so tightly his fingernails dug deeply into its leather cover, he agonized over the impossible paradox he faced. Could he afford to accept the free gift of eternal life in heaven, which could wind up costing him absolutely everything on earth?

Aaron, on the other hand, was angry, as angry as he had ever been in his young life. He was angry with Pastor Bobby for shamelessly subjecting them to so much emotional pressure. Everyone knows there's an unwritten law that prohibits anyone from interrupting or speaking out when someone else is praying. So, there he sat, held prisoner by Bobby's prolonged and passionate intercession on behalf of their eternal souls, being absolutely powerless to do anything about it.

He was also angry with himself for ever getting mixed up with these Gentile infidels in the first place, making it possible for Bobby to take advantage of him like this. If he were honest with himself, he would have to admit that he was angry with God as well. Who else could he blame for his mind's insatiable hunger for knowledge about Jesus Christ, and, at the same time, his soul's absolute absence of faith in Him?

But mostly he was just angry. Angry about the uncomfortable outpouring of emotion, angry about the unnecessary delay keeping them from the fascinating things they were supposed to be studying, and most of all, angry about the horrible emptiness he felt crying out from deep within his heart.

After what had actually been only a few minutes, Bobby realized he had forgotten where he was, and with whom he was. He hadn't planned this episode at all. He had simply become so absorbed in his conversation with the Lord that he had forgotten that anyone else was even there.

He quickly regained his composure and apologized profusely to everyone in the room for his inappropriate actions. He defended his passionate prayers on behalf of the four young men, but he asked them to forgive him for airing them before them in such a way as to put them under undue pressure. He could see from the expressions on their faces that none of them was pleased with what he had done, and he promised them nothing like that would ever happen again.

His humility and obvious sincerity disarmed those whom he had offended, and they all began to relax. Marcus made some comment about expecting Bobby to start speaking in tongues at any moment, and that brought nervous laughter from everyone, even though a few of them didn't even know what he was talking about.

Bobby took control of the meeting again by asking them to turn in their Bibles to 2 Thessalonians 2:1–12. He had requested them to read it beforehand, and they all had done so, even Tony, who had been known to come to class unprepared on other occasions. The passage hadn't set well with some of them, and they had come prepared to take Bobby to task on it.

Bobby asked Scott to read the passage as the rest of them followed along. Scott really didn't want to read it because he didn't like what it said, but he didn't want to appear as intimidated as he felt, so he started in without objection. But before he had finished reading, his hands were trembling and his voice was shaky. It was as though he had been reading his own death sentence. "I don't agree with what this last part says," he added, trying to sound confident, but failing to do so.

"Yeah, neither do I!" agreed Tony.

"Me neither," Marcus added.

"Okay, then," said Bobby, "let's take a look at what Paul was telling the Thessalonian saints about the coming of the Lord, and I think it will clarify the parts you're having trouble with. We already learned a few weeks ago that the rapture won't take place until there's a major religious apostasy and the antichrist sets himself up as God in the temple. That's what the first four verses here are talking about. And with the World Church of Humanity deceiving people all over the world, and the new temple built by Constantine Augustus about to be dedicated in Jerusalem; that day could be just around the corner.

"Then in verses six and seven, he tells us that the force which is restraining the working of lawlessness will continue its restraining efforts until it's taken out of the way. I think it's clear that the force which restrains the working of evil in the world today is the true evangelical church. When it's taken out of the way at the rapture, the antichrist will be free to reveal himself as God in the temple. And in verses eight through ten, through his miraculous powers, he'll deceive the multitudes of those who have refused to believe the truth that they might be saved. But in those verses, Paul also tells us the antichrist won't have long to work his will before Christ destroys him when He comes back to set up His kingdom."

"Yeah, I think I understand all that pretty well," Scott said, "We've studied most all of it before anyway. It's that part about deceiving those who had refused to get saved that bothers me. It's especially verses eleven and twelve that I'm having trouble with. If I'm readin' this right, it says God Himself will deceive people so they won't believe. How could He do that? Why would He do that? I thought He wanted everybody to be saved. Surely it doesn't really mean what it appears to say. Does it?"

"I'm afraid that's exactly what it means, Scott," Bobby said. "In the King James Version it comes across even stronger. Listen to this: '*And for this cause God shall send them strong delusion, that they should believe a lie: that they might be damned who believed not the truth, but had pleasure in unrighteousness.*'"

"So, I wanna make sure I get this right," Scott replied. "What you're saying is, those of us who don't believe on Christ and don't receive Him before the rapture, won't be able to after it happens. You're saying God Himself will make it so we can't be saved. He will cause us to believe the devil's lies and be damned to hell. Is that really what you're saying?"

"No, that's not what I'm saying. If it were up to me, I would never say a thing like that. But I'm afraid that's *exactly* what *God* is saying."

"Well, I don't believe it!" Scott almost shouted. "There must be some error in translation. I'm sure there isn't anything like that taught anywhere else in the Bible."

"Oh, but there certainly is," Bobby replied, quickly turning pages in his Bible. "In fact it's taught throughout both the Old and the New Testaments. Here, let me read what Paul writes in Romans 9:14–18:

> *What shall we say then? Is here unrighteousness with God? Certainly not? For he says to Moses, "I will have mercy on whomever I will have mercy, and I will have compassion on whomever I have compassion" So then it is not of him who wills, nor of him who runs, but of God who shows mercy. For the Scripture says to the Pharaoh, "For this very purpose I have raised you up, that I may show My power in you, and that My name may be declared*

in all the earth." Therefore He has mercy on whom He wills, and whom He wills He hardens.

Bobby went on to say, "Paul teaches us a great deal about the sovereignty of God in Romans, chapters nine through eleven; but especially in this passage, we see it demonstrated. God chose to show mercy to Jacob, but He obviously hardened Esau's heart of unbelief. The same is true of Pharaoh, who didn't want to let the children of Israel go free, so God hardened his heart so he couldn't. Even when God's plagues were destroying Pharaoh's nation, and his own people were begging him to let the Hebrews go free, his hardened heart wouldn't allow him to do it. God Himself prevented him from releasing the Jews until He had thoroughly punished the Egyptians for their many centuries of cruelty toward His people."

"So," asked Candi, "you're saying God hardened Pharaoh's heart to keep him from letting the Jews go free, even though it would have been better for him and his people if he would have?"

"Exactly. And in the same way, He will harden the hearts of those who have heard the gospel and repeatedly refused to accept it. After the rapture, when you would think they would be eager to change their minds and accept Christ, they won't be able to, because God Himself will harden their hearts in their unbelief."

"No way, man!" Tony objected. "Nobody's gonna tell me when I can believe and when I can't. I'm free to choose not to accept Christ right now for my own reasons, but I'll also be free to change my mind whenever I darn well please. If you dudes get raptured outta here and the tribulation starts comin' down, the first thing I'm gonna do is get on my knees and accept Christ as my own Savior, and nobody's gonna stop me."

"That's where you're wrong, Tony," Bobby said matter of factly. "I'm going to tell you something I'm sure you're not going to like. You don't have the power in yourself to receive Christ anytime. Not now, and certainly not then. Paul tells us in Ephesians 2:1, '*And you were dead in your trespasses and sins.*' A dead person can't act, he can't speak, he can't even think. There's no way a dead person can respond to anything. The only way for the dead to respond is for life to be breathed back into them. And that's exactly what Paul says God did for us in Christ."

"Wait a minute there, Dad," Marcus interrupted. "I always thought we all had a free will. Can't we choose or not choose whenever we want to? Doesn't God just sorta set everything out there, smorgasbord-like, and let us pick and choose whatever and whenever we please?"

"That's what most people think, alright," replied Bobby, "but it just isn't the way it is at all. Jesus told His disciples in John 15:16, '*You did not choose me, but I chose you, and appointed you.*' The disciples only responded to His calling. And that's all we can do. We don't initiate anything. That's why the Bible warns us over and over again not to ignore or disregard it when He calls."

"Yeah," said Marcus incredulously. "Where does it say that?"

"Well, for example, in Isaiah 55:6 it says, *'Seek the Lord while He may be found, call upon Him while He is near.'* In Hebrews 4:7 we read, *'Today if you hear His voice, do not harden your hearts.'* And again in Hebrews 2:3 it says, *'How shall we escape if we neglect so great a salvation, which at the first began to be spoken by the Lord, and was confirmed to us by those who heard Him?'*

"These are just a few of the many warnings that are found in Scripture," continued Bobby, "but maybe the strongest one is found in Proverbs 1:24–32, where Solomon warns the scoffers not to play games with God. He says that since there are those who refuse His counsel and neglect His reproof when He offers it, He will not respond when they cry out to Him in their hour of desperation."

"Pastor Bobby, that's so hard to believe," Sarah protested. "Are you sure you're interpreting that correctly?"

"Well here, let me just read verses 26–30, and you all can interpret it for yourselves:

> *I will laugh at your calamity; I will mock when your terror comes, when your terror comes like a storm, and your destruction comes like a whirlwind, when distress and anguish come on you. They will call on me, but I will not answer; they will seek me diligently, but they will not find me. Because they hated knowledge and did not choose the fear of the Lord, they would have none of my counsel and despised my every rebuke.*

"Wow, I never knew verses like that were in the Bible," said Jamal. "It almost sounds like God's saying, 'Look, I'm giving you this chance, now don't blow it. If you don't respond now, there's gonna come a day when you will want to come to me, but you won't be able to.'"

"That's exactly what He's saying," confirmed Bobby. "A man is a fool to play games with God, thinking he can reject Him as long as he likes, and then accept Him whenever he feels like it. I think that's why Paul's so emphatic in 2 Corinthians 6:2 when he says, *'Behold, now is the accepted time, behold now is the day of salvation.'* When Jesus comes a-knockin' on your heart's door, you better open it and invite Him to come in. Because if you ignore Him long enough, He'll go away and won't knock no more, then He'll be forever outside, no matter how much you might want Him in."

"Hey, don't look at me!" Jamal said emphatically. "I know I kept Him outside knocking for a long time, but I finally wised up. I opened that door and He came in, and He's livin' in me right now. I can't believe I was so stupid for so long."

"I know, Son, and I thank God for your decision with all my heart. But there're still some here who haven't made that decision yet. My prayer every day is that they'll make it before it's eternally too late."

"But how can you tell when it's too late?" asked Candi. "Remember, I asked you about the thief on the cross? He was an evil man who had rejected God all his life, but just before he died, he cried out to Jesus in faith, and God saved him. Isn't that right?"

"Yes it is," Bobby agreed, "and that's an excellent point, Candi. Nobody knows when that point of no return comes in each person's life, so we keep on hoping. As long as there's life, there's always the hope that they will change their mind and get saved. But there's a definite exception to that general rule."

"What's that?" Marcus asked, but not sure he really wanted to know.

"It's just what we've been studying about for the last hour. When the rapture comes, it marks a definite cutoff point for all those who have previously rejected the gospel. Their window of opportunity will forever be closed. Their hearts will be hardened and they will accept the deceiving lies of the antichrist in spite of any preconceived plans they might have had."

"I can't believe that!" Marcus almost yelled. "Me and Tony and Scott have learned all this stuff you've taught us. We won't listen to the lies of the antichrist. If we see the rapture takin' place, the first thing we're gonna do is accept Christ. I'd say we have an excellent chance of gettin' saved."

"No offense, Marcus, but if you're still rejecting Christ at the time of the rapture, you won't have a snowball's chance in hell of ever gettin' saved afterwards."[5]

"Did you hear that, Snowball?" Jamal asked, catching his father's play on words. "The great Snowball, who's always beaten the odds, won't have a snowball's chance on that day. You better get saved now, brother."

"Very funny," Marcus shot back defiantly, "but you don't know that for sure. I'm still willing to take my chances. I'll bet there'll be a whole lot more people saved then than you think."

[5] See Appendix Four for a more detailed examination of the hardened heart.

"Yeah, what about all the people we've studied about who'll get saved during the tribulation?" asked Scott with more than a little desperation showing in his voice. "It looks to me like they'll be given a second chance. Why couldn't we be among them?"

"They really aren't those who get a second chance, Scott," Bobby said. "It's true, people will be saved during the tribulation, multitudes of them. But they won't be those who've heard about Jesus Christ before and rejected Him. They'll be the people who've never heard a clear presentation of the gospel before. They'll come from pagan countries all over the world, and even from so-called Christian countries like the United States. There're millions of people in our own nation who've never really heard the good news before. The only possible exception will be the 144,000 Jews saved at the beginning of the tribulation. I think it's likely they'll know a lot about the gospel of Christ before the rapture. That way, when God does save them, they'll be able to hit the ground a runnin'."

"Hey, didja hear that, Aaron?" Marcus butted in. "You can relax, man. You don't have to sweat it like the rest of us pagans."

Aaron didn't laugh like some of the others. He didn't even deny Marcus' claim. He just rolled his eyes a little and shook his head slowly back and forth. It was clear he wasn't buying any of it.

"I know you're just clownin' around, Marcus," Bobby said, "but you may have just illustrated what I've been talking about all afternoon. The chosen 144,000 Jewish young men, who'll be unbelievers at the coming of Christ, are apparently those on whom God will choose to have mercy. Even though they will have rejected the gospel up to that point, God will apparently open their eyes at the time of the rapture and they will all be saved en masse. But the rest of those who've heard the gospel and rejected it before the rapture are those He'll harden. If they don't accept Christ now when we tell them, they'll have no chance at all after Christ comes."

"Then why tell 'em?" Tony wanted to know. "If you'd kept your mouth shut, ignorant guys like me would have had a shot at getting saved after the rapture, but now, supposedly, you've robbed me of that. I know the gospel now, but I'm not at all sure I want to commit my whole life to something still so unproven. True, the rapture and the tribulation would most surely get my attention, and I would be open to the gospel then, and I would respond to it by accepting your Jesus. But now I'm doomed unless I make this leap of faith in the dark and surrender my life to someone who might not even be there to receive it. I don't think you've done me much of a favor."

"That's crazy talk, and you know it, Tony," chided Bobby. "Nobody in his right mind would want to go into the tribulation, even if during it he might have the chance of getting saved. But even if you were willing to go through that kind of hell, the problem remains that no one really knows when the rapture's comin' down. If you knew it was scheduled for next week you might be crazy enough to wait and see what happens, but you don't know that, and you just might die while you're waitin'. Just suppose we didn't tell anybody about the gospel in hopes of not spoiling their chances of getting saved after the rapture, and then the Lord decided not to come back for another twenty years. Everybody who died during that time would go straight to hell because they hadn't accepted the gift of salvation through Jesus Christ. No, we can't play that game. We gotta preach the gospel to everyone we can while we can, cause no one knows whether or not he'll even live to see tomorrow."

"Well," sighed Tony, "I guess I'll just have to take my chances. I'm still not convinced this whole thing is true, and I'm not willing to put my faith in it until I am. But I still say I'll be able to make up my own mind and get saved afterwards if the rapture should take place. I would never be so stupid as to believe the antichrist's lies, not after knowing everything I know now."

"That goes for me too," Marcus agreed, thankful to have someone as smart and articulate as Tony to bolster his shaky position of procrastination and infidelity.

Tears began to well up in Bobby's eyes, and he dropped his head and couldn't muster a response. However, in a few moments he was able to master his emotions and suggested they take a break for ten minutes. Everyone seemed to welcome a chance to break the tension that had been building in the room. Bobby was the first to leave the conference room. He went to his office and managed to close the door before he collapsed to the floor, his body racked in convulsive sobs.

"Oh, dear God!" he cried out. "Don't forsake them! Don't give up on them! Don't let them harden their hearts! And please, Lord, don't You harden their hearts either. Dear Jesus, save those poor boys!"

CHAPTER TWENTY-THREE

THE SURRENDER

Aaron sat at the table alone. Everyone else had left the room for one reason or another. Some had gone to the restroom. The others had gone outside, either to get some fresh air, or to pollute it with a cigarette. Aaron just sat there, having neither the need nor the desire to go anywhere.

He was no longer angry, nor was he under conviction. He didn't feel much of anything. What was wrong with him? He had just heard the most convincing argument for accepting Christ he could possibly have imagined, and yet he felt absolutely nothing inside. The others had heard it too, and some were incredibly glad because they had already accepted its truth. Others were downright mad, because they felt they had been pressured to accept it against their will. And at least one of them was visibly sad, because he wanted to accept it but could not bring himself to do so. But Aaron felt neither glad, nor mad, nor sad.

He didn't know what to think about his feelings, or the lack of them. For someone who loved God as much as he did, and was as willing as he was to do anything for Him, he surely wasn't getting much feedback. It was as though the heavens had turned to brass and God had refused to answer the phone. Aaron didn't have a clue what, if anything, God wanted him to do.

Scott was just the opposite. He knew exactly what God wanted him to do. He needed to surrender to Jesus Christ, and that fact was burning itself deeply into his conscience. He had become fearful that the Lord might come back before he made his decision, or worse yet, he might die. In either case, his heart told him he would be eternally without hope.

He stood with Candi outside the church, trying to make small talk, but he could think of nothing but the hopelessness of his own soul's condition. He was dreading the resumption of the Bible study scheduled to begin again in a few minutes. He wasn't sure he could stand any more conviction. His heart had been beating like a jackhammer during the previous session. He took some consolation in the fact that if he could just tough it out one more hour, the Bible study series would all be over. Then he would be free to sort things out for himself without the constant bombardment of scriptural arguments hurled at him by Pastor Bobby and the other believers.

The rest of them were also looking forward to the completion of the study. Tony and Marcus were tired of being under so much pressure to get saved, and they were ready to get back to their former lives without feeling guilty all the time. Carl and Sarah were anxious to have their Sunday afternoons back again. They felt they had been neglecting Tamika on the only day they had off together. Even though he had been under heavy conviction previously, Scott had persisted in his unbelief, and Candi had finally given up on him ever accepting Christ. She just wanted it all to be over. She could no longer stand the pain and frustration she had experienced waiting and praying for him to make his decision. Jamal had been thrilled with the study, but he had become even more fascinated with what God was doing through the one he was leading in his dorm room on Monday nights. He was looking forward to the extra time he would now have each week to prepare for it.

Bobby was the only exception. He dreaded seeing the Bible study come to an end. He was haunted by the fact that the four boys who had been unsaved when they had begun five weeks before were still without Christ today. But he also realized that he had done about all he could do. It would be counterproductive to try to force a decision now. He was simply going to have to give them all over to the Lord, and trust that the Holy Spirit would use what they had learned to bring about their conversion in His own time. In fact, for lack of any other pressing doctrine to teach, he had decided he was going to cut the next session short and send everybody home a little early.

Bobby waited patiently as the various members of the Bible study took their time resuming their places around the table. The ten-minute break had lasted nearly twenty, but he didn't mind. They were at a stopping point anyway. He announced his intention of letting them go early and there was no objection raised. But before he dismissed them, he asked if any of them had any questions about anything they had studied over the past several weeks.

"I do," Scott said, surprising himself by his response. He had intended to keep quiet and try to figure things out for himself later. His response came not from his head but from his heart. For deep within, he knew if he didn't work through his spiritual dilemma right then, he probably never would. It was his tortured soul crying out for help through his otherwise stubborn lips.

"Sure Scott," Bobby responded, intrigued by the seriousness he detected in his voice, "what's on your mind?"

"Oh, I . . . uh . . . don't know," Scott stuttered, trying to find the words to express what was on his heart. "I was just wondering what's required of a person if he wants to get saved. I know it's a free gift and all, but surely you can't just accept Christ and be saved, and then go right on living the same way you were before, can you?"

"That's a good question," Bobby answered, sensing that Scott's question was much more than a mere intellectual curiosity. "What do you think the answer is?"

"I don't know, that's why I asked," Scott said, disappointed in Bobby's response. "I want to believe there're no strings attached, that you can just get saved without giving up or changing anything, but something tells me that's not so. I can't imagine a drug dealer accepting Christ and then going on with his dope sales, or a Mafia hit man becoming a Christian and continuing to kill people for money."

"No, and neither can I, nor does the Bible allow for such thinking," Bobby agreed. "Jesus said in Matthew 16:24–25, '*If anyone desires to come after Me, let him deny himself, take up his cross, and follow Me. For whoever desires to save his life will lose it, but whoever loses his life for My sake will find it.*' He meant you have to be willing to give up your self-will. You have to recognize that your old life was crucified with Christ on the cross and that your life from that point on belongs to Him. The only way you can really find your life is to be willing to surrender it to Christ. Paul told some Christians who were trying to live self-centered lives in 1 Corinthians 6:19–20, '*Or do you not know that your body is a temple of the Holy Spirit who is in you, whom you have from God; and that you are not your own? For you have been bought at a price; therefore glorify God in your body and your spirit, which are God's.*'"

"How can it be called a gift, then?" Scott argued. "It sounds more like a purchase to me."

"It's actually both," Bobby reasoned. "Salvation is a gift, in that it is bought and paid for by the giver, not the recipient. It's received freely by faith, and it's not earned of deserved. But it's also a purchase, in that Jesus didn't just purchase the sinner's salvation by dying for him on the cross. He actually purchased the sinner himself. The only way a sinner can identify with the life of Christ is to first identify with His death. His old self is put to death with Christ on the cross in order that he might be recreated as a new man through Christ's resurrection. Paul spoke of this new life in Galatians 2:20 when he said, '*I have been crucified with Christ; and it is no longer I who live, but Christ lives in me; and the life which I now live in the flesh I live by faith in the Son of God, who loved me, and gave Himself for me.*'"

"Maybe I can help you to understand it better, Scott," Jamal said. "I'm really new at this myself, but I think I know what my dad is talking about. It fits right into something I wanted to discuss today anyway. I'm facing a really tough decision right now, and the fact that I'm a Christian puts a whole new perspective on it. I need some advice from some other believers."

"Jamal!" Marcus gasped. "Don't you be talkin' about that here!"

"I'm sorry, bother, but this is too important not to talk about. Besides, we're all sworn to confidentiality here. Nobody's going to be talking about anything we say outside this room. Right, everybody?"

Everyone voiced his or her agreement, and Marcus knew he was outvoted. He shook his head and scowled, but he consented to let his brother continue on down the path he was sure would lead to disaster.

Jamal left out many of the details, but he briefly told them of the predicament he had gotten himself into with the mob and of his agreement to throw the Houston game back in January. He hadn't wanted to do it, but his career had been more important than anything else at the time. The Kid had gone ballistic and had pulled the game out after Jamal had been forced to leave with an injury. The only thing that had saved him with the mob was the fact that he had tried to fulfill his end of the bargain, and that he had agreed to throw an undisclosed game in the future. But that had all been before he had become a Christian and had won several of his teammates to the Lord.

"I had gotten so excited about the things of the Lord," he said, "that I had temporarily forgotten about the deal I'd made with the mob. But now they've decided to collect on their investment. They're insisting I throw the game with Stanford this Friday night. I've told them no, but they're not going to accept that for an answer."

"What will they do to you if you don't go along with them?" Candi asked. "Will they beat you up, or what?"

"No, they won't beat him up!" snapped Marcus. "They'll kill him! That's what they'll do!"

"How do you know so much about all this, Marcus?" Bobby wanted to know.

"Because I've been with Jamal in this from the beginning. I was with him in Vegas when he dropped all that money in that poker game. The mob's been working through me to get to Jamal all this time. If he doesn't throw the game this Friday, we'll both be dead meat."

"Then you gotta do it, Jamal," Tony blurted out. "It's a meaningless ball game anyway. You'll still win the conference title and probably go on to win the national championship as well. Then you got the pros next year and a multi-million dollar contract. You can't afford to risk all that, not to mention riskin' both of your lives."

"That's what I would have thought a few weeks ago, Tony," Jamal replied. "But that was before I became a Christian. If I throw this game I'll be lying, cheating, and stealing from myself, from my God, from my teammates, and from every fan who loves the game of basketball. Besides that, the mob would own me. I'd be their *boy* for the rest of my career. I'd never be free from them. I belong to God now, not to the Mafia. I won't have them controlling my life."

"But they *are* in control," Marcus insisted. "Can't you see that? And it's not really your fault. That card game in Vegas didn't just happen. It was me who set you up."

"What're you talkin about?" Jamal demanded.

"I had to do it or they woulda killed me. I dropped a ton of cash I didn't have the week before in the same kind of phony game, and the only way they were willing to let me walk was if I'd set you up the next week. They musta had it planned all along."

"You mean you knew I was gonna get framed before we ever set foot in that casino?"

"Yeah, I'm really sorry, Jamal. They had me then just like they got you now. I didn't wanna do it, but they woulda killed me for sure if I hadn't."

Jamal sat quietly for a few seconds as the reality of what Marcus had just confessed sank in. "That's okay," he said in resignation. "What's done is done. I guess you didn't really have much of a choice. In fact, I'm relieved to find out that you did it. Now I don't feel quite so bad about putting your rotten, conniving life in jeopardy when I tell those thugs what they can do with their precious ball game."

"Oh, no, you don't wanna be doin' that," Marcus pleaded with his brother. "You got a right to be sore at me, but don't be getting us both killed over it. Just do what they say this one time, and then you can go back to walkin' the straight and narrow. I don't think God's gonna send you to hell for one little mistake. Don't be thinkin' just about yourself here, man."

"Wrong! Wrong! Wrong!" Jamal responded loudly. "I'm not just thinking of *myself*. I'm thinking of everyone I ever hope to influence for Jesus Christ, including you. It wouldn't be a *little* matter either. It would be a major breach of ethics. And it wouldn't be a *mistake*. It would be a deliberate act of sin. The only thing you *are* right about is that God wouldn't send me to hell for it. His gift of salvation is permanent. I'm His son forever, and that's just the reason I don't want to dishonor His name by committing this sinful, selfish act."

"But if you don't do it," Tony reasoned, "you'd be throwing your life away, and Marcus' too. What good's that gonna do anybody? You can't serve God if you're dead, can you?"

"No, of course not," Jamal agreed, "but that's not my call. Since I accepted Christ, my life belongs to Him. If He wants me to lay down my life for Him by standing up for what's right, then I'm willing to do it. But if He wants to use my life for His glory, then I think He's big enough to protect it from those who might want to take it from me. I don't know what His will is for me concerning my future, but I'm positive it doesn't include denying everything that's right and godly and throwing that basketball game in an effort to save my own skin."

"As much as it scares me, Son," said Bobby, "I have to agree with you. I just lost my mother a few weeks ago and I don't think I could bear the thought of losing either or both of my sons too, but it doesn't seem you really have a choice here. If I really believe what I've been preachin' for years, I have to be willing to trust God in this matter. If you do what's right before God, you can trust Him to do what's right by you. If I don't believe that, then everything I've been talking about for the past five weeks is just a scam."

"Does it have to be a life or death matter, Jamal?" asked Candi. "Couldn't you go to the authorities and tell them what the syndicate is trying to force you to do? Wouldn't they put a stop to them?"

"It's obvious you don't know how the mob works, girl," Marcus butted in. "Sure the feds would launch an investigation into the matter and put pressure on some of the local hoods, but those in charge would put a contract out on me 'n Jamal so fast it would make your pretty little head swim."

"But couldn't you go into the witness protection plan or something?" she wanted to know.

"Yeah, right." Marcus said sarcastically. "Who would ever notice a coupla seven foot black men, standin' out in an Amish corn field in Pennsylvania? We'd fit right in."

"That's enough, Marcus," scolded Bobby. "But he's right, Candi. There's no place they could hide, especially Jamal. His face has been plastered all over the TV, newspapers, and magazines for the past four years. He's almost as recognizable as the president of the United States."

"I'm just a dumb motorcycle cop," said Carl, "but I'm smart enough to realize you're caught between a rock and a hard place, brother. If you do what the mob says, you might be savin' your life, but you'd be throwin' away your Christian testimony and any chance of ever bein' an effective witness for Him. On the other hand, if you refuse 'em, you'd be signin' your own death warrant. It's gonna take a real miracle to get you outta this mess."

"And I thought I was the only one here who had a problem," Scott said almost apologetically.

"What do you mean?" asked Bobby.

"I've been struggling with the same type of problem for about the same length of time, and I thought I was the only one in the world going through anything like it."

"Don't even think about going there, Scott!" warned Tony, jumping to his feet.

"What's this all about?" Bobby demanded to know.

"I'm warning you, Scott!" Tony went on, totally ignoring Bobby. "You keep your mouth shut!"

"No, Tony," replied Scott, with amazing calmness, "for once in your life, you keep your mouth shut. I'm tired of listening to you, following you, being intimidated by you. Maybe life to you is just a matter of self-promotion and self-preservation, but it's not to me. Not anymore. If Jamal's willing to lay down his life for what's right, it's about time I quit thinking about myself and only what's good for me."

"Okay, punk," snarled Tony, "have it your way!" But remember, you're not just talkin' about flushin' *your* life down the tubes here. You wanna take me with you, and I'm not gonna stand for it. I'm not gonna stay here and listen to you spill your guts, just because you're not man enough to take control of your life. But you haven't heard the last from me, no sir, not by a long shot!"

With that, Tony wheeled and headed for the door. As he reached it, he turned around and spoke more calmly, "If you ask me, you're all a bunch of fools. Marcus, you're the only one here who has a clue what life's really all about. Let's get outta here so we can figure out what we're gonna do about this mess."

"No way, man," Marcus said, shaking his head. "Apparently you must know what Scott's gonna say, but I don't. I wouldn't miss this for the world. You go ahead. I'll catch ya later."

"Suit yourself!" Tony growled, and slammed the door behind him.

After a few moments of stunned silence, Bobby looked at Scott and asked, "What in the heck was that all about?"

"I'm sorry about all that," Scott said. "I guess it's been building up for a long time. I don't blame Tony for blowin' up at me, and I don't think you will either once you hear what I've got to say. I can't believe I've been such a fool and waited so long."

"Go ahead, Scott," encouraged Bobby. "We're your friends here, and remember, nothing you say here will leave this room."

For the first time in weeks, Candi began to have some real hope that Scott might finally be ready to make things right with God. She scooted over a little and reached out and took his hand and smiled to encourage him to continue.

But strangely, Scott withdrew his hand and stood to his feet. He was having trouble controlling his emotions, and he took a moment to regain his composure. He looked around the room at people he had grown to love, and he knew what he was about to tell them would both hurt and anger them, but he could no longer contain the spirit inside him. He had to try to make things right with them as best he could or he knew he could never hope to make things right with God.

"You've all been really kind to me," he finally said, "and I want to tell you everything. But before I do, I've got to tell you something really horrible. You may all hate me when you hear it, and you may not want to hear any more. So, I need to get it out now, and then you can decide if you want to hear the rest of the story."

"Okay, Scott, go ahead," Bobby said. "I'm sure whatever it is, we can handle it. Remember, some of us here lived some pretty rough lives too before we came to Christ."

"Okay, here goes," Scott said, with a strange mixture of hesitancy and determination in his voice. He took a deep breath and then blurted out, "It was me 'n' Tony who robbed The Corner Store back in January! It was Tony who hurt Papa Saul and shot Carl, and it was me who killed your mother and wounded Aaron! I'm so sorry! We never meant to hurt anybody . . ."

He couldn't talk anymore. The words stuck in his throat. He hung his head as he struggled to keep from breaking down completely.

For what seemed like a long while, no one said anything. They all knew Scott and Tony had been questioned by the police concerning their possible involvement in the crime, but with the exception of Candi, they had long since dismissed any possibility of their involvement. Now, no one knew quite how to respond to such a confession and revelation. It hit so closely to home. There wasn't a person in the room, again with the possible exception of Candi, who hadn't been traumatized and devastated by what had happened on that fateful rainy night. Now, to have standing before them one of those responsible for causing it all was more than any of them had been prepared to deal with.

Finally, it was Bobby who rose to his feet and looked Scott squarely in the eye. He said, "For weeks I have struggled with my mother's death. To have her taken so suddenly and so violently was extremely difficult for me. I didn't even have a chance to say good-bye, or I love you, or nothin'. I wondered what I would do if I ever had a chance to get my hands on the one who took her from me. Now here you are . . . not a heartless thug, but a sensitive young man whom I've grown to love. I don't know how to feel. But I'm reminded of the promise in Romans 8:28 that says, *'All things work together for good to those who love God, to those that are the called according to His purpose.'*

"My mother's death wasn't a good thing. It was a terrible and inexcusable thing, but I've already seen it working together for good. Both Carl and Jamal have become Christians as a result of her death, as well as several of Jamal's teammates, and a bunch of people in our church. I cannot absolve you of your responsibility before the law for what you've done, but as the only child of the woman you killed, I forgive you."

Having said that, he walked over and wrapped his big arms around Scott and hugged him to his chest. They both began to weep simultaneously, and they stood there, holding each other up as they shared their sorrow and love together.

That seemed to be the cue for the others to join in. They were out of their chairs and gathering around Bobby and Scott, laying their hands on them and joining in the weeping and the rejoicing. Candi was embracing both Scott and Bobby, weeping unashamedly for joy on Scott's broad shoulder. Even Aaron and Carl were there. The spirit of love and forgiveness had so filled the room, there was no room left for bitterness or revenge.

Marcus stood at the outside of the gathering, filled with mixed emotions. He felt no hatred toward Scott, but he wasn't completely ready to shower him with forgiveness either. He didn't understand how the others were so eager to embrace the man who had just admitted killing the sweetest, most godly woman he had ever known.

After a short time of hugging and crying, Bobby brought it to a close with a resounding, "Amen, thank You, Jesus!" He turned Scott loose and suggested they all return to their seats.

"Before we do," asked Scott, "can I do something I've been wanting to do for the past six months?"

"Sure, son, go right ahead."

With that, Scott dropped to his knees and prayed from the depths of his soul, "Dear God, forgive me for not trusting you. Forgive me for going my own way for so very long. I'm a worthless sinner, and I know it, but thank You for loving me and sending Your Son to die for me anyway. If those who I've offended most can forgive me, I know You will too. I accept Your Son as my own Savior and Lord. Thank You for giving Your all for me. I give my all to You. Do with my life as You will. Amen."

Scott managed to get to his feet, and there followed another session of crying and laughing and hugging. Finally, again Bobby gave words of praise and thanksgiving and asked everyone to return to their seats.

"Okay, Pastor Bobby," said Candi through her tears, "but first can I do something *I've* wanted to do for the past six months?"

"I don't know if this old heart of mine can stand much more of this," replied the preacher, holding his chest in simulated distress, "but go ahead. What could you possibly need to confess?"

Candi didn't answer. Instead, she turned to Scott and threw both her arms around his neck and placed a huge kiss squarely on his mouth. Her kiss was long and hard and wet, from both their tears. Scott was surprised and almost overwhelmed. He just stood there, his response not nearly equal to her advance. He couldn't believe the woman he loved was kissing him, instead of kissing him off, now that she knew what he had done.

Just as abruptly as she had embraced him, Candi released him, smiled sweetly, patted him on the cheek, and took her seat, amid a chorus of shouts and cheers from the rest of the group. They all returned to their chairs as well, leaving Scott standing in shocked silence.

Bobby laughed and cried a little more and asked Scott to sit down. He led them all in a prayer of thanksgiving, and then asked him to fill them in on the rest of the details. How had a couple of good kids like Scott and Tony ever gotten themselves into a mess like that in the first place?

For the next thirty minutes, Scott relived the events of the past six weeks. He told of Tony's plan to win an easy ten grand by betting on Houston in that fateful game, and of his own willingness to go along with the scheme in an attempt to gain some independence from his parents, and to help him win Candi's love. He told them of their desperation after The Kid pulled the game out, and of their attempt to recover the money they had both taken from their parents. His story went on to tell of their final decision to rob The Corner Store based on the information Aaron had inadvertently given them. They had convinced themselves that Papa Saul needed to retire, and they would actually be doing him a favor by taking his money and accelerating the process. They were determined that no one would get hurt, but everything went crazy when Carl showed up, and the unthinkable happened.

He told them of their wild flight from the police and of their plunge into the icy waters of the harbor. He continued with their efforts to cover their trail and to avoid being arrested. He left out some of the details, and concluded with telling them of the hell he had gone through since that time, trying to find a way to God and obtaining His forgiveness without destroying his own life in the process and losing Candi forever.

If there had been any remnant of animosity toward Scott when he began his story, it had all been removed by the time he ended it. Even Marcus, though an unbeliever, was absolute in his forgiveness and support of Scott after he heard everything he had been through.

"Thank you for sharing that with us, Scott," Bobby said, wiping his eyes again for the umpteenth time. "I know that wasn't easy for you, but it sure clarified a lot of things for me, and answered a lot of questions I had. I know more than ever now that God doesn't make mistakes. There isn't a day that goes by that I don't miss my mom, and we've all been through a lot of pain and suffering because of that night, but so much good has already come from it, I wouldn't go back and change it, even if I could."

"Thank you, Pastor Bobby. Thank you all," said Scott. "I never in my life expected this kind of response. I thought you'd all hate me forever for what we did."

"We probably would have if it hadn't been for Jesus," Jamal pointed out. "I know He's changed my entire outlook on life, and I'm sure He's done the same thing for all of us here. I memorized a new verse this past week, and boy is it ever true. In 2 Corinthians 5:17 it says, *'If anyone is in Christ, he is a new creation; old things have passed away; behold, all things have become new.'* And now, Scott you're a new man too. Welcome to the family, brother!"

The others started to join in and express their agreement, but Bobby held up his hand and called for their attention.

"I'm sorry to break this up, folks," he said apologetically. "There's nothing I like better than welcoming a new member into the family of God, but we're plumb outta time. But before we go, there's something we have to address. Scott, because of your repentance from your sin and your acceptance of Christ, God has forgiven you, and we have forgiven you, but unfortunately, the State of California won't be so inclined."

"I know, sir, believe me, I know," Scott agreed. "That's been on my mind every day ever since that terrible night it happened. And I'm ready to face up to my responsibilities, but I would really like some advice from you guys before I actually do anything."

"I agree completely," Bobby said. "Both you and Jamal need some real direction from above. We're gonna have to wrap it up right now so I can go preach, but let the three of us get together tomorrow night and seek God's answers for the both of you."

"Dad, tomorrow night's not good for me," Jamal said. "I've got that Bible study in my room, and things are going so well, I really don't want to miss it."

"Me too, Pastor," Scott agreed. "We've got a swim meet tomorrow evening, and I really need to be there. Besides, I have to talk to Tony. He was awful mad at me when he left here, and I've got to try to patch things up with him."

"Okay, let's make it Tuesday night then. Will that work for you guys?"

"Yeah," said Jamal.

"Me too," Scott added.

"Then it's settled. We'll meet at Reverend Wilcox's retreat off Rosecrans, a couple of miles west of here. The church still keeps it available for me when I need to get away from everything and spend some time alone in study and prayer. I think it would be best if we met there, rather than here at the church. Tony was really upset when he left here, and no telling what he might do, or who he might tell about what we discussed here today. I'd feel better meetin' in a place he doesn't know anything about. You remember where it is don't you, Jamal?"

"Sure, I've been there with you several times. Scott, I'll meet you here at seven o'clock, and then we can go over there together, okay?"

"That'll be fine," agreed Scott, "but I'd like for Aaron to come with us, if that's okay with everybody."

"Me?" asked Aaron. "Why me? I'm not even what you call a believer."

"I'm afraid I have to agree with Aaron on this one, Scott," Bobby said. "I don't see how his presence would be of any particular advantage."

"Look, I don't know what's going on in Aaron's heart and mind," Scott replied. "I'm not sure he even does. God only knows for sure what He has in mind for him. But of this I am sure. Aaron Muller is the most sincere, dedicated follower of Jehovah God that I've ever met. He is absolutely committed to doing what he believes is right, regardless of how it might reflect on him personally. I value his wisdom and counsel."

"Come to think of it," reasoned Bobby, "you're absolutely right. We could use a cool head and some objective counsel. Aaron, could you arrange to meet with us Tuesday night?"

"Yeah, I guess so, but are you sure you really want me there?"

"Yes, I do. We all do," Bobby assured him. "Scott's right. There's something quite unique about you, Aaron. God has laid His hand on you for some special purpose, and though you haven't received Jesus as your own Messiah yet, you have an unmistakable spiritual quality about you. Your insight and recommendations will be most welcome."

"Well, okay, if you're sure. I guess I'll meet Jamal and Scott here at the church, and then we can all go over to your place together."

"It's all settled then," Bobby concluded. "I'll see you guys at the retreat a little after seven on Tuesday night."

With that, Bobby led them all in a prayer of thanksgiving over Scott's decision to accept Christ; and in supplication for the imminent salvation of

Tony, Marcus, and Aaron; and finally, for wisdom for Jamal and Scott as they considered the profound decisions they both had to make.

They all exchanged farewells, and as they were filing out of the room, Candi took hold of Scott's arm and placed her head on his shoulder.

"Thank you, Candi," he said, still overwhelmed that she had forgiven him, and had expressed her love for him so openly.

"You ain't seen nothin' yet, pardner," she said with a coy smile. "As they say, 'One good turn deserves another!'"

CHAPTER TWENTY-FOUR

THE CROSS

There was indeed an enthusiastic display of affection taking place between Scott and Candi on the way home that Sunday evening, but there was even a greater exchange of words. It seemed as though they were attempting to make up for all the time they had lost over the previous six months of his procrastination. In the weeks before, there had been little conversation between the two of them because of the tension that had existed over his unwillingness to accept Christ. Now that he had made his decision, it was as though the floodgates had been opened and there was no stopping the flow of words that came gushing forth.

Candi wanted to hear all the details Scott had deleted from his previous confession. She was fascinated with hearing about everything her friend had experienced, leading up to, and including, that fateful night, and everything he had gone through since then. It also took him some time to explain that the only reason he hadn't confided in her from the beginning, wasn't because he hadn't trusted her, but because he had been afraid of losing her.

Scott asked her if he could take her out to eat on what would be their first official date in over six months of seeing each other. She readily accepted, and over a lavish meal at a pricey restaurant, their courtship and conversation continued. They sat there long after they had finished eating, discussing what Scott was going to do in the future.

"Scott, I really don't want you to turn yourself in," Candi said, sipping from the refilled Diet Coke the waitress had just brought her. "After waiting so long, I've finally got you, and I'm not willing to let you go again."

"And I don't want you to," he agreed. "The last thing I want to do now is to face a murder rap, and maybe spend the rest of my life in prison."

"Georgia Davis' death was actually a tragic accident," she insisted. "The family all knows that, and they've already forgiven you for it. Carl and Aaron have forgiven you for what happened to them as well, and from what I understand about Papa Saul, I bet he will too. If you and I and Tony all work and save, we should be able to pay back the money you stole from him before too long. I don't see why the police have to be brought into this at all."

"What about the car we stole and demolished?" Scott wanted to know. "How are we going to repay the owner for that? The newspapers said it belonged to a single young woman who was a schoolteacher in Santa Monica or somewhere. How are we going to identify and locate her and then pay her back without anybody figuring out who we are?"

"I don't know, but there has to be a way. Maybe we won't even have to pay it back at all. Her insurance company has surely already reimbursed her for it."

"Candi, you're talking with your heart now, not your head," Scott said, reaching out and taking her hand, "I've only been a Christian for a couple of hours, but I know God's not gonna let me walk away from this thing that easily. What I did was a terrible thing, and in my soul, I know He wants me to face up to my responsibilities."

"But what about your responsibility to yourself, to your family . . . and to me?" she wanted to know. "I love you, you big dummy, and I want to spend the rest of my life with you. If you love me too, I'd think you'd want to be with me as well. What good would it do anybody for you to leave me and go off to prison?"

"Candi, believe me, I don't ever want to leave you, but what I do really isn't up to me. After running from God for all these months, I've finally given my life to Him. It's really His call now."

"Well, I think He's telling you to put your old life behind you, and to begin brand new."

"What if it was Tony talking to you right now, instead of me?" asked Scott. "Would you be giving him the same advice? Or what if it was you? Would you believe God would just want you to walk away from what you did and to pretend it never happened?"

"Well . . . uh . . . yes . . . I . . . uh . . ." was all she could get out before she began to cry. She buried her face in her hands, and she sobbed as discreetly as she could.

"That's not fair," she managed to say at last. "I don't love Tony like I love you. I don't even love myself like I love you. I can't imagine going on without you now."

"I don't know what God's ultimate will is for me in this matter," Scott reasoned, "but I just trusted Him with my eternal soul back there at the church. I think I can trust Him with the rest of my life now as well. He knows our hearts' desire. I'm sure He'll lead us to do what is best for His glory, and for what is ultimately best for us too."

"But how are you going to know what His will is? I've been a Christian most of my life and I have trouble figuring it out most of the time. I begged Him for six months to reveal His will to me about you, but I never heard a peep. You're a rookie. You said so yourself. How are you going to determine His will in this matter in just a couple of days?"

"I don't know," he admitted, "but I'm sure gonna give it a try. Tomorrow I'll talk with my parents about it. They're both Christians, and besides, my dad's a shrewd defense attorney. He'll be able to advise me as to what might happen if I do turn myself in. Then I gotta talk to Tony. Maybe he'll get saved too and we can figure out together what we need to do."

"I wouldn't count on that happening," Candi said, stiffening. "You saw how angry he was when he stormed out. I'm worried about what he might do if he thinks you're going to go to the police. You may want to do God's will even if it means getting arrested and going to prison, but he's not about to go along with that."

"I know, but if God could change my heart, then surely He can do the same with his too."

"I know He can too . . . but I don't know that He will. God doesn't always do what we think He should."

"Yeah, I know," Scott agreed. "That's why I'm glad I'm meeting with Pastor Bobby and Jamal and Aaron Tuesday night. By then, we'll know a lot more, and I'm trusting that God will give us the wisdom to make the right decisions for both me and Jamal."

They left the restaurant and continued their conversation as Scott drove Candi home. They sat in his Blazer for a long time outside her dorm, but when it finally came time for him to leave, they were still not completely agreed on what course of action would be best for Scott to take. He promised to see her the next evening after the swim meet, and after he had talked with his parents and with Tony.

He walked her to her door and there he held her close and kissed her just like he had done a hundred times in his dreams, but had begun to doubt whether he would ever do in real life.

The next day dawned with the threat of yet another storm blowing in from the Pacific. El Niño was back, and that winter had been one of the wettest ever-recorded in Los Angeles. The weatherman predicted mostly wind and clouds for Monday, with the rain arriving sometime Tuesday afternoon.

Scott had arrived home late the night before and his parents had already gone to bed. Now they were both sitting at the breakfast table when Scott entered the room. He was already shaved, showered, and dressed, which was unusual for him at 7:00 A.M., especially when he didn't have a class until nine. Florence Graham looked up and smiled at her son and greeted him warmly. Bruce nodded and grunted something, and went back to reading his morning paper.

"Hi Mom and Dad," Scott replied, and then went into his prepared statement. "I have some important things I need to discuss with both of you. It includes some very good news, and I'm afraid, some very bad news as well. Is this a good time for us to talk?"

His tone arrested their attention, and other priorities suddenly lost their importance. Bruce put down his paper and removed his reading glasses and looked at the serious expression on his son's face. "Sure, Scott. What's on your mind?"

"Well, first the good news. Yesterday, at our Bible study I prayed to receive Jesus Christ as my own personal Lord and Savior."

Florence said, "Oh, Scott, that's wonderful!" as she gave him a big hug and kissed him on the cheek. She was already beginning to cry when she added, "We've been praying for you to make that decision for such a long time."

"Son, that's great," his father added, shaking Scott's hand, and then giving him an awkward hug of his own. "You're a smart kid. I figured you'd come around sooner or later. But what took you so long?"

"Well, that brings me to the bad news. I knew I needed to get saved a long time ago, but at first it was just my own foolish pride that kept me from it. Then, when I became convinced of the claims of Christ, and really wanted to accept Him, I kept putting it off because I wasn't prepared to pay the price."

"What price?" Bruce wanted to know. "What have they been teaching you at that Bible study? The last time I checked, salvation was a free gift. Since when do you have to pay the price for a free gift?"

"Oh, I knew I could never pay for my salvation," Scott agreed, "but I knew that if I was really going to come to Christ, I had to be willing to be completely honest with God. I had to repent of my sin, and be willing to confess it, and to turn from it, and I wasn't willing to do that."

"Oh, that's silly, Scott," his mother said. "What possible sin could you have been so guilty of that you felt you couldn't confess it. God forgives us of all our sin the moment we accept Jesus."

"Yes, I know that. I wasn't worried about how God would handle my sin. He knew all about it already. My big problem was with how people here on earth would deal with it."

At this point, the attorney in Bruce Graham began putting things together. "What are you saying, Scott?" he asked suspiciously. "Does this have anything to do with that botched robbery back in January?"

"Yes, Dad," Scott admitted, relieved that now what he had to say would not come as a complete surprise, "it *was* Tony and me that robbed that store up in Los Angeles. It was us who shot those people and killed that old lady. It was a horrible nightmare. We never intended to hurt anybody, but things went crazy, and that's what happened."

"Oh, my God!" Florence moaned, "Oh, my God!" She collapsed into a chair and stared at her son in disbelief, unable to grasp the full ramification of what she had just heard.

"What?" Bruce gasped. "No way! You gotta be kidding! How could you? Why would you? This just doesn't make any sense!"

"Sit down, Dad," Scott said, with more authority in his voice than he had ever used with his father before. "I need to tell you the whole ugly story."

"Yeah, okay," his father said weakly, as he pulled up a chair beside his wife. "I can't believe this is happening."

For the next hour, Scott told his shocked parents everything. He held back nothing and made no excuses for his actions. They interrupted him several times with questions. Why did he feel he needed all that extra money, and why did he try to get it by betting on a rigged basketball game? Why didn't he just tell them he had lost the money rather than resorting to robbing a poor old man to get it back? Didn't he know he could always talk with them about anything?

For some of the questions he had no answers, except that he had been proud and had wanted to achieve a measure of self-sufficiency. He hadn't wanted to appear as weak or as a failure, especially in his father's eyes. He had kept thinking that there had to be a way to fix things. He had kept getting deeper and deeper involved until there had been no turning back.

When he had finally finished his explanation, and had answered all their questions, his mother just sat there with a dazed look on her face. She still could not comprehend that her little boy could have possibly done all the terrible things he had just confessed to them.

His father, on the other hand, was dealing with an assortment of conflicting emotions. He was angry with Scott that he had lied to him, had stolen from him, had invaded his privacy, had seen his *Playboy* magazines, and had continued to deceive him for weeks on end. At the same time, he was secretly in admiration that his, heretofore unimpressive son had the brains, guts, and fortitude to pull something like that off. He was also fearful of what the future might hold for all of them as this ugly thing finally played itself out.

"Who else have you told about this?" he wanted to know.

"Just those in my Bible study group, and they're sworn to silence."

"Yeah, right," Bruce said sarcastically. "If I remember right, you said some of them are members of the woman's family. Others are those you guys shot during the robbery. And one of them is a cop. Maybe they said everything was fine and dandy when you first fessed up to them, but after they've had time to think about it awhile, they'll realize the pain and loss you've caused them, and they'll turn on you and eat you up."

"No they won't," Scott countered. "You don't know these people like I do. Christianity isn't just a religion to them. It's their very life. It was their example of true Christian love and commitment that finally brought me to follow their example and accept the Lord myself."

"Oh, well, thanks a lot," Florence said, obviously offended by his words. "I guess that means that your father and I failed to influence you at all for Christ."

"No, Mom, I'm sorry. I didn't mean it that way at all. You and Dad have been great. It was my fault. I just wasn't paying attention here at home. But being with these people for a couple of hours every week, studying the Bible and working through some really tough issues, has really made an impact on my life. In fact, I'm meeting with some of them tomorrow night so they can help me decide what I'm going to do now."

"What do you mean, what you're going to do now?" his father asked.

"Well, I've not only broken God's laws, I've broken man's as well. I've made it right with God already, but I don't feel like I can just walk away from what I did. I feel there's a need to face the consequences of my actions before the justice system."

"Oh, no, you don't, young man!" his father thundered. "Now you listen to me. You're not going to tell anyone about this. You already said that the family has forgiven you, and the police have all but dropped the case. I gotta hand it to you and Tony. You covered your tracks really well. No court in the country would ever convict you guys on what the state has on you right now. You just keep your mouth shut and you'll be fine."

"I'm not worried about doing what will keep me out of trouble," Scott said confidently. "I just want to do what's right."

"Well, then you'll listen to your father," Florence said. "The right thing to do is to maintain your good name and to keep from going to prison. How do you think it would reflect on us to have our son a convicted felon doing time in the state penitentiary?"

"No offense, Mom, but my greatest concern here is not how we're gonna appear before our neighbors and Dad's colleagues. My concern is to do what's right before the Lord, regardless of the consequences."

"That's just great!" Bruce said in disgust. "First, you dishonor us and steal from us and do all sorts of despicable things. Then, you lie to us for weeks. Now, you're going to make it all better by throwing your life away in prison and dragging our name through the mud. If you weren't going to take our advice, why did you bother telling us about all this in the first place?"

"For two reasons, Dad," Scott said calmly. "First, because I've sinned against you, and I needed to confess it and ask you both to forgive me. That's what I'm doing right now. I'm so sorry for what I've done. I offer no excuses. Please, I ask you to forgive me for my offenses and for bringing dishonor upon your name."

That request stopped both his parents for a moment. But after an embarrassing period of silence, they realized they had no choice. They loved their son, and they were both Christians, and he had asked for their forgiveness. They embraced him and assured him of it, and of their unconditional love as well. But they both insisted that it would be best for everyone if he let them handle the matter as a family. There was no need for Scott to seek other counsel, or to talk to the police. Bruce even offered to help pay back the store's owner discreetly so everything would be corrected as much as possible.

Scott thanked them both, and there was emotion and sincerity in his voice when he did. He was not disregarding their welfare in the matter, but he was still convicted that he needed to pursue it further.

"How could I possibly profess to be a committed Christian before others," he asked, "and encourage them to walk the straight and narrow, when I would be concealing such great matters of sin myself?"

"But once you accept Christ, all your sins are forgiven," Florence reminded him. "Didn't they teach you that at that Bible study?"

"Of course they did, but that still doesn't absolve me of my obligations before the law. The thief on the cross was forgiven of all his sins, but he still had to suffer the consequences of his transgressions against the state."

"That's not the same thing at all," Bruce protested.

"I know it isn't exactly the same," Scott admitted, "but it's the same principle. When I got home last night, I studied my Bible a lot on the subject of honesty, and it was really convicting. In Acts 24:16 Paul says, '*I myself always strive to have a conscience without offense toward God and men.*' In Hebrews 13:18 it says something like, '*Pray for us; for we are confident that we have a good conscience, in all things desiring to live honestly.*' Then, the whole book of Philemon is a lesson in honesty. According to the footnotes in my Bible, Onesimus was a slave who stole from his master and ran away to Rome. There, he met the apostle Paul and got saved. Instead of telling Onesimus to forget about his obligations to his former master, Paul sent him back to Philemon to make things right, even though he was risking his life in so doing. For in those days, death was the typical punishment for slaves who had done what Onesimus did."

"We know the Bible, Scott," Bruce said, clearly irritated by what his son was implying. "You don't need to preach to us about honesty. We're not asking you to continue to do anything wrong. We're just asking you to think before you throw your life away over something that's in the past, and something you can't make right anyway no matter what you do. Besides, this isn't just about you. Tony's involved in this up to his eyeballs. What does he think about you going to the authorities with all this?"

"I don't know for sure yet. He left before I got saved yesterday, but he wasn't very happy about me even sharing it with those in the Bible study. I'm going to talk with him about it today. I'm praying he'll come to the Lord too, and then we can decide together what we're gonna do."

"I wouldn't hold my breath," Bruce said emphatically. "Tony has always been a young man thoroughly caught up in himself and with this present world. I can't see him being even willing to consider running the risk of going to prison over an issue of ethics or biblical protocol. As a matter of fact, I would be concerned about what he might do if he knew you were thinking about it. Because, whatever the courts might wind up doing to you, they would also inevitably do to him. I can't see him just sitting idly by and letting that happen."

"That's why I'm praying God will change his heart. Believe me, God has performed so many miracles in the past few weeks, this one would be no big deal for Him to pull off. But that brings me to the second reason I needed to talk with you today."

"Oh yeah, I almost forgot," Bruce said with mock enthusiasm. "What else can you share with us to make our day?"

"Dad, seriously, I'm sorry for all of this, and I'm not trying to make things worse. I just want to do the right thing. That's why I need as much information as I can get before I talk with Tony. You're an attorney. If we should turn ourselves in, what kind of sentence do you think we'd get?"

"A stiff one. They'd lock you in and melt down the key."

"No, I'm serious."

"So am I," the elder Graham said. "They probably wouldn't go for a murder one conviction because of the circumstances involved, but they'd stick you with armed robbery, assault with a deadly weapon, and probably second-degree murder. I'd say you'd be looking at fifteen years at least, more like twenty-five to life."

"Oh, Scotty," Florence cried, "you can't do this to yourself. You can't do this to us. Promise us you won't do it!"

"I'm sorry, Mom. I can't promise you that. Don't get me wrong. I have no desire to go to prison, not even for one day, but I can't help thinking about what the Lord told Peter and the other disciples about denying themselves, taking up their crosses, and following Him. If I insist on maintaining my freedom, how am I denying myself? If I refuse to suffer for my sin, how am I taking up my cross? And if I'm not willing to walk by faith into the unknown future, how am I following Jesus?"

"I don't know," she admitted. "I don't think He expects us to take those things so literally. Besides, how could you expect to follow Jesus anywhere if you were to spend the rest of your life in prison?"

"It wouldn't be for the rest of my life. Dad, even if I did get convicted of all those things you mentioned, wouldn't I be eligible for parole in seven years?"

"Theoretically, yes," Bruce conceded. "That's assuming you didn't get yourself killed in there first. Even if you did manage to survive, you'd probably get beaten up and raped repeatedly, and who knows what else. Prison is a horrible place. Believe me, you don't want to go there. I forbid it!"

The conversation continued on for another fifteen minutes, with neither side giving in. Scott did promise them he would not make a final decision until after he had talked with his friends Tuesday night, and that he would talk with his parents again before he did anything, even if he did decide to go to the authorities.

He broke off the conversation with the excuse that he had to leave for school. He did have a class to attend, but he could have skipped it. The main reason he chose to leave was that he could see no reason to continue the debate.

Although he could appreciate his parents' concern for him, their reasoning was purely emotional and personal. They offered him no spiritual or biblical advice at all. He had a life-changing decision to make, and they simply were not helping him make it.

His mother clung to his neck and sobbed, begging him not to do the wrong thing. His father gave up in anger and disgust, and went to his room to get ready for work himself. Scott pulled himself away from his mother's grasp and hurried out the door. As he backed out of the driveway, he could see her standing in the doorway in her housecoat, weeping and looking more pitiful than he could ever remember.

As he drove down the hill, Scott felt a strange conflict within. He felt miserable for causing his parents so much distress, but he also experienced a certain inner peace and sensed the presence of the Lord with him. He had no idea what lay in store in the future, but he felt a confidence that if he were obedient to the Lord's leading, he could count on Him to see him through it, whatever it was.

After his last class, Scott set out to find Tony. He had to talk with him and share what God had done in his life. He didn't have long to search, for just outside the building, Tony was sitting on a low brick retainer wall, waiting for him.

"We gotta talk, Scott."

"Yeah, I know."

As they headed for the parking lot, Tony minced no words. "What happened after I left? You told 'em didn't you?"

"Yes, I did," Scott admitted, "but it wasn't like you think. I wish you would've stayed. It was wonderful."

"How wonderful could it have been? You spillin' your guts, and them takin' mental notes so they can turn you in to the cops?"

"No, it wasn't like that at all. I did tell them everything that happened, but they didn't turn on me. They forgave me . . . and you too. They aren't going to tell anybody."

"I don't believe that for a minute. Right now that big dumb cop I shot is probably telling those two detectives the whole story."

"No he's not."

"How can you be so sure?"

"Because, he's a Christian, and he gave me his word."

"Oh, I can't tell you how much better that makes me feel," Tony said sarcastically. "The next thing you're gonna tell me is that you're a Christian now too, right?"

"Yes, as a matter of fact, I am. I finally made the decision I knew I should have made months ago."

"Terrific. I'm happy for you. They forgave you, and now He's forgiven you too. We can drop the whole matter now, right?"

"No."

"Whaddya mean, no?"

"Well, for one thing, you still haven't accepted Christ yet. It can't be over until you become a Christian too."

"Oh no you don't, buddy boy!" Tony bristled. "You may have decided to go that route, but I'm not ready yet, and I'm not sure I ever will be. You get all torn up with guilt over that woman's death, and all goo-goo eyed over Candi, and so you decide to become a convert to win forgiveness and love. Fine, that's your business, but don't expect me to be in a hurry to follow you."

"But, Tony," Scott pleaded, "you studied the same stuff I did. You read all the same Scriptures. Surely the Lord convinced you of its truth just like He did me. How can you continue to reject it?"

"I wouldn't say I'm rejecting it. I'm just not ready to accept it yet. I've got a life to live, and being a pious Christian doesn't fit into my plans for living it right now. I've adopted a wait-and-see policy, and that's what I recommend you do as well."

"Too late. I've already given my heart and life to Christ. My days of waiting and hesitating are over."

"I'm not talking about religion now, Scott," Tony said, his voice low and deadly serious. "I'm talking about that information you so blatantly shared with all those people. I'm telling you to sit on it. I think I understand why you told the others about what we did, but don't you be tellin' anybody else about it. You've done enough damage already. It'll be a miracle if one of 'em doesn't turn us in, as it is."

By this time, they had arrived at Tony's Mustang. Tony unlocked and opened the driver's door, but he didn't get in. He stood, holding the door open, looking at Scott. "You're my friend," he said. "We've been through a lot together, we've got to keep covering one another's backsides on this thing."

"Tony, I was wanting to talk to you about that," Scott said imploringly. "I don't expect you to fully understand, but I'm really struggling with this thing. As a believer now, I have an obligation to live honestly before the Lord and before my fellow man."

"Well, you go ahead and live honestly about everything else, but this is one thing that has to be kept quiet. Go struggle with something else, something that doesn't include me. Surely you've got some other hidden sins that you could confess that won't get either of us in too much trouble. But if you go confessing this one, they'll take you down hard . . . and then they'll come after me. I'm just not willing to let that happen."

"Believe me, I don't like the idea of turning myself in anymore than you do, but I'm committed to doing what I feel the Lord wants me to do. I'm getting together with Pastor Bobby, Jamal, and Aaron tomorrow night to seek their advice. Why don't you meet with us?"

"No way. I already know what I'm gonna do, and if you know what's good for you, you'll do the same thing. Why do you wanna meet with them anyway?"

"The Bible talks about there being safety in having many counselors. I need their counsel, and Jamal needs it too."

"What for?"

"You know. He told us he was being pressured by the mob to throw another game, and as a Christian, he doesn't feel like he can do it. He's considering whether or not he should go to the authorities about it. We're all going to meet together and pray and try to figure out what God would have us do."

"It sounds to me like you've both already made up your minds," Tony said in disgust.

"I think we both have a feeling as to what we ought to do, but we want to make sure we've considered all the options and their possible consequences before we decide on a final course of action."

"What does Marcus think about all this?" Tony asked. "If Jamal turns in the mob, they'll be all over the both of them. It's not just about you and Jamal, you know. If you guys go down, you take me and Marcus with you. I, for one, am not willing to let that happen. And I bet he isn't either."

"I don't really know where Marcus is in all this," Scott admitted. "Personally, I think Marcus is real close to giving his life over to the Lord. He's fighting it real hard, just like I did, but I'm praying he'll make that decision soon. "I'm praying for you too, Tony."

"Save your breath. You're gonna need it, cause I'm gonna knock it right outta you if you even think about goin' to the cops. Where're you guys meeting tomorrow night, anyway?"

"Why? You thinking about planting a bomb there so you can make sure we don't blow the whistle on you?"

"Now why didn't I think of that?" Tony said laughing. "No, my friend, I think I'll talk to Marcus, and we may just drop by after all and try to talk some sense into the rest of you. Lord knows somebody needs to."

"You'd be welcome," Scott responded enthusiastically. "I think it would be great if you guys came. We need everybody's input before we make any final decisions. Unfortunately, I don't know where it is we're actually meeting. It's at a retreat or something Pastor Bobby has somewhere. Jamal knows where it is and we're going with him. But if you're coming with Marcus, he'll know too. Apparently, they've both been there with their dad before."

"Okay. Look, I gotta go," Tony said, looking at his watch. "Promise me you won't do anything stupid until we have a chance to talk about it tomorrow night, okay?"

"Sure. You've got my word on it," Scott promised, extending his hand.

They shook hands and Tony got into his car and drove out of the lot. He didn't appear angry or very upset. Scott stood and watched him drive away, surprised and overjoyed by his friend's apparent change in attitude. Instead of being infuriated, he seemed reasonable and approachable. Scott was becoming excited about what the Lord was doing in the heart of his friend.

"Dear Lord," he prayed, "please continue to soften his heart. Open his eyes and bring him to Yourself tomorrow night."

CHAPTER TWENTY-FIVE

THE DOUBLE CROSS

The swim meet against UC Irvine was the only Monday contest Scott and Tony had all season. It was a blustery night, the swirling wind and chilling air a sure harbinger of the powerful storm brewing off the coast in the nearby Pacific Ocean. In spite of the weather, the building was nearly full of hometown hopefuls, anxious to see if their Forty-Niners could keep their slim hopes alive for an invitation to the national championships later on that month. Irvine had one of the strongest teams on the West Coast, and it would not be an easy victory, especially considering the lackluster way in which the local squad had been performing in the recent past.

But perhaps it was due to the unusual day of the meet, or perhaps it was the nasty weather outside, or more likely, it was due to the change in attitude of certain members of the team. At any rate, after a close and hard fought contest, CSULB pulled off an upset victory.

Tony won all his events, which surprised no one; but so did Scott, which surprised almost everybody. He swam against two of the best sprinters in the nation on the Irvine team, but he rose to the occasion. His times in the 50 and the 100-meter freestyle events were his best ever. And what astounded everyone was the fact that his time of 47.36 seconds in the 100 was the second fastest in the nation that year. Also, in three out of the four relays he anchored, he found himself trailing the competition at the beginning of his leg, but he was not to be denied. He managed to overtake his opponent in all but one of the races, and secured three more victories for his team.

His teammates mobbed him at the end of the meet, and Coach Englehart lavished him with praise. But surprisingly, less enthusiastic was his friend Tony D'Angelo. Partly, it was because Scott was getting the attention that was normally reserved for him. In addition, he was somewhat resentful that Scott hadn't swum that way all season, which would have given their team a much higher position in the national rankings. But mostly, he was reserved in his praise because of what he knew Scott was considering doing. After they had showered and dressed, he called Scott aside in the locker room. He looked around to make sure everyone else had left before he began his conversation.

"You were great out there, man," he said, trying to sound enthusiastic. "I knew you had it in you. You keep that up and we might have a shot at the nationals after all."

"Thanks, Tony, you didn't do bad yourself. I don't remember the last time you lost a single event."

"Scott, with everything we got goin' for us, surely you can forget about talking to anybody about what happened back in January, can't you? We've got nothin' to gain by it, and everything to lose."

"I know. Believe me, I know," Scott said sympathetically. "I would love to forget about the whole thing, but the Holy Spirit won't let me. He keeps reminding me that if I really am a new man in Christ, then I need to deal with all the junk the old man left behind."

"So, you're still plannin' on meeting with those guys tomorrow night, huh?" Tony asked, the disappointment and anger showing in his voice.

"Yeah, I really need their advice on this thing. You're comin' too, aren't you?"

"Yeah, I'll talk to Marcus tomorrow and see if he'll come too." Then Tony lost control of his emotions and demanded, "Scott, for God's sake, don't go to the cops! I can't let you ruin my life over some wild religious obsession you've got . . ."

"If I do go to the cops," Scott cut him off, "it *will be* for God's sake. That's the only reason I'd do it. I don't want to ruin my life, and I especially don't want to ruin yours. You don't know the Lord yet, and you can't possibly understand everything I'm going through here."

"No, I don't understand, and I'm really not interested in finding out. But here's something I want you to understand, and understand well: *I won't let you turn us in to the police!* Do you understand that?"

"Tony, please, let's talk about this," Scott pleaded. But Tony was in no frame of mind to talk. He spun on his heel and walked toward the door.

"You think about what I said," he called over his shoulder, "and we'll do our talkin' about it tomorrow night."

Scott gathered the rest of his things together and also left the building. There, Candi met him just outside the door. She jumped into his arms and hugged him tightly. She had been so reserved for so long, Scott didn't quite know how to respond to her present enthusiastic display of affection.

"You were sensational!" she gushed. "I knew you were good, but I've never seen anybody swim like you did tonight. What got into you? Was it me? It was my love pushing you on, wasn't it? C'mon, say it was me," she urged him playfully.

"Yes, my love, it was you," Scott laughed, finally breaking her grip on him and leading her toward the parking lot. "But there was something else, something more. Do you remember that old movie *Chariots of Fire*, where that Scottish sprinter told his sister that he knew the Lord had made him for Himself, but He had also made him fast? He said he felt God's pleasure when he ran. I never understood what he was talking about before, but I experienced it tonight. I felt His pleasure when I swam tonight, Candi. It was as though the Lord was in my body, swimming through me, and enjoying every second of it."

"Oh, Scott," she said, snuggling up to him as they walked, "I can't tell you how good it is to hear you talk about the Lord that way. I prayed for so long for it to happen, and I almost gave up. Now, finally, I got what I prayed for: a man who loves me completely, but also one who loves Him even more."

The Bible study had outgrown Jamal's dorm room, and they had to move it to the lounge area downstairs. Over twenty young men gathered to study the word of God with the all-American athlete, newly adopted into the family of God. The study was made up primarily of members of the UCLA basketball team, but several of them had invited friends to join them. Jamal was a natural leader on the basketball court, but he felt out of place leading these people in a study of the Scriptures.

The lesson for that evening was on answered prayer. They went through the prescribed study as outlined in the *Navigator* booklets, and then branched out on a discussion of their own. Jamal asked those in attendance, most of whom were even younger in the faith than he was, and some not even saved yet, how they could know what God's answer was when they asked Him for wisdom.

"What do you mean?" asked The Kid, "Wisdom for what?"

"Oh . . ." Jamal said, acting as though he were searching for an illustration, when actually, he knew exactly where he was heading, "suppose you have a really tough decision to make, and you ask God to give you wisdom to make the right one. How do you know if He's given it to you, and how do you go about making your decision?"

"Wow, that's a tough one," Sammy mused. "I suppose you just have to go with your feelin's. You know, if God gives you peace in your heart about a decision, then it must be His will."

"But couldn't our own desires and preferences cloud the picture?" Jamal asked. "How can we be sure what we decide to do isn't the result of our own will, rather than God's?"

"You know, I'm really new at this stuff," Sky King said, "but I think the only safe way to approach such a decision is to study the Bible, and see what light it can shed on the subject. Then, you gotta talk to as many wise and godly people as you can, and listen to what they have to say about it. Then, I guess you gotta pray a lot and make your decision, and trust God to give you the wisdom to make the right one."

"That sounds like pretty good advice to me," The Kid agreed. "Why, Jamal? Are you facing a decision like that, or is this just a hypothetical question to jerk us rookies around?"

"No, this is the real thing alright, but I can't really talk about it with you guys right now. I'm meeting with some Christian friends tomorrow night to seek their counsel, and I'd really appreciate it if you'd all pray for us. Whatever we decide will be life changing . . . and it could be a matter of life and death."

"Hey, let's do it right now," Sammy suggested. "God's been answering so many of our prayers already, I'm sure He can handle this request too without much of a problem at all."

The others agreed, and twenty-two young men knelt around Jamal, many of them with their hands on his head and shoulders, and prayed earnestly that God would give him wisdom and help him to make the right decision. The two non-believers there were so impressed with the sincerity of the faith of the others that, before the evening was over, they had both prayed to receive Christ into their own lives as well.

Candi had just effortlessly delivered a beautiful baby boy, and was sitting up in bed eating a hearty breakfast of biscuits and gravy and country sausage. The nurse handed Scott his newborn son, clean as a whistle, wrapped in a cuddly blue blanket, and smelling like baby powder. Scott looked down into his beautiful blue eyes, set in an angelic face, framed by soft golden curls. His infant son looked up at him and smiled, cooing with delight.

The cooing began to give way to the sound of windows being rattled in their frames by the wind, and by tree branches scraping against the screens outside. Thus, was Scott awakened from his pleasant dream. Not willing to let it escape, he willed himself back to sleep, trying to recapture the scene. But it was to no avail. The images faded into the recesses of his emerging consciousness, and he opened his eyes to the gray reality of his bedroom. The sun should have been shining by that time, but it was still nearly dark outside. Thick, heavy clouds had sneaked up on the darkness during the night, and had trapped it beneath their folds, and now they were doing their best to keep it from escaping.

Becoming aware of the chill in the room, Scott stretched and rolled over; pulling the covers he had kicked off during the night back up around his shoulders. For a moment he entertained the thought of trying to go back to sleep, and of pursuing his vision of marriage and parenthood, but he realized it was pointless. It was Tuesday morning, and he was neither a husband nor a father, and no amount of sleeping would ever make him either one. But he did have a huge decision to make, and how he made it might well affect whether or not he ever realized his dreams.

He arose and got ready as quickly and as quietly as he could, not wanting to alert his parents of his activity. They had lectured him for nearly two hours the night before, trying to convince him not to mention anything about his criminal activities to the police, and he didn't want to give them an opportunity to pick up where they had left off. He slipped out of the house quietly, and was backing out of the driveway when his father awoke and realized that he was leaving.

After their last classes of the morning, Scott and Candi met and went out for lunch together. What could have taken less than an hour stretched into a three-hour session in a back booth at a Denny's Restaurant near the university. They consumed a nondescript lunch and engaged in some small talk as they watched the rain begin in earnest outside their window. When all the dishes had been cleared away, and the waitress had dropped off their check, and Candi was relatively sure they would be left alone, she changed the subject and began to talk seriously about their future.

"Scott, I've been doing a lot of thinking and praying and reading my Bible, and I believe I know what God wants you to do about what happened back in January."

"I know what you're going to say, Candi," he said, "and I really appreciate it, but I just don't feel right about trying to live the Christian life without dealing with the garbage I left in my unsaved past."

"Now, hold on there, mister!" she said curtly, a little anger showing in her voice. "You're not the only one here with a conscience. You're not the only one willing to consider doing what's right rather than what's most convenient or pleasant. If you had let me finish, you would have found out that I believe you should turn yourself into the authorities just as soon as possible."

"What? You do? But I thought . . ."

"I know what you thought," she said, lowering her voice and speaking calmly, "and it's true. I do love you, and I want to marry you, and to bear your children, and to live happily ever after with you, but I also want to do what's right. There's no way we could ever really live for God and raise our children properly, knowing that you had a clouded past. How could we ever teach them about morality and honesty, knowing that their father was a criminal who had never dealt with his crimes?"

"Wow, I can't believe it!" Scott said in amazement. "I thought I was the only one who felt that way." He reached across the table and took her hands in his. Then suddenly a look of concern came across his face and he withdrew his hands.

"Then does that mean you'll want to break up with me?" he asked tentatively.

"No way, you dumb ox!" she scolded, reaching across and taking his hands again. "I've waited all my Christian life to find a man who's willing to be completely committed to Christ, and now that I've found him, I'm never gonna let him go."

"But you said . . ."

"I know what I said," she cut him off. "I said I think God would want you to turn yourself in. You'll go to prison, but they surely won't keep you forever. The Davis family will testify in your behalf, and so will the Singletons. I'm sure Aaron will too, and maybe even his grandfather. Since there won't really be anybody against you, I'm sure the judge will take all that into consideration, and give you a lighter sentence."

"My dad says I wouldn't be eligible for parole for about seven years," Scott said, "but I think it might be sooner than that considering all the unusual circumstances."

"Even if it's longer, I'll wait for you. I graduate next year, and my dad has already offered me a position in his accounting firm. I could live at home and save my money so we could have something to get started with when you do get out. You could finish your degree in prison through correspondence school, and maybe even get a seminary degree there as well. But we'll have to figure out some way we can pay back the money you and Tony stole from Aaron's grandfather."

"I've already thought of that. I'll sell my Blazer, and we should get enough out of it to repay him. We might even have some left over to help pay for the car we trashed. Besides, I don't think I'm going to need transportation where I'm goin'. The last time I checked, they didn't allow inmates to maintain automobiles in prison."

"I know it will mean a real sacrifice," Candi said, "but I really believe these are things we have to do. If we can trust God with our eternal souls, we ought to be able to trust Him with our lives here too, even if part of that life has to be spent in a prison. It didn't seem to hurt the apostle Paul that much."

"Yeah, I've been thinking the same thing. Maybe God has a real ministry prepared for me there. He sure used prison to change Pastor Bobby's life for the better. I bet He can do the same thing with mine."

"Besides," Candi added, "if what we've been studying is true, the rapture could occur real soon, and we won't have to worry about the next seven years. But I sure wouldn't want to stand before the Lord and try to explain why we were so busy trying to secure our own happiness and freedom that we failed to face up to our responsibilities."

"Yeah, I know what you mean. I would much prefer to have the Lord come and find me serving Him honestly in prison rather than living on easy street, running from the truth."

"Okay, but what about Tony?" she wanted to know. "He seemed pretty angry Sunday about you even talking to us about it, much less to the police."

"Yeah, he's pretty upset alright, but I'm still praying he'll come around. I know the Lord's working in his heart. He said he and Marcus were going to meet with us tonight, so maybe we can all come to an agreement on the matter."

"Good, I'll really be praying about that meeting. Both you and Jamal have really tough decisions to make. His might be even more difficult than yours. At least no one's threatening to kill you if you go to the police."

"Not yet anyway," Scott added lightheartedly. "Tony made some really ominous threats, but we've been best friends for years. When the chips are down, I don't think he'd really do anything stupid. Down deep, he knows what's the right thing to do, just like I do. I just believe God's gonna change his heart like He did mine."

The two of them stayed at the restaurant for a good while longer as the strength of the storm continued to build outside. They talked and planned and prayed together until it was time for both of them to go to their respective practices. And they agreed to see each other again before Scott went to his meeting later that night.

Tony D'Angelo hadn't slept well. He had tossed and turned, worried about what Scott might do. He tried to convince himself that his friend would never really be so stupid and so calloused as to actually turn them in to the cops. But he kept reminding himself how determined Scott had sounded, insisting on "doing the right thing."

He was also bothered by what Jamal had said Sunday afternoon about going to the police over the pressure the mob had been putting on him to throw another basketball game. If Jamal was willing to risk his life, and that of his brother, over a stupid ball game, then perhaps Scott was serious about going to the cops too. After all, robbery and murder were more serious crimes than that of trying to fix the outcome of a sporting event. Tony just could not understand the mentality of his friends who seemed to be willing to throw away the lives of four promising young men so easily. If that's what becoming a Christian did to you, then he was more convinced than ever that he didn't want to become one.

He knew he had to get Marcus to take him to that meeting that night so they could try to talk some sense into Scott and Jamal. But he didn't have a good feeling about their chances. He was afraid that Pastor Bobby and Aaron would agree with the others, and he and Marcus would be voted down. He had to apply some pressure on them . . . but how?

Then it came to him in a sudden moment of inspiration. "Of course!" he thought. If he could just take some members of the mob with him to the meeting that night, they would know exactly how to convince Scott and Jamal to keep their mouths shut. They certainly had reason to be concerned. If Jamal ratted on them, they would face some very serious charges of racketeering and extortion. He was sure they would be interested in helping him and Marcus apply the necessary pressure to keep things quiet.

He had heard Jamal mention the name of a certain Mr. Apparicio, and he was sure he had heard his father talk about him as being somehow connected with Global Imports. If he could contact him, he was sure the mobster would be interested in what he had to say.

Tony left for school at his regular time, but he didn't go far. He waited at a McDonalds and ate a portion of an Egg-McMuffin and read the paper until he was sure both his parents had left the house. It was his plan to return home and search through his father's desk until he found a phone number or something that would put him in touch with Mr. Apparicio.

He noticed on the front page of the paper that the date for the dedication of the temple in Jerusalem was all set for the coming Friday morning. Constantine Augustus was going to be there to give a speech since it was funds from his U.S.E. that had paid for the temple's construction. Even though there still remained some detail work to be completed, the priests had pushed for the early dedication date. Passover was going to occur early that year, and they needed as much time as possible in the temple to prepare for what they planned to be the biggest celebration in the history of Israel's four thousand-year existence.

Tony found the article a bit unnerving, especially since Pastor Bobby had told them that the completion of the temple could very well lead to the coming of the Lord and the beginning of the tribulation. But he looked at his watch and tossed the paper aside. It was time now to take care of his present situation. If he didn't, he wouldn't be in any kind of a position to do anything about what might possibly happen in the future.

He returned to his house and, as he had expected, he found that both of his parents had already left, his father to work and his mother to the hairdresser. A quick search of his dad's desk uncovered an address book. On the first page, he noticed the name of Paul Apparicio and three phone numbers listed beside it. He copied them all down and returned the book where he had found it. It was too early to call right then, but he would try to get through later that morning.

He left the house as he had found it and began his commute to school, nearly two hours later than usual. He would miss his first class, but he wasn't concerned. At that moment he had much bigger fish to fry.

Indeed, Mr. Apparicio was extremely interested in what Tony had to say. Tony had a little trouble getting through to him. The first number he called yielded only a recorded message on an answering machine. He hung up without leaving a message and tried the second number. The pleasant voice of an obviously young woman answered on the second ring and identified the company as United Investments and asked how she might direct his call.

Tony asked to speak with Mr. Apparicio, but the receptionist inquired into the nature of his request before she would transfer his call. Thinking of nothing better to say, he told her that it was about the upcoming basketball game between UCLA and Stanford. She thanked him and placed him on hold, where he remained for several minutes, no doubt while several underlings passed the message up the line to Mr. "A" himself.

Paul Apparicio personally came on the line and identified himself. He was understandably cautious and noncommittal, but he was obviously interested in knowing what the mysterious caller had in mind.

Tony couldn't think of any diplomatic way to approach the subject, so he just waded right in. He told Mr. Apparicio that he knew about the fix that had been arranged to guarantee the outcome of the game, concerning which the older man denied any knowledge. Then Tony really got his attention when he told him he knew that Jamal Davis was about to renege on his agreement to throw the game, and that the athlete was also about to go to the police and tell them everything he knew.

Trying not to sound too interested, Mr. Apparicio said he still didn't know what Tony was talking about, but he would be willing to arrange a meeting between some of his associates and the young man to discuss the misunderstanding, and to clarify the matter once and for all. A meeting was agreed upon at three-thirty that afternoon. Tony was to sit in his red Mustang at the northeastern corner of the parking lot behind the Red Lobster Restaurant, near the intersection of Lakewood Blvd. and the Pacific Coast Highway in Long Beach. He would be contacted there and further instructions would be given to him.

The rain was pounding relentlessly on the canvas top of Tony's convertible as he sat waiting in the parking lot. The noise was deafening, making it necessary for him to turn the volume nearly as high as it would go in order for him to listen to Hank Williams sing about *Your Cheatin' Heart* on a CD. The moisture in his breath fogged up his windows, making it almost impossible for him to see what was going on outside.

Tony had gotten hooked on classic country music back in high school when he had dated a girl who had transferred in from Oklahoma. The girl was long gone, but her music remained. He listened to it often, even though he certainly didn't fit the typical stereotype of a country/western buff. He liked it, not so much because of the twangy style of the music itself, but because of the true-to-life stories the artists wove into their songs. Now, he thought about the haunting words of the classic ballad as he sat there waiting to be contacted by the mob. Yes, in a way, he was cheating on his friends by bringing the mob into play, but their foolish schemes had to be stopped, and the end would surely justify the means. When everything settled down and got back to normal again, he was sure his friends would thank him for saving them from making the stupid mistakes that would have destroyed their lives. So, he rationalized, he was really doing it for their benefit.

He jumped, startled by a sharp rap on the driver's side window. He bolted upright and pushed the button to lower the window. Outside, he saw a shadowy face, concealed in part by the turned-up collars of a raincoat and a floppy hat pulled down nearly to his eyes.

"Please get out of the car," he said politely. "Mr. LaMata would like for you to join him in our vehicle, if you don't mind."

Tony wasn't real comfortable with the idea, but the man seemed cool enough, and he had a feeling it would be best not to appear uncooperative. He agreed and raised the window, turned off the ignition and removed the key, and got out of the car. He pushed the little button on his key fob and heard the reassuring *beep beep* as the car locked both its doors and set the alarm. The Shadow opened the back door of a black Lincoln Town Car and motioned him inside. He got in and the Shadow closed the door behind him.

Once inside, the first thing Tony noticed was the foul stench coming from the huge man sitting in the seat next to him. It was a combination of odors, each one unpleasant in its own right, but together they were almost overpowering. The smelly one reached out a big hand and introduced himself as Salvatore LaMata, but gave Tony permission to call him Sal. He didn't bother introducing the two men in the front seat. He acted as though they weren't even there.

Tony noticed the mousey little man behind the steering wheel. He didn't even turn around to acknowledge the newcomer's existence. He kept his hands on the wheel and his eyes straight ahead even though the car was parked at the time. It was not a friendly environment, and Tony was already looking forward to taking care of business and getting out of there.

Sal got right to the point and wanted to know exactly who Tony was and why he had placed the call to Mr. Apparicio. Tony summarized the happenings of the past six weeks into a monologue of about ten minutes. He assured Sal he didn't want to cause any trouble and he didn't care anything about the fixing of ball games, or anything else Sal's people might be involved in. He simply didn't want to go to prison, and he needed some help to convince his friends not to go to the police.

Sal followed his story carefully and concluded the nervous young man had to be telling the truth. The story was too complicated and bizarre to be fabricated. No one would have had the imagination to make it up. He couldn't have cared less about the troubles Tony had gotten himself into, but he was extremely interested in the predicament he said Jamal was facing. If the athlete really was about to go to the cops, he and his associates could be in a lot of trouble.

But how could that be? He had just talked with Jamal on the phone a few days before, and had been assured the game was in the bag. Or had he really talked to him? The voice on the other end of the line had identified himself as Jamal Davis, but come to think about it, there was something a little fishy about the way he sounded.

"That stinkin' nigger!" Sal yelled, slamming his fist down on his briefcase. Then he followed with a string of profanity that shocked even Tony, who had heard and used swear words all his life. "Marcus couldn't get his brother to agree to throw the game, so he called me himself and made like he was Jamal. That lyin' no-good . . . wait'll I get my hands on him!"

Just as quickly as he had exploded, Sal seemed to come to his senses. He quickly calmed down and started to put a preconceived plan into action. He told the Mouse to start the car and head north on Lakewood Blvd. He took a cell phone from his briefcase and punched in a series of numbers and waited for a response.

"Mr. Apparicio, Sal here. The kid's story checks out. It looks like Davis has been shinin' us on. He's talkin' about goin' to the cops and tellin' 'em everything . . . . Yeah, we're gonna go with my friend here and talk to him . . . Yes, sir, I know what to do . . . . Don't worry, Boss. I'll take care of it."

He pushed the end button and replaced the phone in his briefcase. For a moment he seemed lost in thought, then he turned to Tony and said, "Where, and when are these friends of yours meetin' tonight to decide on what they're gonna do?"

"They're meeting at seven o'clock. I don't know exactly where," Tony admitted. "But Marcus does," he quickly added. "It's at some office or apartment or something like that where the pastor goes to get away to study and pray and stuff . . . ."

"And meet girls, maybe," the Shadow volunteered, with a snicker.

"Shaddup!" Sal warned in a menacing voice. "Go ahead, Tony. How can we get over there? Mr. Apparicio wants me to talk to 'em and convince 'em not to do anything stupid. He doesn't want anybody to get hurt, but he has to protect his interests, y'know."

"Yes, sir," Tony agreed nervously. "I can call Marcus and arrange to meet him, and then we can all go over there together. I've got his phone number in my wallet somewhere."

"Okay. Here, use my phone," Sal said, removing the instrument once again from his briefcase and handing it to Tony. "Only don't tell him you're with us. We don't want to make him nervous or anything. And tell him you'll stop by his place after he gets off work and pick him up."

Tony fished the card out of his wallet, on which he had written both Marcus' work and home phone numbers. He punched in the work number and soon made connection with the wrecking yard, which was all but closed down because of the rain.

Marcus, who would normally have been out in the yard, answered after the first ring. Tony asked if he was where he could talk, and Marcus assured him that he was. Gil had gone to pick his children up from school so they wouldn't have to walk home in the downpour, and Marcus was alone in the office.

Tony asked if Marcus was planning on going to the meeting that night, to which he received an affirmative answer. Marcus felt that he had to try to talk Jamal out of going to the police. Tony commended him for his decision and asked if he could tag along. He too had to try to talk someone out of doing something stupid. Marcus readily agreed and asked where Tony wanted to meet.

Tony asked his friend when he would be getting off work. Marcus said he had agreed to close up at six o'clock, and that he should be home about thirty minutes after that. That was fine with Tony and he volunteered to stop over at Marcus' place at about six-forty-five and they could go to the meeting together.

After he had hung up with Marcus, Tony handed the phone back to Sal and waited for further instructions. Sal told him to direct the driver to Marcus' place, saying they might as well wait there for him. Tony agreed, and gave the Mouse directions as the little man maneuvered the big car cautiously through the driving rain.

On arriving in front of the rundown apartment building in Compton, Sal ordered everyone out of the car, saying it would be more comfortable waiting inside the building rather than in the crowded and humid car.

Once inside the building, Sal went immediately over to the bank of mailboxes on the far wall. After identifying Marcus' apartment as number 216, he led them up the stairs. Tony thought it strange that they should want to stand out in the hall for almost two hours, waiting for Marcus to show up. But before he could question Sal's decision, he discovered what the big man had in mind all the time.

The Mouse looked up and down the hall to make sure no one was looking, and then he pulled a small pouch out of his coat pocket. Having retrieved some delicate little instruments from it, he knelt down and inserted two of them into the keyhole and began manipulating the inner workings of the lock. In less than five seconds the lock clicked open, the Mouse stood up and opened the door with a little rodent smile, and motioned the others inside.

After everyone had entered the room, the Mouse closed and locked the door after him. The Shadow removed his coat and hat, revealing a rather good-looking young man in his early thirties. He had a calloused and sinister look about him, too much so, Tony thought, for one so young. He immediately went over to the bed and sat on it. He pulled his shoes off and lay down, ignoring the other occupants of the small, but tidy apartment. Soon he had drifted off to sleep, his soft snoring keeping time with the sound of the rain coursing down the gutter outside the window.

The Mouse also removed his coat and hat, revealing a man even mousier than he had appeared before. His beady eyes darted back and forth, animating his narrow face with its long pointed nose. His narrow mustache twitched as he moved his tiny mouth in rapid chewing motions. He went directly to the telephone beside the bed and began making some adjustments there, careful to keep his back to Tony, thereby concealing his exact activities.

Sal took a seat at the small table in the kitchen area. The apartment was a studio, thus everything, with the exception of the small bathroom in the rear, was all located in one central room. The huge Italian motioned Tony to take a seat across from him as he retrieved a deck of cards from his inside coat pocket.

"Take a seat, Tony," he said, with a relaxed smile. "You don't mind if we play a little rummy while we wait, do ya? We might as well get comfortable. It's miserable outside, and I don't think Marcus will mind us making ourselves at home till he gets here."

As Tony sat down and pretended to be agreeable, his mind was racing. What had he gotten himself into? These men had thought nothing of breaking and entering and tampering with Marcus' phone. What else were they prepared to do?

There was no way he could call and warn Marcus, or anyone else for that matter. He had created this monster, and he was going to have to stay with it until it had fulfilled its destiny. He hoped desperately that it would perform as he had expected it to, but he knew he had no control over it and, down deep in his gut, he feared the worst. He felt his confidence draining from him, even as the swollen gutters drained the torrents of rainwater from the flat roof of the old building that temporarily housed them.

CHAPTER TWENTY-SIX

THE CHANCE

Scott thought it strange that Tony had not been at practice that afternoon. The latter was the most dedicated swimmer on the team and was virtually always there. However, the weather was really rotten, and a couple of the other guys had also failed to show up, so Scott didn't think too much about it. He figured his friend had probably gone over to talk with Marcus about the meeting that night, and had decided it wasn't worth driving through all the snarled traffic just to make it to what was going to be an abbreviated practice anyway. Either that, or he had skipped town.

Not likely, he concluded almost immediately. Tony was too selfish, too competitive, and too smug to risk losing everything he had achieved by panicking and running away. No, he would definitely stay put and try to protect his interests.

Candi was waiting for Scott after practice, and they went over to a nearby fast food restaurant to grab a bite to eat before Scott had to meet the other guys at the church. Their conversation was alive with talk of their future together. Both of them had been thinking and praying about their previous conversations, and were more convinced than ever that going to the police was the only right thing to do. They were actually excited about it. It was true, it would put them in a desperate position where they would have to be completely dependent upon the Lord, but that was exactly where they wanted to be. They were eager to see how God was going to provide for them during their coming ordeal, and how He was going to use them for His glory as they served Him through it.

When it came time for them to part, Scott held her close to him. He didn't want to let her go. Strange, he was going to call her right after the meeting and, if it wasn't too late, he was going to stop by her dorm and tell her all about it. At any rate, they were going to spend the next afternoon together deciding just how, and when, he should turn himself in. Yet, he felt a strange sense of finality about their parting. It was almost as though he was never going to see her again. It reminded him of how he had felt at the hospital when he was in junior high school.

He had been there visiting his favorite grandfather who had undergone a routine knee replacement operation two days previously. Grandpa Graham was due to be transferred to a rehabilitation center the next day, and was in great spirits. He joked with Scott about being able to beat him in a foot race in a month or two, but his grandson had an ominous sense of doom. He clung to him, and had to be reprimanded by his father for being such a baby about it all. When he left the room he was in tears. That was the last time he saw his grandfather alive. Later that night, an undetected blood clot in his leg broke loose and traveled to Grandpa Graham's heart. He died instantly and quietly in his sleep.

As he held Candi in his arms, Scott was now experiencing that same familiar sense of doom. He shrugged it off, telling himself that his fears were groundless and way premature. Nevertheless, he took an extra long time telling her goodbye. He thanked her for coming into his life and for her consistent Christian witness, which had been the main factor leading him to give his life to Christ. He promised her his undying love, and sealed it with a long and passionate kiss. Candi kidded him for being so melodramatic, but she responded to his display of affection and appreciation by returning his kiss with equal enthusiasm.

As they left the restaurant, they had to sprint to their respective cars because of the pouring rain. Once Scott had gotten himself buckled in, the car started, and the windshield wipers going, he looked up to see Candi backing out and making a turn in front of him. She sounded her horn and waved at him as she drove out of the parking lot. Scott felt a lump rising in his throat and he had to fight back the tears as he watched her go. "Please, God, keep her safe!" he prayed. "Don't let it happen again!"

At the same time, Marcus was locking up at the wrecking yard, getting soaked as he secured the chain between the two huge gates that sealed off the establishment. Once in his old Duster, he was relieved when it fired up on the first try. The battery had been acting up on him and he'd had to get a jump to get it started on a couple of occasions. He certainly didn't need to be out in the rain, he thought, trying to flag somebody down on a night like this.

As he drove home, with his worn-out wipers trying unsuccessfully to keep the windshield clear of the watery onslaught attacking it, his thoughts returned to the upcoming meeting that night. Such thoughts had accompanied him all day, retreating only when other things demanded his immediate attention, but creeping back in again just as soon as there was an opportunity. He had never been so torn apart in his entire life as he was over this situation.

He had a strong sense of self-preservation, and for that reason, he desperately didn't want Jamal to go to the authorities. He knew just as soon as the underworld found out about it, a contract would be placed on both their heads. Yet down deep, he realized that Jamal was struggling with a matter of Christian conscience. His brother had absolutely sold out to the Lord, and doing what He wanted him to do was of the utmost importance to him. Though Marcus didn't share his brother's commitment, he respected and admired him for it. He just couldn't see himself trying to coerce him into making a decision that would go against everything he had sworn himself to uphold.

What was even worse was the fact that Tony was counting on him to back him up when he tried to persuade both Scott and Jamal to keep quiet. He had already indicated to Tony that he would be there for him, but as the time of the meeting grew ever closer, Marcus became less and less sure of what he was actually going to do. Although he found trying to drive home in the rain and the traffic to be difficult and frustrating, it wasn't nearly so hard as he anticipated his negotiations to be in the dreaded upcoming meeting.

A few minutes later, Scott pulled up in front of the Antioch Baptist Church, having driven through some of the worst weather he had ever remembered. Jamal and Aaron were already there. They were sitting in Jamal's car, engaged in a heated conversation about the Messianic claims of Jesus Christ, and didn't even notice Scott's arrival. Scott pulled in behind them, got out and locked his Blazer, and made his way to Jamal's back seat as quickly as he could.

"Sorry I'm late," he said as he closed the door and shook the rain off his bare head.

"Whoa!" Jamal gasped, "Where'd you come from?"

"Oh, I'm sorry. I didn't mean to scare you," Scott apologized. "I thought you saw me drive up."

"No way," Jamal said. "Me and Aaron here were talking about Jesus, and I guess we weren't payin' much attention to anything else. Besides, with all that commotion going on out there, the Lord Himself could have come with ten thousand of His saints, and we probably wouldn't have noticed."

Scott laughed as he buckled his seat belt and Jamal started the car. Scott and Aaron exchanged greetings as Jamal maneuvered his older Dodge Intrepid out into the rush hour traffic. Still a student, Jamal couldn't afford a new car, but he had managed to come up with some hard-to-come-by cash to buy this larger sedan. His oversized body simply would not fit into a smaller, less expensive car.

As they drove the short distance down Rosecrans Ave. toward the retreat where they were going to meet with Pastor Bobby, there was an almost festive mood in the car. Both Scott and Jamal had already independently made their decisions to go to the police, and the Holy Spirit had given them peace about the outcome, whatever it might turn out to be. Aaron, though still not a believer, was in complete agreement with their decisions. The only thing that might possibly change their minds would be if Bobby came up with some clear scriptural principles that forbade their intentions, but none of them expected such an occurrence.

Marcus turned the key and unlocked the door to his apartment. He was eager to get out of his wet clothes and change into something dry before Tony showed up. He hadn't noticed the big Lincoln out front, or anything else unusual, and was totally unprepared for what was waiting for him inside.

As he started to step into the room, a big hand grabbed him by the lapels and pulled him inside and closed the door.

"What the . . ." he started to yell, but another big hand was clamped tightly around his mouth.

"Hello, Snowball," Sal said sarcastically, "come on in. Tony here invited us to the party, and we didn't want you to miss it."

Sal half led, half dragged, Marcus over to the table where he and Tony and the Mouse had been playing cards. "Now I'm gonna remove my hand," he said sternly, "and when I do, you're not gonna holler or nothin'. Understand?"

Marcus' eyes were wide with a combination of surprise and fear, but he managed to keep his wits about him. He nodded his head up and down in compliance to Sal's demands, and then gulped in a welcomed breath of air when Sal removed his hand. The big man's grasp had closed off both his mouth and nose, making it impossible for him to breathe.

Sal pushed him down in the nearest chair, and then sat down in the one next to him. He was comfortable and confident. He had been handling punks like this for years, and he knew how to go about it. He had to show Marcus who was in charge. The more intimidated he could make him, the more quickly he could get out of him what he desired.

"Tony here told me a funny story today, Snowball," he said, eyeing his captive carefully. "You wanna hear it?"

"Yeah, sure, Sal," Marcus replied weakly. "Make yourself at home. You want to tell me a story, go right ahead. I don't think I'm going anywhere at the moment . . . am I?"

"You got that right," confirmed the big man. "You're gonna stay right here until we get a coupla things straightened out. For instance, how come a few days ago I get a phone call from your brother, just like we agreed, and he tells me he's all set to throw the game on Friday night. Then Tony here tells me today that Jamal ain't plannin' to do no such thing. Instead, he's plannin' on goin' to the cops with his story. Now, can you tell me how come he changed his mind so quick like?"

"I don't know, Sal. Honest, I thought he was all set to throw the game too. I don't know where Tony got the idea Jamal had changed his mind."

"I'll tell you what I think, punk," Sal shot back with contempt in his voice. "I think Tony got the idea from Jamal himself at your little Bible study. Oh yeah, he told me all about it. He says Jamal's got religion now, and he said he wasn't ever thinkin' about throwin' that game. You know what else I think? I think it was you that called me the other day and pretended to be your brother cause you wanted to get me off your back. You was hopin' to get Jamal to change his mind before the game, and you was just buyin' yourself some time. Is that about right, punk?"

"I don't know what you're talkin' about, man," Marcus lied, glancing over at Tony with a look of disbelief in his eyes.

"Well, in that case," Sal smirked, "you won't mind takin' us over to that secret meetin' they're havin' tonight so we can hear it right from the horse's mouth, so to speak."

"I don't know anything about any meeting . . ."

"Don't lie to me, Snowball!" Sal yelled, as his big right hand lashed out and slapped Marcus on the left cheek, almost knocking him out of the chair. "Tony told us all about it . . . how you and him are goin' over there together to try to talk Jamal and that other punk outta going to the cops. He was in my car, talkin' on my phone, when you agreed, so let's stop playin' games. We all want the same thing. Tony here just figured you guys could use a little help convincin' those boys to keep their mouths shut, so he invited us along. So here we are. Now stop foolin' around, and take us over there."

"I don't know where they're meeting," Marcus lied again.

"You lyin' dog!" Sal bellowed, this time hitting Marcus in the jaw with a massive fist, sending him sprawling to the floor.

"Hey!" Tony protested, trying to sound authoritative. "Take it easy! You promised nobody was gonna get hurt."

"You shut up, Tony!" Sal growled. "I'll handle this. There's only one way to get the truth outta lyin' punks like this one."

"Marcus, why are you doing this?" Tony pleaded with Marcus, bewildered at his friend's behavior. "All they want is to talk to Jamal and Scott. They might threaten them a little, but that's what we want. None of us can afford for them to go to the police, and they just need to be convinced not to do it."

"Tony, I can't believe you're so stupid!" Marcus said in exasperation, sitting on the floor and rubbing his throbbing jaw. "Remember, I've lived on the streets for years. I know how the mob operates. These animals aren't goin' over there to talk to nobody. They're goin' over there to eliminate some loose ends. Jamal's become a liability, and they're going to take him out, and everybody associated with him. If we take 'em over there, we're all dead men! Do you understand me? Everybody dies!"

"You're the one's that's stupid, Snowball," Sal said. "Nobody's gonna die. We just wanna talk to 'em, maybe rough 'em up a little bit if they have trouble seein' it our way, but we ain't gonna kill nobody. Now get up and let's all go on over there before the meetin's over."

"No way, Sal," said Marcus defiantly. "You think I don't know who Pretty Boy over there is?" pointing to the Shadow, who was sitting on the bed with a dispassionate look on his face. "He's one of your mechanics. He does people for hire. You didn't bring him along to negotiate nothin'. Sure, he's here to make sure that nobody talks . . . ever!"

"You stupid nigger!" Sal hissed, reaching beneath his coat and retrieving an automatic pistol. "If you don't take us over there right now, I'm gonna do you myself . . . right here . . . right now! Do you understand me, boy?"

"Perfectly," Marcus said with surprising calmness. "I don't want those guys to go to the cops either, but there's no way I'm gonna sell out my own father and brother just to try to save my own butt. Besides you'd never let me walk anyway . . . . So, I guess it's a matter of 'kill me now' or 'kill me later.' You might as well make it now."

"As you wish," Sal stated matter-of-factly as he pulled the trigger. The hefty weapon in his hand exploded to life, sending the 9mm bullet knifing its way instantly through Marcus' abdomen, piercing his spleen and small intestine before exiting out his back.

"NO!" Tony screamed in horror as he watched his friend crumple on the floor. "Oh, my God, Marcus, I'm so sorry!"

"Shut up, Tony," Sal warned, "or you're really gonna be sorry. Come on. Let's get outta here."

"But we can't just leave him here like this!" he protested.

"Sure we can. With all the thunder and lightning goin' on out there, nobody probably even noticed the sound of the shot. Come on. We gotta get to that meeting while everybody's still there."

"But I don't know where it is!"

"You let me worry about that, kid. Now come on. Let's get goin'."

With that, the three gangsters headed for the door, with Sal forcefully leading Tony by the arm. Tony glanced back over his shoulder as he left the room with a look of shocked disbelief as he saw his friend writhing on the floor in a gathering pool of his own blood.

It was well past seven o'clock, and the four men were seated in the little room on the second floor of a low-rent hotel on Benton Street. Jamal and Scott and Aaron had arrived twenty minutes earlier and had been greeted by Bobby, who had been there most of the afternoon, giving himself to the study of God's word and prayer.

As much as he loved his own two sons, and had grown to love Scott and Tony, and wanted to keep them all out of harm's way, he could not find anything in Scripture, or in his heart, to justify them not going to the authorities. He told them of his opinion, and was reassured when both Jamal and Scott told him they had independently reached the same conclusion. Now the only problem that remained was the convincing of Tony and Marcus.

They discussed one strategy after another, but in each case, they finally had to concede that their friends weren't going to agree with their reasoning. The other two wanted to stay out of jail, and out of trouble with the mob, and nothing short of that was going to satisfy them. They concluded the only thing that would change their minds was a change in their hearts. Bobby suggested they make good use of the time they would spend waiting for Marcus and Tony to show up by spending it in prayer for their salvation.

As the four of them knelt in front of various articles of furniture, three of them led out in heartfelt audible prayers. Aaron prayed too, only silently. He sincerely believed something supernatural had happened to Jamal and Scott, and he prayed that Jehovah might grant Marcus and Tony the same thing so they too would be able to make the right, though painful, choices. It never really dawned on him how inconsistent he was, praying for a conversion to Christianity for others, when he hadn't experienced one himself. He considered himself as being an exception to the rule. It indeed seemed that Gentiles needed to believe on Jesus Christ in order to get God in their lives; but he was a Jew, a Son of Abraham, and he had established a right relationship with the Lord years ago. He still persisted in the belief that he could love God and serve Him with all his heart without the relationship Gentiles seemed to need to have with that Prophet from Galilee.

Suddenly, the phone rang and interrupted their prayers. Bobby was surprised because the number was unlisted and few people knew it. He was the one praying at the time the phone rang, so he quickly terminated his prayer and got up to answer it. He assumed Marcus had forgotten how to get there and was calling for directions. That would explain why he and Tony had been so late.

"Hello," he said cheerfully.

"Dad, you guys gotta get outta there," Marcus' voice came labored and slow. "They're comin' after you. They're on their way over there right now."

"Marcus, what's wrong?" Bobby demanded. "Who's coming over here, and why?"

"It's the mob, Dad . . . . Tony brought 'em over to my place so they could go over there with us and talk Jamal and Scott outta going to the cops. But they had a hit man with 'em . . . . They're plannin' on wasting everybody . . . . You gotta get outta there!"

"What's wrong, Marcus?" Bobby pleaded with his son, fear rising in his voice. "What have they done to you?"

"I wouldn't go with 'em, and I wouldn't tell 'em where you are . . . . They shot me, Dad . . . . I'm hurt bad . . . . But you gotta go!"

"Oh, my God, Son! Hang on! I'm calling 911 right now! We'll be there in a minute!"

"No!" Marcus groaned. "It's too late for me . . . . They musta hit me in an artery in the stomach or somethun . . . . I'll bleed to death before anybody can get here. Forget about me . . . . You get outta there. They're on their way . . . . I don't know how they know where you are, but . . . . Oh! No!"

"What is it, Son?"

"Of course! I can't believe I'm so stupid! That's why they shot me in the guts, instead of the head!"

"What're you talking about, Marcus?"

"Dad, I'm on the floor . . . . I'm looking under the table my phone sits on, and there's some sort of a device here . . . . They've tapped my phone . . . They were countin' on me calling you . . . . They're tracing the call right now . . . . I gotta hang up!"

"No! Wait!" Bobby begged, his voice breaking up. "Don't hang up! They've already made the trace by now. We still have time. It'll take 'm forever to get here in this weather and traffic . . . . Marcus, you've got to accept Christ as your Savior right now! That's the most important thing!"

"That's right, keep him talkin'. Give us time to get a fix," Sal said anxiously. He and the other three sat in the big Lincoln, parked alongside the curb just down the street from Marcus' place. They had been listening to the entire conversation while watching the flashes of lightning strikes and hearing the sounds of crashing thunder as the freak storm unleashed her fury.

"Help him get religion," Sal went on, "so he can go to that big junkyard in the sky when he croaks. Take your time. Give us time to get over there, and we can arrange for all of you to go together."

Sal congratulated himself for his sagacity. He had figured that Marcus would refuse to take them over to where the meeting was taking place. That's why he had ordered his phone tapped. He had also purposefully shot him in the abdomen and left him wounded, knowing he would call his father to warn him, giving them a chance to trace the call. He also figured the preacher man would try to give last rites, or something, to his dying prodigal son, allowing them time to get over there and finish the job. So far, everything was working precisely according to plan. He had even had his man change the license plates on his car while they waited. In case things got messy over there, he didn't want to run the risk of the getaway car being traced back to him.

"Got it, Boss!" the Mouse said triumphantly as he sat watching the electronic equipment beside him on the front seat. "They're on Benton Street, just off Rosecrans, not too far from here."

"Excellent!" Sal crowed. "Get us over there on the double! This deathbed conversion outta take a while . . . just like I planned. We should be able to make it before they have a chance to get away."

The Mouse fired up the slumbering V8 and punched it into drive. The massive engine responded instantly and catapulted the big sedan out onto the street. The car's rear end fishtailed on the wet pavement as it accelerated into the gathering darkness.

"No, Dad, it's too late for me," Marcus said weakly. "Save yourselves while you've still got time."

"No way! I'm staying right here till you come to Christ. Your salvation is much more important than our safety right now. Marcus, you know the gospel inside and out. Just ask Jesus to save you, and He will!"

"But, I don't deserve it. I've been so rotten."

"Yeah, just like your old man. Look, if God could save one drug-dealin', car-stealin', woman-chasin' lowlife like me, I think He can save another one like you, don't you?"

"Yeah, I guess so," Marcus agreed, and started to laugh, but he winced with pain and his words were choked off.

"Marcus, if you're dying," Bobby was weeping now, "you're headed for the devil's hell, but you don't have to go there. Down deep you've got a good heart. Remember what I told you at Mama's funeral? Jesus said, '*Greater love has no man than this, than to lay down one's life for his friends.*' That's what Mama did for Aaron, and that's what you just did for us. And that's what Jesus did for you on the cross. If you turn to Him right now, He'll forgive you, just like He did the thief on the cross. You can cheat the devil at his own game too, and wake up in paradise with God."

It all seemed to click in Marcus' fading consciousness, and without introduction, he began to pray, "Lord Jesus . . . I don't deserve to go to heaven . . . . But if you'll have me, please receive my soul . . . . I'm sorry for all the rotten things I've done . . . . Please forgive me . . . . I receive You, and give my life to You . . . . I wish I could live to serve You like I've been servin' the devil for so long, but I guess I'm not gonna get that chance . . . Watch out for my family and friends, Lord . . . You know I love 'em . . ."

"Oh, thank You, Jesus! Thank You, Jesus!" Bobby prayed, through tears of intense emotional release. "Receive my boy, Lord. Watch over him and Mama till I get there. Oh, thank You, Jesus! Thank You!"

"Hey, Dad," Marcus whispered, "here's one snowball who's gonna have a chance after all."

"He sure is, Son! He sure is!" Bobby laughed and cried, his voice revealing the intense joy and sorrow he was experiencing simultaneously.

"Now go, Dad. Or else you . . ." Marcus started to whisper, but his voice trailed off. There was a brief rattling sound, then there was nothing.

The silence at the other end of the line screamed at Bobby. He held the receiver to his ear and sobbed his son's name over and over again, but he knew in his heart that he was gone.

The Snowball had leapt the gates of hell, and landed safely in the arms of God.

CHAPTER TWENTY-SEVEN

THE BEGINNING

Tony heard the whole conversation sitting beside Sal in the back seat of the speeding Lincoln, and he was weeping openly by the time he heard the click on the line as Bobby hung up his phone.

"This is disgusting, Boss," said the Shadow. "Do you want me to do him right now and put him out of his misery?"

"No. You know what Mr. "A" said," Sal scolded him. "His old man keeps the books for us, and we don't want him gettin' upset or suspicious or nothin'. Besides he's not gonna tell nobody nothin'. Isn't that right, Tony?"

"Yes sir," Tony complied, and he knew he was telling the truth. He was up to his eyeballs in the underworld now. If he ever thought about going to the police with what he had witnessed, he would never be afforded the luxury of going to prison. He would be gunned down without mercy just like Marcus had been . . . . No, he loved life too much to think about becoming an informant. Like Sal had said, "He wasn't gonna tell nobody nothin'."

"Step on it, willya!" Sal shouted. "Now that the punk is dead, they'll be leavin' up there. We gotta cut 'm off before they get away . . . or worse yet, before they go to the cops."

"We're almost there, Boss," the Mouse said through clenched teeth. "That's Benton up ahead, and then it's just a coupla blocks down on the right."

"Okay, get ready up there," Sal barked.

"You got it, Boss," the Shadow said as he bent down and retrieved an automatic assault rifle from under the front seat and worked the action, loading the first cartridge into the chamber.

"Oh, my God!" thought Tony to himself. "When is this nightmare ever going to end?"

While Bobby had been on the phone with Marcus, Scott and Jamal were praying for the young man's salvation. They also used their cell phones to try to get some help. Jamal called Carl, and found him at a Wendy's, trying to stay out of the weather. Jamal told him of their situation and asked him to get some of his buddies over there to provide some protection. Carl assured him of his support, and after calling for backup, he got on his motorcycle, storm or no storm, and sped off in that direction himself.

Scott took the card Sergeant Spangler had given him out of his wallet and dialed the number. Spangler had told him it was a direct line to him, and he could reach him day or night. The information had been accurate, for the detective answered on the second ring. Scott told him he was coming in to make a full confession, but that he might need some help getting there. Spangler wanted much more information, but Scott cut him off. He gave him their location and their need for police support and the route they planned to take to the station. Then he hung up.

Scott also thought about calling Candi, but there was nothing she could have done, and it would have worried her to death, so he decided against it. Besides, there wasn't time.

Now, the four men were bounding down the stairs of the old Padre Hotel. They had to get to the police station as quickly as possible. No telling how close their adversaries might be by now, and they needed a place of asylum, as well as a place of confession. As they burst through the door, Bobby yelled for them to get into his car, which was parked right next to the curb.

He pushed the button on his key fob that unlocked all four doors and they all headed for his older model Ford Taurus. Bobby ran around the car and got in behind the wheel, as Jamal slipped into the front passenger seat beside him. Aaron slid across the back seat behind Bobby, and Scott jumped in after him and closed the door. As the rest of them buckled themselves in, Bobby started the car and turned on his headlights and windshield wipers. He was just starting to pull out into the street, when a big black Lincoln passed them by, going in the opposite direction. The driver instantly slammed on his brakes and spun around in the middle of the street.

Bobby mashed the gas pedal to the floor, and the much smaller Taurus accelerated down the short street toward Rosecrans. In his rear view mirror, he could see the headlights of the pursuit vehicle as it fishtailed on the pavement less than half a block behind them.

"Quick, call 911!" Bobby instructed Jamal as he tossed him his cell phone. "Those guys back there aren't here on a social call. They killed Marcus, and they know we know it. They're gonna try to shut us up one way or another. You guys hang on back there," he warned those in the rear seat. "It could get pretty hairy for awhile."

Jamal punched in the three digits on the phone as Bobby steered the Ford through a sliding, screeching, reeling turn from Benton onto the westbound lanes of Rosecrans Ave. The traffic was fairly heavy on the main thoroughfare, and it was amazing that they didn't hit another car. Several drivers had to brake and swerve, but there were no collisions.

A few seconds later, the Lincoln negotiated the same turn, but with far different results. The bigger car had to make a wider turn, carrying it over into the eastbound traffic lanes. The Mouse yanked the wheel hard to the right and managed to pull his car back across the centerline, narrowly avoiding a head-on collision with a minivan. The driver of the other vehicle also swerved to her right to avoid the crash, but in so doing, sideswiped a Volkswagen and went into a spin.

All the drivers in the immediate area slammed on their brakes, and the wet pavement sent their vehicles careening off in all directions. Like bumper cars at an amusement park, the out-of-control vehicles randomly collided into one another. Fortunately there were no direct head-on collisions, and the cars were all traveling at a reduced rate of speed because of the weather. Therefore, although eight cars eventually sustained some damage, no one inside them was seriously injured.

Up ahead, Jamal was able to raise a 911 operator and reported their gut-wrenching circumstances and their precise location. He told her they were trying to make it to the downtown headquarters, and requested immediate police assistance. She assured him she would see that units were dispatched right away and requested he stay on the line. He declined and pressed the end button. They were fleeing for their lives, and potential disaster lurked at every intersection. He had neither the time nor the interest to be talking on the phone.

Bobby was pushing his car to its limits, driving much faster and more aggressively than he ever had in his life, but he only had four cylinders in his engine, and he couldn't shake the dark mass behind him. The big Lincoln steadily ate up the distance between the two vehicles, slicing around the slower cars between them, until it was positioned directly behind his Taurus.

He kept looking for police cars speeding to their rescue, but he realized everything had happened so quickly there hadn't been enough time for anyone to arrive at their location, especially under these adverse driving conditions. They were not likely to get any human assistance. He prayed God's avenging angels would deliver them from the evil threatening to overtake them.

"We gotta take 'em out now!" Sal yelled. "This whole area's gonna be crawlin' with cops any minute. Gino, you know what to do!"

"Okay, Boss," the man whom Tony had labeled the Shadow responded, "but it could get messy."

"I know, but we got no choice. Do it!"

Gino pushed the button that retracted the cover for the sunroof, and immediately, wind and rain began to enter the cabin of the vehicle. However, they were going fast enough, and the little spoiler worked efficiently enough, that most of the weather was deflected over the top of the opening.

Gino brought his weapon up to his shoulder, and then he stood upright in the seat, thrusting his upper torso above the roof of the car. He had planned to commence firing immediately, but he had not allowed for what he would encounter. The wind and rain hit him with such force that it stung his eyes and literally bent him over backwards. It took him several seconds to brace himself and get in a position where he could actually shoot with some hoped-for degree of accuracy.

Scott, who had assumed the self-appointed role of lookout, was watching through the rear window when he saw Gino's silhouette emerge above the glare of the headlights behind them. He couldn't see the weapon, but he sensed immediately what was about to take place.

"They've got a gunman on top of the car!" he yelled. "He's gonna open fire! You gotta do somethun', Bobby!"

Instinctively, Bobby slammed on the brakes and turned the wheel hard to the left. The agile Ford responded by sliding broadside across both of the eastbound lanes. There was a break in the oncoming traffic, and they made it across without incident. Bobby gunned the engine and the spinning front wheels finally gained traction and the struggling car shot down a narrow alleyway, lined by brick buildings on either side.

The Mouse swore as he tried to duplicate Bobby's maneuver, but the bigger car wasn't as responsive, and he shot right past the opening to the alleyway, almost ejecting Gino through the sunroof in the process. He spun the Lincoln around in the middle of the street, again sending cars scurrying in all directions. No crashes were heard this time, but the Mouse couldn't have cared less. He was intent on getting his vehicle into position behind the other car, and nothing else mattered. He swung the big car into the alleyway, hardly slowing down; sending a couple of garbage cans flying as he narrowly missed the building on his left.

Now it was Sal's turn to swear. "I just got that fender fixed after the last time you wrecked it. Watch where you're goin'!"

"Sorry, Boss . . . but we got 'em now," the Mouse said as he gunned the engine. "There's no place for them to go and they can't outrun us."

"Good! Gino, get ready! We gotta do it right this time!"

Again Gino readied his weapon and braced himself, waiting until the Mouse had narrowed the distance between the two cars, then he stood up to open fire.

Tony buried his head in his hands. He couldn't bear to watch what was about to take place. He knew he ought to pray for God's divine intervention, but the words would not come. All he could do was sob and put his fingers in his ears.

Scott again saw the shadowy silhouette emerge above the glare of the Lincoln's headlights, but this time there was no sense of panic. There was nothing that could be done anyway. Buildings lined the alley on both sides, and there was no place to go. A heavenly peace came over him as he turned around and spoke, more to the Lord than to his friends.

"It's comin', boys! I think this is it!" he yelled. "Lord, forgive whoever it is back there for what they're about to do, and Dear Jesus, into your hands we commend our bodies and our souls!"

"Amen!" Bobby and Jamal said in unison.

Aaron didn't agree with some of the particulars of Scott's prayer, but he too experienced an overwhelming sense of peace and spiritual well-being. He nodded in general agreement with the others.

Suddenly, the rear window exploded as fiery bullets riddled the interior of the Taurus. Instantly, the air was filled with flying pieces of glass, metal, and fabric. Along with that were bits of flesh and bone and splashes of blood.

One bullet hit Scott in the back, breaking his spine, and another one struck him in the neck, blowing out the front of his throat as it exited. He slumped forward against the back of the front seat, dying almost instantly.

Jamal was struck in the shoulder by the same bullet that passed through Scott's throat. It broke his shoulder blade but didn't cause any mortal damage. However, another slug hit him in the upper back, piercing his right lung before shattering the front windshield on its way out. He grabbed his chest in pain, struggling to breathe.

Another bullet passed less than a quarter of an inch above Aaron's left ear and struck Bobby squarely in the back of the head. It blew out a large hole in his forehead as it exited, splattering the fractured windshield with blood and bits of bone and brains.

Killed instantly, his body slumped over the steering wheel, and his foot let up on the gas feed. The car lost speed and drifted to the left, sideswiping the back of an old brick apartment building. It rebounded to the right and plowed into a similar building on the other side of the alley. The impact spun the car around and it slid to a stop, facing into the headlights of the oncoming Lincoln, braking to a stop in front of it.

It was two minutes after six o'clock on Wednesday morning in Jerusalem. The sun was just emerging over the top of the Mount of Olives on the east, and through the broken clouds, its rays reflected off the magnificent spires of the newly completed Jewish Temple, and off the golden dome of the newly restored Mosque of Omar.

It was shortly after eight, on Tuesday evening, in South-Central Los Angeles. In a driving thunderstorm, what appeared to be a flash of lightning lit up the entire night sky. Or was it a flash of lightning? Maybe it was an exploding electrical transformer? Whatever it was, it didn't matter. It was over, and there was still work to be done.

Sal ordered Gino out of the car to make sure everyone was dead in the other vehicle. They needed to get out of there quickly, but they couldn't afford to leave any loose ends. They hadn't gone to all this trouble, and taken all this risk, just to leave a live witness behind in the wreckage.

Gino was already soaked from standing through the sunroof, so he didn't mind the present assignment at all. Actually, he rather looked forward to it. He derived a strange sense of power and superiority when he gunned down human beings. He went over to the stricken Taurus and threw open the driver's door, his weapon ready to pour yet a few more slugs into the hapless bodies of its occupants. But instead of firing his rifle, he stood transfixed, staring open-mouthed into the car.

"Well, get on with it, Gino, We ain't got all night," Sal yelled through the lowered window to his left."

"Uh, Boss, I think you oughta take a look at this," Gino answered back, not at all sure of himself.

"What the . . ." Sal started to say, but caught himself. He decided he had best humor Gino so they could get their job done and get out of there before the cops showed up. They were somewhat protected down there, out of the way, but he didn't want to push it. Back down the alley on Rosecrans Ave., he could hear the sound of screeching brakes and what sounded like automobiles slamming into one another. With all that commotion, the cops couldn't be far behind.

"Okay, I'll be right there," he called back.

As he got out, he insisted the Mouse and Tony accompany him. The Mouse readily complied. He was used to obeying orders without question. But Tony begged to stay in the car. Already nauseous, he was sure he would throw up at the first sight of what he anticipated seeing in that car. But Sal wouldn't hear of it. Tony had a choice: either he come over and look at what he had participated in doing, or he could suffer the same fate as his former friends.

When it was put to him that way, he agreed to go. He climbed out of the car and walked on unsteady legs, mentally trying to prepare himself for the gore he was about to see. But when he got to Bobby's car he saw what the others were already staring at . . . nothing.

The front seats were completely empty. There were fragments of glass and fabric and what looked like quarts of splattered blood, but there were no bodies at all. In near panic Sal threw open the rear door and almost screamed. The rest of the back seat was empty, but there sat Aaron, seemingly oblivious to Sal's existence and that of the others, staring toward the heavens, and having a silent conversation with an unseen visitor.

His clothes were covered with bits of shattered glass, and there were splotches of splattered blood, but he was otherwise apparently unhurt. He was obviously in some sort of ecstatic state, staring intently, with rapt and upturned eyes. His mouth was moving, but no sound issued forth.

"Where'd the others go, Boss, and what are we gonna do with this one?" Gino wanted to know.

"I don't know, but they couldn't have gotten far. They had to be hit bad. Look at all this blood. Finish him off, and we'll take a quick look for the others. Manny, you keep a sharp lookout for the cops. We don't want no surprises."

"Okay, Boss," the Mouse said, as he turned and looked back up the alley.

"Manny. So that's his name," thought Tony. "Manny Mouse." If he hadn't been so sick and so terrified, he might have found that amusing.

Gino lifted his weapon and pointed it squarely at Aaron and pulled the trigger. Instead of the burst of gunfire everyone expected, there was only the sound of a hollow click. Gino swore and ejected the not-empty clip, and inserted a new one. He worked the action and loaded the first shell and pulled the trigger again. Again, there was only a click. He swore again and worked the action again, ejecting a perfectly good shell, and inserting one just like it in its place. He pulled the trigger again, and again there was only a click.

Gino swore even more vehemently, and swung the rifle away and pointed it toward the side of the building next to him. He worked the action again, throwing out the good but rejected shell, and pulled the trigger again. This time, the weapon exploded into action, and a dozen bullets riddled the side of the building before Gino let up on the trigger. He swung it back again and pointed it at Aaron and pulled the trigger one last time. Again it only clicked.

Gino threw the rifle to the pavement, and kicked it in fury. He pulled his pistol from its holster and clicked off another round . . . and another . . . and another . . . . Finally, he limply dropped his pistol, and just stood there, staring blankly at Aaron, mumbling incoherently.

Sal, by now in a rage himself, pulled his own weapon and clicked off a few rounds of his own before he too stopped and stared at the strange young man in the back seat, who had still not so much as acknowledged their existence.

Suddenly, and without warning, Aaron unbuckled his seatbelt, swung his legs over, and stepped out of the car. The two men jumped back instinctively, expecting swift and brutal retaliation, but Aaron simply looked at them. It was not the look of anger or hatred they might have expected. Instead, it was a lingering look of pity and deep sadness. He stepped toward them, and they fell over backwards.

Lying in the rain-soaked alley, they were unable to move. They lay there, completely powerless to defend themselves, expecting to be consumed by fire or something even more hideous. Their tortured minds struggled with confusion, frustration, and fear, and then they lost their grip on consciousness.

But Aaron ignored them and turned back toward Tony and Manny. Tony alone was there, petrified with fear. Manny could be seen, over a hundred yards away, running like a man possessed, his coattails flapping like sails behind him, his feet making tiny little splashes in the flooded alley, hardly seeming to touch the surface as he fled in stark terror.

Ignoring Tony, Aaron turned and began walking down the alley in the opposite direction. He was a man on a mission, and his face was set with determination.

Tony, a trembling mass of fear and confusion, finally found his voice and called after his former friend. "Oh, my God, Aaron, don't go!" he managed to get out weakly. "It happened, didn't it? It really happened! What am I gonna do now? Is this it? Is this the end?"

Aaron stopped, and slowly turned around and faced the hollow man who had once been the handsome, self-assured athlete. “No, Tony, this is only the beginning.”

He turned and walked briskly and confidently into the night, leaving Tony shivering in the rain, feeling helplessly alone . . . and empty . . . so very empty . . . .

. . . to be continued

Appendices

APPENDIX ONE

THE INVASION OF GOG AND MAGOG

One of the most controversial of all prophetic passages in the Scriptures is the one in Ezekiel 38–39, which describes what is commonly referred to as the Battle of Gog and Magog. The invasion has been studied carefully by Bible scholars for generations, and they are in general agreement in their interpretation of most of it.

One of the things they all agree on is that the invasion will come from the north. *"Then you will come from your place out of the far north"* (Ezek. 38:15). Scholars have done an excellent job of identifying the land of Magog as modern-day Russia. They have also identified Gog as the leader of the invasion, and they have identified his ancient allies with modern-day counterparts. The question is not a matter of *who* will invade.

Neither is it a question of *why* will they invade. It is clearly stated that the raiders will come, *"to take plunder and to take booty, to stretch out your hand against the waste cities that are again inhabited, and against a people gathered from the nations, who have acquired livestock and goods, who dwell in the midst of the land"* (Ezek. 38:12).

Neither is there any question as to the outcome of the invasion. The end of chapter thirty-eight and the beginning of chapter thirty-nine describe the absolute destruction God will bring upon the invading armies. There is really no battle at all. God overthrows them before the battle is ever joined.

The only question over which the scholars remain divided is *when* it will occur. The invasion described is so massive and the results so cataclysmic that it defies being identified with anything that has happened in history thus far. Therefore, it must be yet in the future, but when in the future? Scholars are divided over three different possibilities, all of which seem equally untenable.

Before the rapture

LaHaye and Jenkins, in their *Left Behind* series, would lead us to believe that the invasion by Russia and her allies will occur before the rapture takes place. Their story begins with the rapture, and the invasion has already been miraculously overthrown by divine intervention. Their timing of the event fits in conveniently with the development of their plot, but it doesn't fit in so well with the facts of Ezekiel 38–39. They make no attempt to support their claim from Scripture, but if they were to attempt to do so, they would encounter three major obstacles.

The first roadblock they would have to try to hurdle is the setting in which Ezekiel describes the invasion. From the middle of chapter 33 to the end of the book at chapter 48, the context is purely that of the future millennial kingdom. Throughout those sixteen chapters, the prophet predicts the kingdom blessedness of the regathered peoples of Israel, their subjugation of the heathen nations around them, and the greatness of the kingdom temple and its worship system. Events from this present age, or even from that of the tribulation, would be completely out of context.

More specifically, the conditions in Israel described by Ezekiel at the time of the invasion could not possibly be conditions existing there now, nor anytime in the foreseeable future, for that matter. The prophet describes Israel as being in a state of absolute peace and safety:

> *After many days you will be visited. In the latter years you will come into the land of those brought back from the sword and gathered from many peoples on the mountains of Israel, which had long been desolate;*
> *they were brought out of the nations, and now all of them dwell safely.* (Ezek. 38:8)

> *You will say, "I will go up against a land of unwalled villages; I will go to a peaceful people, who dwell safely, all of them dwelling without walls, and having neither bars nor gates."* (Ezek. 38:11)

> *Therefore, son of man, prophesy and say to Gog, "Thus says the Lord God: On that day when My people Israel dwell safely, will you not know it?"* (Ezek. 38:14)

It is inconceivable that Israel could be described in such terms today. The nation is dwelling in perilous times, and is armed to the teeth. The

Israeli military is one of the most formidable in the world, and it is only because of her superior firepower that she continues to exist.

She is surrounded by militant Arab nations who overwhelmingly outnumber her. Granted, there have been many conferences to discuss peace between the Jews and their neighbors, and there will doubtlessly be many more. But the Jews know their only real hope for survival is to remain strong enough militarily to discourage any attack against them.

Only after her Messiah comes and sets up His kingdom, will Israel finally be comfortable laying down her arms and dwelling safely in unwalled villages, having neither bars nor gates.

The second hurdle one would have to scale, if he were to hold to a pre-rapture date of the invasion, is the aftermath. What Ezekiel describes after God utterly destroys Gog's invading armies simply will not fit into the context of the rapture and the following tribulation. The tribulation will be a time of chaos and turmoil, with people hiding among the rocks and in the caves of the earth for survival. But Ezekiel describes a setting of peace and tranquility following Gog's destruction. The primary activity of God's people is cleaning up the evidence of the overthrow:

> *Then those who dwell in the cities of Israel will go out and set on fire and burn the weapons, both the shields and bucklers, the bows and arrows, the javelins and spears; and they will make fires with them for seven years.* (Ezek. 39:9)

> *It will come to pass in that day that I will give Gog a burial place there in Israel . . . For seven months the house of Israel will be burying them, in order to cleanse the land.* (Ezek. 39:11–12)

The whole context of chapter 39 is one of peace and order following God's overthrow of the invading armies. The unmolested citizens of the land go about their business of burying bodies for seven months and burning weapons for seven years. There is no continuing threat of any kind. In fact, clear to the end of the book nothing is described apart from kingdom abundance and blessing.

The third problem one would encounter, holding to a pre-rapture invasion, is the composition of the weapons of war mentioned in the above verses. Granted, the language may be figurative, and the prophet would have described future weapons in language the hearers of his day could understand, but the fact remains, the weapons will burn for seven years.

Modern weapons of war are made primarily of metal, which does not burn. True, there are elements of rubber and plastic in modern weaponry, which will certainly burn, but they would never make an acceptable substitute for firewood. Ezekiel clearly points out that the Jews will use it explicitly for that purpose:

> *They will not take wood from the field nor cut down any from the forest, because they will make fires with the weapons; they will plunder those who plundered them, and pillage those who pillaged them, says the Lord God. (Ezek. 39:10)*

What the weapons will be like at the time of Gog's invasion, we cannot be sure. But whatever they are, we can be sure that they will be made of materials perfectly suited for firewood. Nothing in today's arsenals would possibly meet those requirements.

No, the attempt to place the northern invasion prior to the rapture is completely untenable. It makes for very great drama, but it also makes for very poor doctrine.

During the tribulation

Most scholars of Bible prophecy realize the problems with the prerapture position, but they still want to place the northern invasion within the context of the tribulation. And indeed, the circumstances of the overthrow of Gog and his forces sound very apocalyptic. Ezekiel 38:18–23 speaks of a mighty earthquake, which topples mountains, and of God raining down from heaven great hailstones and fire and brimstone upon Gog. Such activity would fit perfectly in the context of the tribulation.

Besides, if the invasion were overthrown at the end of the tribulation, then Christ would be setting up His millennial kingdom after that, and the peaceful burying of bodies and the burning of weapons would fit perfectly into such a context.

Finally, advocates of this position point out, the antichrist will have established a peace treaty with Israel and its Arab neighbors, and the Jews will be dwelling safely under his protection at the time of the invasion. That false security would disarm the unsuspecting Israelis and make them sitting ducks for the greedy pillagers from the north.

But before we assume we've solved the problem, let us examine some of the problems with this view.

In the first place, the beginning of the tribulation will hardly be the period of peace and safety spoken of by Ezekiel in chapter 38. Granted, most scholars contend that the first three-and-a-half years of the tribulation will indeed be a period of peace, orchestrated by the antichrist through his treaty between Israel and its Arab neighbors. But such a treaty is not even mentioned anywhere in the New Testament, nor does the Book of Revelation describe any such period of resulting peace. Scholars all agree that the beginning of the tribulation is described in Revelation, chapter six. But how does it describe it? The four horsemen of the apocalypse begin to ride, and the world is plunged into global conquest, horrible warfare, indescribable famine, and unprecedented pestilence; so much so that one-fourth of the world's population is eradicated.

Does that sound like a time of peace and safety? Hardly. One would have to stretch his imagination to the breaking point to conceive of Israel disarming herself and dwelling unprotected during such times.

The other problem is even more difficult for advocates of this view to answer. They insist the invasion must occur during the first half of the tribulation in order for Israel to be dwelling at peace and without protection of any sort. But they also maintain that it isn't concluded until the Lord returns at the end of the tribulation so there can be a peaceful and thorough cleanup afterwards. In that case, Gog's invasion from the north would have to last a minimum of three-and-a-half years, and more likely, nearly seven years. As rapidly as conditions will deteriorate during the tribulation, the only time when there could possibly be any conceivable period of peace would be at the very beginning of the antichrist's covenant with Israel.

If that were the case, the invasion could not be considered a battle at all, but rather a lengthy campaign, lasting not days or weeks, but years and years. But how does Ezekiel describe it?

The prophet describes it not even as a battle, much less a campaign. God says He will, *"put hooks in your jaws, and lead you out"* (Ezek. 38:4). God will draw Gog and his hoards to Israel only to destroy them. The Jews won't have to fire a shot, neither will they suffer any casualties. God will destroy the invaders with a cataclysmic overthrow as clearly described in Ezekiel 38:18–23. It will probably be all over in a matter of hours. How long did it take God to destroy Sodom and Gomorrah?

The proponents of this view find it extremely difficult to support their position. They are hard-pressed to find any period of peace wherein to launch their invasion, and even if they do, it is simply too far removed from its dramatic conclusion at the end of the tribulation. Its logistic impossibilities make this view completely untenable as well.

At the end of the millennium

Some scholars recognize the same problems with the aforementioned views that we have pointed out, and they have adopted a logical, but equally doomed, alternative. They have turned to the twentieth chapter of Revelation and equated Ezekiel's invasion with the one described by the apostle John at the end of the millennium:

> *Now when the thousand years have expired, Satan will be released from his prison and will go out to deceive the nations which are in the four corners of the earth, Gog and Magog, to gather them together to battle, whose number is as the sand of the sea. They went up on the breadth of the earth and surrounded the camp of the saints and the beloved city. And fire came down from God out of heaven and devoured them.* (Revelation 20:7–9)

There are many characteristics listed by John that would cause us to believe he is describing the same invasion as did Ezekiel hundreds of years before. The names of Gog and Magog are common to both. The rapid fashion in which the invasion is put together is also similar. So is the devastating way in which it ends. Why then would we maintain the view also has to be rejected?

It all has to do with the aftermath. In Ezekiel 39, the invasion is overthrown, and then the saints of God go about cleaning up the mess, which takes seven years to accomplish. And then the prophet goes on for another nine chapters describing the joys and blessings of the kingdom that will follow. But such is not the case in John's account in Revelation.

John describes an invasion at the very end of the millennium, which culminates in three events of ultimate finality. The devil is taken and thrown into the lake of fire to be tormented there forever and ever (Revelation 20:10). All the ungodly from all the ages are brought before the great white throne and are judged, the condemned suffering the same fate as that of the devil himself (Revelation 20:11–15). The existing heavens and earth are destroyed by fire, and new ones are created to take their place. The eternal state of absolute perfection is thus ushered in (Revelation 21:1–4).

The two endings could not be more dissimilar. Why would God have anyone spend seven months burying bodies, much less seven years burning weapons, when He was about to destroy the entire universe and create it anew? No, this theory, although admittedly attractive at first, must also be rejected.

What then is left? Is Ezekiel's account to be rejected altogether as merely an allegory, like his vision of the valley of dry bones in chapter 37? Are we to conclude that, because of the many discrepancies we have pointed out, the invasion he described will never actually take place at all?

No, there remains yet another possibility. True, it isn't a view held by many scholars, but it may actually be the one that best conforms to the characteristics revealed by the prophet so long ago.

At the beginning of the millennium

Granted, some problems with this view appear immediately, but before we dismiss it, let's consider its merits.

In the early weeks or months of the millennium, Israel would be in a situation exactly like Ezekiel described it in chapter 38. Israel would have returned to a land that had been devastated by war. Christ would have returned and would be there to guarantee their safety; therefore, they would be dwelling without natural defenses. Also, with the blessings of their Messiah, great wealth would be returning to the land along with its people. Restored and replenished Israel would make a tempting target for would-be invaders.

The outcome of such an invasion would also be predictable. The returned Christ would not tolerate any threat to His emerging kingdom. His retaliation would be swift and devastating, just as Ezekiel describes it.

The weapons and mode of warfare described by Ezekiel also conform to what we might expect to find after long years of tribulation and the devastating judgment at the Battle of Armageddon. The reigning Christ could easily order the destruction of all conventional weapons. Therefore, any remaining weapons would be for the most part crude and handmade. Those made partly or mostly of wood would not only be possible; they would almost be expected.

The aftermath of the battle also fits perfectly within the setting at the beginning of the millennium. After the utter destruction of Gog's invading armies, the inhabitants of Israel would naturally go about the business of cleaning up the residue of the conflict and preparing for the long and glorious reign of their king just as Ezekiel describes it in the remainder of his book.

But many would be quick to point out that such a massive invasion, after the cataclysmic Battle of Armageddon, and after the glorious return of Jesus Christ, is almost unthinkable. They insist that two ironclad arguments disallow any such idea.

The first thing they would have us to consider is that every unsaved person left on the earth at Christ's return at the end of the tribulation will be destroyed with the brightness of His coming. There are Scriptures that seem to support such a conclusion:

> *And I saw the beast, and the kings of the earth, and their armies, gathered together to make war against Him who sat on the horse and against His army. Then the beast was captured, and with him the false prophet who worked signs in his presence, by which he deceived those who worshipped his image. These two were cast alive into the lake of fire burning with brimstone. And the rest were killed with the sword which proceeded out of the mouth of Him who sat on the horse. And all the birds were filled with their flesh.* (Revelation 19:19–21)

Because of passages like these, it is assumed all the unsaved in all the world will be killed in like fashion, and the only ones left alive will be believers who have managed to escape the antichrist and the plagues of the tribulation. Therefore, only saved people will enter the millennium.

If that were the case, then an invasion of Israel like Ezekiel describes would be impossible. There simply wouldn't be any ungodly people left alive on the earth to stage it. But does the Bible really teach that none of the unsaved will survive the tribulation? Not really.

The Bible often uses absolute terms when it is referring to a more limited concept. In Luke 2:1 we read, *"And it came to pass in those days that a decree went out from Caesar Augustus that all the world should be registered."* Now we know that people from Southeast Asia, Australia, and the Americas were not included in the phrase *"all the world."* It referred only to all those in the Roman world. So it is in the description of the tribulation.

In Zechariah 14:1–2 we read, *"Behold, the day of the Lord is coming, and your spoil will be divided in your midst. For I will gather all the nations to battle against Jerusalem."* Are we to believe that the more than six billion inhabitants of the more than two hundred nations of the world will be gathered in Jerusalem? Certainly not. Large armies of representative nations will be there, but most of the world's inhabitants will stay home.

When Christ returns, all the ungodly who are gathered in Israel to do battle with the returning King will indeed be destroyed, but multitudes will doubtlessly remain in their own countries, and will thus be spared. In Zechariah 14:16–17, we read that after the final battle is all over, there will still remain inhabitants in those pagan countries who will have to be forced to comply with Christ's demands. It reads:

> *And it shall come to pass that everyone who is left of all the nations which came up against Jerusalem shall go up from year to year to worship the King, the Lord of hosts, and to keep the feast of Tabernacles. And it shall be that whichever of the families of the earth do not come up to Jerusalem to worship the King, the Lord of hosts, on them there will be no rain.*

If everyone who entered the millennium were saved and loved the Lord, why would they have to be coerced into worshipping Him? Indeed, why will Christ have to rule with a rod of iron if everyone loves Him with all his heart? No, it appears multitudes of the unsaved will survive the tribulation, and since most of them will not actually be among those attacking Jerusalem at the time of Christ's return, they will be spared. There will be plenty of unsaved people on the earth at the beginning of the millennium, and they will be primed to join in with Gog as he seeks to attack Israel.

But that brings us to the second big objection to this view. Why would God ever allow such a thing to happen? Isn't the Battle of Armageddon the war to end all wars? What could possibly be God's reasoning for allowing such a massive invasion as Ezekiel describes to follow so closely behind Christ's glorious return?

Those are good questions, and the answers are not easy ones. But since when has God been easy to figure out? Does not Romans 11:33–34 read *"Oh, the depth of the riches both of the wisdom and knowledge of God! How unsearchable are His judgments and His ways past finding out! For who has known the mind of the Lord? Or who has become His counselor?"* Let's consider a possible solution to the question at hand.

Could it not be that the invasion of Gog and his hordes will actually be part of God's plan, not something thrown up against it? At the end of Revelation chapter nineteen, the beast and the false prophet are thrown into the lake of fire, and the devil himself is cast into the bottomless pit. None of them will even be around to foment such an invasion.

In fact, in Ezekiel 38:4 it says it is God Himself who draws Gog and his allies down to Israel. He says, *"I will turn you around, put hooks in your jaws, and lead you out."* God Himself orchestrates the invasion of Gog and the resulting overthrow of his minions, but why? Could it not be for the purpose of venting the remainder of His wrath upon the wicked and the ungodly?

As we already pointed out, simple logistics would not allow for all of the ungodly to actually participate in the battle of Armageddon. Hence, they will not be destroyed by the Lord at His return. But they will not be converted either. They will crawl out of their caves, and from under their rocks, hissing and spitting out blasphemies against the reigning Christ. God will simply lure them into attacking the peaceful and prosperous inhabitants of Israel so He will be justified in delivering a final blow against the remaining forces of evil.

Is it not possible that God will start the new millennium with a display of His wrath and power to bring the inhabitants of the earth into complete submission?

They will know, in no uncertain terms, that the Prince of Peace is no pushover. He will establish a reign of peace and prosperity, but He will make it abundantly clear that rebellion against Him and His people will absolutely not be tolerated. Ezekiel records in 38:22–23 God's own words as to why He will do what He will with the forces of Gog:

> *And I will bring Him to judgment with pestilence and bloodshed; I will rain down on him, on his troops, and on the many peoples who are with him, flooding rain, great hailstones, fire and brimstone. Thus I will magnify*

Myself, and I will be known in the eyes of many nations. Then they shall know that I am the Lord.

Conclusion

The prophecy of the invasion of Gog and Magog in Ezekiel 38–39 still remains a difficult one to pinpoint on the prophetic timeline. But we have demonstrated that it just refuses to fit nicely into the slots so many scholars have carved out for it.

The context in which it is revealed, and the particular characteristics of the invasion itself, argue strongly for a post-tribulational, early-millennial fulfillment. Such a conclusion may not be ironclad, but one thing is quite clear: it is virtually impossible for the invasion to occur before the rapture. We have many signs to look for that are clear indicators that the coming of the Lord is near, but the invasion of a peaceful and unarmed Israel by a huge confederacy from the north simply is not one of them.

APPENDIX TWO

DANIEL'S SEVENTIETH WEEK

Virtually everyone who writes prophetic literature or speaks concerning future events will mention something about the seven-year tribulation as though the fact were axiomatic. Brilliant scholars disagree over almost everything else in prophecy: the time of the rapture, the occurrence of the invasion from Russia, the nature of Christ's return, and that of the millennial kingdom; but they all agree that the tribulation will be precisely seven years long.

By the unanimity of their agreement, one would expect to find a plethora of Scriptures supporting their position; but surprisingly, there is only one passage, and it is anything but absolute in its interpretation. The prophecy about the seventy weeks appointed for Israel found in Daniel 9:24–27, is the only place in the entire Bible that even suggests that the tribulation will be seven years long. And that conclusion has to be deduced from a rather complex series of future events revealed by the prophet.

We will examine the passage in some detail shortly in an attempt to reveal a completely plausible alternative to the accepted viewpoint; but first, let us take a look at it in the way so many have, for so many generations.

The Traditional View Explained

The following is what the Holy Spirit had Daniel record some 2600 years ago:

> *Seventy weeks have been decreed for your people and your holy city, to finish the transgression, to make an end of sin, to make atonement for iniquity, to*

bring in everlasting righteousness, to seal up vision and prophecy, and to anoint the most holy place. So you are to know and discern that from the issuing of a decree to restore and rebuild Jerusalem until Messiah the Prince there shall be seven weeks and sixty-two weeks; it will be built again, with plaza and moat, even in times of distress. Then after the sixty-two weeks, the Messiah will be cut off and have nothing, and the people of the prince who is to come will destroy the city and the sanctuary. And its end will come with a flood; even to the end there will be war; desolations are determined. And he will make a firm covenant with the many for one week, but in the middle of the week he will put a stop to sacrifice and grain offering; and on the wing of abominations will come one who makes desolate, even until a complete destruction, one that is decreed, is poured out on the one who makes desolate. (Daniel 9:24–27, NASB)

All scholars agree that the seventy weeks Daniel introduces here are not to be understood as normal seven-day periods of time. If that were the case, all the things that the prophet predicted would have had to be fulfilled in 490 days, or about sixteen months. Obviously that didn't happen. Some of the events haven't even occurred yet. So, what everybody agrees on is that the weeks are to be understood as weeks of years: periods of seven years, not seven days. Therefore, the seventy weeks are actually seventy periods of seven years each, or 490 years in total.

The countdown was to begin when a decree went out to rebuild Jerusalem, and since Daniel wrote in the sixth century B.C., we know the decree had to be issued sometime after that. There is a small problem, in that there were actually four decrees issued that had to do with rebuilding and repairing in Jerusalem. But scholars have almost unanimously agreed on the last one. It was issued in 445 B.C. by the Persian King Artexerxes, allowing Nehemiah to return to Jerusalem and rebuild the walls of the city. This can all be confirmed in the first and second chapters of the Book of Nehemiah.

Most scholars point to Robert Anderson, in his classic work *The Coming Prince*,[6] for the explanation of the exact dates and their fulfillment. He insisted that the years in question were not to be understood as ordinary 365-day years, but what he called prophetic years of only 360 days. Since Daniel said there would be exactly seven weeks and sixty-two weeks, or a total of sixty-nine weeks, between the issuing of the decree and the appearance of the Messiah, Anderson did the math. He multiplied 69 X 7 X 360, and came up with exactly 173,880 days.

Then, he identified the exact date in the spring of 445 B.C. when Artexerxes issued the decree to rebuild the walls of Jerusalem. Next, he

[6] J. Dwight Pentecost, *Things to Come,* (Grand Rapids, Mich.: Zondervan, 1958), 245-246.

pinpointed the exact date that Jesus Christ rode into Jerusalem on the back of the donkey on Palm Sunday in the spring of 32 A.D. He insisted that the Palm Sunday event had to be the ending point of the sixty-ninth week because it was then that the people of Israel publicly proclaimed Jesus to be their Messiah. In Matthew 21:9 they cried out, *"Hosanna to the Son of David, blessed is He who comes in the name of the Lord. Hosanna in the highest."*

Assuming his calculations were correct, he claimed he had proved his point when he counted the number of days between the two events and found them also to be exactly 173,880.

We cannot be certain of the absolute exactness of his dates and figures, but we have to admit that the impression he made is pretty amazing. Most prophecy buffs agree. They accept Anderson's conclusions as valid without much further investigation. They maintain that figures so specific and so precise could not be coincidental. They are so phenomenal they must be true.

With that assumption firmly in place, scholars go on to make several other conclusions. They conclude the Messiah was cut off immediately after the end of the sixty-ninth week when Christ was crucified the Friday following Palm Sunday. And, they maintain, the seventy-week time clock stopped ticking a few days later when Jesus arose from the dead and initiated the New Testament church age.

The seventy-week prophecy was purely Jewish in nature, they say, and when God temporarily set aside the nation of Israel as His agent on earth and replaced it with the church, the prophecy too was interrupted and put on hold. They contend that the remaining seventieth week will not commence until such a time as Israel is reinstated as God's primary agent in the world.

Therefore, it is to be understood that when Christ returns and takes His church out at the rapture, God will once again deal directly and exclusively through the nation Israel. The church will be gone during the tribulation. God will deal with the Jewish nation and the world of the Gentiles, but there is no mention of the church.

That is the point at which the prophetic clock starts ticking again, and the seventy-week prophecy resumes. And since there is only the seventieth week remaining, it is a logical conclusion that it will play out during the tribulation period. It will conclude with the glorious return of Christ to the earth, exactly seven years later.

In Daniel 9:26, it says that after the Messiah is cut off, *"the people of the prince who is to come"* will destroy the city and the sanctuary. Since it was the Romans who destroyed Jerusalem and its temple in 70 A.D., they must be the people of the coming prince. The antichrist is, of course, thought of to be that prince, and since it appears he will rule over a revived Roman Empire, it is safe to say that he will be the one to initiate the seventieth week. For in the next verse, Daniel 9:27, it says that, *"he shall confirm a covenant with many for one week."* It doesn't matter whom you read, the scholars all seem to agree that the seven-year tribulation will begin when the antichrist orchestrates a peace treaty between Israel and its Arab neighbors. That peace treaty is what everyone is looking for as the unmistakable sign of the beginning of the seven years of tribulation.

Admittedly, so far, it all makes perfect sense. If all the calculations are correct, the conclusion is unmistakable. But, before we congratulate ourselves on having answered all the questions, perhaps we should go back through the passage in Daniel and reevaluate it. Such an investigation could change the picture entirely.

Problems with the Traditional View

Anderson's calculations

The first thing we should look at is Anderson's theory of when the seventy weeks began, and when the sixty-ninth one ended. He said they began in 445 B.C., and ended in 32 A.D. That may be exactly 173,880 days as he says it is, but it's definitely not sixty-nine weeks of years like the Bible requires. Sixty-nine times seven is 483 years, and if you subtract that from 445 B.C., you come up with 38 A.D. That's long after Christ was crucified, buried, and resurrected. The numbers just don't match up.

To get around that, Anderson arbitrarily decided the years of Daniel's prophecy were not ordinary years, but they were *prophetic years* of only 360 days. That way, when you multiply 7 X 69 X 360, you come up with the necessary 173,880 days; but it's only 476 actual years, instead of the required 483. He justifies that by telling us that the Jewish year was made up of twelve lunar months of thirty days each, thus their typical year was only 360 days long.

That's all true, but what Anderson didn't bother telling us, is that the Jews had a system to accommodate for the difference between their lunar year and the standard solar year. You see, every year they would lose over five days because of the difference between their 360-day lunar year and the standard 365-day solar year. After six years, they would be a month behind the solar calendar. After thirty-six years, they would be a full six months behind. That means they would be celebrating their Passover in the fall, and their harvest feasts in the dead of winter.

Obviously, they would never have allowed that, so they compensated by adding a full lunar month about every fifth year or so. That year would be 390 days long, which would more than make up for the days that had been lost in the preceding years.

The point is, the Jews would naturally have thought of their years as being 360 days long for three or four years, but never for three or four centuries. They would have automatically added the extra months periodically to keep their lunar years compatible with the regular solar calendar. So, sixty-nine weeks of years would have been exactly 483 years, regardless of whether you were reckoning them by means of a lunar calendar or a solar one. It appears Anderson performed his numerical gymnastics only because the numbers didn't work out for him by using ordinary logic and subtraction.

Actually, there are several other reasons why we ought to question Anderson's conclusions. Even if we were to accept his suspect calculations and agree that the sixty-ninth week ended in the spring of 32 A.D., there are questions remaining that just simply do not have a satisfactory answer. For example, even though Anderson was able to shave off a good number of years, the date is still too late.

The 32 A.D. date

If we assume that Jesus was born around the time of the B.C./A.D. transition, and he was about thirty years old when he was baptized (see Luke 3:23), then the date of 32 A.D. would be a fairly accurate one for his entry into Jerusalem on Palm Sunday after three-and-a-half years of public ministry. But Christ was born well before that hypothetical date.

We must realize the ancient calendar that determined the date of Jesus' birth was at least four years off. But the ancient scholars didn't figure out their mistake for about a thousand years, and by then everybody was so used to the wrong dates they didn't want to change. Besides, there were so many monuments and records with the wrong date attached, they could never change them all, so they just never bothered to correct the calendar.

Reliable secular records establish the death of Herod the Great in the early months of 4 B.C., probably in the month of March.[7] And we know from Matthew, chapter two, that he was the wicked king who sought to kill the baby Jesus right after he learned from the wise men that He had been born. Allowing time for the Magi to journey from Persia to Jerusalem to find the newborn King, and a month or so for Herod to get sick and die, that would put the birth of Jesus several months prior to Herod's death, probably in the late fall of 5 B.C.

7 Alfred Edersheim, *The Life and Times of Jesus the Messiah*, (Grand Rapids, Mich.: Wm. B. Eerdmans, 1974), 218-219.

Now we know Jesus began his public ministry when He was baptized by John in the Jordan River. In Luke 3:23, we read that He was about thirty years old when that took place. So, if we add thirty years to 5 B.C., we come up with Jesus getting baptized in the fall of 25 A.D. Actually, the more correct date is 26 A.D., because we have to add a year when crossing the B.C./A.D. line. You see, when calculating dates, there is no year 0. We count from 1 B.C. to 1 A.D. as just one year, not two. So, by adding the extra year, Jesus, at age thirty, would have begun His ministry in the fall of 26 A.D.

The great majority of Bible scholars who have studied the life of Jesus agree that His ministry was three-and-a-half years long. Therefore, He would have died no later than the spring of 30 A.D. By the way, that's the date upon which virtually all scholars agree for the end of Christ's earthly ministry, that is, all those who aren't trying to make the date conform to Anderson's calculations.[8]

Some would say that Luke tells us that Jesus was only *about* thirty years old when he was baptized. If He were thirty-two at the time He began His ministry in 28 A.D., then the date of 32 A.D. for his crucifixion would fit.

That is possible, but hardly likely. Young Jewish men weren't allowed to enter a spiritual ministry until they were thirty,[9] so we know Jesus would have waited until then, but His sole purpose in coming to earth was to give Himself to and for His people. It is hard to imagine Him building furniture for two more years when He had such a passion to become the Shepherd to the lost sheep of Israel. But even if we were to concede an extra two years, there are a couple more reasons the year 30 A.D. looks to be the far better choice.

We know the biblical record states that Jesus was crucified on a Friday, and that it was at the same time as the Passover. According to findings published by the Astrological Society of Berlin, the Passover occurred at that time in the year of 30 A.D., which is in complete accordance with the Scriptures.[10] But other experts have verified that the Passover occurred on a Sunday or a Monday in the year 32 A.D.[11] A crucifixion so early in the week would have been absolutely impossible according to the details given to us in the gospel accounts.

Not only that, we must also consider the fact that the number 40 has special significance in the Bible. Every time we see it used, it speaks of a

[8] Phillip Vollmer, *The Modern Student's Life of Christ,* (Old Tappan, New Jersey: Flemming H. Revell, 1962), 45-47.

[9] H. D. M. Spense, "Luke" in *The Pulpit Commentary,* (Grand Rapids, Mich.: Wm. B. Eerdmans, 1962), 70.

[10] Harold W. Hoehner, *Chronological Aspects of the Life of Christ,* (Grand Rapids, Mich.: Zondervan, 1977), 137.

[11] Ibid., 124-126.

time of testing and trial. It rained exactly 40 days at the time of Noah. Moses was on Mt. Sinai for 40 days waiting for God to give him the Ten Commandments. The children of Israel wandered in the wilderness for 40 years because of their rebellion against God. Jesus was tempted on the mountain for 40 days by the devil.

After their rejection and crucifixion of Christ, God tested and tried the nation Israel for 40 years. He gave them time to repent and turn back to Him, but they refused, so He brought the Roman armies against them. The Romans destroyed Jerusalem and the temple, and burned them to the ground in 70 A.D.; exactly 40 years after the Jews crucified Jesus in 30 A.D.

It appears clear that Christ was crucified no later than 30 A.D. But, through further investigation, we can demonstrate that Anderson was off, not by two years, but by an additional three-and-a-half years as well.

When the sixty-ninth week ended

Let us turn back to Daniel 9:25, and take a look at it again. The decree to rebuild Jerusalem was not necessarily and exclusively the one given to Nehemiah in 445 B.C. Artaxerxes, the same King of Persia, issued an earlier decree in 457 B.C. authorizing Ezra the scribe to gather necessary materials and workmen to repair and refurbish the house of God. The account is recorded in Ezra, chapter seven. It was an official proclamation from the king, but it is usually overlooked by prophecy scholars because it refers to the temple specifically, rather than to the city walls, as was the case in the later proclamation recorded in the Book of Nehemiah.

But is it not reasonable that God would have been more interested in spiritual things than He was in material things? Could not His reference to the rebuilding of Jerusalem have been more about the restoration of the temple, the real heart of the city, than merely with the restoration of its crumbled walls?

Besides that, the math works out perfectly without the need for any creative manipulation. If you subtract 483 years from 457 B.C., you come up with 26 A.D. The sixty-ninth week ended exactly the same year Jesus was baptized and began his public ministry.

But you might say, "Wait a minute there, don't you have to add a year when you cross the B.C./A.D. line because there's no such thing as a year 0? If you did that year, wouldn't you actually come up with an ending date of 27 A.D.?"

It is correct, that you do gain a year because of that phenomenon, but you also lose a year because of a different one. The Jews had an unusual custom of reckoning time. If they were recording the number of years a certain king reigned, they would count the beginning year as year number one, and then number the following years consecutively. So, if a king reigned for what we would consider ten years, they would record it as eleven years because they would always count both the beginning and the ending years in their tally.

That is why Jesus is said to have been in the tomb for three days, when actually, it was less than two. He was placed in the tomb on Friday afternoon, and he rose early Sunday morning, less than two days later. But in their minds, He was in the tomb three days: Friday, Saturday, and Sunday.

So, by the Jewish method of recording time, the 483 years of Daniel's sixty-nine weeks would have been counted, beginning with the year 457 B.C. as the first year, and ending with 25 A.D. as the last one. But since you gain a year at the B.C./A.D. transition, the period ends in 26 A.D.; right at the time Jesus began His earthly ministry.

That brings us to our next question. When was Jesus of Nazareth recognized as the Messiah of Israel?

When Christ was proclaimed the Messiah

Daniel 9:25 tells us that sixty-nine weeks will separate the issuing of the decree to rebuild Jerusalem and the emergence of Messiah the Prince. Jesus was not initially declared to be the Messiah when he rode that donkey into Jerusalem on Palm Sunday in the spring of 30 A.D. Actually, he was declared to be the Messiah by at least three different individuals three-and-a-half years prior to that time.

First of all, when Christ was baptized by John in the Jordan River, God the Father confirmed that Jesus was His divine Son. In Luke 3:22 we read, "*And the Holy Spirit descended in bodily form like a dove upon Him, and a voice came from heaven which said, 'You are My beloved Son; in You I am well pleased.'*" Then, the next day, John the Baptist confirmed what the Father had said when he saw Jesus coming toward him. In John 1:29, he said of Him, "*Behold the Lamb of God, which takes away the sin of the world.*" Lastly, a few weeks later, Jesus Himself announced that He was the Messiah in the synagogue in his own hometown. In Luke 4:18–19, Jesus stood up and read this messianic prophecy from Isaiah 61:1–2:

> *The Spirit of the Lord is upon Me, because He has anointed Me to preach good tidings to the poor. He has sent Me to heal the brokenhearted, to proclaim liberty to the captives, and recovery of sight to the blind, to set at liberty those who are oppressed; to proclaim the acceptable year of the Lord.*

After He had finished reading, He closed the scroll and gave it back to the attendant and sat down and said, "*Today this Scripture has been fulfilled in your hearing.*" The Jews understood exactly what he was claiming because they became enraged that He would have the audacity to claim to be the promised Deliverer of Israel, and they sought to throw Him off a cliff for His blasphemies.

Anderson and those who subscribe to his theory all point to Christ's triumphant entry on Palm Sunday as the fulfillment of Daniel's promise that the Messiah would be revealed after the conclusion of his sixty-nine weeks. But that's impossible. Christ had been revealed as the Messiah by God the Father, by John the Baptist, and by Himself, a full three-and-a-half years prior to Palm Sunday. Furthermore, throughout the rest of His entire ministry, He proclaimed himself to be the Messiah, as did His disciples who followed him, and the multitudes to whom He ministered. That is what so enraged the Jewish leaders and caused them to seek His death.

Perhaps an event from recent history will help illustrate this truth. President George Bush addressed our nation in 1991 after our smashing victory in the Gulf War. The American people responded to him with great enthusiasm, his approval ratings skyrocketed, and he was recognized as a great leader on that day. But when history books introduce the presidency of George Bush, they will record not that incident toward the end of his administration, but rather his election and inauguration, more than two years earlier. Likewise, Jesus' messiahship began, not at the great triumphal entry at the end of His earthly ministry, but rather at His humble baptism at the beginning of it.

The Alternate View Presented

So, if the sixty-ninth week of Daniel's prophecy ended at the beginning of Christ's ministry, not at the end of it, that greatly affects the nature of the seventieth week which follows. Although there were several scholars in the past who concluded that the sixty-ninth week ended at the beginning of Christ's ministry, they all seemed to see the entire seventieth week as having been played out in the first century. They saw Christ being crucified in the midst of the week, and the week ending at the stoning of Stephen and the conversion of the apostle Paul, three-and-a-half years later, in 33 A.D.[12] But critics have rightly pointed out that those events, significant as they were, did not even remotely conform to the cataclysmic ones at the end of the seventy weeks recorded in Daniel 9:27. Virtually all modern scholars have correctly dismissed that theory as untenable.

It seems apparent that there has to be a gap somewhere between the end of the sixty-ninth week and the end of the seventieth week. The final

[12] Ibid., 124-126

events of the seventieth week haven't been fulfilled yet, and we have to account for the past two thousand years of history somehow. For generations, scholars have virtually all agreed that the gap began when Jesus Christ was crucified, buried, and resurrected; at which time the Lord replaced Israel with the church as His primary instrument on earth. The scholars have also agreed that the gap occurred between the end of the sixty-ninth week and the beginning of the seventieth week, thus leaving a full seven years yet to be revealed. But, if what we have said is true, that can't possibly be so.

We can agree with the experts that the gap occurred after the Jews rejected and crucified their Messiah, and God turned to the Gentiles and established His church. But that occurred three-and-a-half years after the sixty-ninth week ended. So the only conclusion we can logically come to is that the seventieth week began when Jesus was baptized, and the first half of it was the three-and-a-half years of His public ministry here on earth. The second half of it remains to be fulfilled, and it will be, when the Lord raptures out His church, and the three-and-a-half-year tribulation runs its course.

But before we can expect anyone else to agree with this conclusion, there are some obvious problems with the theory, and some questions that have to be answered.

Objections Answered

The conflict with an established historical date

Some would be quick to point out that according to Luke 3:1, John the Baptist began his ministry in the, "*fifteenth year of the reign of Tiberius Caesar.*" According to historical records, Octavian Caesar, also known as Augustus, died in 14 A.D., and his stepson Tiberius succeeded him. Thus, the fifteenth year of the latter's reign would have been around 29 A.D. Since John the Baptist was six months older than Jesus, and began his ministry before our Lord did His, Jesus would have completed his three-and-a-half-year ministry no earlier than 32 or 33 A.D. Such scholars would insist that it would be impossible for our Lord to have begun His ministry in 26 A.D. and completed it in 30 A.D. as we have suggested.

They have a good point, and a convincing one, until we look a bit closer at the historical facts. Octavian indeed died in 14 A.D., but he had appointed Tiberius to be his co-regent nearly three years prior to that time. Alfred Edersheim, the foremost authority on Jewish history, insists that Luke would have reckoned the reign of Tiberius from the earlier date, not the later one. Thus, the fifteenth year of Tiberius would have been in 26 A.D., the exact year we have maintained that both John and Jesus turned thirty and began their ministries.[12]

The chronology of events

Another obvious difficulty with the suggested interpretation of Daniel's Seventy Weeks is that the order of events appears to be out of sequence. In the first place, in Daniel 9:26, it says the Messiah will be cut off after sixty-nine weeks, not after sixty-nine and a half weeks. Then it says the city and temple will be destroyed, which actually took place forty years after Christ's death. Then it says, in verse twenty-seven, that the covenant will be signed to start the seventieth week. We have the sixty-ninth week ending in 26 A.D., and then we jump ahead three-and-a-half years to the crucifixion, and then ahead another 40 years to the destruction of Jerusalem, and then drop back to 26 A.D. again to start the seventieth week in verse twenty-seven. That appears to be entirely just too much jumping around.

Yes, that does present a problem, but not one that is unprecedented in Scripture. Actually, the prophets did that sort of thing fairly often in the Bible. For example, let us take another look back at Isaiah 61:1–2. This is that passage from which Jesus was reading back in the synagogue in Nazareth. He was reading about all the things He, the Messiah, was going to accomplish. The list goes something like this:

> *The Lord has anointed me to preach good tidings to the poor; He has sent me to heal the brokenhearted, to proclaim liberty to the captives, and the opening of the prison to those who are bound; to proclaim the acceptable year of the Lord, and the day of vengeance of our God; to comfort all who mourn.*

If you will notice, all the things He listed initially are things He did at His first coming almost 2000 years ago, but He stopped right in the middle of the second verse. By comparing Christ's words in Luke, we see that He didn't finish the part about, "*the day of vengeance of our God.*" That, of course, is because vengeance wasn't a part of His ministry at that time. He will indeed exercise vengeance when He comes back again at the end of the tribulation. But Isaiah recorded it as though there were no gap at all. But in the next phrase, "*to comfort all who mourn,*" he again refers back to things that characterized Christ's first coming. That constitutes a bit of jumping around as well.

The Old Testament prophets couldn't see the New Testament church age. They saw all the events of Christ's two comings as occurring generally at the same time.

For another example of the same sort of thing, let us consider another passage in Isaiah, this time the sixty-fifth chapter. The prophet begins by describing events that will take place during the thousand-year reign of Christ on the earth. They will occur after He comes back the second time at the end of the tribulation period. But in verse seventeen he says, *"For behold, I create new heavens and a new earth: and the former shall not be remembered or come to mind."* When we compare that with Revelation chapter twenty-one, we see that the new heavens and new earth are to be created after the millennial reign of Christ is over. Revelation goes on to tell how perfect conditions will be at that time, with no suffering of any kind and no experience of death. But back in Isaiah sixty-five, the prophet reverts back to the millennial reign in verse twenty, where he says, *"No more shall an infant from there live but a few days, nor an old man who has not fulfilled his days; for the child shall die one hundred years old, But the sinner being one hundred years shall be accursed."*

So, we can see, Isaiah again jumps back and forth through the ages. He begins talking about the blessings of the coming kingdom age, and then jumps ahead to the eternal state, and then back again to the kingdom age. The prophets didn't really understand much of what the Holy Spirit inspired them to record, so they didn't notice their own discrepancies. Obviously, the Lord isn't bound by the limitations of time like we are, so He sometimes revealed things in a logical or spiritual sequence, rather than in a strictly chronological one.

Here in Daniel 9:24–27, the prophet brings us up to the introduction of the Messiah at the end of the sixty-nine weeks, then he jumps ahead to His death because of His rejection by the Jews. Then he moves on even further to reveal God's judgment on Israel for their continued rejection of their Messiah. After that, he returns to pick up the narrative in verse twenty-seven where he introduces the *"covenant with many"* that marks the beginning of the seventieth week.

That may suffice to answer the objection about the interrupted sequence of events, but that very covenant presents us with another problem that would seem to defy explanation.

The covenant with many

If what has been presented is true, it would appear that the antichrist would have had to make a treaty between Israel and its Arab neighbors back in 26 A.D., at the beginning of the seventieth week. Of course history records no such treaty. And besides, one might say, since the antichrist hasn't even yet made his appearance on the earth, how could he have been back there in the first century to initiate such a treaty?

That does present a problem, but not an insurmountable one. Let us dissect this verse and see what it really says before we throw up our hands in surrender.

In the first place, the one who initiates the covenant is, *"the prince who is to come,"* referred to in verse twenty-six. It can be demonstrated that this coming prince is ultimately the devil, not the antichrist. Three times in John's gospel, the devil is called, *"the prince of this world,"* and in Ephesians 2:2, Paul calls him, *"the prince of the power of the air."* Certainly we can agree that the devil was present and active back in 26 A.D., just as he is today, and will be during the tribulation period to come. He just uses different people to carry out his dirty work on earth during various periods of time.

The one whom the devil used in the first century was Judas Iscariot. He was never loyal to Jesus from the beginning. The Lord knew from the outset that he was going to betray Him, and in John 6:70, He said he was a devil. In John 12:6, Judas is condemned as a thief. In John 13:27, it says that Satan actually entered into him. And finally, in John 17:12, Jesus calls him the son of perdition (or destruction). Interestingly, Paul uses those exact words to describe the antichrist in 2 Thessalonians 2:3.

The devil, through Judas, confirmed a covenant with many, that is, with Christ and His other disciples, when he committed to become one of His chosen twelve. Three-and-a-half years later, he broke that covenant when he betrayed his master and delivered Him over to be crucified.

But you might be asking, "What covenant?" There is no biblical record of Judas ever making a seven-year agreement with Christ and His disciples, much less signing any covenant to that effect. But before you dismiss the idea as untenable, consider these facts.

The Bible is full of covenants, but how many of them were ever signed in document form? God established a covenant with Noah not to flood the earth again. He established a covenant with Abraham when He called him out of Mesopotamia. He repeated that covenant with Abraham's descendants, Isaac and Jacob. He established the old covenant with Israel through Moses. He promised an eternal kingdom through a covenant He established with David. He established the new covenant with all of us through the blood of Jesus Christ. But never once did he draw up a document and have the different parties sign it. A covenant, throughout the Bible, was simply a promise or a commitment between two or more parties. Why should this one in Daniel 9:27 be any different?

As far as the breaking of the covenant goes, we are told that it will occur when the antichrist turns against the Jews halfway through the tribulation and ends the period of false peace and initiates the period of great tribulation. But there is a much simpler and more plausible answer than that.

When Judas betrayed Jesus, he brought about His death. It was the devil's attempt to destroy God's plan of redemption, but it backfired. Christ's death actually satisfied God's justice and paid the final price for mankind's sin. After His death, there was no more sacrifice necessary, nor was any accepted by God. In Hebrews 10:14 it says, *"For by one offering He has perfected forever those who are being sanctified,"* and then in 10:18 he adds, *"Now where there is remission of these, there is no longer an offering for sin."* Just to prove His point, the Lord caused the veil in the temple to be torn in two from top to bottom immediately after the death of Christ, thereby signifying that the way to God no longer went through the temple and its sacrifices.

Of course, the Jews sewed up the rip in the veil, and went right on offering their sacrifices until the temple was destroyed by the Romans in 70 A.D. But as far as God was concerned, the sacrifices were over. Jesus stated just that fact a few days before He was crucified. In Matthew 23:37–39, He was weeping over Jerusalem and its temple because of the unbelief of the people and their rejection of Him in spite of His many attempts to nurture and care for them. Knowing they would soon demand His crucifixion, he said in verse thirty-eight, *"See! Your house is left to you desolate."*

When Judas betrayed Jesus, he broke his covenant with him, and brought about Christ's death. God accepted His Son's sacrifice as full payment for our sins, and rejected all other animal sacrifices as invalid after that. The temple had no more significance thereafter, so God's presence left it, and it became spiritually desolate, even though it continued to be in operation in man's eyes.

Even if it can be accepted that the covenant of Daniel 9:27 was actually a spiritual agreement between Judas and Christ and his disciples, there remains the problem of split personalities. How could Judas be the wicked prince in the first half of the week, and then two thousand years later, the antichrist be the same prince during the second half? We will discuss that matter next.

The identity of the prince

Is it really possible for two different people, living centuries apart, to fulfill the same role in biblical prophecy? It is indeed a strange concept, and we are tempted to dismiss it as an impossibility, but that sort of thing isn't unprecedented in Scripture. Let us consider the last two verses in the Old Testament. There, in Malachi 4:5–6, the prophet promises that Elijah will come to the people of Israel before the end of the age. The Jews have anticipated the return of Elijah for the last 2400 years. They believe he will have to come before the Messiah can be revealed.

The Jews in Jesus' day were expecting their Messiah to come soon, so they were anxiously looking for the appearance of Elijah, the forerunner. When John the Baptist came on the scene, they were hopeful that he might be the one, and asked him if it were so. But in John 1:21, the Baptist emphatically denied being the Messiah, or Elijah, or any of the prophets. He said he was simply a voice crying in the wilderness.

But after John had been beheaded, Jesus himself had some very interesting things to say about him. The disciples were questioning the Lord about the scribes' insistence that Elijah come before the Messiah be revealed. Jesus said to them in Matthew 17:11–13, "*Indeed, Elijah is coming first and will restore all things. But I say to you that Elijah has come already, and they did not know him but did to him whatever they wished. Likewise the Son of Man is also about to suffer at their hands.*" The next verse says the disciples understood that He had spoken to them about John the Baptist.

How can that be? John insisted he was not Elijah, but then Jesus says that he really was. Can we really have it both ways?

That's just the point. John wasn't actually Elijah, but like we read in Luke 1:17, "*He will also go before Him in the spirit and power of Elijah.*" As far as Christ was concerned, John the Baptist fulfilled the prophecy concerning the return of the prophet. In a similar way, Judas and the antichrist are not the same person, but they both go forth in the spirit and power of the devil, and thus fulfill the prophecy of the, "*prince who is to come.*"

Conclusion

The seven-year tribulation and the seventieth week of Daniel's prophecy have for generations been considered synonymous, but we have demonstrated that such a conclusion is far from proven.

As we shall see in the next appendix, the scriptural account of the tribulation lends itself much better to a period that is three-and-a-half years long, rather than it does to a seven-year period. Daniel's seventieth week is indeed seven years long, and it is divided in the middle. The first half of it was played out during Christ's three-and-a-half-year ministry on earth, and the second half will be played out during the coming three-and-a-half-year tribulation period. To try to force both halves into the narrow confines of the tribulation is neither necessary, nor is it supported by a comprehensive examination of the Bible.

APPENDIX THREE

THE NATURE OF THE TRIBULATION

No matter which book on prophecy you pick up, when you get to the part about the tribulation, you will likely find it described in terms similar to these.

It will be a period of seven years, which begins with a seven-year, Middle East peace accord, orchestrated by an emerging leader from a confederacy of ten European nations. This charismatic man, the antichrist, will quickly become a dominant world leader, who successfully crushes what little opposition is thrown up against him. The first three-and-a-half years will be a time of relative peace and prosperity on the earth. He will use this time to consolidate his power and rebuild the temple in Jerusalem. The unsuspecting earth-dwellers will herald him as a magnanimous humanitarian and philanthropist, even a religious man, supporting an emerging one-world church.

But at the mid-point of the treaty, he will break his covenant with Israel, and will begin an intense persecution of the Jews and other people of orthodox faith. He will set himself up as God in the temple and demand that he be worshipped. He will destroy the one-world church, and anything else that dares to oppose him. He will possess miraculous powers and will deceive the multitudes. He will control both the world's military and economic power. None will be able to resist him. None, that is, but God.

Most scholars agree that the tribulation will begin with a series of great devastations, as described in Revelation chapter six. Yet, somehow, the first three-and-a-half years will still be considered a time of relative peace. But during the second half of the tribulation, God will really turn up the heat.

Toward the end, He will devastate the earth, and ultimately destroy the antichrist and his forces, and will defeat the devil himself at the glorious return of Jesus Christ to the earth.

Not all scholars agree with this part, but the general consensus is that the people who are left behind after the rapture will at least have the first half of the tribulation to prepare for that which is to come. They will have time to get saved, prepare their defenses, and plan their strategy to resist and escape the wrath of the antichrist, which will be hurled against them during the last three-and-a-half years.

Admittedly, that is an over simplification of their view of the tribulation period, but it generally conforms to what is commonly taught by the majority of the prophecy scholars. However, it can be demonstrated that much of it is pure fabrication and wishful thinking. But if it is not as we have been led to believe, how then does the Bible describe that awful period we call the tribulation?

It won't be seven years long

As we discussed in the previous appendix, the prophecy of Daniel's seventy weeks does not necessitate a seven-year tribulation. It can be readily understood to teach that the first half of the seventieth week has already been fulfilled during the earthly ministry of Jesus Christ. Only the second half remains to be played out during the coming time of tribulation.

If the seventieth week in its entirety, and the tribulation period were to be understood as being synonymous, as virtually all scholars believe, then you would expect to read elsewhere of a seven-year period of time in the future. But you do not. The number seven occurs over fifty times in the Book of Revelation alone. It speaks of seven of about everything you could imagine, but not once does it mention seven years!

However, there are at least seven different places in the Bible where the length of the tribulation *is* mentioned. In Revelation 11:2 and 13:5, it mentions a period of forty-two months in duration. That's three-and-a-half years. Then in Revelation 11:3 and 12:6, it says the period is 1260 days long. The typical Jewish lunar month was 30 days long, making a typical year 360 days in length. If you divide 1260 by 360, you again come up with three-and-a-half years. Then in Daniel 7:25 and 12:7 and Revelation 12:4, we encounter the strange phrase, "Time, times, and a dividing of times (or half a time)." If we understand a time to be one year, then times would be two years, and a dividing of times would be half a year. If you add all of them together, you get three-and-a-half years again. Is it not strange that the Bible mentions a three-and-a-half-year period at least seven times, but it never mentions a seven-year period at all, nor any hint that there are two consecutive three-and-a-half-year periods?

Actually, the Bible never divides the tribulation into two halves at all. It is divided by three different series of judgments, and again by three distinct "woes," but it is never divided into two separate periods. Scholars assume it is divided because the seventieth week is divided, and they even arbitrarily assign one event to the first half, and another event to the second half; but the New Testament never even hints that there are two different periods in the tribulation.

To illustrate how inconsistent those scholars are in their attempt to separate the tribulation into two separate halves, let us look at the way they interpret Revelation 11:2–3. In verse two, John mentions the holy city being trodden under foot by the Gentiles for forty-two months. The scholars insist that particular abomination could not occur during that first half of false peace, so they relegate it to the second half of the tribulation after the antichrist has broken his covenant with Israel and has unleashed his wrath upon the Jews. But in the very next verse, John introduces us to the ministry of the two witnesses who will prophesy 1260 days in Jerusalem clothed in sackcloth. The same scholars see the ministry of those two witnesses, further described in verses four through twelve, as being compatible with that period of false peace, so they insist it will occur during the first half of the tribulation.

But how could that be? How could a thinking person believe that the three-and-a-half-year period mentioned in verse two refers to the last half of the tribulation, and the following three-and-a-half-year period, mentioned in verse three, refers to the first half? Such an interpretation is a logical and biblical absurdity, and it is insisted upon only because those scholars feel compelled to fit everything into their seven-year model, divided into two halves. Why not take the revolutionary approach and conclude the obvious: the reason all the events John describes in the tribulation seem to take place during the same three-and-a-half-year period of time is simply because they do? It is not divided in half, and it is not seven years long.

There will be no three-and-a-half years of peace

Obviously, if the tribulation is not seven years long, it can have no first half of false peace as virtually everybody else teaches. Such a period seems to be the delight of scholars everywhere, and admittedly, it would really come in handy. It would provide a very convenient buffer zone between the present church age and the the period of great tribulation, which follows.

It would keep the doctrine of imminence in tact as well. The rapture could occur any day, and there would still be three-and-a-half years to set the stage for the really heavy stuff to come. During that time of relative inactivity, the little-known antichrist could rise in power until he was in a position to take over the world. Also the temple could be rebuilt, and those left behind after the rapture would have time to get their act together in anticipation of what was to follow.

Everyone seems to want that three-and-a-half years of peace. But one is hard pressed to find its existence identified in God's order of things to come. As pointed out in the dialogue of *A Snowball's Chance*, Revelation chapter six, which everyone admits details the beginning of the tribulation, is anything but peaceful. It describes world aggression, warfare, famine, pestilence, persecution, death of the saints, and it ends with a description of worldwide devastation. Reading that chapter will reveal nothing resembling a period of peace of any sort.

It is true, the antichrist will present himself as the world's champion for peace, but nothing but destruction will follow in his path. It will be as Paul describes the day of the Lord in 1 Thessalonians 5:3. He says, *"For when they say, 'Peace and safety!' then sudden destruction comes upon them, as labor pains upon a pregnant woman, and they shall not escape."*

The reason so many insist on this period of peace is because the time of actual tribulation in the Bible is repeatedly limited to three-and-a-half years. Whether it is 42 months; 1260 days; or a time, times, and a dividing of times; it still adds up to just three-and-a-half years. So, if all the really bad stuff is confined to just one-half of the tribulation, then they assume the other half must be a lesser period of relative peace and safety. But there is no necessity for them to embarrass themselves by manufacturing such a period when there is no biblical support for it. The reason the Bible fails to describe any three-and-a-half-year period of false peace at the beginning of the tribulation is simply because there will be no such period.

It won't start with a Middle East peace treaty

Virtually every prophecy book on the shelf confirms the belief that the tribulation will begin with an antichrist-designed treaty between Israel and her Arab neighbors. That, of course, comes from a very imaginative interpretation of Daniel 9:27. But, is it not strange that such a treaty is never even hinted at elsewhere in Scripture?

The synoptic gospels all mention certain signs that will precede the tribulation. The faithful are to look for them and be forewarned of the coming of that great day. But none of them comes close to referring to anything that might be interpreted as a Mid-East treaty.

The Scriptures do, however, tell us of something entirely different that *will* mark the beginning of the tribulation. In Matthew 24:15–21, Jesus told his disciples:

> *Therefore when you see the Abomination of Desolation, spoken of by Daniel the prophet, standing in the holy place . . . . then let those who are in Judea flee to the mountains . . . . For then there will be great tribulation, such as has not been since the beginning of the world until this time, no, nor ever shall be.*

Later, in 2 Thessalonians 2:3–4, Paul confirms what his Lord had revealed. He wrote the following words to inform the saints what would precede the day of God's wrath:

> *Let no one deceive you by any means; for that day will not come unless the falling away comes first, and the man of sin is revealed, the son of perdition, who opposes and exalts himself above all that is called God or that is worshipped, so that he sits as God in the temple of God, showing himself that he is God.*

In both cases, the day of the Lord begins, not with a treaty, but with a traitor. The thing the saints were to look for was when the man of sin (also called the son of perdition) would set himself up in the temple as God. That indeed would be an abomination to the Jews, desecrating their temple and leaving it desolate.

Please take note that the one event that will precede the revealing of this man of sin in all his blasphemy, is not the signing of a peace treaty, but the rapture of the church. In 2 Thessalonians 2:6–8, Paul tells the faithful in that city exactly what to expect:

> *And now you know what is restraining, that he may be revealed in his own time. For the mystery of lawlessness is already at work; only He who now restrains will do so until He is taken out of the way. And then the lawless one will be revealed, whom the Lord will consume with the breath of His mouth and destroy with the brightness of His coming.*

It is generally understood that the one who is restraining the full manifestation of evil in the world today is the Holy Spirit working through the evangelical church of Jesus Christ. Once the church is taken out of the way at the rapture, immediately, the lawless one is to be revealed in all his abominable wickedness. But this simple truth is quite different from what most of the prophecy scholars tell us.

They say the church is indeed restraining the evil working of the devil, and they agree it will be taken out of the way at the rapture. But then they take a big detour from what the Scripture says here. They say after the rapture, the next thing to occur is the illusive Mid-East peace treaty. Even then, the antichrist is not revealed for who he really is. He goes on for another three-and-a-half years deceiving the nations. Only after the dubious first half is over, does he break his covenant with Israel and set himself up in the temple as God.

Such a conclusion may be the scholars' logical deduction, based on their interpretation of Daniel 9:27, but it is not justified by the honest interpretation of 2 Thessalonians, chapter two; nor indeed, of any other New Testament passage. As admittedly fascinating as it may be, the idea of the tribulation beginning with a peace treaty between Israel and the Arabs must be discarded in the name of honest biblical interpretation.

There will be no consecutive series of plagues

One of the main reasons scholars insist on a seven-year tribulation period is because that much time is deemed necessary for all the many plagues to run their course. The Book of Revelation discloses four series of judgments (though no details are given for the thunder judgments in Rev. 10:3–4), and three-and-a-half years just isn't enough time for all of them to occur consecutively. And most scholars agree with LaHaye and Jenkins that they will indeed occur one after the other.

They maintain that the seven seal judgments occur over the first twenty-one months of the tribulation. Those are followed by the seven trumpet judgments, which continue on until the forty-second month, or the half-way mark. Then the terrible bowl judgments are unleashed on the inhabitants of the earth over the last forty-two months, or what is called the great tribulation.

If all the judgments actually did occur one after the other, then one might expect them to require more than three-and-a-half years to run their course, but there is strong evidence to contend that, instead of consecutively, they will actually occur concurrently.

It is clear, admittedly, that the judgments differ from each other, and cannot be considered three different accountings of the same series of events, but that doesn't mean they can't occur at the same time. Because the judgments were revealed to John one after the other, we assume that they must also occur in the same fashion. But that simply isn't necessary at all.

The four gospels differ from each other significantly. Each one of them has considerable information unique to itself. We find sermons, miracles, and conflicts in one, that we do not find in another. But we all recognize that the events recorded in Matthew did not precede the events recorded in Mark, and those before Luke, and so on. Though all of the records differ, we agree that all the information contained in the gospels about Christ's adult ministry occurred during the same three-and-a-half-year period of time when Christ was ministering here on the earth.

In similar fashion, we ought to be able to accept the fact that all of the various events and judgments that are recorded in Revelation, chapters six through nineteen, occur during the remaining three-and-a-half years of Daniel's seventieth week, the coming period of tribulation.

The reason the judgments differ from each other is that they are not all global in their scope. What occurs in one judgment may not affect the whole world. It is entirely possible for John to record a great asteroid falling into the sea in Revelation 8:8–9 as the second trumpet judgment, and for him to record how a third of the marine life died and a third of the ships were destroyed in that particular ocean. Then he could record the second bowl judgment in Revelation 16:3 where an angel poured out the contents of his bowl into the sea, causing it to turn as to blood, killing everything in that area. The two events could be taking place at the same time, in two different oceans, halfway round the world from each other.

It is probable that the seal judgments will begin first, but the trumpet judgments will commence shortly thereafter, and the bowl judgments will start not long after that. They may well begin at different times, but it is clear that they all have a common ending. Let us just compare some of the descriptive language John uses to reveal the last of the three sets of judgments:

> *I looked when He opened the sixth seal, and behold, there was a great earthquake . . . .and the stars of heaven fell to the earth . . . .and every mountain and island was moved out of its place . . . .and the kings of the earth . . . .hid themselves in the caves and in the rocks of the mountains, and said to the mountains and rocks, "Fall on us and hide us from the face of Him who sits on the throne and from the wrath of the Lamb! For the great day of His wrath has come, and who is able to stand?"* (Revelation 6:12–16)

> *Then the seventh angel sounded: and there were loud voices in heaven, saying, "The kingdoms of this world have become the kingdoms of our Lord and of His Christ, and He shall reign forever and ever!" . . . . Then the temple of God was opened in heaven, and the ark of His covenant was seen in His temple. And there were lightnings, noises, thunderings, an earthquake, and great hail.* (Revelation 11:15–19)

> *Then the seventh angel poured out his bowl into the air and a loud voice came out of the temple of heaven, from the throne, saying, "It is done!" . . . .and there were noises and thunderings and lightnings; and there was a great earthquake . . . .Then every island fled away, and the mountains were not found. And great hail from heaven fell upon men . . . . Men blasphemed God because of the hail, since that plague was exceedingly great.* (Revelation 16:17–21)

These three passages are almost carbon copies of each other. All of them describe the same horrible combination of calamities in the heavens and on the earth, and a declaration that all things have come to a final conclusion. They all describe the same cataclysmic period of time, and all come to the same confirmation, "Judgment day has come. Prepare to meet thy God!"

The antichrist will not control the whole world

It is commonly assumed that the antichrist will control the entire world of the unsaved. Supposedly, only those who get saved will escape his domination. There are indeed verses that lead us to draw that conclusion, verses like Revelation 13:8. It reads, *"All who dwell on the earth will worship him, whose names have not been written in the Book of Life of the Lamb slain from the foundation of the world."*

But, as pointed out before, sometimes the writers of Scripture used absolute words to describe situations that were limited in scope or magnitude. The antichrist will certainly exercise great control, even absolute control in certain areas, but that cannot be said to be true concerning the entire unbelieving population of the planet.

The main reason we can be confident that the antichrist will have limited power is that the Bible defines the tribulation as a time of war. Persecution requires only the powerful forces of evil terrorizing the weaker forces of good, but war requires two opposing sides in military conflict. The second seal judgment describes such a condition with these words, *"Another horse, fiery red, went out, and it was granted to the one who sat on it to take peace from the earth, and that people should kill one another; and there was given to him a great sword"* (Revelation 6:4).

This great sword of war is further revealed in the eleventh chapter of the Book of Daniel. There, the antichrist is seen as the same blasphemous demigod as he is described in the Book of Revelation. There too, he seeks to conquer the whole world, but there also, it describes those forces which will rise up against him. Verses 40–45 contain these convincing words:

> *At the time of the end the king of the South shall attack him; and the king of the North shall come against him like a whirlwind, with many chariots, horsemen, and with many ships; and he shall enter the countries, overwhelm them, and pass through. He shall enter the Glorious Land, and many countries shall be overthrown; but these shall escape out of his hand: Edom, Moab, and the prominent people of Ammon . . . . But news out of the east and the north shall trouble him; therefore he shall go out with great fury to destroy and annihilate many. And he shall plant the tents of his palace between the seas and the glorious holy mountain, yet he shall come to his end, and no one will help him.*

The antichrist will face opposition in his obsession to subdue the whole world. Especially toward the end of the tribulation, he will be opposed by armies from nearly all directions. He will take his stand in the heart of Israel to do battle with those who will dare oppose him. When Christ returns to the earth, it appears that all the armies, which had previously gathered to battle each other, will, in unison, turn their hostilities toward the Lord. They will all, of course, be destroyed by the Lord, simply by the power of the word of His mouth (see Revelation 19:11–21).

The antichrist will indeed be powerful, but he will not be absolutely sovereign. He will not only face opposition from the God of heaven, he will also face opposition from other ungodly rulers on the earth.

Conclusion

This has been, by no means, a thorough discussion of the coming tribulation period, but hopefully it has been sufficient to point out some of the errors that are commonly held concerning it. It will not be seven years long, and thus, it will not begin with three-and-a-half years of peace. The antichrist will not initiate it by orchestrating a peace treaty between Israel and the Arab nations around it. And it will not be characterized by three separate series of judgments, each played out, one after the other. Powerful as he may be, the antichrist will not control the entire world of the unsaved.

What the tribulation will be is three-and-a-half years of hell on earth. It will start out with the antichrist in the temple, proclaiming himself to be God, and setting out to destroy everyone and everything that opposes him. He will be very successful in his efforts for a time, but many on this earth will oppose him. God will respond by pouring out a barrage of judgments on him and his followers in such increasing magnitude that, in the end, the antichrist, the devil he serves, the whole earth, and all its ungodly inhabitants, will be defeated before Him. That will happen when Christ returns in glory to reclaim the title deed to the universe, and to set up His millennial kingdom.

APPENDIX FOUR

THE HARDENED HEART OF UNBELIEF

Certainly one of the most controversial ideas set forth in *A Snowball's Chance* is that of the hardened heart. It presents the idea that a person can reject God's truth only up a point. After that, God quits seeking his conversion altogether. Not only that, it suggests the concept that eventually God Himself will turn from that apostate and harden his heart so that he could not respond in faith even if he wanted to.

We can see apparent evidence of hardened hearts in the lives of people around us. Even though we have known of apparently hardened sinners coming to Christ late in life, even on their deathbeds, some of us have also seen other doomed souls go off into eternity without Christ in spite of the prayers and testimony of many believers in their behalf. They may even have expressed a desire to believe, but they could not bring themselves to exercise saving faith, and they died without hope of eternal life.

It can be demonstrated that the Bible clearly states that, at the time of the rapture of the church, those who have heard the gospel and have refused to accept it will be doomed to eternal separation from the Lord. They will not be saved during the tribulation; indeed, it will not be possible for them to do so. The devil, through his antichrist, will deceive them. Even more condemning is the fact that God Himself will confirm their hearts in their unbelief. Let us consider carefully what Paul says in 2 Thessalonians 2:9–12:

> *The coming of the lawless one is according to the working of Satan, with all power, signs, and lying wonders, and with all unrighteous deception among*

those who perish, because they did not receive the love of the truth, that they might be saved. For this reason God will send them strong delusion, that they should believe the lie, that they all may be condemned who did not believe the truth but had pleasure in unrighteousness.

The Scripture is clear and straightforward. Yet most scholars try to find some way around it. They just can't bring themselves to believe that God would do such a thing. It seems to fly in the face of everything we have been led to believe about Him. Doesn't He give everyone a will completely free, either to accept or to reject whenever he might decide to exercise it? Isn't it His desire for all people to be saved? Wouldn't He do everything He could to give them another chance, especially after the horrors of the tribulation begin?

Although this subject is dealt with at some length in the novel, let us look at a couple of these questions in a little more depth. It is indeed possible to demonstrate that what Paul told the Thessalonian saints is to be understood exactly as he made it sound.

Does God really will everyone to be saved?

Scholars are quick to point out the Scripture that tells of God's great desire to see everyone eventually saved. In 2 Peter 3:9, the apostle shares with us these words, "*The Lord is not slack concerning His promise, as some count slackness, but is longsuffering toward us, not willing that any should perish but that all should come to repentance.*" The context is of the coming of the Lord and the judgment of the earth. Scholars tell us that Peter makes it clear that even during the period of intense judgment, God is still in the business of saving souls and that He hasn't shut the door on anyone. How then could He harden the hearts of millions and condemn them to eternal destruction?

That is an interesting question, and a convincing one; convincing that is, until you realize there's a significant difference between what God desires and what God decrees. God certainly is not a man, but He does have a personality. In that sense we were created in His image. He has the same attributes of personality that we have: intellect, emotions, and a will. They are distinct attributes, and we must not confuse them.

With His intellect, God knows all there is to know in the entire universe. With His emotions, He deeply feels such diverse emotions as love, compassion, jealousy, and wrath. With His will, He decrees, either directly or indirectly, all that comes to pass. Unfortunately, we often confuse His emotions with His will.

When the Bible says that God is unwilling for any to perish, and wills rather that everyone come to repentance, it is referring to His emotions.

God takes no delight in the death of the wicked. His heart's desire is that everyone would respond to His grace and be saved. But that is not to say that He will always act according to His emotions. On the contrary, He often decrees things that are not to His liking. His decrees are subject to His sovereign and righteous will, not His compassionate emotions.

In Matthew the seventh chapter, Christ informed His listeners in His *Sermon on the Mount* that He will be harsh and unbending concerning those who fail to respond to His grace. In verses 21–23 He says:

> *Not everyone who says to me, "Lord, Lord," will enter the kingdom of heaven, but he who does the will of My Father in heaven. Many will say to Me in that day, "Lord, Lord, have we not prophesied in Your name, cast demons in Your name, and done many wonders in your name?" And then I will declare to them, "I never knew you; depart from Me, you who practice lawlessness."*

If God simply acted according to His emotions, His great heart of compassion would surely have given those sincere seekers an opportunity to find His grace, but He does not. They have refused His will; therefore, they will suffer His wrath forever.

In the Book of Proverbs, Solomon confirms that truth when he warns his son not to presume upon the longsuffering of God. He tells him that those who have rejected God's appeals repeatedly will later find Him unresponsive when they cry out to Him in their time of trouble. We read in Proverbs 1:28–31:

> *Then they will call on me, but I will not answer; they will seek me diligently, but they will not find me. Because they hated knowledge and did not choose the fear of the Lord, they would have none of my counsel and despised my every rebuke. Therefore they shall eat of the fruit of their own way and be filled to the full with their own fancies.*

Many other passages can be found in Scripture where God does the same thing. Just because God doesn't want sinners to perish, that doesn't mean He will always keep the door open for them to respond to Him whenever they get around to it. His will is sovereign, and there are times when it will close the door on those whom He loves, but who have transgressed beyond the ultimate boundary He has established.

Does God close the door before death?

If we really believe the Bible, we have to admit that God does go against His emotional desires, and, at the judgment, condemns those who have rejected Him. But we find it extremely difficult to entertain the notion that He could do that while the person is still alive. There is a perfect example of just such a person in the Scriptures.

Rebecca gave Isaac twin sons, Esau and Jacob. Their story can be found in Genesis 25–27. Esau was the older of the two, and he was in line to receive the greater portions of all of Isaac's inheritance. But he despised all things spiritual, and he sold his priestly birthright for a pot of porridge. Because of his profane heart, God rejected Esau from that day forward. God knew Esau's heart before he was ever born, and Paul records the Lord's condemnation of him in Romans 9:10–13:

> *And not only this, but when Rebecca had conceived by one man, even our father Isaac (for the children not yet being born, nor having done any good or evil, that the purpose of God according to election might stand, not of works but of Him who calls), it was said to her, "The older shall serve the younger." As it is written, "Jacob have I loved, but Esau have I hated."*

This is a harsh passage of Scripture, and many choose to pretend it isn't there. But it is, and so are others that confirm that God does indeed close the door on certain ones who reject His truth. The writer of the Book of Hebrews warns his readers not to presume upon the grace of God. He too uses Esau as an example of one who was rejected by God because of his profane heart:

> *Looking carefully lest anyone fall short of the grace of God; lest any root of bitterness springing up cause trouble, and by this many become defiled; lest there be any fornicator or profane person like Esau, who for one morsel of food sold his birthright. For you know that afterward, when he wanted to inherit the blessing, he was rejected, for he found no place for repentance, though he sought it diligently with tears.* (Hebrews 12:15–17)

This too is a tough passage, but we must not ignore its message. Esau rejected God's will for His life, and while he yet lived, God rejected him. He wanted to receive certain material blessings, but he was able to gain no audience with God even though he sought it diligently and emotionally. There was no faith in his heart, and God closed the door. This brings us to another question.

How free are we to choose?

We naturally assume we have a totally free will, and we can choose to accept or to reject Christ whenever we want to. But is that the extent of the message taught in Scripture? Certainly, the Bible places on us the responsibility to respond to God's grace and to exercise personal faith in Christ in order to be saved. And indeed the appeal is universal. We read such verses as:

> *But as many as received Him, to them He gave the right to become children of God, to those who believe in His name.* (John 1:12)

> *Believe on the Lord Jesus Christ, and you shall be saved, you and your household.* (Acts 16:31)

> *For whoever calls on the name of the Lord shall be Saved.* (Romans 10:13)

God also holds all of us accountable for our own decisions, and He judges us accordingly. It appears that God simply waits to see what we're going to do, and then He deals with us according to the decisions we make. But a careful reading of Scripture reveals that God is a whole lot more active in our coming to Him than we might want to think.

Paul tells us we were dead in trespasses and sins and totally unresponsive to His call. We had to be made alive by His Spirit before we could even come to Him (Ephesians 2:1–5). Jesus told His disciples that it was He who had chosen them, not the other way around (John 15:16). In fact, He insisted that no one could even come to Him unless the Father draw them first (John 6:44, 65). Perhaps we're not as free as we think we are.

Paul gives a good picture of the heart of the natural man. He describes us as we all were before we came to Christ. We can read His summary in Romans 3:10–18:

> *There is none righteous, no, not one; there is none who understands; there is none that seeks after God. They have all turned aside; They have together become unprofitable; there is none who does good, no, not one. Their throat is an open tomb; with their tongues they have practiced deceit, the poison of asps is under their lips, whose mouth is full of cursing and bitterness. Their feet are swift to shed blood; destruction and misery are in their ways; and the way of peace they have not known. There is no fear of God before their eyes.*

Since none of us is good, and none of us fears God and seeks after Him, is it any wonder that God has to take the initiative and seek after us? That is why He is described as the one standing outside the door of our lives seeking entrance: "*Behold, I stand at the door and knock. If anyone hears My voice and opens the door, I will come in to him and dine with him, and he with Me*" (Revelation 3:20).

The sad part about all this is, if we keep refusing to open the door, He will eventually stop knocking and walk away. And since we have neither the inclination nor the ability to seek after Him, He will remain forever outside. That is why He gives us so many warnings in His Word not to neglect the calling of God.

As already pointed out, there are passages like Proverbs 1:24–32 that teach us that if we reject God's invitation long enough, He will eventually reject us and refuse to respond in our day of trouble, even when we cry out to Him in pain and fear. Just like with Esau, God will harden our hearts and we will find it impossible to cry out to Him in faith, which is the only call He will answer.

But there are still those who insist that they will be able to turn to God and sincerely believe in their time of trouble and be saved. Especially, they claim, if the rapture were to occur, they would be convinced of the truth they had previously rejected, and would turn in faith to Christ and be saved. That seems logical enough, but the Scripture says otherwise.

Can knowing people really be that deceived?

As we have already seen in 2 Thessalonians 2:9–12, the antichrist will deceive those unbelievers left behind after the rapture, and God Himself will delude them that they should believe the lie. Yet, there are those who still maintain that it couldn't possibly happen to them.

They insist that they will be free to make their own decisions, and no amount of deception will convince them to follow the antichrist after the rapture. They say they will know that Christ has come for His church, and nothing will keep them from turning to Him and believing on Him to the saving of their souls. But what they don't understand is the deceitfulness of their hearts and the intense power of the devil's deception.

Jesus Himself told His disciples in Matthew 24:23–24, *"Then if anyone says to you, 'Look, here is the Christ!' or 'There!' do not believe it. For false christs and false prophets will rise and show great signs and wonders to deceive, if possible, even the elect."* Christ's own words are that the only thing that will keep people from being deceived during that time is if God personally elects them and protects them. But we already know that He will not do that for those who have previously refused to believe on Him. Instead, He will harden their hearts in unbelief and confirm their deception. In the end, it all boils down to one final question.

Who is ultimately in charge?

Many, perhaps most, scholars believe each person has the final say as to his own soul's destiny. They say God may make salvation available, and even encourage us to accept it, but He exerts no compelling force one way or the other. He remains neutral and allows each of us to make the final choice.

If that were so, then we would all agree that a person could be saved whenever he got good and ready to do so, either before or after the rapture. But we find that the Bible paints it quite differently. It states clearly that God alone is in charge.

He chooses us: *"Just as He chose us in Him before the foundation of the world, that we should be holy and without blame before Him in love."* (Ephesians 1:3)

He saves us: *"For by grace you have been saved through faith, and that not of yourselves; it is the gift of God."* (Ephesians 2:8)

He keeps us: *"Now unto Him who is able to keep you from stumbling, and present you faultless before the presence of His glory with exceeding joy."* (Jude 24)

But some He hardens: *"Therefore He has mercy on whom He wills, and whom He wills He hardens."* (Romans 9:18)

Nebuchadnezzar, the great king of ancient Babylon, considered himself to be the master of his own destiny. He became lifted up with pride and self-importance until God brought him down. He took from him his reason, and the king became like a brute beast for seven long years. When God, in His grace, restored Nebuchadnezzar's reason to him, the humbled king records in his own words:

> *And at the end of the time I, Nebuchadnezzar, lifted up my eyes to heaven, and my understanding returned to me; and I blessed the Most High and praised and honored Him who lives forever; for His dominion is an everlasting dominion, and His kingdom is from generation to generation. All the inhabitants of the earth are reputed as nothing; He does according to His will in the army of heaven and among the inhabitants of the earth. None can restrain His hand or say to Him, "What have You done?"* (Daniel 4:34–35)

Nebuchadnezzar learned the hard way what we must accept as well. God is sovereign. He is in charge. He is the *"Author and Finisher of our faith"* (Hebrews 12:2). We don't make the rules. We don't call the shots. We must determine what He decrees and accept it whether we understand it or agree with it or not. To do otherwise is to court eternal disaster.

We are now living in the day of God's grace. He is patient and longsuffering with us. He invites us to come to Him and be saved. He invites again and again, and still He waits. But if we persist in our unbelief, the day will come when He will turn His back and walk away, and then it will be eternally too late.

Conclusion

If you should die without a saving knowledge of Jesus Christ, you will be condemned to a Christless hell, no matter what good or religious things you may have done, or how much you may beg to be forgiven and accepted into heaven.

If you should reject Christ long enough, you may reach that point where God will turn away from you while you are yet alive. Your heart will be hardened and you will not be able to respond to God in faith, even in a time of great pain or fear. You will be confirmed in your unbelief and will face eternal condemnation.

If the rapture should occur and find you knowing clearly the way of salvation, and yet not possessing salvation, you will not get saved afterward. You will be deceived. You will believe the devil's lie. You will follow the antichrist. You will be condemned and spend eternity in hell.

God, of course, does not want that to happen, but the only way to be sure you avoid any such eventuality is to confirm your faith in the finished work of Jesus Christ *today*! Make sure you have acted on what Paul said in 2 Corinthians 6:2, *"Behold, now is the accepted time; behold now is the day of salvation."*

Don't try to justify it, or sift it through the filters of your own reason. Just accept it. That's the way God revealed it to us in His Word, and as a great news commentator used to say at the end of each of his broadcasts, "And that's the way it is!"

WHAT TO EXPECT IN THE FUTURE FROM THE PEN OF TED DUNCAN

Aaron's Rod, the gripping sequel to *A Snowball's Chance*, begins when the Lord returns for His church at the rapture, and when Aaron Muller, a handsome young Jewish athlete, is sealed as one of God's chosen 144,000 witnesses. Aaron and his fellow witnesses contend for righteousness during the following three-and-a-half-year period of tribulation. They preach the word of God to those tortured souls who are left behind. They also enter into deadly conflict with the forces of evil, orchestrated by the antichrist, Constantine Augustus, and his minions.

Follow the triumphs and tragedies, both in heaven and on the earth, of many of the characters introduced in *A Snowball's Chance,* and grow to love and hate new personalities as they are introduced. Experience the horrors of the great tribulation as they unfold, and the incalculable toll it will take on this earth and its inhabitants. Also thrill to the heroic evangelistic triumphs of God's chosen witnesses, and the miraculous ways in which God delivers His own. Follow Aaron and his family as they struggle to survive the devil's onslaught and to live to see the coming of their promised Messiah. And as you near the end of your journey, prepare for another cliffhanging ending that will absolutely blow you away. (Expected in the summer of 2003)

Gog's Revenge, the last book in the trilogy, begins with the final months of the tribulation, and then launches you into the return of Christ to the earth and the resulting Battle of Armageddon. After the antichrist and his ungodly multitudes are destroyed in that cataclysmic overthrow, and the devil himself is bound, the returned Messiah welcomes His chosen people back to their Promised Land from all over the world. And with them, they bring incredible resources and wealth. Old friends are united as they join in to assist their Savior in preparing for His millennial kingdom. But one last battle must be fought before swords can be beaten into plowshares and spears into pruning hooks.

Gregor Odin Galinikov, the ruthless Russian czar, rejects the stringent rules of the new King of Israel, and goes about gathering the world's remaining forces of evil to launch a massive attack to dethrone the reigning Christ and to seize His enormous wealth. Learn the outcome of the sensational Battle of Gog and Magog, and discover the final destinies of the characters whose lives have unfolded before you in the preceding books. (Expected in the spring of 2004)

To order additional copies of

A SNOWBALL'S CHANCE

Have your credit card ready and call:

1-877-421-READ (7323)

or please visit our web site at
www.pleasantword.com

Also available at: www.amazon.com

Printed in the United States
206324BV00001B/166/A

9 781579 216221